BEFORE GIRL

KATE CANTERBARY

VESPER PRESS

Editing provided by Julia Ganis of Julia Edits.
Proofreading provided by Marla Esposito of Proofing Style.
Cover design provided by Sarah Hansen of Okay Creations.

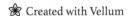 Created with Vellum

ABOUT BEFORE GIRL

She'll juggle your balls.
For Stella Allesandro, chaos is good. She's a rising star at a leading sports publicity firm. She's known throughout the industry as the jock whisperer—the one who can tame the baddest of the bad boys in professional sports without losing her signature smile.

But Cal Hartshorn is an entirely different kind of chaos.

He'll fix your broken heart.
This former Army Ranger and now-famous cardiothoracic surgeon fails at nothing...except talking to a woman he's adored from afar. Whether on the battlefield or operating room, he's exacting, precise, and efficient, but all of that crumbles when Stella is in sight.

Cal always knows—and gets—what he wants, and now he wants all of her. His forever girl.

But Stella isn't convinced she's anyone's forever.

For big girls who like getting some.

1

CAL

IT STARTED OUT AS A GAME, AN EXERCISE IN OBSERVATION NOT unlike assault drills from Army Ranger school. It kept my mind from wandering to surgeries and patients, and since I couldn't simply go on an early morning run without a mental task to keep my head busy while my body worked, I started tracking the targets.

The moms with jogging strollers were the arms dealers.

The serious runners and fitness freaks—the ones lunge-walking—were the insurgency.

The rowers on the pond were the counterintelligence.

The birds and animals were the civilians.

And then...then there was the dark-haired woman with golden olive skin and *that ass*. She was built like a pinup, thick and round in all my favorite ways.

At first, she was a welcome reminder that, even at forty-two, my libido was very much alive and I could still appreciate a beautiful woman...even if only from a distance. She walked at a brisk pace, but when I was running a five-minute mile, I had the luxury of passing her twice if I pushed hard and timed it right. I'd get her once from the back and then reverse course and get her again from the front.

I couldn't determine which side I admired more and I thanked the god of ripe rear ends that I didn't have to choose.

Even bearing the winter's dark, wind-chilled mornings was worth it to catch a glimpse of her and that flash of recognition in her smile.

She was the asset.

But it wasn't only her body that caught my eye. It was everything about her. She looked people in the eye and smiled before sunrise. She walked with her chin up, her hips swinging. Sometimes her shoulders shimmied with the music coming through her earbuds or she moved her hands with the beat. The girl had swagger and that—*that* was captivating.

One frosty morning in January, I'd jogged by her and our eyes met. She'd smiled at me and called "Good morning." I couldn't wipe the sloppy grin off my face for the rest of the day. My third-year residents thought I was having a stroke. They tried to run a brain bleed protocol on me. One of them went so far as to lobby for an MRI. I let them buzz around me all day as they ran down wild diagnoses, never telling them the strange face was the result of a smile that warmed me through and through and a backside that kept me up nights. Kept me *up* most mornings too.

No, I didn't tell them that. I didn't tell them anything.

But after that smile, she became a fascination bordering on flat-out obsession. Instead of maintaining my routine of rotating through Boston's Emerald Necklace parks for my morning workouts, I stuck with Jamaica Pond. I couldn't tear myself away. Not when that meant risking a chance at saying "Good morning" back to her. Or asking her name and how she liked her coffee and which side of the bed she favored and if she'd take my name when we married.

Despite my preference for scheduling six a.m. surgeries on Tuesdays and Thursdays, I pushed them back to eight after missing her on those days for three straight weeks. The way some relied on a morning jolt of caffeine to get them going, I needed to share that brief, anonymous connection with her. Without it, I was edgy and distracted. My residents interpreted that behavior as evidence of a frontal lobe tumor. Cardiothoracic surgical residents were off the deep end like that. They even dragged my neurosurgeon friend Nick into that go-round. He enjoyed the consult far too much.

I didn't explain away my mood or tell them about the woman at the pond. Not to my residents. They survived on RXbars and hospital gossip, and I wasn't giving them any of the latter.

And now, after all those mornings, all those runs spent imagining everything about this woman—her name, her voice, her interests, her history, and her future—now she was here. Perched on the back of my Jeep, smiling like she knew a secret but had no plans to share it, and bleeding in several spots.

Yeah, bleeding. I couldn't claim credit for the smile or the secret but the bloodshed was all on me.

2

STELLA

FEELIN' THE BURN.

Sweatin' to the oldies...because late nineties boy bands now qualified as oldies.

Gettin' my fitness on and loving every damn minute.

Okay, none of that was true. I was dragging my ass around the Jamaica Pond path, sweating like I had a fever and pretending I loved all this healthy, outdoorsy, exercise-y crap.

Not that I hated it. I mean, who could hate this quiet, beautiful space just minutes from the hustle and bustle of Boston? It was an oasis of green and water and calm. Now that spring was breaking through winter's stranglehold, the trees were filling in and the pond felt even more secluded and secret.

And I needed every step in this one-and-a-half-mile path to keep my ass in check. I was in a serious, committed relationship with cheese. And wine. And my mother's Dominican cake with pineapple filling. Always the pineapple filling, never guava.

I reserved my serious and committed for carbs and fat.

There was also the task of preventing my brain from overheating into nuclear reactor-level stress meltdowns. Occupational hazard. My boss could give a master class in the art of tyranny. Most of my clients too.

I'd tried gyms, including the one in my office building, but I was not interested in shvitzing all over my coworkers. Something about gym treadmills felt utterly hopeless to me, like I was a little drone walking on a mechanical road to nowhere. I couldn't do that.

So, this was my routine, rain or shine: one full loop around the pond at six every morning, Do Not Disturb mode on, The Backstreet Boys blasting. Get my steps in and get ready for the day, even if that meant waking up, getting dressed, leaving my house, boob-sweating around the trail, and *then* going home only to shower and dress and leave the house all over again. All while pretending that I loved exercising at the ass-crack of dawn. It made sense in some strange world.

There was one definite drawback to the ass-crack of dawn: some of the woodland creatures were still living it up and popping out of the bushes like they were at a fun little forest rave with a sticky-fingered toad on the turntables. On most days, it was nothing more than a squirrel or pair of mourning doves, and I could handle those dudes. Today wasn't one of those days.

A raccoon-possum-evil-monkey-stegosaurus hybrid darted out from the brush, stopped in the middle of the path, and hissed at me. It was possible that I peed just a tiny bit.

"Oh hell no," I screamed.

I stopped in my tracks, holding my breath while I waited for the beast to run off but it went right on snarling at me.

"Okay, this must be the day when the animals rise up and enslave humans because you, sir, are possessed by—"

The words stuck in my throat as a pile of bricks slammed into my back and knocked me to the ground. Then again, maybe it wasn't a pile of bricks because bricks weren't known to have arms or chin scruff, and bricks didn't smell like sweaty pine trees.

Sweaty. Pine. Trees.

Yeah, I said it. Thought it. Whatever. It was one hundred percent accurate.

I barely had time to register the shock of hitting the ground before the man-brick was muttering to himself and running his hands over my arms, legs, and torso, and bless us, oh Lord, for granting us these hands from your bounty.

"Unffff," I sigh-groaned as his fingers moved over my ribs.

His hands stilled, and then he pressed my sides again. "Did that hurt?" the man-brick asked.

I shifted away, suddenly aware of the stinging pain in my knees, palms, and chin. My breasts took most of the impact, but several layers of fabric protected them from the trail. And it wasn't like boobs bruised. Right?

"Just tell me the beast is gone," I said, teetering into a sitting position to tend these scrapes. "I can live knowing it's still out there, but I can't handle it being in my line of sight."

Man-brick was suddenly beside me, hooking his arm around my waist and bringing me to my feet. *Oof.* That hurt. Standing, breathing. Everything hurt in that glorious everything-was-worse-after-turning-thirty kind of way.

"I need to take care of this." He frowned at the battered skin on my hands and thin trails of blood running down my legs. "For fuck's sake. I can't believe I did this to you."

"Can we focus on the real priority? Seriously, tell me that creature scurried back into the pits of hell," I said.

He blinked as if he hadn't heard me correctly and then glanced from side to side. "We're about a quarter mile from the trailhead. Do you think you can make it? Is that too far? I want to know if it's too far," he said.

"Not too far at all," I lied. "I'm fine. I can walk."

He stared at the scrape on my chin, his jaw locked. This man-brick, he was a looker. Square jaw straight out of the Disney princehood, long limbs, frown for days. And everything he said was rumbly-grumbly. Mutters and murmurs and growls. But for all his Prince-Hans-of-the-Southern-Isles-ing, he was gentle. He brushed his thumb over my chin, his touch little more than a mild breeze.

Please don't be a Prince Hans. Only Kristoffs allowed here.

"Okay. We'll walk," he said. "But you'll stop me if anything hurts."

"You can bet on it." He shouldn't bet on it because that was another lie. I didn't have a reason for this tough girl routine but I was committed to it, and sticking with things long past the point of reason was my most charming trait.

His grip on me was fierce, and despite the fact I was not a small woman, he was shouldering the majority of my weight while also walking faster than I could run.

He toggled between asking whether I was all right and apologizing for knocking me to the ground. He led me to an older SUV, opened the tailgate and directed me to sit while he rustled in the back seat for his first aid kit.

I expected a wallet-sized container of bandages and out-of-date antibiotic ointment. Instead, I got a battlefield backpack stocked with more equipment than most ambulances.

"This is handy," I said, my eyes wide as he pulled on a pair of gloves. He snapped those babies on like he meant business.

"Started out as a medic. Army Rangers. Some habits are hard to shake."

He pressed a gauze pad to my bleeding knee and in the process, he stroked the back of my calf with his free hand. It tickled in the best way and I yelp-squeaked. For that one moment, I studied the sweaty-pine-scented man-brick with the squee-inducing hands. And *brick* wasn't too far from the truth: he was broad and strong and could probably run through a fucking wall.

More Hulk, less Kool-Aid Man.

Oh, yeahhhhhh.

In the morning sunlight, streaks of gold shone in his dark hair and scruffy chin. I couldn't make out the color of his eyes with his dark athletic sunglasses separating us, the type you saw on snowboarders and surfers. Neither option was likely here, a hot second outside Boston.

"These days, I'm a surgeon," he said, interrupting my inspection of his tanned arms and decidedly ring-less fingers. I was pleased on both counts.

"And trail savior," I added, gesturing to the gauze on my knee. "Don't forget about that."

He chuckled, nodding, and met my gaze with a wide, warm smile. Such a nice smile. You could tell a lot about people by their smiles. This guy was honest, kind. A little reserved but not everyone needed to live their life balls out.

"Anytime," he said. "I'm Cal."

"Stella," I replied.

Cal glanced off toward the trail, shaking his head before looking back at me. "Wow," he said, squeezing my calf. "It's nice to finally put a name to the face. After all this time."

I smiled but it was one of those I-don't-get-it smiles. "'All this time'?"

He gazed at me, frowning as if he didn't understand what I didn't understand. "I've been hitting this trail almost every day for months." His voice faded and he stopped himself. He stared at the ground for a long moment, blinking as a blush crept up his neck and across his cheeks. This sweaty pine man-brick had a shy side. "I've seen you out here a lot. I thought—I don't know. I thought you'd seen me too."

Oh.

Ohhhh.

Oh.

3

CAL

Most guys started off with a quippy line. I waited a handful of months to approach Stella and then I knocked her to the damn ground. That was just great. Real fucking awesome.

After that smooth move, it was no wonder I didn't know what to say. It was easier to talk about her contusions; I owned that territory. But when I palpated her knee and ankle for more serious injuries, I couldn't keep my touch clinical. Even with gloved fingers, her olive skin felt exactly like the perfection I'd imagined.

Yes. Fine. All right. Half of those thoughts were filthy, sweaty, skin-slapping fantasies. She was the star in every one of my dirty dreams, and until now, I hadn't even known her name.

"Wow," I said to myself, my fingers curling around Stella's calf. "It's nice to finally put a name to the face. After all this time."

Her nose wrinkled and she tilted her head, confused. "'All this time'?" she repeated.

"Yeah," I said, stealing another moment to caress her leg. Memorize the feel of her. Imagine those legs wrapped around my waist. "I've been hitting this trail almost every day for months." I should've stopped right there and been done with it. I should've picked up the clear cues and choked myself with them to keep my mouth shut. I should've stopped digging myself deeper into this big, awkward hole just like I should've stopped before slamming all two hundred pounds of me into her. But I didn't. Nope. Couldn't help myself out of this mess with both hands and a shovel. "I've seen you out here a lot. I thought —I don't know. I thought you'd seen me too."

Her eyes widened and she pulled on a tight, cautious smile. "Um, yeah. Right. Definitely."

Ah, hell. There was a reason I didn't talk to women. It had something to do with always saying the wrong thing at the wrongest moments. And when it came to this woman? Wrong, wrong, all fucking wrong. If I could've hightailed it out of the situation, I would've. But I had wounds to tend and I didn't know how to walk away from a patient. Not even when my life depended on it. There was a bullet hole through my left leg to prove it.

"Oh, no, no. It's okay," Stella said, leaning forward and angling her face to catch my eye. "I'm in my own world when I'm walking, you know? I get into the tunes and block everything else out. I'm sure I've seen you a hundred times. I'm positive. It just took me a minute to catch up. And everyone looks different up close. I notice shoes more than anything else." She glanced down at my sneaks. "Oh, right. Yes! Yes, of course. Orange with the blue laces. I've seen those plenty of times. From a distance, I thought it was orange and purple. Clemson colors. I don't know how you feel about Clemson but I'll just say I'm excited it's blue and not purple."

A noise signaling some form of agreement rumbled in my throat, and I turned my attention to cleaning and bandaging her knees. My brain was on lockdown and I couldn't gather a single thing to say to the curvy, confident woman I'd been lusting after for months. I couldn't tell her my blue laces came with the sneaks and I'd never given any thought to coordinating my collegiate pride with my running gear.

As if sensing my wordless panic, Stella filled the silence with her thoughts on the weather and the Red Sox's prospects this season, her joy in seeing early buds on the lilac trees around town, and the new ducklings she noticed in the pond last week. I was nearly finished cleaning the scratches on her chin when she leveled her dark-eyed gaze on me.

"So, Blue Laces," she said, her smile deepening until dimples appeared. "How can I thank you for peeling me off the trail and patching me up?"

"No, that's not necessary. It was my fault to begin with." I stared at the birthmark beneath her ear. Too light for a freckle, too dark for a scar, too flat for a mole. It looked like Turkey. The country, not the bird overtaking the streets of Cambridge. "You don't have to thank me. I'm the one who knocked you over."

Stella nodded. "Right. Coffee sounds great. How about Seven Pond? It's a cute little spot. Do you know where that is?" She patted her hips until her fingers located her key fob. Goddamn, there were hidden pockets in those leggings and now I needed to find out what else she had in there. "Either way, you can follow me."

"You, uh—you really don't have to do that," I stammered. "You don't have to do this, Stella."

I wasn't due in surgery until the afternoon and I had another three hours before rounds. I didn't have any reason to turn down her offer, other than my complete inability to form sentences around this woman.

She smiled and those dimples popped again. They were deep enough to hold the entirety of my heart, soul, and being, and I was ready to claim my place in there now. Did she know what she was doing when she hit me with that sunshine? Did she understand?

"I really do, Cal," she said. "The raccoonasaurus was probably going to tear off my leg and run back to the forest with it, and you prevented that situation. And..." She offered a little shrug. "We're trail buddies. Trail buddies get coffee. It's the rule, Cal."

"It's the rule?"

She bobbed her head, the movement sending her ponytail swishing over her shoulder. I stared at those silky strands, wondering what they'd feel like between my fingers. Over my bare chest. And then, lower. "Yep, it is."

I couldn't argue with that. I could not.

"Let's go before that creature comes back for my leg. Today's one of those days where I know I'll need both of them."

I shouldn't have said anything but I couldn't stop myself. "What creature?"

A blank expression pulled her smile into a flat line.

"The giant beast that ran out from the woods and hissed at me. I'm sure you saw it."

I scratched my chin. "I saw a little beaver but I can't say I noticed anything else on the trail. I could've missed it." My gaze dropped to the flare of her hips. "I'm sorry. I was a bit preoccupied."

Stella crossed her arms over her chest with a huff. "I know beavers and that was no beaver."

"Maybe you're not used to seeing them from that angle." I took a step back. Ran my hand down the nape of my neck. Hoped she was experiencing some momentary deafness or temporary amnesia because what the fuck was wrong with me?

"Really, Cal," she replied, dragging a slow gaze over the length of me. "Really."

"I'm not going to say anything else because it's going to come out very wrong and I will continue fucking everything up."

"I'm not sure you can stop yourself." She hopped off the tailgate and slammed me with a gut-stirring smirk. "Let's go. We're getting coffee."

I followed her red Volkswagen around the corner, gazed at her while she chatted with the barista about coffee beans, and when we sat down at a table by the window, I couldn't stop myself from blurting out the only question I needed answered.

"Who are you, Stella? I want to know everything about you."

4

STELLA

CAL LAID HIS THICK FOREARMS ON THE TABLE, HIS TAWNY EYES wide as they dug straight into me, and he said, "I want to know everything about you."

Oh, he was a treasure. All that wide-shouldered strength and those soulful gazes. He was sweet in a quiet, bashful way. He was also built like a wide receiver and that made his sweetness just a touch more endearing.

And he'd been watching me?—*following* me?—for months.

That was a fun little recipe for early morning oddness. When viewed under a certain light, it was creepy. But that wasn't this morning's light. Cal didn't worry me. If anything, I was fascinated. A bit flattered too. And I could handle myself.

"Mmhmm." I stirred my matcha latte. He was still doing it—watching me—but now that I knew, I warmed under the attention. "Spoken like a true stalker."

His gaze snapped away from my hands and up to my face.

"No, no, that's not it," he stammered. "What I said back there, I know it sounded bad. That's not what I meant. Honestly, it never went beyond noticing you on the trail. Lime green Asics." He laughed, nodding toward my shoes. "I'd never do anything, you know, I'd *never*." He dropped his head into his hands and huffed out a long sigh as he rubbed his eyes. "I'm not a stalker. I'm sorry about all of this. I should go."

His ears were pink. He was blushing, and even though he was waiting for the earth to open up and swallow him whole, I was charmed. "No, don't go," I said, touching my fingers to his forearm for a second. "You have a nice, big cup of coffee here and I really can't eat this scone by myself."

Cal looked up at me, then he eyed the lemon scone smothered in blueberry glaze. I was sure it would be a two-biter for him. He looked like the kind of man who could actually, truly eat a horse and then ask for the dessert menu. He'd demolish a tray of my mother's meat pastelitos before they cooled from the fryer. "I don't want you to feel uncomfortable."

"It takes a lot more than that to make me uncomfortable. Really, I've seen it all. I'm good," I said, waving him off. "Anyway, I took a picture of your license plate and texted it to my assistant in case you decide to torture me in your basement or kill me in the woods." Cal rapid-blinked at me as his mouth fell open. "It's too early to joke about that? Okay. I'll hold off a little longer."

I broke off a corner of the scone for myself and passed the rest to Cal. He gave the pastry a resigned grin and said, "Can we start over? Please? You're so beautiful and I can't think. I've wanted to talk to you for the longest time and you'd think that would've been enough to decide on something smooth to say but nothing is coming out right."

Biting my lip to keep my dimples under control, I studied Cal. How did I miss this man at the pond? There were laugh lines around his eyes and just a few silver-white hairs on his temples, and the hint of a tattoo hiding under the sleeve of his old t-shirt. How could I have missed this?

"Okay, let's start over." I reached across the table, my hand outstretched. "I'm Stella Allesandro and I zone all the way out on my morning walks. I blame *NSYNC."

Cal laughed, but he didn't release my hand. "I'm Cal Hartshorn and I approach women by mowing them down to see if they like being underneath me."

A shocked laugh burst from my lips and I felt heat rising to my cheeks but I couldn't focus on the obvious innuendo he offered when there was more curious business at hand.

"Hold it right there," I said, leaning closer to peer at him.

"You can hold it anywhere you want it," he murmured.

"I'm sure." I held up a finger as my shoulders shook with silent laughter. "You keep them coming, Cal Hartshorn."

"I keep them coming like you wouldn't believe, Stella Allesandro," he replied. "Like you would not *believe*."

Laughing, I said, "Stop being obscene for a minute."

He had the balls to pull an appalled face. As if I was the one with all the bawdy comments here. "Obscene? I'm not obscene at all."

"You hide behind all your shy-boy awkwards but you're filthy," I said.

"Would you rather I hide with you in your cool-girl

pretties? It might not look like I'll fit but you let me worry about that."

Another surprised laugh rumbled in my throat. "You... you should've talked to me a long time ago."

"I suppose that's as good as I'm going to get this morning," he said. "I mean, you haven't dumped coffee in my lap or run screaming."

"Not yet," I said. "But—wait. Go back. You're *Doctor* Hartshorn? The one on the cover of *Boston Magazine's* Best Doctors in the Bay State edition? The one who worked on the Patriots' defensive line coach when he had a heart attack last winter?" I tapped my hand—the one not currently swallowed by Cal's bear paw—to my breast, as if he didn't know how to find the organ in question. "You're *that* cardiothoracic surgeon?"

"Oh, hell," he muttered, cringing. I thought he was going to crawl back into his shell again and take his fresh comments with him but he didn't. And he didn't release my hand. "You saw that?"

"Did I *see* that?" I cried. "Hate to break it to you, but that magazine is on every newsstand and checkout line in New England. But I didn't recognize you without the scrubs and white coat and the *I really hate this pose but I'm trying* smile."

He hummed in agreement as his thumb passed over my palm in a smooth, rhythmic motion that sent goose bumps down to my toes and...other places.

"On behalf of the Patriots Nation, I want to thank you for looking after Coach Torres," I said, and it was a weak attempt at preventing myself from turning into a pile of pudding in this man's hands. All it took was his thumb stroking my palm and my game was crumbling like the scone between us. "And you've got the perfect name for cardiology. *Hart*-shorn."

"I've heard that once or twice," he said with a wry laugh. "But I'm not interesting at all. I want to hear about you. What do you do? Where are you from? What are your favorite flowers and now that I've nearly assaulted you, when can I take you for a proper night out?"

I reached for my latte with my free hand because I needed more palm rubbing in my life. The entirety of his focus was on me, completely ignoring the morning rush around us. If there was a world beyond this table, he was unaware of it and I wasn't far behind.

I hadn't felt this inkling—the little tingle in my chest, the swoop and roll in my belly—since my twenties. Early twenties. Sitting here today, a thirty-five-year-old woman, I couldn't reach back far enough to grab those memories. I couldn't hold them up alongside this morning and deter-mine whether they were the same or different. And I wasn't sure that mattered. I was different now. Even if these inklings and tingles were the same, I didn't experience them the same way anymore. I didn't melt into them, didn't let them surround me like a shawl.

I didn't want them.

But I didn't want to stop them either. I didn't remove my hand from Cal's grip, I didn't grab my latte and go back to the comfortable, organized life I'd created for myself. I stayed. I stayed because I wanted his thumb on my palm and I wanted to share this scone with him, and I didn't want to think beyond those simple desires. There was no room between his thumb and my palm for my work, my stress, my no-strings, no-futures relationships, my history of holding on too long or fucking it up with good guys who deserved more.

"Tell me something, Cal."

He replied with a crisp nod and I saw a quick flash of that military discipline in the gesture. "In my wallet, in the glove box, and in my first aid kit. Always prepared."

I blinked. "Excuse me?"

"Nothing. It's nothing." His ears were pink again and— oh shit, was he talking about condoms? "Go ahead. What did you want to know?"

I eyed him. "You keep them in the first aid kit, huh?"

His shoulders lifted and fell. "Never know when you'll get banged up."

"Wow," I said, a laugh cracking out of me, "you're gifted. This is a talent you have, Doctor Hartshorn." I took a sip of my latte and set it back down. "Why have you been watching me at the pond?"

"I wasn't watching you. Not exactly. I saw you one day and then again, and...I wanted to keep seeing you. I liked it. I liked you." He swallowed. "You're gorgeous and fascinating and it brightened my day every time we crossed paths. I was trying to figure out the best way to approach you, but— but I didn't know what to say. I thought you might be spoken for."

Yeah, no. None of that. I snatched my hand back because nope.

"Let me stop you right there, chief." I held my index finger up, laughing without humor. "I speak for myself, thank you very much."

It was true—no one spoke for me. No prevarication, no half-truths. I wasn't dating anyone, I wasn't looking, and I didn't belong to anyone. Didn't want to. I'd foreclosed that option long ago and never looked back. But the reality came with more layers than I was willing to share right now.

"Right, my bad. Figure of antiquated speech," Cal said. His smiling eyes never left mine as he took my finger-wagging hand, lifted it to his lips, and pressed a single kiss just past my knuckles. "Go ahead, then. Speak for yourself. Tell me everything."

"I'm in public relations," I started, amazed that I could form words after Cal killed me with the last great act of chivalry. *My god.* I didn't believe there were still men out there who kissed a woman's hand as if he was bowing at her feet before riding into battle. And yes, feminists could enjoy acts of chivalry. I could open my own doors but I could also appreciate a man opening one for me when it was done out of deference rather than some old-fashioned concern over my skirts being too big for me to reach on my own. "I manage publicity and communications for professional and collegiate athletes. I specialize in crisis management messaging and total image overhaul. I'm from around here. Quincy, to be exact."

Cal's fingers started moving up my wrist, toward my elbow, and I had to stop speaking because my words were dissolving like salt in stew. This wasn't me. Not at all. Not how I rolled. I didn't get lovestruck or smitten. I didn't *fall* for guys.

I had a healthy handful of men in my life and each of them understood the name of the game. They'd have to after the lengths to which I went to establish expectations up front. Stephen, Leif, Harry. I didn't have the time or interest in cultivating a relationship with any of them but I did have a color-coded Google calendar reminding me of my meetups. I wasn't dating them. They weren't my boyfriends. They barely qualified as friends with benefits.

Harry and I met up once a week and we'd been on that program since last fall. We didn't have any mutual friends and shared few interests but our evenings together didn't require any of those things because he was a big believer in the two-to-one ratio and he didn't get his until I got both of mine. Leif traveled a solid forty-five weeks out of the year but we managed to get ourselves in the same place about once every other month. He had a few kinks that didn't interest me but he always came with his A game and I admired that. Stephen lived in London but his firm shipped him off to Boston for a week each quarter. The man was a beast in bed but drier than a week-old biscuit.

Those guys didn't need relationships, exclusivity, feelings. They were predictable and reliable, and I never worried about my world collapsing because I figured out all the important things a minute too late.

And none of them ever kissed my hand or dragged their fingers up the inside of my wrist like they were amazed by the feel of my skin.

Stopppppppppp, Stella. Just stop. Throw a flag. Call a penalty. Get out of here.

Cal wasn't following any of my rules. He was already two thousand percent more invested than I wanted him to be but I couldn't stop him. Couldn't stop myself. I didn't pull my hand back or edge away. I didn't shut him down. I scooted my damn chair closer to his side and—and yeah, this was un-fucking-believable—I dropped my hand to his thigh.

Stelllaaaaaaaaaa.

What the actual fuck was I doing? What was I thinking? Was I thinking or had I fallen into some kind of hand-kissed dream state where I made moves on a man without first communicating the rules and boundaries? Because I always laid down the rules and boundaries. No one walked away bitter and bruised and hating me when there were rules and boundaries in place.

Cal glanced down at my hand. His brows pitched up. Then he shifted his chair toward mine, closing the whole damn distance between us. Boundaries? Gone. Rules? Nowhere to be found. And those inklings? They were everywhere. *Everywhere.*

"And what about the flowers and your first available evening?" he prompted. "Tonight comes to mind. You'd be doing me a big favor if you agreed because I don't think I can go back to lurking around you at the trail. If you think this has been awkward, I've got some news for you about the way tomorrow morning is going to shake out."

I wanted to touch him. More than resting my palm on his leg. I wanted to feel him. It was an urge twisting deep inside me. I wanted him to hold me the way he did when we stumbled away from that raccoonasaurus on the path, his arms around me and his big body making me feel small and precious. Even though I was neither of those things. I wanted to spend time cataloging every inch of him, feel the places where he was hard and soft.

Stelllllllllla. Noooooooooo.

"I'm not really a flowers-and-proper-dates girl," I said,

fully aware of his thigh muscles tightening under my hand. "I'm more of a burgers-and-football girl, to be honest. Baseball or hockey since we're in the off-season. Basketball too. Burgers, sports, nothing proper. I'm not proper."

Cal rested his forehead on my shoulder with a quiet groan. That sound, it was more intimate than a kiss. It belonged to private spaces where no one else could listen in. But we'd already forgotten about the rest of the world. We were alone here, me and Cal, and I wasn't smitten. I wasn't lovestruck. "Marry me, Stella. Marry me and bear my children."

His hand skated up my arm and over my shoulder to cup my face, and just like that, I was kissing a man I'd met an hour ago.

5

CAL

I was forty-two years old.

I'd studied in the most demanding cardiothoracic surgical residency program in the country.

I'd done two tours through an active war zone as an Army Ranger.

I'd hiked the Appalachian Trail straight through from Maine to Georgia. Twice.

But all of that age, experience, and constitution of will faded away when I dragged Stella into my lap and nestled her sweet curves over my crotch. For the first time since my gangly teen years, I was suffering from a very prominent, very public erection, and the tender sweep of her lips against mine was making matters worse.

And when I said worse, I meant better than anything else in the known world.

"Stella." It was spoken as a broken plea. I was aching for her, for anything she'd give me, and desperate enough to beg.

Her fingers moved up my chest, my shoulders, my neck,

and her touch was like coming home. It was a comfort and a craving like I'd never known before.

She was tiny in my arms and as soft and sweet as springtime. The faint scent of citrus echoed from her skin. Her ponytail tickled my wrist and though I wanted nothing more than to wind those silky strands around my fist and tug until I was drowning in her big, brown eyes, my hands weren't leaving the safe harbor of her hips.

No, ma'am. I'd met my daily quota for shameful and indecent acts. I was not mauling this angel in a coffee shop. I'd knocked her to the ground, confessed my obsession, and asked for her hand in marriage, all within an hour. *An hour.* She deserved better than the live-action version of the fantasies currently on heavy rotation in my head.

I was going to find some decency even if it took sheer force of will now and an ice-cold shower later.

"Stella." Her name was delicious on my lips. It was meant to be moaned, gasped, fucking howled. "*Stella.*"

She giggled against me, driving her fingers into my hair. It was cut close—Army habits weren't meant to break. Her nails on my scalp were whittling away the very last of my civility, my hands gripping her hips as if I had a mind to mark them, and her little sounds—the laughter, the sighs, the hums—were the only thing in my universe.

The barista called out several orders like the bang of a drum—tall Americano for Barry, tall coconut milk capp for Serrai, short half-caff macchiato, extra foam for Linus, tall extra shot non-fat latte for Tayla—and those shouts brought Stella's attention away from the thorough inspection she was giving my mouth.

"Oh," she breathed, pressing her fingertips to her lips.

She knew. She knew, she felt it—and not just the erection throbbing against her rear end, begging for her attention. This was it, she was it.

I needed my mother to meet her yesterday. I could have Mom on a flight from Oregon this morning and gushing over Stella before nightfall.

By all accounts, I could get a ring on Stella's finger as early as this weekend.

"Tonight," I murmured as I leaned into her, desperate to feel her skin beneath my lips again. "Stella, tell me I can see you tonight."

"Not tonight," she said.

"Tomorrow," I said. It was not a question.

"It's the craziest time of my year. You know, aside from all the other super-crazy times."

I tilted my head to the side, studied her. "What makes this so crazy?"

She reached up, brushed a few loose strands behind her ears. Sucked in a shallow breath and blew it out. "It's signing season and the NFL draft day is next week. I can't even tell you how much I'd love to see anything other than the inside of my office tonight, but I'm barely able to take this hour in the morning without drowning in drama when I get to work. I'll let you in on a little secret."

"You can give me your big secrets too," I said. "I'll keep them safe."

She gifted me with a quick smile. No dimples this time. "Athletes tend to be nervous nellies who need their hands held and egos stroked when it comes to their place in the draft." She blinked twice, drew another short breath. "Give me some time to think about everything, okay?"

"If not tonight, tomorrow morning, then," I said. "On the pond."

"Will you return to your regularly scheduled stalking," she started, a sly smile tipping up her lips, "or will you be walking with me?"

"Stella. If you're walking at the pond, you're walking with me now."

She gazed at me, her eyes as wide as they'd been when I confessed to watching her for months. If not for those fast, shallow breaths, I might've mistaken her for a statue. "Oh, really? That's how it's going to be?"

I gave her a quick nod. "Someone has to keep an eye out for that beaver of yours."

6

STELLA

THERE WAS A LOGIC TO IT ALL. THIS MAN, THIS MORNING, this overwhelmed thrill coursing through me. Oh yes, most definitely. It made all the sense in the world when I squinted from the right angle.

But when the man-brick—err, *Cal*—returned me to my seat, I was struck with an overwhelming shortage of warm, solid man beneath my buns, and the logic didn't feel too logical anymore.

However.

Aside from all that, I had a to-do list of epic proportions on my desk today and the draft next week, a genetically modified raccoon on the loose, and a man-brick growling all over me while he proposed marriage and promised an eternity of beaver protection.

"Stella," he rasped, and that was the sound of a rumbly, grumbly bear. He snaked one arm around the back of my chair while he dipped his head in search of my eyes. He brought his free hand to my leg, squeezing just above my knee.

Holy Hannah. Those...those were forearms. Thick, ropey, dusted with dark golden hair. For all his thickness, his fingers were long and—dare I say?—elegant. Yes, those were elegant man fingers. Nothing sausage plump here. I figured it made sense since those hands mended hearts. Actual human organs. They had to be elegant.

"I'm going to need a minute here." I pressed my hand to my breastbone, gulping down a breath. An hour after running right into me, Cal had succeeded in knocking the wind out of me. "I need—just give me a minute."

"Take two," he said. "Take two hundred. There's no rush. I'm not going anywhere."

"I'm sure you have places to be."

A warm laugh whispered over my ear. "Even if I wanted to leave right now, I don't think I should."

His hand came to my back, resting between my shoulder blades for a second before moving in slow, soothing circles meant to calm this percolating panic, but it only solidified the fact that I was developing feelings—*feelings*!—for a man after nothing more than an eye blink in time. But this wasn't feelings. This was adrenaline. Shock from the scare, the fall. None of this was real. Couldn't be.

This man had asked me to marry him and that wasn't even the crazy part. No, it was that, for one crazy minute out of all the crazy minutes in this crazy morning, it didn't feel crazy. My heart was burrowing straight out of my chest and into my throat, and there was a goddamn unicorn chasing butterflies around my stomach, and my head was full of fizzy bubbles like New Year's Eve, and for one tiny, tiny second in the middle of this crazy, I wanted him to mean it. To ask, to want me for always.

Now that was *crazy*. I didn't want that. I didn't want any of that. I loved my life. I had everything I needed, everything I wanted. Cute, shy heart surgeons who kissed like that and made me feel like this were unnecessary.

Stella. No no no no. No. No, Stella.

"And it's not like I can walk out of here in this condition," he continued, the fine bristles of his chin scruff brushing against my neck and his thumb gliding over the tender spot behind my knee. He knew right where to find me at my most sensitive. "Or drive. Not without some, uh, rearrangement."

I stared at him for a beat before glancing down at the erection trapped under his track pants. "Jesus," I rasped.

"It's not a big deal, honey, but I prefer Cal," he replied.

"And you went there," I said, mostly to myself.

Cal shrugged. "That could apply to everything that's happened this morning."

"You went there and I can't decide whether to laugh or —I don't know." I lifted my wrist, squinting at the freckles there because I hadn't worn a watch since my iPhone became my most essential accessory. "Thank you. For everything. Especially with that raccoonasaurus, even if you think it was a beaver. You're wrong but I still owe you for that one."

"You don't," he replied, his fingers tight around my thigh. "You...you don't owe me anything, Stella."

I murmured in disagreement. I wasn't done with this man-brick. It didn't matter how many times I silently screamed at myself, I wasn't done. "Another coffee maybe? A muffin too. What kind of muffin do you like? No, wait. Let me guess." I stared at him as I tapped my index against my lips. "You're a corn muffin kind of guy, aren't you? Maybe corn and jalapeño? Or corn and blueberry? Oh, yeah. Corn and blueberry all the way. That's you."

"Tomorrow," he said, blowing right past my name-that-muffin trick. "I'll see you tomorrow, Stella."

"You're very direct," I said. "When you're not busy being shy."

"All I'm saying is the only *muffin* I want to bite is yours," he replied. "Forgive me if that's a bit forward."

With that idea planted in my mind, I stared at his mouth, my own lips pursed together as I forced air in and out. Legs pursed together too. I thought about kissing him again. I thought about sending a group text to Stephen, Leif, and Harry, ending our color-coded arrangements because their come-and-go companionship was no longer needed.

Stelllllla. No, dammit, no.

Wait. I didn't want to do that. No, I liked my life *just* the way it was. I had good things going. I didn't need any of this. Early morning trail rescues and emotionally demanding scones and surgeons with cocks the size of cruise missiles weren't part of the plan.

There was an alarm bell pealing in the distance, urging me up, out of this coffee shop, into my car, away from this man, back to my chaos-but-I-love-it life. Because I controlled that shit. This? The man-brick and the raccoon and the feelings? Nope, I controlled none of this.

But I ignored the unpredictable, saying, "Okay, sure. Tomorrow. The trail, not the muffin." Nodding as I granted myself permission, I brought my hand to the back of his neck and tugged him closer. *Stelllllla.* "Would you—"

"Yes," he said, that single word at once a twisted plea and gracious sigh. His lips crashed over mine, and he dragged me right into the deep end with this kiss. It was heavy and desperate and I didn't think I'd ever come up for air again, but then he retreated only long enough to lift me onto his lap. *Where I belonged.* He didn't have to say it. I knew what he was thinking. The hand that was once fixed on my thigh was now tucked between my knees and squeezing hard enough to tell me that he wanted to slide it higher just as much as I did. Just a bit more. *Come home, Cal. Come to me. Come for me.*

His lips mapped my jaw and neck, and he said, "You can't work all night. You have to eat at some point, don't you?"

"You've seen my ass. It is substantial proof that I eat," I replied.

Cal leaned back, regarding me for a moment. He eyed my scraped chin, my undoubtedly messy ponytail, my kiss-swollen lips, my fingers tangled in his shirt. A low, hazy smile lit his eyes. It was as if he was taking stock of everything but my curves. It was nothing like the bold-faced ogling I got from most men. No, this appreciation was built on much more than standard-issue admiration for tits and ass, and if I never felt a man's eyes on me like this again, I'd still talk about it to anyone who listened. I'd start a new urban legend, the one about the man-brick who found a woman sexy without mentally molesting her.

"Even more reason for me to keep you fed. Isn't that right, sweet thing?"

Sweet thing. That wasn't supposed to sound like perfection in my head, but it did.

As I nodded and agreed to meet him late this evening, I curled into his chest, listening to his heartbeat while he asked after my burgers and beer preferences. I felt dazed, nearly drunk, and even though he was with me now, I was counting the minutes until I'd have him again.

I wasn't falling. I wasn't smitten. I wasn't lovestruck. Not at all.

I MARCHED DOWN THE HALL, A BURST OF STEAM FUELING every step. My residents were trailing behind me like always. Never had I sympathized with mother ducks until I had ducklings of my own. Most days, I enjoyed my ducklings. I liked teaching them. I liked learning from them.

This wasn't most days.

When I reached Nick Acevedo, I turned back to them. "Labs," I barked. "Get them."

Like always, O'Rourke was quick to respond. "Already done." He waved his tablet.

I liked the kid. I really did. He was meticulous about prep work and thorough in the OR. Two things I appreciated. But I didn't have it in me to reward him for his attention to detail this morning.

"Get ready for rounds. If you're under the impression you're ready, you're not even close," I replied. "Now. Go."

They snapped into action, my words a quick whip.

"What was that all about?" Nick asked. He spared me a glance before returning to his phone. He was chained to that thing anytime his wife Erin was traveling for work. She was a climate scientist. The planet was keeping her busy these days.

"I talked to her." The reality of that statement left me a little breathless. "This morning, I talked to her."

"Talked to who?" he asked, his thumbs flying over the screen.

"*Her*," I replied. "Her name is Stella Allesandro and I talked to her."

He dragged his gaze up to meet mine. He stared at me for a long moment, disbelieving. Hell, I barely believed it. "The girl from the park? You spoke actual words to her? Not just in your head? Or out loud when she was half a mile away? Because we've talked about this, Hartshorn. It doesn't count if she can't hear you."

I started to respond but dragged my hand over my head, rubbed my neck instead. "I bumped into her. She tripped. On the trail. She tripped because I ran into her," I admitted. "It wasn't my best moment but we did talk and...and yeah. We talked. A lot."

The parts about kissing her and damn near dry humping her backside weren't up for discussion. Nick and I didn't get into the details like that, even though we'd known each other for years. Before he and his wife bought a house in Cambridge, we lived in the same apartment building across from the hospital. For as long as I could remember, surgeons had lived in the three apartments carved out of that old brownstone. A trauma surgeon lived on the third floor now, a surly guy from California. He didn't talk to anyone about much of anything.

"You—ran into her?" He blinked at me for a second, his

brows knit together. "How hard are we talking? Is she all right?"

"Uh, yeah. She's okay. It wasn't that bad," I hedged. I rubbed the back of my neck again. I hated that I'd injured Stella. "A couple bruises. Some scratches. I took care of it."

"And this didn't result in her calling the police? Because stories about strange men accosting women in parks don't usually end with polite conversation."

"We got coffee and talked for an hour," I said. "It went surprisingly well, all things considered. I'm seeing her again."

"Oh, this is gold." Nick pushed off from the wall, peering at me. "Where's Emmerling? She needs to hear this," he said, looking up and down the hall. "She should be done with the hot gallbladder that came through first thing this morning. I'm texting her right now. Prepare yourself to tell this story again."

Alexandra Emmerling was the gastrointestinal surgeon who lived in the apartment above mine. She was one of the best surgeons I knew and a better friend. Within seconds, she jogged around the corner, her scrub cap in hand and red clogs squeaking against the linoleum floors.

"What's going on?" she asked. "What's wrong?"

Nick pointed at me. "He tripped the woman at the park so he could talk to her."

Alex dropped her hands to her hips. "That's not normal, Hartshorn. Not normal at all." She shook her head. "Where are your residents? We need them to get you a psych consult."

"That's not funny because they'll do it and I didn't intentionally trip her," I argued. "It was an accident. There was an animal on the trail and she stopped suddenly. It was a raccoon but she thought it was some kind of wolf, I think. I didn't notice she'd stopped and I ran into her. And then I was on top of her and that wasn't the way I wanted to start things."

Nick shook his head at that. "Even better."

"Let me get this straight," Alex said. "You didn't just trip her, you slammed into her and took her down to the ground. Is that right?"

"Yes, but then we went out for coffee. The coffee was her idea. I was going to die of mortification or something but she insisted on coffee. With me. At a coffee shop. Where we drank the coffee and talked and, you know—" I hesitated. "Yeah. That's what we did. At the coffee shop."

Nick and Alex exchanged a dubious glance.

"Her name is Stella Allesandro and she's a sports publicist, and she's from Quincy and I'm seeing her again tonight."

Another dubious glance.

"Did you tell her you've been watching her for a short eternity?" Alex asked.

With a grim smile, I nodded. "Yeah. That part didn't go over too well."

"Imagine that," Nick said.

"And she still wants to see you again?" Alex asked. "You're sure about that?"

Of course I was sure. I pressed the heels of my palms to my eyes. I knew the taste of her mouth, the way her fingers felt on my scalp, how her backside was the sweetest agony against my cock. Of course I was sure. "We're meeting downtown at nine thirty."

"I gotta get to post-op but I want the whole story over lunch," Alex said. "I'm expecting a minute-by-minute accounting of these events and I want to understand how this chick could survive you tackling her to the ground. If you did that to me—"

"Riley would kill you with his bare hands," Nick said.

I didn't doubt Alex's fiancé would do just that. He was a deceptively chill guy but he would clean my clock if I harmed her in any way.

Alex laughed, nodding. "Riley would kill you but I'd also be calling Shap to put my face back together."

"Shap?" Nick asked.

"Sara Shapiro," Alex replied. "The new reconstructive surgeon. The one we poached from Sloan Kettering."

"Oh, I didn't hear about that," Nick said, mostly to himself. "When Erin gets home, we'll have to invite Doctor Shapiro over. A little welcome-to-the-surgical-wing dinner. I'd like to hear the details of this poach."

"I love poaching," I said. "We don't do enough of it."

"And low-key attacking women because that's easier than starting a normal conversation," Alex added. "But I think you've done plenty of that."

"Wait a second," Nick said as he rubbed his knuckles down his jaw. "Did we ever invite Stremmel over? We said we were going to but then—then Erin was tied up with that report and then she was traveling again. I don't think we ever did it."

I held back a groan but just barely. Sebastian Stremmel was a problem child. More specifically, my problem child. I'd championed his candidacy as the hospital's new trauma surgeon and I was thrilled when he moved his practice here from Southern California last fall but the shine wore off quickly. What I'd interpreted as a serious, to-the-point attitude during interviews was actually a persistently bad mood. He didn't like anyone or anything and he complained about Boston's weather like it was his calling in life.

But he was a talented surgeon and an adequate teacher and I didn't want to see him shuffled out because he couldn't get along with anyone. And that was how he became my problem child. Not that anyone else knew about the arrangement. I took it upon myself to keep an eye on Stremmel, get him into Nick's old apartment in my building, and mentor him wherever possible. But he wasn't making it easy on me, not at all. His primary forms of communication were scowls and grunts.

"No," I replied. "Perhaps we should have a gathering for Stremmel. A little 'congrats on the first six months' thing. We want him to feel welcome, right?"

"Better yet," Alex started, wagging her finger at Nick, "an end of winter event. He'll love that because we all know how much he hates anything below seventy degrees and sunny."

"If you're asking whether my wife wants to throw a vernal equinox party, I think we all know her answer will be yes," Nick replied. "If she was in town often enough to host new moon and assorted planetary alignment parties, she'd do that too."

Alex stared at him for a beat. "I don't know how to respond to that."

He waved her off. "You don't have to."

"We should work on bringing Stremmel into the fold," I

said, turning the conversation back around. "I'll see if he wants to join us for lunch."

Alex nodded, her lips pursed as she hummed to herself. "Yeah, I'm good with that. Especially now that he's stopped flirting with me. Mostly."

Another barely contained groan. "I've told him that's completely unacceptable. I'll speak to him again."

Nick shot a glance at his watch and then his phone. "I gotta go pull a meningioma. We can cover the rest of this over lunch. With or without Stremmel." He clapped me on the back, smiling. "Good job on beating up your girl from the trail and then convincing her to give you a shot. That is some kind of miracle."

"If anyone knows how to work them, it's Hartshorn," Alex said as she backed down the hallway. "He's going to need them."

Of that I was certain.

8

STELLA

I was never late.

I didn't make out with strange men over scones either. By most measures, this day was already unusual, but it wasn't as though my boss would appreciate that explanation.

When the elevator doors opened on the fifteenth floor, I knew I'd find Flinn and Tatum waiting for me in the foyer. He was chewing his thumbnail and she was pacing, and both were clutching their phones as if they were waiting for Moses to tweet out his new rules.

"Thank god, you're alive!" Flinn yelled, pushing away from the wall as I stepped into the foyer. He waved his hands at me, wanting details. "You send me a license plate photo and tell me to call the police if I don't hear from you before noon, and—*what* is this? What happened to your face?"

Marching through the glass-walled offices and pod-shaped cubicles with Flinn and Tatum, my dynamic administrative support duo, hot on my heels, I said, "Tripped on the walking path. No biggie."

"Should I run down to Whole Foods and get some aloe?" Tatum asked. "Or call one of the team docs and get a B12 shot sent up?"

"I don't need a B12 shot," I replied. "Some aloe wouldn't hurt but it's not a top priority."

"Yes. Aloe. Lovely. But the license plate picture?" Flinn said. "Shall we revisit that? Can we take a moment to regroup here? Your knees are bruised too."

Dammit. Should have worn trousers. But dresses were easy. It was a single item of clothing, no prints or textures to coordinate, no layers to balance.

"Like I said," I smiled over my shoulder, "I took a tumble. I'm good."

"Rebecca is waiting for you in the conference room," Tatum whispered. She was a serial quiet-talker, and though I'd spent the past two years coaching the timid out of my account coordinator, we were no closer when it came to audible speech. She had no trouble hollering at Flinn so I knew she had it in her. "There's a client—"

"—and you look like you've been working out with the Fight Club," Flinn interrupted.

Where Tatum was quiet, Flinn was bold and more than a little abrupt. He'd been assisting me for almost four years now, and while he was desperate to manage clients of his own, his edges were still too rough to turn him loose. That was the Catch-22 of attaining a certain level of success: you could be an asshole, but not until you were indispensable and irreplaceable. He had work to do on all fronts.

"—the client is waiting too. With Rebecca. And his agent. In the conference room," Tatum continued.

"The client is also Lucian McKendrick," Flinn said. "If my sources can be trusted, ol' Lulu's publicist dropped him last night after he got up on the bar at Grand Ten, stripped down to his nakeds, danced around, and had to be dragged out of there by Boston's finest. Homeboy spent a few hours in lockup. Another drunk and disorderly but everyone expects he'll get off with a fine. Does he realize it's not a froyo punch card? There's no prize for racking up ten arrests." He sighed and shook his head. "They should've called me. I would've helped keep that issue under control."

"With your mouth," Tatum quipped.

"To start, yes," Flinn said with a shameless grin.

"McKendrick is the top relief pitcher in the league," Tatum said. "His current contract is worth a little more than eleven million dollars per year plus bonuses and endorsements, and he's currently out on a personal conduct suspension. That suspension came with a fine to the tune of two hundred and fifty thousand—"

"I know. I got it," I replied. It came out snappier than I'd intended, and when we reached my office, I turned and held up my hands for silence. Their eyes darted to my scraped palms and they shared another open-mouthed *what the fuck* glance. "Everything is fine. Thank you for worrying about me and getting me up to speed on McKendrick. That's why I love you both and please believe I'll give you an update on me and the client after my meeting."

Flinn motioned toward my raincoat and tote bag, and when I'd surrendered both, Tatum supplied me with my tablet and phone. Neither of them were perfect, but they made this job fun and easy, and I wouldn't trade them for anything.

With a deep breath and smile fixed on my face, I stepped into the conference room. My boss, the managing director of the Boston Sports Management Group, shot a pointed glance at the wall clock before acknowledging me.

"Thrilled you could join us," Rebecca called as I settled into a seat across from McKendrick and his agent. Many agents were based in Florida or California but Travis Veda was a local boy and he liked it that way. "Thank you for squeezing this convening into your schedule at the last moment."

There were many amazing things about Rebecca Breverman. To start, she wasn't exactly human. As far as I could tell, she didn't sleep, didn't eat, and didn't age. But right now, the most amazing thing was that she said all of those passive-aggressive words without even a hint of shade. She was furious that I was eleven minutes late for an impromptu meeting, but she sounded genuinely gracious and that required talent.

She also rocked a vaguely English-but-also-maybe-Australian accent that was almost definitely fake and that required a version of talent. I'd once heard it referred to as a New Hampshire accent by someone who obviously hadn't visited New Hampshire.

"I'm thrilled to be here," I said, swiping open my tablet and nodding at McKendrick and Veda. "Please, continue. I'll catch up."

"Hey, nice lady," McKendrick drawled, scooting his chair

closer to the table as he eyed my cleavage. "What's your story, honeycakes?"

"Shut *up*, Lucian," Veda cried, slapping his hand on the shiny tabletop. Where his client was bright-eyed and bouncing in his seat with the overflowing energy of a child in a man's body, Veda's suit was wrinkled and his face matched. He looked like he hadn't slept in weeks. "Just *shut up*. If you fuck this up, you're on your own. I'll walk, bro, and I won't look back."

Rebecca clasped her hands and glanced back and forth between Veda and McKendrick. It didn't show but she was boiling with rage over the disorderly nature of this gathering. This wasn't a typical pitch session. She wasn't showing off the wonderful things we'd do to solidify his brand or how we'd triage pesky issues.

But this was typical for me. Much like Lucian, I was a closer. I stepped up to the plate only when it was time to bring the heat and shut it all down. Hot messes and train wrecks and zombies pouring out of the closet were my specialties.

The only difference was Lucian wasn't closing anything right now. Not when he wasn't allowed on the field.

"Thank you for that segue, Mr. Veda. Mr. McKendrick, I understand that you're in a spot of trouble with the league. Is that correct?"

He offered little more than a flippant shoulder lift. This was nothing new, not for McKendrick, not for any athlete who came through these doors. Many—definitely not all, but enough—were well acquainted with being exceptional and with that exceptionalism came entitlement.

"Hmm. Yes. That's what I thought," Rebecca said,

tapping her fingertip to her lips. It was her way of communicating she'd had enough of this shit. "You've made the rounds, I see. Six publicists in the past two years. That's a new record. And it's all water under the bridge now, isn't it? The team won't trade you. They'll get you back soon enough, god willing, and they're looking for you to close for them all the way to another World Series win. Isn't that right?"

McKendrick turned to stare at Veda. "See?" he said, pointing at Rebecca. "That's what I've been telling you."

Veda shook his head. "Like I've been telling you, the owners called me this morning. If you can't clean up your act and keep it clean through the end of your suspension, they're dropping you. They don't care if you can win them twenty more pennants. They're sick and tired of all the bad press."

"The fuck they did," McKendrick grumbled, but it was a losing battle. The wrinkle in his forehead and downcast eyes told me that he knew where the chips were falling.

In recent years, the league had been quietly shifting its position on the so-called bad boys of baseball. Rather than watching the antics with amusement and welcoming the publicity, they were now taking aggressive steps to penalize unbecoming conduct and looking to make an example of a few players.

They probably didn't bet on that example being the relief pitcher who sewed up series after series, but the dark cloud of negative press was hanging heavy around McKendrick. They couldn't let him off the hook for multiple drunk-and-disorderly arrests, a DUI, and an unpleasant collection of public indecency charges while hammering the next guy for smoking a little weed.

"That's where Ms. Allesandro comes in," Rebecca said. "She has a gift for turning around the worst public images in professional sports and breathing new life into flailing brands. She'll be managing all of your appearances, social media, and other public statements. She'll be the angel on your shoulder, reminding you to keep your knickers on and your todger out of sight. She'll get you back on the field at the end of your suspension, Mr. McKendrick."

McKendrick swiveled toward Veda. "What's a todger?"

"Your dick, you dickhead," Veda snapped.

McKendrick scowled at the table. "I don't need a fuckin' babysitter," he grumbled.

"Yes, you do," Veda replied. "I'm hiring two full-time personal assistants to keep you out of the bars and away from the press, and you're doing everything that Stella instructs unless you want to go back to alfalfa farming in Blythe."

"They better be hot," McKendrick said. "*Girls Gone Wild* hot."

"They're going to be former defensive tackles who will have no problem laying you out," Travis said under his breath.

"Outstanding," Rebecca said, ignoring their comments. "Very productive. We'll ring you for a chat on progress next week, Mr. Veda. I trust you'll keep your shoes shined and your nose clean, Mr. McKendrick. You'll need both for all the charitable appearances you'll be doing."

McKendrick followed his agent out of the conference room, grousing, "What does that even mean?"

"Talk less," Veda replied.

The glass door thunked shut behind them, and Rebecca tapped her pen against the table to draw my attention.

"I'm sorry I was late," I said, pointing to the abrasion on my chin. "I had an accident this morning, and—"

"Keep McKendrick on the roster and out of trouble, and you'll find yourself with a promotion to partner and a thirty-three percent bonus. There's a corner office with your name on it if you get this right."

I curbed the desire to bust out a huge *fuck yeah*! grin followed by an *it's about damn time* side eye, instead nodding as if the suggestion mildly intrigued me. "What makes McKendrick such a priority?"

Rebecca tucked her glossy black hair over her ear. I was pretty sure it was a wig but I had no hard evidence on the matter. I always watched to see if I could catch it wobbling on her head. "The team is betting on him to get them through the post-season and bring home another World Series appearance. They have no one to replace him. They've picked up a few from the farm teams, but without McKendrick, they need a miracle." She hit me with her frosty-yet-fiery smile, the one I was certain she'd picked up from Cruella de Vil. "Be the miracle."

...or be gone. In the same way Rebecca didn't have to tell me that she was annoyed at my tardiness to an unscheduled meeting, she didn't have to tell me there was no room for error. Rebecca didn't believe in second chances. You either got the job done or got the hell out.

The only reason I'd survived eleven years at Boston Sports Management Group was because I was a closer. I nailed it every time, brought home the win, shut it all down. But I'd been on a plateau for the past year. I was getting the job done with the problem cases but I was overdue for a big score. If I wanted to level up, McKendrick was the way to do it.

After discussing strategy and logistics with her, I returned to my narrow office overlooking Copley Square. Flinn and Tatum shared a cubicle suite near my door, and they were hunched over their laptops when I appeared.

"Can we keep him?" Flinn asked. "We've never had a baseball player who can't keep his pants on in public before. Please tell me we can keep him."

I snorted as Tatum handed me a takeout menu. "We're keeping him," I said, pointing to my regular—a BLT with avocado in a spinach wrap—before handing the menu back. "Let's just pray he's willing to play nice."

Flinn and Tatum high-fived at this news.

"I'll see what I can do about scheduling visits to the children's hospital and assisted living facilities," Tatum said. "Those grannies just love pinching some MLB ass."

"I'll see what I can do about getting the photos and video from last night removed," Flinn said. "After I study them for a minute or two."

"For authenticity, right?" Tatum asked.

"I'm a fan of the human form. Man, woman, everything in between and none of the above. I admire all of them," he replied.

"But you're really fond of the male form," Tatum countered.

"The chromosomes don't matter to me," he said. "I'm attracted to people, not parts."

"You're telling me you're attracted to Lucian

McKendrick as a person?" she argued. "His kind heart and giving soul, the one that urinates all over the subway while smiling for photos?"

"Listen, I never said I was perfect," he replied, laughing. "He's nice to look at but that doesn't mean I want to drink piña coladas and get caught in the rain with him."

Tatum shook her head. "But how is that—"

Ducking out of another sermon from Flinn on pansexuality, I headed into my office. I settled into my desk and scrolled through sports highlights and social media for the next two hours while returning the calls that had piled up while I was meeting with McKendrick and sharing a scone with Cal.

Cal.

That boy knew how to start a heart. Even a heart hidden under a thick, protective layer after one bruising too many. And those self-inflicted bruises, those hurt the worst.

"In four years, this is the first time that I'm seeing you daydreaming," Flinn said as he pulled a chair up to my desk. "There was that one time when you were glazed over, but you had the flu."

"Good memory." I turned my attention back to approving or deleting my clients' tweets.

"About the license plate you texted me," he prompted. "Whose car was that? Is someone bothering you? I can call up that private investigator we used when our favorite running back had all that baby mama drama. Or the bodyguard we used when the power forward's half-brother lost his damn mind."

"You have a stalker?" Tatum squeaked from the doorway, her tablet in hand. "Is that why you were late getting here?"

"I bumped into a guy on the trail this morning," I said, omitting the part about the Mesozoic Era creature—which was not a beaver—and my boob-crushing fall. "We grabbed coffee and got to talking."

"This is the guy with the license plate?" Flinn asked. "The one you texted me?"

"What happened with the license plate?" Tatum asked. "You didn't text me about a license plate."

"There's always a story about some otherwise normal person who turns out to be running a human smuggling ring and you can never be too careful." I shrugged. "That's why I sent you his license plate. Sorry, Tate. Didn't mean to exclude you."

Flinn ran his fingertip over his eyebrow as he stared at me. "Coffee. How'd that go?"

Tatum settled into a chair beside him, nodding for me to continue.

I scanned a few more tweets before responding. I wasn't sure how to describe this morning and I wasn't convinced that I wanted to share it just yet. It was flirty and fun, and seriously overwhelming. I had buckets and buckets of big thoughts today but I didn't have room for any of them right now. These kinds of big thoughts required a big basement or a big storage unit, a place to keep all of this big stuff from creating a big logjam in my head.

"It was good," I said. "We're getting dinner. Later tonight, after the West Coast conference calls."

Tatum frowned. "Isn't Harry on your calendar tonight?"

And this, my friends, was what you got for sharing your personal calendars with your assistants. They didn't make the mistake of double booking me for calls or events but they also knew about the Stephens, Leifs, and Harrys of my life.

"I canceled with Harry," I said.

Tatum tapped her tablet, shaking her head as she asked, "When? I'm still seeing it here. Did you cancel on him after making plans with this guy or before?"

"Not that it matters," I started, "but I texted him last night. I thought I adjusted my calendar but I must've only done it in my head."

I didn't have a good reason for canceling on Harry. I hadn't had a good reason in the past two weeks but I'd canceled on him both times. He was attentive and attractive and carried a decent conversation but I couldn't get myself excited about seeing him for drinks, dinner, and dick. No good reasons, no good explanations. Just not feeling it right now. And that was fine. I didn't need a reason. As much as I was down for a good time, I was allowed to politely decline a good time too.

"Should I keep him on your calendar for next week?" she asked, still staring at her tablet.

"Please don't devote any time to worrying about Harry," I replied. "I'll handle him."

"Let's set the man-handling logistics aside for a second," Flinn said, picking up the invisible issue and moving it away. "You thought he might sell you into the sex trades. The dude from this morning. Meeting him for dinner is a curious choice given that concern."

"No, I didn't think that. Not really. I was being excessively cautious," I said. "There was a weird moment before we got to talking and I wanted to cover all bases. I don't really pay attention to anything while I'm walking. It's like meditation for me. He said he'd noticed me before, but I hadn't noticed him. Not beyond his running shoes. I thought he was a Clemson fan. You can see why I'd avoid that. But he's not a stalker. I would know."

Flinn and Tatum shared a brow-furrowed glance before turning back to me.

"Confirm this for me one more time. You're seeing Stalker Boy again tonight?" Flinn asked. I nodded.

"Is that what we're calling him?" Tatum asked, shifting toward Flinn. "Stalker Boy?"

"I gather from your tone you have a problem with that," he replied.

She held up her hands before crossing her arms over her chest. Nice and defensive, almost as if I hadn't taught her how to maintain an open face when people said things you didn't want to hear. "It's fine if you don't mind it sounding like an early 2000s Avril Lavigne song."

"Let me know when you come up with a better option," he said. "Until then, we're sticking with Stalker Boy." He propped his elbows on his thighs, his fingers steepled under his chin. "You're seeing him tonight?"

"You're both overreacting," I said. "We're getting dinner and drinks, and that's it. I'll be home by midnight."

"If you are ri-fucking-diculous enough to go anywhere alone with Stalker Boy, get a picture of him and his driver's license," Tatum said.

"And text it to both of us," Flinn added. "And your location. We need to know where you're going with him so the sniffing dogs can start at the right place."

"Maybe we should come with you," Tatum suggested.

"We'll sit a few tables away and keep an eye on things. He'll never know."

"I'll know," I objected.

"Then you need to work on your open face. Stage presence too. Fix your face and get your shit together," Flinn said.

I rolled my eyes at that. There was no hierarchy in my office. Not one bit. Not that I minded. I appreciated people who told it to me straight but it wasn't every day they were telling it on the topic of my love life.

Love life. What a funny phrase. I had a life and I could catch a dick whenever I wanted but love...that didn't enter into the equation anymore. I loved my sisters and my parents but I wasn't looking for more. I had friends, I had family, and I had regular visits with Stephen, Leif, and Harry. I didn't need anything else.

Until this morning, I'd believed that the same way I believed the earth was round. I still believed the earth was round but now I had a few other questions brewing.

Flinn leaned back and patted Tatum's shoulder. "I think this conversation is closed, Tate."

She nodded. "I think you're right, Flinn."

I glanced at my phone and then my assistants. "Let's get back to business. We have to divide and conquer because Lucian McKendrick isn't going to make it easy on us."

9

CAL

I PACED IN FRONT OF JM CURLEY, THE TAVERN I'D SUGGESTED a block from Boston Common. I was early—really, really early—and that free time was growing my doubts like a petri dish loaded with listeria.

Would Stella like this place? She liked burgers, I knew that much, but what if this wasn't her style? Not everyone was up for Russian dressing running down to your elbows or a fistful of slaw under the bun. What the hell was I thinking? Oh, fuck. This was a bad idea.

Was this too late? She'd agreed to meeting me at nine thirty, but she was also a fan of first thing in the morning walks. Maybe she was an early to bed, early to rise kind of girl. If that was the case, I was ruining her day. Her night. Whatever. All of the above. Everything. Why stop with knocking her down on the trail when I could rip her whole damn day from stem to stern?

Was I clinically insane? Was this entire day nothing more than a series of delusions predicated on the undeniable truth that I hadn't had a woman in a long, long time?

Was I overdressed? I'd spent half an hour contemplating my usual day-end uniform of scrubs, running shoes, and a Massachusetts General Hospital fleece jacket, and decided that would not do. The suit I wore when I arrived at the hospital this morning was my only other option. It was appropriate for the day's cases but seemed woefully out of place on a casual date. Despite the excess of time, it hadn't occurred to me to stop at home and agonize over my clothing choices there. At least, not until I'd arrived here and a return trip was out of the question.

And what if this wasn't a casual date? If that was the case, I had no hope of selecting the right attire. What did I know about dating and its clothing protocols? Clearly, nothing.

Would she come? This was all rather quick and unusual, and given twelve hours to contemplate, it was possible—if not probable—she was rethinking. Stella didn't strike me as a woman of whimsy, regardless of whether she was rocking some lime green Asics.

But then again she seemed playfully pragmatic: she maintained a fiercely disciplined morning routine but also insisted on taking semi-random dudes out for coffee.

What if she *did* come? How could I sit across a table from her without succumbing to the desire to touch her? I wanted to know absolutely everything about her and I wanted to feel her.

It was shameful.

The more I thought about it, the greater the shame. A decent, respectful man didn't look at a woman and hear the slap of bare skin in his head. He didn't imagine the sounds she'd make when pinned beneath him, her body soft and welcoming and needy. He didn't dream up filthy things to whisper into her ears. He definitely didn't take himself in hand under the shower's spray and pretend the warm, wet heat was her mouth.

Turning on my heel to pace back toward the tavern, I shoved my hands into my pockets to prevent another glance at my watch or phone. When she'd agreed to dinner with me, I was too dumbstruck to ask for her number. I couldn't text or call her to confirm the time or place or whether she'd given any thought to that marriage proposal because I hadn't stopped thinking about it.

But then I heard it—*her*. I swiveled in the direction of her voice. She walked toward me in a short green trench coat, belted at the waist, with earbuds tethered to the mobile phone in her hand. Her dark hair was loose around her shoulders, and I couldn't remember ever seeing it that way before. She was moving her hands while she spoke, and it had the effect of rippling through her entire body.

I loved it. So much it hurt.

"I know we haven't been working together long, but I'm going to be straight with you. My advice: don't show up at Icon or Guilt or Storyville tonight. The last thing you need is to be photographed in a bottle service booth with all the chickies hanging on you and a magnum of Dom in your hand. That isn't painting a remorseful picture and you can bet your balls the judge and the team's owners will hear about it."

Stella came to a stop in front of me, close enough for me to hook my fingers in that belt and tug her to me. It was a move I never would've attempted before today. It wouldn't have occurred to me to physically drag a woman into my space but here I was, not sorry about it in the least.

She inclined her head toward the phone and gave a nod-shrug combo that suggested she'd be finished quickly.

"Listen, I know you've been off the field since last October and you're itching to get back. Unfortunately, you're only eight or nine games into a suspension that won't end until summer's here to stay. If that's what you want and this string of stunts isn't a ploy at getting out of the game, you need to get comfortable with your home gym and Netflix, my friend," she said.

Greedy, impatient feelings started filling my chest. I'd waited all day for her, and now I wanted her to myself. It was rude and wrong and entirely unnecessary but the pressure to wrap her up in my arms and tell everyone she belonged to me was oppressive.

"Netflix is actually pretty great," she continued. "I'm especially fond of several original series, and I need someone new to talk them over with. Does it even count as binging a series if you don't analyze it to death with someone? I don't think so."

Marry me, Stella.

She paused, nodding, and met my eyes as if she'd heard my thoughts. Her lips curled into a smile that fired up those sweet dimples, and I reached for her again.

Closer, pretty girl. Closer.

Her shiny yellow ballet flats carried her forward, and she pressed a finger to my lips while she finished her conversation. There was a tremendous quantity of restraint involved in preventing me from sucking on that finger. I couldn't explain why I'd want to suck anyone's finger, but some fuzzy, prehensile portion of my brain gave zero fucks about all the microbacteria thriving on the average fingertip and simply wanted to taste her.

"Okay, that's fine," she said, her shoulder lifting. She was right here, my hand still gripping her belt and her scent filling my lungs. "I don't care whether you watch Netflix, Hulu, HBO GO, or PBS fucking Kids, McKendrick. Irrelevant. Keep your ass out of the clubs, your dick in your pants, your hands to your everlovin' self, and let me and your agent work on convincing the owners that you've learned your lesson and deserve to come back from this suspension. Otherwise, you need to learn how to enjoy retirement."

Oh, I knew all about Lucian McKendrick. Any New England sports fan knew about the relief pitcher's penchant for drunk groping, drunk driving, drunk strip teases, drunk Red Line riding, drunk pissing on walls and fire hydrants and people. He was awaiting sentencing for his most recent debauched behaviors, and though I barely had time to skim the national headlines, I'd heard that McKendrick was bollicky bare-ass in the Back Bay last night.

"That's wonderful. That's a great idea. When we're done, hand over your phone to one of your new personal assistants. Tell them to lock it up for the night. Veda and I know how to track you down and there's nothing you need on social media, my friend. It's all trash and rage. You don't need that in your life."

The guy was a handful, an overgrown and overpaid toddler, and Stella was charming him right into submission.

And he wasn't the only one.

When the conversation ended, Stella tugged her earbuds loose and stuck her phone in her pocket before looking up at me. My eyes landed on her dimples first, and then those perfect heart-shaped lips.

Under normal circumstances, I would have said hello and asked if this restaurant sounded good to her, and maybe asked about her call.

But these were no normal circumstances and I did none of that. I cupped her face, drove my fingers through her silky hair, and brought her lips to mine.

This was no simple chemical reaction. This wasn't a basic attraction. There was a string tied between us, a fine thread drawing us together. It reminded me of the old transatlantic telegraph cables, the ones originally laid in 1858. They ran from Valentina Island in western Ireland to Heart's Content, Newfoundland. Those cables reduced the travel time of communication from ten days via steamship to minutes. Those cables shrunk the world. They changed everything.

That was how I felt right now. Like I was connected to Stella in ways I couldn't see and barely understood but I knew it changed everything.

My hands moved down her back to her waist. Her coat was knotted too damn tight for my tastes. "Stella," I whispered against her mouth.

"Whatever you need to tell me," she started, her teeth scraping over my jaw until lust was chasing heat down my spine, "it needs to involve a burger and a truckload of fries unless you want me yelling at another client."

I brought my hands back to her face, gazing into her

eyes before I spoke. "Yes, we're going to eat. But then," I said, pausing to breathe. "Then I want to take you home with me. I want to see you in a place that's just ours. I don't want anyone else around."

Stella's fingers trailed up and down my chest, over my tie, and she smiled. "I have a question for you."

Yes, I'll marry you tonight.

Yes, you can name our babies whatever you want. But not Melvin, please.

Yes, I'm feeling a bit snarly about you handling pro male athletes all day—actual specimens of human excellence—but more than that, it impresses the hell out of me.

Yes, your ass is a deity in my world.

Yes, I'm disease-free and can name my sexual partners on my fingers.

No, I don't think any of this is moving too quickly.

My thoughts flew back to those transatlantic cables, the protection of which featured in several Ranger school drills. The original cables only lasted three weeks before the hostile environment of the North Atlantic destroyed them.

I blinked, forcing that thought away. "Anything," I whispered against her jaw.

"What if I want to take you home with me?" she asked.

10

STELLA

"WHAT IF I WANT TO TAKE YOU HOME WITH ME?" I ASKED.

Yeah, it was bold. It was brazen. It was even a bit ballsy.

But that was how I was feeling today. I'd started the day by narrowly avoiding death by raccoonasaurus, followed that up with the most intense, panty-melting cup of coffee this side of Ryan Reynolds, and then I kicked some ass at the office.

I'd earned some bold, brazen, and ballsy. It was mine and I was keeping it. Even if I'd never invited a man to my home before. Never once. It seemed I was crossing a lot of nevers off my list today.

Lust-fueled hunger washed over Cal's face and his lips parted with an eager breath. "Anything, Stella," he said, his grip on my waist impossibly tight and his erection nudging my leg. That was a lie. It wasn't in nudge territory anymore. It was straight-up knocking on my leg, impatiently waiting for me to open the door and invite him inside. "Anything."

He looked up and around, as if seriously considering some biblical acts right here, a block from Tremont Street and the Common. His hazel eyes moved quickly, assessing everything around us. Looking for a dark alleyway, no doubt. Eventually, his gaze tracked down to my level and he offered a wobbly smile. "Would it be too forward to ask to go there now?"

My stomach rumbled in response, long and loud as if I had some sort of unpleasant gastric situation, and we shared an uncomfortable laugh at that.

"I'm fine. I swear," I said, gesturing to my torso. "There's not a lot of things I take more seriously than food and I've been thinking about this meal all day," I said, drinking up the sight of Cal in a suit.

Oof. This man knew how to wear the shit out of track pants but the expertly tailored suit was an entirely different level. Working with athletes, I'd often run across big guys who wore suits like straightjackets—stiff, forced, uncomfortable—but Cal wasn't one of them. There was a thick cloud of strength and power around this man-brick, and I'd spotted it from two blocks away. That and a cloud of testosterone that seemed to beam off his tanned skin.

"Eat first. Go later." I tilted my head toward the restaurant's dark door. "Don't let me forget. I'm supposed to text my friends a picture of you and your driver's license if I make the quote-unquote ri-fucking-diculous decision to go anywhere alone with you."

A smile pulled at one corner of Cal's mouth and his tongue darted out, painting his upper lip. Another *oof*. I felt that tongue, its quick flicks. I felt it on my lips, my skin, between my legs. And he knew it. The way his smile turned into a smirk said he knew it all.

"You told your friends about me," he said, and for such a

shy guy, he had no problem squeezing my ass right here in the middle of downtown Boston. "But they think I'm..."

"A stalker," I supplied. "Not a legit stalker, like one who'd hide under my bed for six months or steal my panties—"

"Oh, I'll steal your panties," he murmured.

"Or build a creepy shrine out of the takeout containers and wine bottles you scavenged from my trash," I continued. "They have very active imaginations. They're obsessed with true crime podcasts. Maybe a bit too much."

We weren't talking underwear yet. Nope, nope, nope. If all I wanted was for Cal to take me to Pound Town, we would've checked that box earlier this morning. Right there in the back of his SUV, nice and proper like the goddamn lady I was.

Cal's eyes drifted shut as he nodded. He brought his lips to my forehead. "My friends, the people who've busted my balls for months because I couldn't figure out how to talk to you, they didn't believe you were going to show up tonight," he admitted. "They figured you'd think it over and come to your senses."

"Why is this so unimaginable? You said burgers and beers, right? If I went up to someone on the trail and said, 'You, me, food, drinks?' They'd say yes. Anyone in their right mind would say yes."

"They'd say yes because you're a walking wet dream."

My lips parted as a small laugh tumbled out but I had no other words. Not for a solid minute. That smirk of his stayed right there, almost challenging me to ask him for details. Not doing that. Nope. It was clear I had some catching up to do as far as this man was concerned. And that was why this trench coat was double-knotted. A mite of distance was necessary to keep myself from diving in headfirst. I knew better than that.

Mostly.

"Yeah. Yeah. So what if I'm having dinner with my stalker? We're in public. It's all good."

"Never going to live down this thing, am I?"

My arms twined around his trim waist. "It all depends on whether I eat in the next five minutes," I said. "Get me my own order of sweet potato fries and I'll spin it into an entirely different story. I'm good at that sort of thing."

He caught my lips in an urgent kiss and if it weren't for my bleating hunger and desire to know this guy before I *knew* him better, I would have pointed us in the direction of my house and saddled up.

But this wasn't going to be a quick and easy hookup. This wasn't a regularly scheduled night with Stephen, Leif, or Harry. I didn't want that. I wasn't certain what this was or what I wanted, but I knew it wasn't that.

"Cal," I gasped against his lips. "Feed me."

"Oh, honey. I will," he promised.

Gulping, I walked my fingers up his tie and over his shoulders until my nails scraped back and forth over the nape of his neck. He purred into my touch. "Food. I need to eat food."

"And then? After the food?" he asked.

"We'll see where the evening takes us." I leaned away and pulled on a stern expression, the same one I used when some of my clients balked at the notion of someone managing their social media accounts. They paid me to be their filter but they often forgot that meant *filtering*. "Now, let's eat."

He held open the tavern's door, motioning for me to step through. "I'd rather eat you," he murmured as I passed.

"I heard that," I said, glancing over my shoulder.

"Good," he replied. "That's why I said it out loud."

There was a comment ready to leap off my tongue but Cal turned his attention to the hostess, gesturing toward an open table near the windows as he spoke. When the hostess nodded in agreement and marched toward that table, he waited, tipping his head in that direction. I waved for him to go ahead—I wanted to get a look at that suit from behind—but he wasn't having it.

"Ladies first," he said.

I waved toward the table again. "I insist."

"Believe me, Stella, *I* insist." He stepped up behind me, his hands on my waist as he pulled my back to his chest. "Get in that seat, sweet thing. If you wait another minute, we're turning around and walking right outta here."

Even the hottest guy with the most incendiary growl-pout couldn't make me miss a meal.

Sorry, no. I was many glorious things. A girl who forgot about food I was not.

And I wasn't taking Cal anywhere unless I had a plan. No plan, no penis.

"Then we'll sit," I said. "We'll stay awhile."

THE BEERS ARRIVED first but Cal didn't seem to notice. He was looking at me in a way no one ever had before. Like he needed to gobble up every inch of me before I disappeared. I didn't know how to make sense of it.

71

So, I didn't. Not everything required analysis.

I lifted my glass. "To sitting," I said with a laugh.

Cal nodded, raised his glass to mine, and then watched while I drank. He went on staring for another second or two but then he blinked away and rubbed his eyes. "Sorry about that," he said. "Whenever I stop to think about this, I realize how crazy it is."

"Don't stop," I replied. "Don't think." *Don't plan.* I shocked myself with that thought but shook it off as quick as it came.

He took one sip, then another before setting it down. He ran his fingers over his lips before dropping his chin onto his fist. "Where did you come from, Stella Allesandro?"

"Quincy. I already told you that. Come on, Cal. You gotta keep up here."

Cal laughed, quick and surprised at first but then deep. As if I'd presented him with true comedy. "That's fair," he said. "That's a fair response. I probably would've said the same thing."

I reached for my glass and gestured for him to do the same. "And where did you come from, Cal Hartshorn?"

"Anywhere you want," he replied.

"No. Nope. Offensive foul. Ten-yard penalty." I shook my head, putting my drink down while the server set our plates in front of us.

"Ten yards?" he asked, his face crinkling in mock outrage. "You gotta be kidding me, ref."

"Illegal play," I replied, stealing some fries from the basket between us. "Sweet talk. Pandering to the receiver." I sliced my hand through the air, the call official. "Ten yards."

Cal brushed his palms together, an inkling of mirth

peeking out from behind the heavy fog of his adoration. I couldn't operate like that. If there was one thing I'd learned from my life before the color-coded calendar it was that relationships required balance. I could be his queen but only—*only!*—if he was my king. Anything less and the whole thing teetered on unsteady legs.

I wasn't saying—after a matter of hours with this guy—he couldn't be my king. But I needed to know my king loved *The Goonies* and understood the happiest place on earth was the fifty-yard line and let me borrow and then slowly steal his t-shirts and never asked whether I was wearing too much mascara because—in the immortal words of *Mean Girls*—the limit did not exist. And my sisters needed to love him. My parents too.

"All right," he muttered, resting his forearms on the table. "What do you want to know, Stel?"

Stel. I'd never heard that one before. It was usually a deep, bellowed "Stella!" or my sisters' favorite, Stellaluna. I'd take *A Streetcar Named Desire* over the children's book about a bat any day.

Fuck plans. Just...fuck plans. I could get away without a plan this one time. What was the worst that could happen?

"I want to know the same things you do," I replied. "Everything."

And that was it. That was the worst thing that could happen—everything.

11

CAL

"EVERYTHING," SHE SAID, AS IF IT WAS THE SIMPLEST REQUEST ever made. *Give me everything you have and don't think twice.*

Where did I even start? What could I say that would allow us to bypass the bullshit and get right down to business? I wanted to know what she loved, what she craved, what she wanted from this life. But I didn't know how to get there from here.

I didn't know when it happened but I was a heathen. I wasn't about to apologize for it either. Stella's presence, it loosened something in me, granted me permission to be— to be a little wild. Then again, maybe it wasn't Stella so much as me wanting to be wild with her. For her.

"I'm from rural Oregon," I said, plunging straight into the bullshit while I arranged my burger. "Went to OSU. Undergrad through med school. Then the Army, Ranger school, two tours in Afghanistan. After that, residency in Minnesota. Attending gig here in Boston. Never married. One sister, older. Mom's a family physician, Dad works with wood."

Her eyes glittered as she asked, "But you're open to the possibility?" I frowned, not immediately understanding her question. "Or was that proposal this morning purely comical?"

There was something to be said for women like Stella. The ones who knew their worth, knew their mind. Who didn't give a fuck what anyone else thought, or so it seemed. Who didn't tap dance around what they wanted. It was a variation on sexy that would hold strong when everything else evolved as the years passed.

"That was completely serious," I said, feigning some indignation for her benefit. That was the game we were playing right now. "Still waiting on a response, Stel."

Her shoulders shimmied back and forth as her gaze swept over the tavern. "We're clearly compatible on the burger front," she said.

I nodded. "Clearly."

"We should see how it goes with pizza," she said with a shrug. "And then a restaurant with really bad service. Like, awful service. Because true colors come out when forced to deal with that kind of situation."

I gestured toward myself. "What? You think I'd lose it over a waiter forgetting about us or a burnt steak?"

She shook her head. "That's just it. I don't know. And you don't know how I'd deal with a two-hour wait to be seated."

It was my turn for the head shaking. "Yeah, I do. You'd find somewhere else to go. There are no two-hour waits for anything in your world."

She seemed to agree with this but barreled on. "The real test is Italian. My dad's great-grandparents came over on the proverbial boat from Sicily so this one is personal. Clams or sausage, linguini or ziti, red or white. That's where it gets tricky. If we aren't compatible on the lasagna front, then—"

"Then we make two different pans of lasagna and life is good," I interrupted. "Lasagna is not a zero-sum game."

She took a big bite from her burger, nodding, her gaze fixed on me. Eventually, she said, "I hadn't thought of it that way. No fighting over the crispy, cheesy corner pieces."

I bobbed my head. "Even better."

"If we wanted to go wild, we could throw in a trip to Ikea. Now that's the proving ground," she said.

I reached for my beer, took a sip. I wasn't sure what I'd ordered but it was fine. A little hoppy but fine. "What do we need at Ikea?"

"Probably an extra lasagna pan." She was busy rearranging her hair and pulling it out from where it had slipped under the collar of her coat.

That goddamn raincoat. I couldn't determine whether it was a dress intended to look like a raincoat—that was a thing, right?—or she really wanted to keep her coat on, but I needed it off. And whatever was underneath, I needed that off too. I didn't want her naked in the middle of this tavern but I couldn't think with all those layers between us.

As if I'd be able to think with nothing between us.

I glanced down at my half-eaten burger and then back up at her. "And then you'll give me an answer?"

Another shrug. "I'll introduce you to my family. They'd guilt the shit out of me if I got engaged before they had a chance to draw and quarter"—her eyes widened as she pressed her fingers to her lips—"I mean *meet* the guy."

"Pizza, pasta, bad service, Ikea, medieval torture," I said, marking the invisible checklist on the tabletop. "Then you'll decide?"

"Yeah, probably." She tipped her chin up, a smile pulling at her lips. "What else do you have for me? What's your everything, Cal Hartshorn?"

You.

The thought came out of...I didn't know where. But now it was here, expanding like a chemical reaction.

"Hearts," I managed. "Hearts are my thing."

"That I know," she said. "Rumor has it you're pretty good with them too."

"I am," I admitted. "But I'd rather talk about you. I'd rather know your everything."

I was waiting—hoping with the most ludicrous hope in the world—for her to tell me I was it, I was her world as of today. It was straight insanity. Instead of shoring up that insanity, she said, "Balls."

"Balls?" I repeated.

She bobbed her head as she sipped her beer. "Balls." Her tongue swept out, over her top lip and I didn't know how to breathe anymore. "All about those balls, 'bout those balls," she sang, wiggling her shoulders. The tune was vaguely familiar but I couldn't focus on anything while her body was moving like that. "Baseballs, footballs, fútbols, basketballs, tennis balls, the occasional golf ball. Pucks are just ice balls so I allow those too."

That made more sense than the scrotal thoughts bouncing around my mind. "How did you get into this work?" I asked. "Pro athletes and everything?"

"Strange but true, women make up a solid portion of

sports fans. It does seem to contradict conventional wisdom," Stella replied. "I imagine that's where the question comes from. People rarely ask the dudes at my firm how they found their profession."

She had me there. I never would've asked a guy how he got involved with professional sports.

"Uh, yeah. You're right about that. Sorry," I said.

"No worries," she replied. "I like sports. College is great. I love college football something fierce. But it's the pro balls that pay the bills."

"Yeah," I said, nodding. "There's a lot of restrictions on collegiate players, right?"

She groaned. "Like you wouldn't believe," she said, launching into a detailed accounting of NCAA restrictions and how they made her life difficult. "But that's a technical conversation for a different day. Tell me something crazy. I'm sure you have some wicked good stories with everything you've seen, everywhere you've been."

She leaned forward to grab some fries. She went for the thin, crispy ones. The runts at the bottom of the basket. When she propped her feet up on my side of the booth, I reached for her bare legs, bringing them to my lap. It was what I'd been missing all this time—touching her.

I traced the socket of her ankle bone, dragging my fingers around and around as if it was something more private. She snagged a few more fries and sent me a curious glance. Brow wrinkled, eyes narrowed, lips pouty. That pout smacked me like a belly flop. Every inch of my skin smarted. I wanted to retreat, curl into myself but also stretch myself out and feel that throb everywhere. Oh, I was a goner. She could've asked me for the entirety of my liver and I would've dug it right out for her.

My thumb and forefinger circled her leg then moved up to the back of her knee. She squirmed, giggling as I touched her. She was ticklish. Very ticklish. That knowledge cracked open a cavern of dark ideas and I couldn't stop myself from saying, "You're my craziest story, Stel."

"Is that so?" she asked, a grin on her face that said, *Yes, I am delightful.*

"You know it," I replied. "Just like you know tomorrow morning's walk is going to be a slow one."

She arched an eyebrow but didn't drop the smile. "And why is that?"

"Because I'm gonna make sure your body knows who it belongs to, sweet thing."

It sounded fantastic in my head. It sounded exactly as possessive and craven as I felt. But oh fuck, the look on her face. It was a cross between complete shock and total horror.

What the fuck was I thinking?

I knew what I'd been thinking. It was Stella in my apartment. Stella in my bed. Stella's legs over my shoulders. Stella in the shower. Stella bent over an assortment of furniture and fixtures. Stella...just Stella.

With me. I wanted her. Simple as that. But broadcasting such a primitive thought was a bad move. This wasn't the straightaway to her heart.

Her lips parted as if she was about to say something, but she stopped herself, instead staring at the bottles of ketchup and malt vinegar between us. A line formed between her brows and she dragged her teeth over her lower lip. She didn't look at me.

Fuuuuuck. Fuck.

This—right here—this was why I didn't talk to women. I didn't know which chromosome carried the ability to speak to women I found attractive without gnawing on my feet but I was certain mine was deficient.

"Okay, so that was direct," Stella said, a laugh rolling through her words.

She shifted in her seat, pulling her feet from my lap, but I tightened my hold on her ankles, keeping her there. And with that, I'd managed the Creepy Guy Hat Trick. Announcing I'd semi-stalked her for months. Proposing marriage. Mouthing off in public *and* holding on when she wanted me to let go. Well done.

Jesus. Who the fuck am I right now?

I held up my hands. She was allowed to say no. "I'm sorry."

"Don't you worry, dearie. If I can handle a D1 locker room after a bowl game, I can handle your pervy tendencies. Go ahead. That calf massage was better than anything I get at my pedicure place."

I reached for her. Didn't have to tell me twice. But I had to make this right. "Stella, I don't—"

"Let me guess. You don't say that to all the girls?" she asked.

Her eyes twinkled with her smile and I had no idea how to respond. Other girls? No, no other girls for me. I barely allowed myself to acknowledge the existence of women in the romantic sense. But here I was, throwing down my carnal desires and hoping they folded neatly into our conversation about alma maters and hometowns.

They did not.

"That wasn't what I meant," I said, the backs of my fingers running up her calf. Her skin was satin and I didn't want to let go. "Or...I didn't mean it like that."

"Now, now," Stella said, her dimples popping as she smirked. "I don't think that's true. I think you meant every word, exactly as you said it."

I did. I absolutely did.

"And if I did? What do you think about that?" I asked.

Her gaze pawed over my features for a heavy beat. When I met her eyes, she arched a brow. "If I had a concern about it, you would've had a heel to the balls by now," she said with a sharp shake of her head.

Her dark hair spilled over her shoulder with the movement, and it sent a twinge to my gut, a fine ache that would only be soothed by dragging my fingers through that hair while I moved inside her.

And there we go: another mark in the Public Erections column for today.

"But I should warn you," she continued, "I don't belong to anyone but me."

I heard it as a challenge. There was a clear warning issued under those words but all I heard was *come and claim me*. Others had tried and they'd failed, that was obvious. I wasn't going to be one of them. For all my awkwardness and fumbled moments, I knew how to set my mind on a target. I knew how to win.

"All right," I said. "Can I belong to you too?"

Stella studied me, her brow still arched up. "You seem like a lot of trouble," she said after a beat.

"More than you know."

"The good kind of trouble?" she asked. "Or are you telling me—reminding me—you're a naughty boy, Cal?"

My jaw locked, the muscles ticking as I fought off the urge to roar. To whip my belt open and rip my trousers off and prove to her that I could be everything she ever needed. But I shook my head. "I'm not saying that at all."

Stella leaned back in her seat, that sparkly smile faltering. "You're trouble," she started, "but not the fun kind? Hmm. Let me think on that for a minute."

"I'm plenty of fun," I said. "But you're wrong about something, Stel."

She snorted out a laugh and made no move to smother it. I loved her. *Loved her*. Not because she was a cool girl but because she didn't give a fuck what anyone thought. "Yeah? What's that?"

"I'm no boy, sweet thing."

I heard her gulp from across the table. Hell, they probably heard it back in the kitchen and down the street. "I don't doubt it, Cal." She held her index finger up, tapping a spot in the air between us. "I don't doubt it at all."

My breath was coming quickly, and I could feel the adrenaline coursing through my veins. "Stella. Let me take you home and—"

"So this fuckin' guy tells me that he worked for Whitey and all the other mobsters back in the day, and he knows where the bodies are buried."

"Let me guess: he was a consultant for *The Departed* too.

Everyone's a fuckin' expert when the film crews are in town."

Stella and I turned in unison, watching as two men settled at the table across from ours. It was less than an arm's length away and their conversation was jarringly loud. It was an inherently Bostonian moment, with these men sporting as much Red Sox- and Patriots-branded gear as they could manage on an evening when neither team was playing, and speaking at a level that superseded private conversation.

The Army was a lot like these guys. This town too. Unapologetic. Unflinchingly loyal. Physically incapable of quiet unless survival depended upon it. Unwilling to embrace newcomers until they'd proven their worth.

If it hadn't been for the Army, my sheltered Oregonian upbringing would have been in for one hell of a culture shock upon arriving in Beantown.

Stella bit her lip to hold back laughter. She slanted a glance at the table across from ours. "Should we—"

"I live on the other side of Beacon Hill," I said, thumbing some cash out of my wallet. "I can have you in my apartment and undressed in five minutes. Four if I throw you over my shoulder and run."

"That was also direct," she said. "For a guy who needed eight months to say hello, you're, like"—she punched her fist into her palm—"not holding back on the strong opinions."

"Come with me now," I said. I dragged my hand up her leg before reaching across the table for her hand. "We'll go somewhere quiet. We'll talk. I have a few other strong opinions to share with you."

"Just to clarify: I'm hearing your strong opinions while naked? Am I the only one naked or will you be joining me in that activity?"

I lifted a shoulder, let it fall. "Yeah," I replied. "If that's how you want it."

"That wasn't a clear answer but let me just say I wouldn't want to be the only one naked. That seems boring and weird," she said. "And I like when you tell me what you're thinking. Even if it knocks me on my ass."

"Don't you know by now?" I laced my fingers with hers. "I won't let you fall. I'll catch you."

She smiled, pointed to the scrape on her chin. "Your maneuvers are a little rough, my friend."

I shrugged. "Never said anything about gentle."

Stella pressed her lips together but she couldn't hold back her dimples. "Five minutes?" I nodded. Staring at our joined hands, she drew in a breath, held it for a beat, and then blew it all out with a tiny shake of her head. "Let's go."

I led her from the restaurant to the sidewalk. It wasn't so much walking as very aggressively striding out of the restaurant and onto the street. My grip moved from her palm to her forearm, then her elbow. I held her like that, like she was my prisoner, all the way through the Common and down Charles Street. She layered her hand over mine as if she was agreeing to this hostage situation.

We didn't speak. I didn't think it was possible. The tension between us was boiling over, a low hissing that required urgent attention. But not until we reached my building. If I forced words from my lips right now, they'd be the wrong ones. I'd ask if she minded ducking down an alley and me sliding my hand into her panties. If I could kneel at her feet and press my face between her legs. If I could take her against my front door, hard and loud enough for the entire building to know she was mine tonight. If she'd stay. Stay and never leave.

No, I didn't say a word on the seemingly endless journey to my apartment. I didn't do anything but place my hand over hers, both of us securing my hold on her.

I lived in an old brownstone, a tall, skinny building that once stood as a single residence but was now chunked into three apartments, one on each level. My problem-child trauma surgeon Stremmel lived on the third floor and Alex lived on the second with her fiancé. For the first time in all the years I'd lived here, I loved my first floor apartment with its street noise and the parade of people past my door. I loved it because it was two steps from the building's vestibule and one more step to be alone with Stella.

Once inside, I curled my hand around her raincoat's belt and backed her against the door. I stared at her while I flipped the locks.

"That was a long, long five minutes," she said.

"It's been a hundred years since we left the restaurant."

She nodded, a smile pulling at her lips. "I saw you eyeing those alleys. I'm beginning to think you're something of an exhibitionist."

A snarl rattled in my throat. "Not nearly, not when it comes to you." Her name was meant to be groaned, growled. I did just that as I bent to taste her lips. "Stella."

"Tell me how you're going to belong to me," she whispered against my neck, her lips moving just enough to trigger a shudder. "I want to know, Cal."

No lights. No need for them.

My teeth closed around the collar of her raincoat because it was the only thing I could do to repress a primal roar. I brought my hands to her ass, squeezing and boosting her up until I could rock against her and find a small shred of relief. I didn't get it but I kept searching, wanting it, wanting her. "I just—I want—I need you, Stella."

"No, no, no," she said. "Don't play shy with me now."

"I want you in my bed," I said, "and I want you to want to be in my bed."

Her lips captured mine, and there was perhaps two or three minutes until I came in my trousers and I made things even more awkward. My hold on her ass tightened and I rocked into her again, harder. I kneaded her backside. God, I wanted to bite it. Sink my teeth right into that supple flesh and then lick away the sting.

I wanted it. I was going to have it.

I leaned back, taking hold of her belt once more. "This thing is evil," I said, scraping a gaze over her. "Just evil. Get rid of it."

Stella had something to say about that—she always did —but I didn't wait to hear it, instead spinning her to face the door. I dropped to my knees and waited while she unknotted the trench. I was both pleased and annoyed to find a dress underneath.

With my hands coasting up the backs of her thighs, I asked, "Is there a reason you kept this coat on all night?"

"Torment, mostly," she replied over her shoulder.

My hands moved up, up, under her dress until her backside came into view. I pushed her panties aside, exposing one cheek. It was luscious. Better than I'd ever imagined and I'd spent a fair time imagining.

"Evil," I repeated. I edged closer, my gaze still devouring the sight of her. My eyes fluttered shut as I dragged my lips over the sweet swell of her ass. It was the trade-off I had to make. I couldn't have all my senses and an erection of this magnitude.

"If all you wanted to do was kiss my ass, I would've taken you up on the offer months ago," Stella said.

I filled my lungs with the scent of her, the one I couldn't place or describe but already knew as *Stella*, and then I did it. I bit her, just enough to leave a mark but not break the skin. Her body pulled tight against the pain but a breathy sigh followed and—and she canted her hips back, toward me. Asking for more. As quick as that, I was addicted and delirious and done for.

A red welt bloomed around the mark I'd made and that sight filled me with a heady blend of contradictions. Never in my life had I considered biting a woman. I wasn't certain I wanted to be in league with men who made a habit of biting women. But I didn't know how I'd draw another breath if I didn't feel her skin between my teeth again, if I didn't hear her sigh or see her wiggling her backside in my face.

At the sound of a shuddering breath, I looked up at Stella. She was gazing at me over her shoulder, her eyes hooded and her lips parted. My cock was burning under my trousers from this moment alone. "Don't stop," she whispered.

I didn't. How could I? I pressed my lips to her skin and nipped, lower this time. Near the junction of her thighs. She was glorious there, soft, smooth, delicious. And the sounds she made, my god.

I nipped again, closer to the heaven covered by that scrap of cotton. Once and then twice, and then my only desire was biting every inch. Turning it hot and red. And that was what I did, hypnotized by her purrs and moans, until a starburst of teeth marks covered her bare cheek.

When I pressed a chaste kiss to her inflamed skin, I battled a surge of arousal and pride and doubt. I didn't understand why this turned me on, why I felt like I owned that ass, or why I struggled to accept what I'd done to her. None of it made sense but instead of puzzling it out, I kissed her again. No tongue, no teeth, just my lips on her throbbing backside.

"Stella," I said, my hands loose on her hips as I turned her to face me. I found her eyes wide and cloudy, somewhere between needing more and not believing she let me nibble her ass. I was right there with her. Couldn't believe it, needed a whole hell of a lot more. I hooked my fingers around the sides of her panties. "I'm taking these off now."

"It's about damn—*ahhhh*." Her words dissolved into a quiet scream as I dragged the fabric over her abused bottom. She beat her fists against the door at her back. "Fuck fuck fuck *fuck*."

I brought my hand to her ankle, squeezing so she'd lift her foot. When she did, I pulled the panties off and moved to her other ankle. With the garment out of my way, I ran my knuckles down the dark thatch of curls between her legs. "I'll make it better, Stel," I promised. "Is that what you want, sweet thing? You want me to take care of this ache? You want me to kiss it better?"

"I don't wax," she announced, her head tilted back

89

against the door and her words shaky. "It hurts and it's expensive and I don't have time for that shit."

I brought a hand to my erection, squeezing it through my trousers. It was all I could do to keep from exploding right here. "Yeah, that's not a problem. I've dropped Blow Pops on the rug, picked them up, and enjoyed them just the same. Spread your legs."

She glanced down at me, at my hand on my cock. "Recently?"

I squeezed again, for her benefit as much as mine. "I don't see how that matters."

With a laugh, she said, "It doesn't but I'm trying to figure you out. I don't know many men who regularly consume Blow Pops. Or lollipops of any variety."

"Maybe they should." With my palms flat on her inner thighs, I pushed her legs apart. Even in the darkness I could see the shine of her arousal. "Where do you think I learned how to bite and lick?"

"Seriously," Stella replied, groaning. "You should've said something to me *months* ago."

Shrugging, I dragged two fingers through her slit. The scent of her was amazing. It wasn't fruit or candy or flowers, nothing that didn't belong in this sacred space. She smelled like a woman, rich and ripe. I breathed her in as I circled the pearl at her apex, tracing around and around while her hips rolled and her stance widened.

Fuck, she made a pretty picture. Bare from the waist down, flushed from the neck up. Lips parted, gaze lowered like she wanted to exist in this narrow space between us and nowhere else.

I spared Stella a quick smile. "Sorry about that. Didn't know where to start."

Around and around. Two fingers now, around and around. Another two fingers at her opening, just barely petting. Only enough for her to know I was there.

She laughed, brought her hand to my head. "You should've started with, 'Hi, I'm Cal and I might look nice but I'm a pervy beast and I'd like to wreck you up against a door.'"

"You would've gone for that?" I asked, sliding those fingers inside her. "Seems...inappropriate."

I didn't even care about my throbbing cock anymore, not with my eyes rolling back in my head at the feel of her muscles spasming around me. No, that wasn't entirely true. I cared a great deal about my cock and his satisfaction but Stella came first.

Her fingers tangled around my hair, gripping as much of the short strands as she could. "Nah, you're right. Tackling me was a much better choice. Your game's golden, sweetheart."

I wanted to laugh at that but the only thing I really wanted was my mouth on her skin. I leaned forward, dropping light kisses up and down her cleft. And she wanted that too. The way her breath caught, her words faltered, her fingers fisted against my scalp, her body pitched toward my mouth for more. No, it wasn't want. It was need. She needed me right now.

That knowledge alone was enough to do me in.

Stella's grip on me tightened. She angled me back, forcing me to look up at her. "I'm going to burst into flame right now," she whispered.

I brought my hand to her thigh, cupped the back of her knee. I pushed it up, settled her over my shoulder. I kept her steady with a hand on her ass—the unbitten side. "Not if I can help it," I replied.

She continued speaking but I stopped hearing, my pulse pounding in my ears and her creamy thigh drowning out everything else. I parted her folds and licked, giving no thought to style or finesse. My only objectives were tasting her and teasing her. Perhaps I should've leaned into my A game but this didn't seem like the moment for that. I had the rest of our lives to wow her with my technique.

It was a good thing we had time on our side because it only took one, two, three flat-tongued licks to set her off. She dropped her hands to my shoulders and pitched forward as I ran the tip of my tongue around her clit and pumped my fingers into her cunt and there was nothing more perfect than this moment. She let me caress her through the rise and fall of her release and then let me build her back up again. She climbed and climbed, her body impossibly tight, and then she broke.

"You're beautiful," I said, the words spoken against the jut of her hipbone.

"You're good with your hands," she panted. "Tongue too."

"If you liked that, I have another appendage you might enjoy."

Her gaze washed over me from head to toe and then back over again. "When I saw you this morning, I thought you were a man-brick." She stared at my zipper and the cock strangled behind it. A laugh burst from her lips. "It looks like I was right about that."

I sucked on a tiny patch of skin below her belly button while her body shook with laughter. I'd never experienced a woman laughing while I had two fingers inside her but I liked it. Didn't want it to stop. This dress though, I hated it with all the fury I could conjure. Not for any reason other than it being in my damn way.

I pushed to my feet and tore at my belt, my gaze fixed on Stella the whole time. "You want this?" I asked, yanking my zipper down. "You ready for this?"

She sucked in a breath, blinked, nodded.

No. That wasn't enough. "Words, sweet thing. Give me your words."

She beckoned me closer. I went, my trousers gaping open and my cock tenting my boxers, and pulled her into my arms. With my palms on her ass, I boosted her up, bringing her right where I needed her.

I'd spent months imagining a conversation with her and now her bare ass was in my hands and her lips on my neck and my cock was sliding over her most intimate places and I couldn't keep up here.

"I burst into flames, I did." She dragged me closer, fused her lips to mine, clawed at my neck and shoulders.

"That's not a yes," I replied, settling myself into the notch between her legs. The layer of fabric separating me from her warm, wet heaven didn't stop me from rocking forward or the tingle of release crawling up my spine. I thrust again, again, again, flattening her against the door and going half blind at the feel of her arousal soaking through my boxers.

"I—I—I," Stella cried between gasps, "I want—"

"Tell me, sweet thing. Tell me what you want."

Her hands shifted from my neck to my shoulders, down to my chest. She stroked her fingertips in tiny circles over the starched cotton. I expected her to reach for the placket and tear it right off but she said, "I want to wait."

She said this as I was rearing back, ready to torture us both with another rough thrust. My reflexes kicked into action and I set her down, stepped back. The rest of me hadn't processed the message. My cock was standing at attention, eager as ever, and the energy I'd gathered to pound her straight through the door was burning in my muscles. I stood before her, my breath snarling out like an angry bull and my body heaving with anticipation.

I reached for her but she held up her hand, warning me off. "No. I want to wait."

"Then we'll wait," I promised. "I'm not asking you to change your mind. And I'm not going anywhere. I know all about waiting for you, Stel. I just—I wanted to hold you. If you're good with that."

She turned the hand she'd held up and pressed it to her chest. She was breathing as hard as I was. "Okay," she said. "Okay. Come back to me."

I folded her into my arms and rested my cheek on the crown of her head. My trousers were still open and my dick was still ready for action but as far as I was concerned, this was a fine substitution. I wasn't smooth or practiced when it came to women. I wasn't a player. I didn't want to spend my time with women who didn't interest me. Or wear lime green sneakers and let me bite her backside. And I didn't want to touch that woman in any way unless it was exactly what she wanted. Not today, not ever.

"You dropped me like a hot potato back there," she said.

"Yeah, you've seen the best of my awkward moments today," I said with a stiff laugh.

"I'm sorry about that," she said. "I'm sorry I let us get this far and—"

"Don't," I interrupted, holding her closer. "Don't apologize. There's no reason for it."

"A really big storage unit. One the size of Vermont."

I tilted my head to catch her eyes but she was staring at my shirt. "We're going to Vermont? Is that like Vegas for New Englanders?"

"No, it's nothing." Then, she whispered, "Shit."

I glanced down, concerned. "What?"

She shook her head against my chest. "I didn't get a picture of your driver's license. My friends are probably freaking out right now."

"Do you want to call them?"

Another head shake. "Not really. They'll be fine. It's not like they can file a missing persons report yet and I can't think of a single reason why I'd ever move from this spot."

"Me neither," I said.

"Except for lasagna," she whispered. "More cheesy than saucy."

"Incidentally, that's how I prefer it."

"Come on now," she chided, her face still pressed to my chest. "You do not. Take the score you earned. There's no need to cheat on the field goal."

"I'm not," I argued. "I'm squarely in the cheesier-than-saucier camp. But I prefer when there's some sauce on the bottom of the plate, just an extra scoop. Like a—"

"Sauce puddle," she interrupted. "It needs a sauce puddle or it's dry and incomplete."

I murmured in agreement. "Better to be saucy on the plate than between the layers."

"Dammit, you're right." She thumped her fist against my arm. "You're totally right. Even if you made it sound so dirty."

"There you go, Stel. One more item off your list. Ready for that trip to Ikea now?"

"We could bring my parents and sisters along and destroy the whole thing this weekend," she said, laughing. "We don't need an extra pan now but I'm sure we could find something complicated to build. Furniture feats of strength, you know?"

"Better yet, I'll fly my mom out from Oregon, we'll head down to Ikea, and stop at a bad restaurant on the way back and then put together some particle board."

"Oh my god, I love it," she said between laughs.

"Then you can say yes to me," I continued. "Or we could skip all that and stay right here."

"Cal," Stella said. "Cal, sweetie, you're vibrating."

I kissed her forehead. "I know, I can't help it."

Stella grabbed my shoulders and forced me back. "No, you're *vibrating*." She patted my chest. "I think it's your phone."

Motherfuck. She was right. There was only one number that vibrated that pattern and I had to answer. I hated it. Of course I did. I wasn't on call tonight. If the hospital was calling, it was to report one of my cases was declining and that was not the news I wanted to hear. Not for the patient, not for me.

"Don't move. Not an inch, not a muscle, don't even blink," I warned her, reaching into my breast pocket with a sigh. I scowled at the screen as if that would change anything. It didn't. "This is Doctor Hartshorn."

I listened as the resident explained the complications he was seeing from yesterday morning's valve replacement case and the interventions up to this point, my chin resting on her head and my arm wrapped around her shoulders. If I was getting called in, I was damn well taking this last moment with Stella and savoring it.

"Thanks, Miller. Good catch," I said. I ended the call and replaced the phone in my pocket.

"You have to go," she said. It wasn't a question.

"I do but you can stay here. You can go through my closets and cabinets, and check out my DVR." I needed a yes. I needed to keep this going with her. If we parted here, it was over. I knew it. This spell would break and I'd never get it back. "I'll be back as soon as possible and we can"—I glanced around, wondering what could happen next. She'd said *wait*, she'd said *no*. I couldn't invite her into my bed after she'd pressed pause like that. She could invite herself but I had to wait until she was ready for my demands, my belt throwing. I couldn't make her ready. "We can watch SportsCenter."

Stella pressed a kiss to my lips and smiled as she shook her head. I wasn't getting what I wanted. Not tonight, maybe not ever. "On the pond. Tomorrow. Same time as always."

"All right," I conceded, still holding her close. "But you're not leaving yet."

She hit me with *what are you talking about, boy* eyes. "I'm not?"

I ran my palm over her backside. She jerked against my

touch. "Not in this condition, no. I'm putting salve on you first."

She peered up at me, a smile tugging at the corner of her lips. "Are we playing doctor now?"

I stepped back from the door and zipped up my trousers. I didn't go looking for the belt. Chances were good I'd be out of this suit and into scrubs within the hour. But I did snatch Stella's undies off the floor. "If by *playing* you mean me treating the welts I left on your skin then yes, we're playing."

"You're a special one, Cal."

I couldn't read the expression on her face and didn't have the time to try, instead leading her into the bathroom. I wet a facecloth and plucked a few sample-sized tubes of cream from under the sink and settled on the lip of the tub. There were perks to being a doctor. One of them was the endless amounts of samples. Gesturing for her to come closer, I said, "Turn around and pull that dress up for me, sweet thing."

Stella stared at me for a moment, her hands on her hips. "You want me to turn around and pull up my dress and—and you're going to put cream on my ass? Is that what's happening right now?"

I nodded. "Pretty much."

"The last time anyone did that was after I doused myself with apple-scented body spray, put on a thong and miniskirt, and went to a party in the woods behind Merrymount Park. I was fifteen and every mosquito in a five-mile radius attacked me. I swore I was never putting myself in another situation that ended with anyone creaming my ass.

Haven't worn a thong since and I have no regrets where that's concerned."

"It was probably the body spray. That attracted the bugs." It was the best I could do to keep myself from diving into the perverted deep end and imagining Stella in a thong. "But—uh—who treated your bites?"

"My older sister. We all shared a bedroom. Me, my older sister, and our younger sister. They saw the fallout the next morning but it was Sophia who busted out the cotton balls and Calamine. I swore I wasn't going through that again and she swore she'd never put herself in the position of being the person applying the cream, and I respect that."

I considered this while trying—and failing—to keep my gaze away from her peaked nipples. God, I wanted to taste them. Lick them. Bite them. *Bite bite bite*. I could already imagine the ring of marks around her nipples. A twin set of devil's halos.

Finally, I said, "That's how I felt about getting shot. I understand. I still want to take care of you. I also want another look at the marks I left on you."

Stella blinked at me. And again. "You've been shot? Where?"

"In Afghanistan."

"That—that isn't the answer I'm looking for," she seethed. "Don't make me strip you naked to find it for myself."

"Really, Stella. That's no threat," I remarked lightly. "I was shot in the back of my thigh. As far as gunshot wounds go, it was a basic one. It went in, missed the femoral by a hair, went out the other side. No major damage aside from a gnarly scar all the way around. I'll show it to you sometime but only if you let me do this. I don't want you hurting tonight."

Laughing, she dropped her hands to her sides and curled them around the hem of her dress. "Only because you have me curious about that scar," she said, pivoting.

"Whatever works for you, Stel." Her bare backside came into view and—fuck me running. I couldn't keep my fingers from tracing the raised marks dotting her cheek. Her skin was hot like a fever and I wanted to feel those bumps on the head of my cock. The longer I stared at her, the more I could imagine my cock rubbing against her, my release splashing over her skin.

"Cal," Stella said.

I cleared my throat but it wasn't enough. "Yeah?" I managed, my voice rough.

"Just making sure you're still with me," she said.

I glanced down at the little tube in the hand not currently occupied with her ass. My grip was fierce. I was shocked it hadn't exploded. "I'm admiring the view," I said, gently running the damp cloth over her. "Your skin blooms like a rose."

"Is that," Stella started, her words hesitant, "is that what you're into? I mean, it's fine. I'm just wondering."

I tossed the towel to the corner and squirted some lotion into my palm. "This shouldn't burn or tingle at all but it is thick. You'll feel it for a bit," I said. "And no, I'm not, uh, I've never bitten anyone before."

"Oh, wow. Okay, then," she said softly.

"Was it all right?"

"Was it all right," she repeated. "Yeah, you could say that. I'm a little surprised your neighbors didn't call the police. I don't usually scream like that. I don't usually scream at all."

"New territory all around," I said, and it was all I could do to keep myself from shaking this woman and shouting at the top of my lungs that she was it, she was everything, and we were meant to collide on that trail this morning. Didn't she see it? Feel it? Didn't she know? Because I knew. I fucking knew.

"You were right," Stella said.

I glanced away from her backside, wondering if I'd spoken those thoughts out loud. I couldn't have. "About what, sweet thing?"

"About tomorrow's walk being a slow one."

Ah, the trail. It was a handful of hours away but I hated the idea of relinquishing her. Just fucking hated it. "We can take it as slow as you want, Stel." I meant that. Sure, my dick and I weren't thrilled about tonight's turn of events but we'd keep the faith. I massaged the remaining lotion into my hands and pressed a kiss to the base of her spine. "You're all set. You might have some bruises but nothing that won't heal within a day or two."

Stella reached for the panties I'd abandoned near the sink and stepped into them before turning to face me. "Walk me out," she said, tipping her head toward the door. "I'll get a car service to take me home."

"Where is home for you?"

She busied herself with brushing a hand down her dress but I didn't miss the way her eyes widened at my question. "Not too far from here," she replied. "But not too close."

"You're not going to tell me," I said.

She shook her head. "A lady needs her secrets, Cal."

I mentally sifted through every cardiothoracic surgeon I knew as we left the bathroom, desperate to find one who could pick up my case and let me see the night out with this woman. Couldn't find one. That wasn't accurate. There were several but none who would handle it the way I would and I didn't know how to get past that issue.

I held Stella's hand as I locked the apartment door behind me and headed through the small vestibule. "Is your phone handy? I'll put my number in there," I said, holding the front door open for her. "Or is that one of your secrets?"

She squeezed my fingers. "Give me my hand back and I'll get my phone."

Before I could respond with an offer to dig through her pockets, I found my colleague and neighbor Alex and her fiancé Riley staring up at us from the sidewalk. "Oh. Hey," I called, lifting my hand in a quick wave.

"Yeah," Alex replied. "Hey."

"Is this what you were telling me about?" Riley asked Alex.

She bobbed her head. "Yeah, I think so." She smiled at Stella. "Where are your manners, Hartshorn? Introduce us."

I pointed at them, saying, "Alex Emmerling. Riley Walsh. This is Stella. Stella, these are my neighbors."

"Sorry, we're androgynously named." The gastro surgeon held her hand up. "I'm Alex. He's Riley."

Stella laughed. "That's helpful, thank you."

"I'm the only person in the building who isn't a doctor so that makes me easier to remember," Riley said. "If you need to remodel a house, give me a holler."

"Also helpful," Stella replied.

Alex touched her fingertips to her lips, pausing a moment. "I feel like I've heard so much about you," she said. "All good, of course. Great. The best. This guy can't stop talking about you."

"Emmerling," I warned.

"I'm just so happy you're a real person," Alex continued. "Not that I thought you weren't but you're so pretty and you were obviously in his apartment just now and—"

"Is she drunk?" I asked Riley.

"—and after the story I heard this morning I wasn't sure what was going to happen—"

He held up his hands. "The champagne never stops flowing when you're getting married." He shrugged. "And I love it when she babbles. It's adorable." He stared at Alex. "Honeybee, you're beautiful and I love everything you do but I think Hartshorn's head is going to explode if you keep embarrassing him in front of the woman he's obviously trying to impress."

Alex's eyebrows pinched upward. "He'll survive." She gestured toward Stella. "I'm not usually this chatty but you are lovely and he is one of the best guys and I want good things to happen. I hope to see you again."

"Absolutely," Stella agreed.

She said it in a way that made me believe she was interested in getting to know my friends. Like she intended to see me again. That was the real mystery here, wasn't it? Whether the bubble would burst and everything would change tomorrow. I couldn't explain why but it seemed we only had today to get this right.

She shifted to face me. "Tomorrow morning. Right?"

Regardless of the audience before me, I drove my fingers through Stella's hair and brought her lips to mine. Her arousal still lingered on my tongue and I was certain she could taste it too. I liked that. Another thing I didn't understand but thoroughly enjoyed.

"Tomorrow," I whispered. "And we'll go as slow as you want, sweet thing. I know how to wait."

She patted my chest as a smile turned up her lips. Her dimples popped and I was powerless. "Yes, it seems that you do."

12

STELLA

IT DIDN'T MAKE SENSE BUT I CHECKED MY PHONE ONE MORE time. Cal wasn't calling. He couldn't. He didn't have my number and I was the one who had to dash off to my Uber like Cinderella at the stroke of midnight without having the presence of mind to slow down and exchange info.

It was ridiculous, really. I had everyone's phone number. Every reporter and radio host and all their bookers, the television commentators and the bloggers, the agents and managers, and personal assistants and security details. Even the governor of a certain southern state who was a closeted Yankees fan.

I wielded the power of the Rolodex but the one time I truly needed a number, I didn't have it.

Ridiculous.

I could've tracked him down. I could've asked some favors, pulled some strings. Everyone knew someone and I knew a lot of people in this town. But there were daytime favors and nighttime favors, and I wasn't ready to wake anyone up to get Cal's number. That felt a bit crazy to me, a bit clingy. And those weren't looks I wanted to wear.

When the call from his hospital came through last night, we separated in the most reluctant manner possible —complete with him backing away while still gripping my belt and taking me with him for several paces until I literally dashed away into the waiting car—but we parted with nothing more than a promise to meet here, at the pond.

Logistics had no place in lust.

Waking up this morning, I was almost convinced that the entire day was a strange, sexy, unsatisfying dream. I would have believed it too, if not for the scrapes on my knees and chin...and the tender side of my ass. All of that and the overwhelming sense that the world as I knew it was shifting. The boundaries I'd drawn, the walls I'd erected, the laws I'd enforced—they were all changing, even as I attempted to strengthen them.

Glancing at the screen one last time, I dragged my tongue over my teeth and tapped my sneakered toe against the trail. It was fifteen minutes past my usual start time at the pond and I couldn't find another reason to wait much longer. My day was packed to the brim, I was due in Los Angeles tomorrow in preparation for the football league's draft day, and my newest and most high-maintenance client McKendrick was busy being a get-the-last-word-in, can't-kill-him-with-kindness, passive-aggressive sumbitch.

That fucker did not know when to shut the hell up and appreciate the PR triage my firm was arranging for him. It was as if he forgot that he hired us for this exact purpose. He reminded me of something my grandmother had often said, that people were less kind and appreciative these days.

That they expected so much but found themselves accountable for little, and true gratitude was found as often as four-leaf clovers.

And he was a spoiled sumbitch. My grandmother hadn't said that but she would've if she'd met Lucian McKendrick.

This morning's dark, drizzly weather meant the trail was less busy than most days. I looked out over the water for a moment, hoping I hadn't missed him again. But there was no man-brick to be seen. After all this time of Cal watching me and me barely noticing his Clemson-ish running shoes, and everything we shared yesterday, we were back to missing each other again.

But I couldn't keep my day on hold any longer. I had a promotion to claim. I pulled up my hood, switched on my playlist, and nudged my earbuds into place. As I moved forward, I forced myself to believe that there was a reasonable explanation for it.

For the whirlwind day we shared yesterday.

For the touches and kisses—*and bites!*—that were too intense to be anything but real.

For the words and promises that followed me into the night and all the way to dawn, and still wouldn't leave me today.

For his absence now.

Perhaps it was for the best. Too much, too fast, and the timing was all wrong. It was always about the timing.

But my younger sister Serina would've called horseshit on that pretty quick, and then my older sister Sophia would have agreed with her. Serina grabbed the bull by the horns and life by the balls, whereas I negotiated with the bull and maintained a respectable distance from the balls. Grabbing wasn't my style. I was all about friendly coaxing followed by a gentle reach-around.

And that was a good explanation for why I'd missed out on this promotion for far too long. Enough with the gentle reach-arounds.

I knew the timing excuse was horseshit too, but there was something helpful about hearing from your baby sister that your entire emotional and relational infrastructure was as sturdy as a pile of sardines. Serina would tell me to march my ass right down to Mass General, storm the cardiothoracic floor, and wait until Doctor McMan-brick showed his face.

Those stunts always worked for her. Serina the Stunt-Puller. Never for me, Stella the Scrupulous.

Even if I could manage stunts like Serina, I didn't know what that would solve. There was no point in guilting a guy into seeing me. If Cal didn't want to meet me this morning, forcing him wasn't going to make the situation any better.

No, I wasn't putting on my ass-kicking heels or barging into any hospitals. That wasn't my style. I didn't wait *on* men and I didn't wait *for* them either. I had my pick of dicks if I needed one and I didn't need one today.

With 98 Degrees blasting in my ears, the man-brick memories were gathering themselves up, putting themselves away. Really, he was nothing more than a flash in the pan. A moment of high heat and then a kitchen full of smoke. I was in need of a good airing-out.

It didn't seem like a great decision at the time but I was thrilled we hadn't slept together. I'd wanted to but I *knew* it wasn't a smart move. Then, I'd worried about falling too far, too fast. Too hard. Now I knew better. I'd allowed those touches and kisses, the words and promises—and the bites —to get the better of me. I'd let them set the terms when I should've known better, done better.

But at least now I didn't have another name to add to my list of men who stuck around just long enough to realize I wasn't the one.

If I walked fast enough, I could ignore the damp and cold, and even the twinge on my battered ass cheek. I could ignore everything—and I needed to. I needed to shake it all off before getting to the office and settling in for a long day of fixing and finagling because I didn't believe in carrying drama around with me. There was no reason to let crazy live in my head unless it was paying rent.

I went on walking, singing under my breath with Nick Lachey—no one wanted me singing full-out; that would only wake the raccoonasauruses—as I chased the trail around the pond. The entrance gate was in sight when I realized the exercise had done me good. Score one for movement.

I wasn't hammering myself over near-regrets and I wasn't wondering what I'd done wrong this time. Because I hadn't done anything wrong. I just wasn't the woman that men returned to, even when they promised they would. I wasn't stressing over McKendrick's whiny boy bullshit anymore and though my heart was still tender from soaring high and then falling hard, I was better.

And then Cal was right beside me.

I stared at him with a boatload of confusion, my mouth hanging open and eyes unblinking. As hard as I tried, I couldn't voice the words, *Where the fuck did you come from*?

All I could do was stare. And trip over my own feet when I failed to notice a sizeable dip in the trail.

Cal's eyes flashed as my stride broke and he reached out to help me but it was no use. Now both of us were snowballing into a tangle of stray limbs. It was a cartoon collision, complete with dust flying and a rough ass-first landing in a puddle.

"Unnff."

And Cal was on top of me once again. Oh, my manbrick.

Stellllllllllla not yours stop it now.

"We have to stop meeting this way," I said, cupping his cheek. Even when I thought my feelings for him were packed up and waiting on the curb, I still wanted to feel him. I still wanted him. "Sorry. This one was my fault. You should've let me hit the ground."

"Never, Stella. Never," Cal said, tugging my one remaining earbud loose as he shifted to his knees. "But tell me something, sweet thing, how loud do you have this? I've been running flat out to catch up to you and I kept calling your name and I thought—I thought you were—wait. Are you all right? Are you *crying*?"

My bum was wet. Puddle water was soaking my workout leggings straight through to my undies and the bottom of my t-shirt was growing damp as his body pressed mine to the ground. I hated being wet like this. It was uncomfortable and unpleasant. Like spilling a drink on your lap and feeling that weird dampness every time you moved. And it never dried. It didn't matter if it was Phoenix in July, it never dried. It was a perpetual state of damp, a reminder of things gone wrong.

"I-I—it helps me clear my," I stammered as hot tears sprang to my eyes, "my head."

I wasn't a crier. I had plenty of misty-eyed moments but actual tears dripping down my face wasn't the norm. And I wasn't going to cry now. Not on the middle of the trail, not in front of a man I barely knew. He was an Oregon State alum and an Army veteran and a doctor, and aside from knowing he preferred to dip his fries in ketchup rather than drizzling it over the top and he ate pussy like a champ, I didn't know him. There was no earthly reason to cry in front of him, over him, or about him, and nothing that'd happened this morning altered this truth. Not even landing ass-first in a dirty trail puddle.

"Oh, shit. Stella, no, no," he said, dragging his fingers through my hair and over my shoulders, squeezing as if he was searching for bones poking through my skin. Just like yesterday. "What did I do this time? Where does it hurt, sweetheart?"

"I'm serious. We have to stop meeting this way." I pushed against his chest, a not-so-subtle order for him to let me up.

"Stay where you are," he barked. He gripped my wrists and pushed them down before his fingers began moving over my sides. "Does anything feel broken? Did you hear anything snap when you fell?

"There's puddle water in my underwear and someone gnawed on my ass last night so I'm a little sensitive this morning," I said flatly. "I'm getting up and you're not stopping me this time."

Cal stood and reached for me, his lips folded together and his brows furrowed. His scruff was thicker than it was yesterday. There were lines around his eyes too. He looked rumpled, tired.

When I regained my feet, a small downpour fell from my backside. Awful, just plain awful. Yet Cal didn't miss a beat. Nope, he scraped his hand over my ass, swatting away the water as if this was an everyday occurrence for him. As if this wasn't weird and awful.

Not. Crying.

"Please don't," I said, slapping his hand away. "Just stop. I'll be fine. Soggy, but fine."

He shook his head and rested his hand on my hip, his fingers curling around the waistband. "Let me see."

"Cal, I'm not going to say this twice. You are not examining my ass on the middle of the trail," I said, prying his fingers off my leggings.

I forced a smile at the pair of nylon tracksuited ladies power walking past us. They appeared as mortified as I felt and the *whish-whish* of their nineties-era outfits only snapped this moment into sharp focus. Here I was, watery-eyed and -assed, and I had a whole mess of unpacked feelings about Cal Hartshorn. I'd halfway convinced myself he and everything that happened yesterday was like a rookie throwing a no-hitter: it just didn't happen.

Cal propped his fists on his hips while he stared at me for a long moment. He nodded, saying, "Okay, then," and scooped me up. He held me like a fireman intent on clearing a burning building.

He jogged past the nylon tracksuits with my size fourteen ass over his shoulder. I waved. They were still mortified but they both gave Cal the elevator eyes. Good for them. What was that old adage? The day you stopped looking was the day you died?

Look all you want, ladies. Live this life up!

"I can walk," I called to him, although I was slightly concerned that the thick, corded muscle of his back would absorb my words. "Put me down, dude. You're going to dislocate something."

He slowed when we reached the sidewalk. "If you don't mind, I'd like to hold you."

"Maybe I do mind," I said. "Maybe having some dude peel me off the trail and lug me to safety two days in a row is messing with my girl power, and if you don't know this by now, I'm rather fond of my girl power."

Cal's fingertips skated over the back of my calf. "I'm not some dude, Stella."

"I determine dude distinctions, thank you," I replied. "I don't even have your number. That's *some dude* territory, Cal."

Yes. Sure. He was the only *some dude* who'd ever given me an orgasm in thirty seconds—no lie—but those were not my problems today.

He fished his keys from his pocket and I heard his car alarm chirp as the door locks disengaged. He set me on the tailgate, where I was rapidly reminded of my wet-not-in-the-nice-way undies, and he rummaged through his road-side disaster bag.

"I was in surgery," he said while he snapped on a pair of gloves. "I wasn't ditching you."

"I know you weren't," I lied.

"No, you didn't. I saw the look on your face. You didn't think you were ever going to see me again." He took my hands, his thumb passing over my palm in search of injuries. Finding none, he examined my arms, legs, and torso. His touch was urgent but still gentle. If not for the gloves, it would have felt like another round of foreplay with my man-brick.

My *man-brick? Goddamn it, Stella. Slow your roll.*

Giving myself a quick shake, I continued, "I wasn't sure whether you missed the fun of stalking. This morning had some extra ripped-from-the-headlines feels to it. I mean, I caused this situation but it wouldn't have happened without you."

Crouched by my feet to study my ankles, Cal raked his gaze up until it landed on my eyes. "Stella."

I smiled, watching as his eyes drifted to my dimples. He liked them and not in that "oh, she's such a cutie-pie" kind of way that everyone else liked them. "Cal."

He was about to say something but then he sighed and shook his head. "Everything looks fine. You're fine, you're—perfect. Let me get in those pants now."

I pressed a hand to my chest, my brow arched up. "This has been a lot of fun and all but I don't do roadside naked."

"Stella." He snapped his fingers and pointed at the vehicle. "Back seat."

For a guy who was shy as hell yesterday morning, he sure was bossy today.

"I'm going to sit right here for a second and then I'm going home to wash this disaster of a morning off me." I glanced into his vehicle and I was reminded of Robbie Prince, my sophomore year of high school, and his mom's old station wagon. As far as back seat romps went, that one was unsuccessful. Robbie claimed "it" couldn't *reach*.

I stifled a laugh at that memory.

"What?" Cal asked.

"Just remembering the last time I was in a back seat with my ass out."

That earned a raised eyebrow. "And you're laughing about that?"

"Not really," I said. "Okay, yes, I'm totally laughing about it. But it was high school. Half a lifetime ago. I'm allowed to laugh about it now."

"I can't wait to hear that story," he grumbled. He balled up the gloves and tossed them in his medical bag. His fingers bare, he reached for my waist, gently pressing and squeezing the skin around my hips, my backside. His brows were pinched and his lips set in a grim line. "I'm sorry about this. I'm sorry about everything back there. I didn't mean to sneak up on you and scare you like that."

Reaching out, I closed my fingers around Cal's hoodie and dragged him between my legs. "I know you didn't," I said. "And I wasn't scared. A little surprised but not scared."

"You don't need to do this for me," he replied. "You don't need to brush everything off and downplay your emotions. Whatever it is you're feeling, I can take it. I work with a guy —actually, he lives in my building too—and every single day is the worst day of his life. Yesterday was bad but today will be worse, and tomorrow will be worse than today. He's always deeply, profoundly miserable." He tipped his forehead to mine and stared into my eyes. "If I can deal with that, I can deal with whatever you have for me. I don't need your publicist face. Okay?"

I laughed, shrugging off his comments. It was the fastest way to make it go away. It was too early—in the day, in the short time I'd known him, in this lifetime—for him to see straight through me. "I'm okay, really," I insisted. "As a rule, don't sidle up to women on wooded trails. That's a one-way ticket to pepper spray and the police, and it's not the way to dodge the stalker label."

A quiet laugh burst from his throat as he kissed me. Quick and sweet, as if he knew it was everything I needed. "I don't know why I can't get my act together around you."

"We can start over," I suggested. "It worked yesterday. At the coffee shop."

He shook his head. "I don't want to start over again. I want to pick up where we left off last night."

I lifted my shoulders. "I'm not sure we can do that," I said softly. "I don't think we can teleport back to that moment or erase all the moments that followed it. But we can make new ones. Preferably ones where I don't end up in muddy puddles."

He looked away and blew out a breath. "I thought you were ignoring me," he said, "and I panicked a little. A lot."

"Why?" I asked. His lips moved over my jaw, down my neck. "Why would I do that?"

He shook his head from the crook of my shoulder. "I was late. I tackled you to the ground yesterday and I kept talking about beavers. I've asked you to marry me repeatedly. I had to leave last night. Now this. I don't know. I've given you enough reasons."

"None of those are *real* reasons," I said, laughing, "and you only asked me to marry you that one time."

He leaned back and pointed to his temple. "In my head. I asked repeatedly in my head. I feel a little possessive when I'm around you, like I want to keep you and never let go."

Oh.

Oh my.

My face must have been painted with all of the overwhelmed emotions that were kicking up a tornado in my belly, because Cal stared at the ground for a beat, scrubbed a hand over his face, and stepped back.

That wasn't what I wanted. I wanted him closer, touching me, whispering those words that made me feel like the center of the universe. Even if the center of his universe wasn't mine to keep, I could steal that feeling for right now.

He returned to me when I shivered, wrapping his arms around my shoulders and kissing the crown of my head like I was small and precious. "Can I take you home now?" he asked. "Wrap you up in pillows and apologize for everything I've ever done? I'll take care of those panties too."

It wasn't lost on me that Cal really liked talking about my underwear. It was why I mentioned them. I liked throwing him those bones and pretending I didn't hear his pervy remarks. "I have to go to work," I said.

"I doubt you're wearing this to the office. Let me help you out of these wet clothes."

"I have to work," I repeated. "This is a hectic time for me, Cal. I have a high-priority client, the draft, I'm shooting for a big promotion, and I need to get my team ready to slay in LA. That's the mantra. Slay in LA. We're doing it. We fly out tomorrow."

He nodded, his chin bumping against my head, and he

reached for the iPhone secured in my armband. I was amazed it'd survived two Cal collisions. He held it out.

"Unlock this," he ordered. He caught my expression—the one that summarized exactly how much of my girl power he was trampling at the moment—and managed a contrite frown. "Please unlock this so I can give you my information, Stella. I tried to call you when I was pulled into another emergency surgery this morning but then I realized that I *still* didn't have your number. Let me tell you, sweet thing, I fixed that heart real fucking fast when I realized I was going to miss you."

"I'm not sure how I should feel about that. Am I allowed to be flattered if you pulled a rush job on someone's heart? Or should I be worried for them?"

"I did that heart just fine," he replied. "I know how to get in, get out, get the job done. Sometimes I take my time doing it and close everything up nice and tidy. Others, it's quick enough to make sure everyone walks away happy and I leave the resident to close."

There was a promise in those words. A commitment.

I keyed in the password and handed it back to him. He set to typing one-handed, the other still tight around my shoulders, but it was far more than a few digits. I figured he was sending himself a text with some smart-assed comment about my skivvies that I'd enjoy later. He showed me the screen again and it revealed an entire page of his contact information.

"Here's my mobile phone, my house phone, my office at the hospital, my head scrub nurse's number, my address, my work email, and my personal email."

"That's very...thorough," I said, tucking my phone back in the protective case.

Cal pinned me with an arched eyebrow and the inkling of a smile. "That's how I operate, Stella."

Yeah, that was the truth. This man knew nothing short of all the way.

13

CAL

I didn't know how I did it but I scored another evening with Stella.

Instead of sitting down in a restaurant, she insisted on walking and ice cream. It was odd but I wasn't arguing. Not when I could get a few hours with this woman before she left me for the West Coast. Not even if it meant feigning an interest in ice cream.

"What do you think?" she asked, tipping her chin toward the chalk-scrawled menu board. The raincoat was back, and with it came an orange scarf printed with tiny red elephants. I had a newfound appreciation for the close-fitting leggings and tight t-shirts she favored for her morning routine. Goddamn, I loved those leggings.

"I, uh." I glanced between sundaes and frappes—which rhymed with *traps* when in New England, I'd learned—and scoops and shakes. "It's all great."

"They have grape-nut," she cooed. "Have you ever tried it? Or heard of it?" Before I could respond, she turned to the server. "Can we get a sample of grape-nut?"

"I haven't," I replied. "Tried or heard."

She held out the plastic sample spoon. "Cal. You have to try this. I promise, it's really good."

When she looked up at me with those big, gleeful brown eyes and an expectant smile, it didn't matter how unpleasant the flavor sounded or that I didn't favor anything in the frozen desserts family, I was eating it. And how could I not?

I swallowed the spoonful down and it was fine. It was ice cream and that wasn't my favorite, but it was less horrible than it sounded and Stella was smiling. Honestly. I'd survived two trips through an actual war zone. I could choke back some weird cereal ice cream for the woman I was going to marry.

"What do you think?" she asked. "My dad is a grape-nut ice cream fanatic so I grew up debating the merits of one creamery's quality over another."

"Not bad." I pointed back at the menu board. "What do you like here?"

"I'm leaning toward black raspberry," she said, her attention still trained on the wall. God, she was beautiful. Just fucking gorgeous. "But I'm also feeling that chocolate with pretzels. I don't think it would make sense to double up though. I don't want my raspberries melting into my chocolate, you know?"

"Yeah. That would be unpleasant." I studied the menu for a minute before looking back at Stella. "You get one, I'll get the other. We'll share. No raspberries in the chocolate."

"Ooh, that's perfect." She tapped her fingertips together under her chin like she'd hatched an evil plan of ice cream domination. "Okay, yeah. Let's get that."

I lingered at her side while she ordered. I didn't touch her but I didn't have to. She was close in a manner that announced she was *with* me and that was everything.

With a loaded cup of ice cream in each hand, she gestured toward a long, narrow table tucked up against the street-side windows. "Stay or go?" she asked.

It was another late evening for us and the streets were dark. After this morning's spectacular turn of events, I wasn't going to complicate matters with walking and eating. I pulled out a chair for her. "Stay," I said. "Then we can go."

She dropped into the seat, letting out the tiniest yelp of pain when her backside met the hard plastic. I had a mess of thoughts about that. First and greatest—fuck yeah. I was the one who left her sore, I was the one who could draw a topographical map of her ass from memory, I was the one who knew how to make her scream.

Next up came the questions. Would she let me under that raincoat tonight? Would she let me taste her tonight? Would she let me keep her tonight?

"Dude, you gotta sit down," Stella hissed. "It looks like we're doing some kind of lady and her manservant role-play. That sounds fun but for someone else."

I yanked a chair out and sat. "Someone you know?"

"I'm willing to bet my boss plays lady-and-the-manservant every night. I bet he's the one keeping her wig in such great condition." She handed me a spoon as she laughed. "Listen, I'm not going to yuck all over her yum but I'm comfortable saying it's not for me."

I was wrong about not needing to touch her. Whatever I'd been thinking a few minutes ago was incorrect. I didn't have the patience or strength necessary to be this close to her without touching her. I'd waited months—yeah, that one was on me—and I didn't want to wait a second longer. I motioned toward her legs and then patted my lap. "Come here, sweet thing," I said.

"Don't mind if I do." She leaned back and settled her legs on me, her ankles crossed. "Careful, Cal. I could start to expect this every night."

"Careful, Stella," I replied. "I could start offering every night."

I glanced up from her legs at the moment her smile flattened, her dimples disappeared. Her eyes flashed dark. She stared at me, pointing with her plastic spoon. "It's always the nice ones. They're the most trouble."

I dragged my fingertips up her calf to the tender space behind her knee. "Is that how it goes?"

She met me with a wide-eyed nod. "Mmhmm. The bad boys have hearts of gold and the rebels just want to be understood. The nice ones though, they show up and cause all kinds of trouble."

"I don't know," I hedged. "I seem to recall you enjoying all kinds of trouble last night."

Bobbing her head from side to side, she replied, "That's where the nice ones nab you. They reel you in with the good-boy manners and complete absence of douchebaggery. Everything is fabulous until you realize you brought a throw pillow to the office because your ass hurts and you've seen him two nights in a row despite your personal commitment against agreeing to back-to-back outings." She drew a checkmark in the air with her spoon. "That's how the nice ones nab you."

I stared at her a moment, not sure which thread to pull

first. She didn't make a habit of seeing the same person on consecutive evenings. That was an interesting nugget. Then there was the entire analysis of nice guys and our faults. Our penchant for nabbing otherwise hard-to-get women. I was starting to see Stella as just that: hard to get. It wasn't a prop so much as the set she'd chosen for herself.

If the past two days proved anything, it was that Stella wasn't nearly as unattainable as she wanted me to believe. And I was holding on to that interesting nugget.

I waved toward her seat. "I'm sorry you're uncomfortable today."

She scooped up a bite of black raspberry, smiling. "I know. You're a good guy. You give a shit about how I feel and you want to make it better when things are bad." She ate that spoonful of ice cream and went hunting for another. "You also want to destroy me on every solid surface in your apartment and meet my parents and build particle board furniture on your day off, and that's why you're trouble."

I couldn't square the circle she'd drawn for me. I was missing something here. "Try the chocolate," I ordered, pushing the cup closer to her. "Then explain why any of the things you just said are problematic."

She reached for the cup of chocolate ice cream and passed the black raspberry to me. "Don't you want to talk about sports?"

I narrowed my eyes at Stella, frowning. "I'm sorry, what?"

Still focused on the chocolate, she said, "I can talk about sports. I can tell you about the players I've met and the games I've seen. I can talk about coaches and stadiums and unusual team rituals and the best place to get a beer in dry counties in the South. I have thoughts on pro football and the changes we're going to see over the next decade as well as some of baseball's more asinine rules and reasons why women's basketball isn't getting the attention it deserves despite being the best game around." She set the cup down and looked up at me. "I can talk about all these things. We don't have to do the personal details and heavy emotional stuff. We don't have to do any of this."

I slipped my palms down the outside of her legs, pausing at her ankles. As far as talocrural joints went, hers were lovely. "Would you like to hear about the hearts or lungs I've fixed? I have thousands of photos of them on my phone. I can tell a damn good surgery story. Or I can talk about the hospitals I've worked in or the ones I've visited to observe or instruct."

Stella glanced out the window at the passing cars on Charles Street. "I think your profession is crazy impressive and I can't imagine how hard you've worked to reach this level in your field," she said, her words tipping into that serene tone I'd come to think of as her publicist voice. I wasn't sure whether she lapsed into it consciously or it had become as natural as a second native tongue. But it was clear she did it when she needed to remedy something. Yesterday it was to determine whether I was the creepy stalker I seemed to be. Last night it was putting McKendrick in his place. And now she was juggling the off-topic balls I'd thrown at her.

She continued, "It's incredible what you do. But I'm happier when I don't think about the precise details of cutting into people's bodies and fixing their organs. I don't think I could handle seeing the photos. It's bad enough when people post their cuts and bruises or IVs on Facebook." She coughed, gagged a bit. "Sorry. Thinking about that is too much for me."

"That's fair. Expected, even. It didn't occur to me you'd want to talk surgery."

She picked up the chocolate ice cream again. "I get what you're doing here but we can still talk sports. It's fine, Cal. Everyone does it."

I wasn't certain whether my mind was leading me to these conclusions or Stella was implying that most of the men she dated kept the conversation confined to her profession. Maybe that wasn't it at all. Maybe she was suggesting *she* kept the conversation confined to her profession.

"Is that what they do with you?" I asked, wading right into that murk. "They test you, right? They doubt your bona fides so they interrogate you and then find out you're smarter than a snake charmer. Is that how it goes?"

Her lips twisted into a fake scowl and she glanced up at the ceiling. "Not sure how I feel about being compared to a snake charmer."

"I'm taking your deflection as agreement," I replied.

Stella ran her spoon around the inner edge of the cup, scooping up the melted ice cream. "I like this one but that one's good too." She jabbed the spoon in my direction. She was finished with the last leg of our conversation. Whatever it was, it was over. "It's early for raspberries. Right? Yeah. Raspberries come out in the summer. But I guess it doesn't matter. They were probably frozen or shipped in from somewhere." She shrugged, repeating the process. "Still good."

I pushed the black raspberry toward her. "All yours."

She nibbled each flavor with tiny spoonfuls followed by thoughtful pauses and commentary, but the only thing I could see was her mouth. The way it curved into a smile or a pout, the way her lips closed around the spoon or folded together, the way I imagined her lips on my cock.

Yeah, I couldn't think about that right now. Not one bit. We weren't talking about sports or why it was bad to be good, and me thinking about cocksucking was the last thing that should've been on my mind.

But there it was, flashing like an oasis in the desert. And I lived in a blowjob desert.

I cleared my throat, asking, "Are you ready for your trip to Los Angeles?"

She frowned. "I haven't packed. I'm a last-minute packer. Everything in, hope for the best. If I screw it up, there will be shops in California. But it would be good to get that done tonight. Knowing my current client list, I'll wake up with my phone on fire because five of them failed their drug tests and I'll have to buy a toothbrush from the hotel gift shop."

"I shouldn't keep you." I glanced at my watch but didn't register the time. It didn't matter. "It's getting late," I said. "Let me take you home."

Stella slowly dragged the spoon from between her lips and then her tongue shot out, tracing the plastic edges. I'd challenge any red-blooded, heterosexual man to watch a show like this one and not find himself at half-mast.

"What if I'd rather," she started, torturing me with another bite of ice cream, "walk for a bit? With you."

I leaned back in my seat, surprised that option was on the table. Shocked. The entire evening was a sampler pack of mixed signals. "I'm always up for a walk around Beacon Hill but I don't want to be to blame for any hotel gift shop purchases."

She considered this, nodding. Her spoon hovered over the duo of ice creams before diving for the remaining portion of creamy purple. One taste of the black raspberry had her eyes fluttering and a low hum of pleasure rumbling in her throat. Torture. Plain fucking torture. She licked her spoon again and I damn near snatched it out of her hand and threw it across the store.

She twirled her spoon in my direction as if she was casting a spell. "Use your words, Cal. I don't speak man-growl."

My gaze was glued to her mouth. If there was anything else in the world to see, I was unaware.

"That was another one of those rumbly-grumbly not-words situations," she said.

The responsible, Army-precise side of me desperately wanted to walk her home, leave her at the door, and allow her to prepare for her business trip. The other side of me, the one concerned with dragging her lower lip between my teeth while my hand slipped under her panties, desperately wanted to get her behind closed doors.

"I can promise you one thing," I said.

"Just one?" Stella asked, a skeptical scowl on her face. "You seem like a multiple promises kind of man. I feel like you've already promised me a boatload of things. Actually, where is my pony?"

I shook my head once. "I expect I'll give you more satisfaction than that ice cream."

She glanced at the cups before her, her lips pursed. She scooped up another bite. The chocolate-pretzel-chaos flavor this time. She damn near sucked the shine off that spoon before asking, "Is that so?"

There was a weight associated with articulating all the things I wanted with Stella. It piled up around us like a drop in the air pressure. My shoulders were bunched tight and my cock was heavy, and I was working hard at keeping cool even when I wanted her to tell me she wanted it too. That was all I needed to hear. Then I'd toss her over my shoulder, hustle her home, and make good on those promises.

"I think you know it is," I said.

Stella smiled down at her spoon. I was really fucking jealous of that plastic. "Where do you come up with all these dirty thoughts?"

Watching your ass for the past eight months.

Stroking myself to memories of your smile in the shower every morning.

Hearing your laugh every time I close my eyes.

Last night. Last fucking night.

"You," I said. "You bring it all out, sweet thing."

She turned her attention to the table and busied herself with balling up the napkins and gathering the ice cream cups, but I noticed a rosy flush creeping across her cheeks. "Always the nice ones," she murmured. "The awkward ones too. Oh, they're even worse."

I stood, squeezing her hand and tilting my head toward the exit. "Come with me. Let's see where the streets take us tonight."

The evening air was cool and damp, and puddles dotted the sidewalk from today's on-and-off rain. Fog and clouds hung low over the city, and it gave me a valid excuse to keep Stella tucked close to my side. It wasn't a good night for walking, no more than necessary. But she asked for this and I was willing to do a great many things to keep this woman in my company.

We made our way around one side of Beacon Hill and down the other. The logical next stop was my apartment, the one I'd selected for its proximity to the hospital. I could be dressed, out the door, and inside the facility within minutes. The greatest variation in my commute time was my willingness to jog through oncoming traffic.

She led the way, urging me down narrow side streets and around corners I'd never noticed. I was certain she was leading us on the most circuitous path to my building but I didn't know whether she was waiting for me to insist on taking her home like I did last night. I wanted to. I wanted her. But with every step we took, one fact became arrestingly clear.

This wasn't last night. The vibe was wrong, the gravity was off. Yesterday was cosmic. It was fairy dust and sliding doors and a rowdy beaver. Today was the hangover. Even if I loaded up on fairy dust and went looking for a beaver, I wasn't getting yesterday back.

When we reached my building, I tipped my head toward the door before wrapping my arms around her waist. "Here we are again."

She hummed in agreement as she stared at the building. "We are. It's funny how we have this small circle of places. The trail, a place to eat, your apartment. We keep going around and around."

"We do." I leaned down and pressed my lips to hers. She tasted of cold and cream and sweet berries, and I kissed her as if I wanted that flavor all for myself. I didn't mind ice cream when it was on her tongue.

But Stella stepped back, denying me those berries. "There are a few things I should tell you."

I gestured for her to continue but she said nothing, instead staring at me.

Finally, she said, "I have to tell you this and I'm sorry it took me so long to get it out." Her expression softened and she tilted her head to the side as if she was looking at a one-winged duckling. "You're such a nice guy and I don't want to hurt you."

Oh, fuck. Not this again. I knew it was going to come back and bite me. I knew there was something I was missing.

"I'm not," I argued. "I'm not even close to a nice guy." I hooked my thumb over my shoulder, toward the hospital complex. "I can get twenty interns and residents over here right now who will tell you I'm an asshole. One of them made a dartboard with my picture on it. Rumor has it someone made a voodoo doll a few intern cohorts back."

"You're a nice guy, Cal," she repeated, laughing. "You're a nice guy and I don't want to give you the wrong idea about me." She circled her hand between us. "I don't do *this*. I do *that*." She pointed toward my building. "I like to keep it casual. I don't do *this*. The relationship thing. I don't talk about feelings or families or—I don't know. Lasagna. I don't do this. I don't do the thing you want."

"How do you know what I want?" I laughed to soften the snap of my words. "You don't know what I want, Stella. You don't."

She clasped her hands under her chin and gave me an evilly angelic look. "You asked me to marry you yesterday."

"You keep mentioning that."

"It's worth mentioning," she replied. "It's kind of a big deal."

"Only because you haven't given me an answer," I said.

"Yeah," she murmured, nodding. "That's the point."

She glanced up at the building again. Stared at the windows, the old brown bricks. Stared so long I thought she was waiting for me to walk away. But I wasn't going to do that. "I hate to break it to you, Stel, but if you're expecting me to leave, you'll be waiting a long damn time."

"And why is that?"

I had to close my eyes to keep from rolling them. "Because I spent eight months trying to figure out the right way to say hello to you. Because you climbed into my lap and kissed me yesterday morning. Because I made you scream the very first time I tried. Because the best and worst thing about me is I don't know how to give up. Because I think we want the same things but we're saying it in different ways."

She waved her hands at me as if she was trying to stop traffic. "Cal, no. We are not saying the same things. I assure you."

This woman was all kinds of headstrong, and I walked a

line between admiring the shit out of it and wanting to club her over the head and drag her back to my prehistoric cave.

"Then help me understand," I said.

Stella stared at the intersection, her gaze far away. Eventually, she glanced back at me and said, "If we go upstairs right now, if we go to your apartment, we'll have sex." She eyed me up and down, giving extra attention to my crotch. "Good sex. Like, phenomenal sex. The kind of sex where you murder my vagina and then shapeshift into a bear."

"I'm not going to shapeshift into a bear," I said.

She held out her hand. "But you will wreck my vagina."

"I—I don't even know what that means," I replied.

She folded her arms across her chest. As if I was the one being ridiculous here. "I had to sit on a pillow today," she said, "and that was just from some light—you know—whatever it was we did last night."

"God help me, Stella," I growled.

"If we go upstairs right now and have vagina-murdering, bear-shifting sex, it will be nothing more than that. Sex. It will be amazing and I'll enjoy the hell out of it and trust me, I'd really love to go upstairs right now. You don't even know how much I'd like that. But it would be sex. In and out. One and done. No lasagna, no Ikea. That's not who I am." She stared at me hard, pushing me to recognize something I was obviously missing. "Just sex. Just the one time."

"I guarantee it will be more than one," I replied.

Her lips tipped up in a coy smile. She winked at me. It zinged right into me, landing somewhere near my belly button and melting me from the inside out.

"I don't doubt that," she replied. "But—but I don't think I can do that with you. I don't think I want that with you."

Her words sent me back a step. Two. "I understand," I lied, my gaze on the sidewalk. I did not understand any of this. "But you're wrong about something."

"What's that?"

"The lasagna, the trip to Ikea. That *is* who you are," I replied. "Those were your ideas, sweet thing. You opened the door. I just stepped through it."

She tossed both hands in the air, waving them as if she was trying to shake something off her skin. I didn't think the truth came away that easily.

"We have a good time together," she said, still ridding herself of my words. "We have chemistry. But you're a nice guy and you need to find yourself a girl in the market for that."

"And you're not? Let me guess, you're in the market for the misunderstood rebel and the golden-hearted bad boy?"

She blinked, her eyes fluttering for a second. Fine dots of mist were clinging to her lashes. Why the fuck were we outside? Why were we talking this over on the damn sidewalk? There was a dry, warm apartment no more than fifteen steps from here but yet we couldn't go there. We had to keep our private conversation public because once that door closed we both knew the clothes were coming off.

Because we knew—regardless of the ways in which we pulled back and leaned in—this was it.

And that made this fucking infuriating. We had chemistry? Yeah? Really? That was like saying Mount Everest was tall. If we had chemistry, it was volatile chemistry. We had to save ourselves from it or run headlong into it.

She brought her fingers to her temples with a harsh sigh. "Actually, no. I have no time for either of those things.

I'm not trying to play the work card here or paint myself as the busy businesswoman who can't live because she's so busy with business, but my job is a lifestyle."

"Yeah." I shoved my hands into my pockets. "I know something about lifestyle careers."

"Yes," she shouted. Heh. She thought I was agreeing with her. "Of course. You get it."

"Okay, Stella." I stepped closer, edging into her space. "You don't want a relationship. Okay. I won't give you one."

Her eyebrow arched up. I moved closer.

"You don't want sex," I continued. "Okay. I won't give it to you."

She glanced down, her gaze on my coat.

"You don't want a nice guy." I shrugged. "Okay. I won't give you one."

I inched closer, all the way into her space now. She sucked in a breath, blew it out slowly.

"I won't give you anything, Stel," I said. "Not until you ask me for it."

Her teeth sank into her bottom lip but then she laughed, a quick, fluttery sound that dissolved as fast as it appeared. "And if I ask you to leave me alone? You'll do that?"

Without conscious thought, my jaw tightened and a steel band of tension pulled my shoulders taut. "I will," I replied, hating the taste of those words. I'd respect her wishes no matter what but goddamn I didn't want that to be her wish.

She reached for my hands, squeezing them as she offered me a watery smile. "Thank you." She released my hands, backed away. "I should go now."

Those were dropkick words. They knocked the wind right out of me.

She slipped her hands into her pockets. The streetlights overhead illuminated the mist, casting her in a sparkling halo. It was strange but fitting. "I won't be on the trail tomorrow morning. I have too much to do before LA and I have to—"

"Slay," I finished.

"Slay," she repeated with a laugh. "But I'll be back on Monday evening and walking Tuesday morning."

"Is that your sweet way of telling me to stay off the Jamaica Pond trail?"

She stared at the night sky as if she was searching for the answer up there before glancing back to me. "Take all the things I've said tonight, all the things you've said. Spend the weekend with them. Come Tuesday, you know where I'll be if you still want to see me."

"All right." My response sounded like a question.

"We could talk," she offered. "Or not. We could just walk without saying anything. I do have some epic playlists."

"All right," I repeated.

Stella stepped toward me but stopped herself midstride, shook her head, and then continued into my arms. She hugged me tight for one perfect moment but quickly untangled herself, turned, and walked away without a word.

I stood there, rooted into the sidewalk as I watched her stride up the hill. The streetlights kept her bathed in golden light and misty halos. She was complicated, of that I was certain. Complicated and once again out of reach.

Yeah. She was the asset.

14

CAL

"Then he leans in and kisses her, *Gone With The Wind*-style, right there on the sidewalk with me and Riley watching. I guess we can say that when Hartshorn goes for it, he goes all the way."

Nick swung a glance in my direction before turning back to Alex. "Wow," he said. "That's unexpected."

"Why, exactly?" I asked.

"It really was," she continued, ignoring me. "And she was into it. I mean, for someone who'd just met her stalker—"

"For fuck's sake, Emmerling," I growled. I glared over her shoulder at the rowing team gliding over the Charles River. I didn't know whose idea it was to eat lunch outside today but that person underestimated the wind chill.

She gave me a *you're not off that hook yet* grin. "—she was shockingly into it. If Hartshorn goes all the way, this chick does too."

"If memory serves, you were champagne drunk on a

weeknight," I said. "Not sure your eyewitness testimony is credible."

A gust of damp air blew her hair into her eyes but that didn't stop her. She held up a finger. "I was tipsy," she argued. "There is a major difference."

Alex stopped analyzing the shit out of me and Stella to zip her jacket all the way up and burrow into the fleece. If only she knew how much had changed in the thirty-odd hours since running into us on the sidewalk.

"She seemed cool?" Nick asked. He watched me, a cautious glint in his eyes. "Of sound mind despite all indicators otherwise?"

"Oh, yeah," Alex agreed, balling her hands inside her sleeves. "Cute, sweet, outgoing. She was great."

"She put up with your babbling," I grumbled.

"Mmhmm," Alex hummed. "And you tackling her on the trail and confessing your not-so-small obsession with her. As far as questionable behavior goes, I think I'm in the clear."

Nick held up a hand. "All right, man. You talked to the girl. You've hit the one in a million scenario where she's not married or awful or insane. I'm happy for you. I'm shocked but I'm happy this epic holding pattern has resulted in something decent. What happens next?"

I stared at my sandwich for a second as I struggled to respond. I still didn't understand last night's conversation. I knew there was something Stella wasn't saying, something big. I knew she was holding herself back, putting up a wall. And I knew this wasn't ending with me on one side of that wall and Stella on the other.

I wasn't exaggerating when I told her I didn't give up. I

didn't know how. I didn't walk away when the going was tough or the odds were low. I didn't abandon my people, and whether she liked it or not I counted her in that group now.

I cleared my throat, meeting their expectant stares. "She has business travel through the weekend. She'll be back in town next week." I hesitated, reaching for my drink but only to buy myself another second. "We'll see what happens when she gets back. No need to dictate the rest of the calendar year."

"Does that mean you haven't convinced her to move in with you yet?" Alex asked.

"Yeah, I was expecting a Save The Date card in my mailbox this weekend," Nick joked. "At least making it Facebook official."

Yeah, me too.

Instead, I said, "I'm not on Facebook."

Nick and Alex shared a knowing eyeroll.

"We're taking it slow," I continued. The vision of her bitten backside filled my mind's eye and no, there was nothing slow about me and Stella. "We're still figuring it out."

"What are you still figuring out?" Alex asked. "Aside from everything because you talked to her for the very first time in your life just the other day."

I do that. I don't do this.

"Where it's going. What we want," I said. The words tasted as lame as they sounded. "We're taking it slow."

"Sure," Alex said. Her tone informed me she didn't believe a word of it. "That's why you were hustling her out of your apartment around midnight and eating her face on

Cambridge Street. That's the textbook definition of taking it slow."

"It's not what you think," I argued. "She—she doesn't do relationships."

Nick and Alex gave each other *that sounds bad* eyes.

"Mmhmm," Alex replied. "Where does that leave you?"

I studied my sandwich. "She asked me to think about it and meet her on the trail next week. When she's back from LA. If I want to see her. If I'm interested."

"You will, you do, you are," Alex said. I nodded because —yeah. She was right on all counts. "Why, Hartshorn?"

"Because I know," I replied, frustrated. "Even if she doesn't know it, or doesn't believe it, I'm willing to wait until she does. And I'll tell you something, Emmerling, I think she's just being stubborn. Set in her ways."

"Yeah," she said, snickering. "Don't mention that part to her. It won't make her any less stubborn or set in her ways. If anything, it makes me sympathize with her."

I replied with an annoyed shrug.

"But why do you want to put yourself through that?" she asked.

"Why not?" I asked. "I mean, I've had months to think about this and—"

"Build her up in your crazy head," Alex interrupted. "To invent her all on your own. You've created an idea of her, Hartshorn, and the complication is that your idea probably doesn't match the reality. You've run off with your fantasy-imagination version of her. I bet she's waiting for you to come down from that cloud and that's why she wants you to think it over."

"Emmerling makes a solid point," Nick said, finally

weighing in. "The information she shared with you—is it difficult to integrate that into your vision of her?"

I don't do this. *I do* that.

I don't do the thing you want.

"Stella needs some time to catch up," I said. "That's what I'm going to do. Give her time."

"What if she doesn't catch up?" Alex asked. "What then?"

I studied my lunch again. "Then...the wait will have been worth it. I'll never wonder what could've been."

Nick crossed his arms over his chest and turned his face to the sky. "Y'all have extremely complex romantic lives." He glanced from me to Alex, then back to the sky. "I don't know how you handle all this drama."

"Dude," Alex said with a sigh.

I leaned forward, my elbow braced on the table as I pointed at Nick and stared at Alex. "Is he for real right now?"

She shook her head. "I hope not."

"Same," I muttered. "Maybe his residents should wrestle him into the MRI this afternoon because there's no way he's forgetting the time he and his wife lived on different continents—"

"For two fucking years," Alex finished.

Nick shook his head, still soaking up the sun. "That situation is nothing like the two of y'all. I met a woman, I married her that day, and I played the long game in getting us under one roof." He shrugged. "Nothing outrageous."

"Um, I'm going to push back on you there, Acevedo," Alex argued. "It's rather outrageous and I do recall you Charlie-Browning your ass around here between your trips to Iceland. And let's not forget the part about you spending every free minute writing emails and ditching us so you could video chat."

"Or all the times you'd sit right there, sniffling over your sandwich because Erin liked bread or some shit like that," I added.

"Yeah," Alex replied, jabbing a finger toward me in agreement. "That. Your wife is the tits and I'm really thrilled she's local but you were too damn emotional over bread to claim you have any kind of experience with normal relationships. Get off the moral high ground for a minute, would you?"

Nick waved a hand at us. "Say what you will but I never sat here and told y'all I was taking it slow and low-key assaulting her in parks."

"No," Alex replied with a sharp nod. "You never did those specific things. However, you did drag me to a jeweler because I had to help you pick out a wedding band for your wife some three months after you eloped. I also had to try on sweatshirts for you even though I have a solid fifty pounds on your wife. I'd argue these things are the same but different. Excessively dramatic and unnecessarily complex."

I stared at the platinum band shining on his left hand. I resented it, just a bit. Like he said, he met a woman and then he married her the same night. I couldn't execute on that move.

"We'll agree to disagree on this point," Nick said.

"It must be a neurosurgeon thing," she mused. "This intractability. It's what happens when you assume one organ system is more important than the others."

"It is," he replied. "When the brain shuts down, the game's over."

Alex squared her shoulders and let out a long breath. "Gastric functions continue, unaided, for at least a week following brain death."

"Yeah. With a ventilator," he snapped.

Because I couldn't listen to this argument without fighting for my service's supremacy, I added, "You're both wrong because none of it matters without a beating heart."

The three of us stared at each other for a second, each ready to drop our specialized hammers. Then Nick said, "We need to get a urologist at this table. Someone to stand up for balls."

Immediately, I thought of Stella and all the balls she juggled.

"That's the lamest argument you've lodged yet," Alex replied. "The last thing anyone needs is balls and the urologist would come down hard for kidneys."

"I'll see her again on Tuesday morning," I said, swinging the conversation all the way back to my complex affairs. "Stella. On the trail. I'll see what happens."

Nick sighed as if I was causing him real pain. "I need you to use an abundance of caution. No more incidents, please. Once is an accident. Twice is cause for concern. Three times is us passing the hat for bail money."

I scowled at him. "You can afford it on your own."

"We're focusing on the wrong things here," Alex said.

"Don't injure the woman again," Nick warned. "Even if she's the one who causes the accident, I need you to be far away from it."

I glanced back to the river. It must've been freezing out

there, with the wet wind blowing right off the water. "I'm working on it."

Behind me, I heard, "It's funny how you people call this spring." Turning, I saw Stremmel jogging toward our table with his head ducked low into his shoulders. "This is winter. Hell, there are still piles of snow around the city."

"Yeah, those aren't going anywhere until June. It will be eighty degrees before the last remnants of blizzard season are gone," Nick said. "Believe me, man, I get it. Coming here from Texas was tough." He gestured around the table. "We're all transplants. None of us natives. It's tough but it grows on you."

"So does MRSA," he grumbled, dropping beside me on the bench. He pointed at the paper-wrapped sandwich on the center of the table. "Is that mine?"

"Yep," Alex replied. "Extra avocado too. I watched them put it on."

"Probably not ripe," he said under his breath.

It took a fair amount of restraint to keep myself from kicking him under the table. But if I kicked him over a snide remark now, I'd have to pound his ass for the truly obnoxious things he said every day. It was like he had a quota to meet.

"Mine was ripe," Nick said. "I'm sure yours will be too."

"We were just rehashing the recent events of Hartshorn's love life," Alex said, gesturing to me. "It's been entertaining."

"I'm certain I do not care," Stremmel replied before biting into his sandwich.

I watched his reaction—we all did—praying that damn avocado was to his specifications. When he went in for another bite without slamming the region's avocado supply chain, we breathed a collective sigh of relief. And that was a fucking problem.

"Well?" Stremmel prompted.

"Well, what?" Nick asked, his Texas drawl thicker than ever.

Stremmel rolled his eyes. "Where are we with Hartshorn's relationship drama du jour? Rumor has it you talked to your mystery woman."

"The avocado is to your liking?" I asked.

He jerked a shoulder up, tipped his head to the side. After a pause, he said, "It'll do."

"You're welcome," Alex said to him. There was a hefty pinch of salt in those words.

Stremmel looked down at his sandwich and then up at her. "My bad," he said under his breath. "Thank you. Let me know what I owe you."

She waved him off. "It's good. We take turns picking up lunch." She tipped her chin up. "Your day will come and you'll hear all about Acevedo's cilantro needs and my mustard-to-mayo ratio requirements."

A slice of avocado fell from his sandwich and landed on the wax paper. He grabbed it, popped it in his mouth. "This is an ongoing thing?"

"Fresh air, sunlight, food," Nick said, ticking off the items on his fingers. "Arguments about the hierarchy of organ systems but mostly surgical services. Why not?"

"That's easy," Stremmel said. "You can't survive without vessels carrying blood from one place to another. Vascular wins."

"Oh my god," Nick said with a groan. "How is that—no. No. That's not a reasonable answer. Try again."

"Is your objective to aim low and finish high?" Alex asked, staring at him with unmasked horror. "Because you can't possibly believe that."

I stared at him for a beat. Blinked. Stared a bit longer. He knew I was keeping an eye on him and he seemed to tolerate me. He knew I had some experience in his specialty—trauma—and he seemed to respect that. If there was anything I knew as well as hearts and lungs, it was treating patients with the worst injuries and the least amount of time. But that tiny bit of respect wasn't going to be enough to tame this shrew and everyone knew he didn't give two shits about positional authority.

But maybe respect and authority weren't the ways to winning Stremmel over. Maybe it was meeting him where he was, misery and all, and accepting that baggage.

"What are you doing tonight, Stremmel?" I asked. "Don't answer that. You're getting a beer with me because I've never heard anyone put vascular ahead of cardio—"

"Or neuro," Nick added. "I'd join that beer but my wife flies in tonight and I'm going to know you're both wrong while spending time with her."

Alex gave him an impatient glare. "I'll be with my fiancé at the ballgame so I'll also skip that beer but I'd like to state one more time that without gastro, everyone would be literally full of shit."

"Goddammit," Stremmel muttered. "I should've kept my mouth shut."

"That's the spirit," I said, clapping him on the back.

15

STELLA

I WANTED TO GO STRAIGHT HOME AFTER ARRIVING BACK IN Boston. Go home, do laundry, change the sheets, shower away the flight, look over my calendar and plan out the week. That was my routine and I loved it. It staved off the jet lag and put me in the right mood to get back to work bright and early. To get back on the trail.

But I wasn't doing any of that. Nope, the car service was driving right past my neighborhood and into downtown Boston where Lucian McKendrick was dirty dancing— pants down—on a bar. Thankfully, it only took me whistling at him from the door and my sharpest glare to get him down and the pants up. I'd called ahead and handled his tab and Flinn already had a jump on minimizing the social media impact.

McKendrick complained about leaving, of course, whining and moaning to his adoring fans as he shuffled toward me. None of that mattered to me. He was allowed to save face. Hell, he could throw me right under the bus for all I cared. I didn't mind being the villain here. If I played this situation right, I'd be the villain with the corner office and the kind of raise that said "vacation in the south of France."

I held the car door open for McKendrick, waiting until he scooted to the far side before climbing in beside him. The driver already had McKendrick's address and orders to take us there regardless of the bribes and promises lobbed at him.

When the car turned onto Storrow Drive, heading out of the city, I glanced at the man to my left. "What was that all about?"

He shrugged. "I'm twenty-seven years old and really fuckin' rich. What am I supposed to do with myself on a Monday night?"

"Honestly, McKendrick, I know a lot of rich dudes. Rich ladies too. You're the first one I've met who entertains himself by gettin' low on a bar, rubbing a bottle of Hennessy on his junk, and then dousing a bunch of chicks in that ball-sweat-anointed Hennessy. But here's how I see it," I continued. "You're an individual. You follow your own drummer. You want to rub your jewels on that whiskey and there's nothing anyone is going to say to change your mind."

"Thank you," he cried, slapping his palms on his thighs. "Thank you. Finally. Someone who gets it."

I didn't get it but I wasn't telling him that. It only mattered that he felt heard, seen. "We're headed to a number of goodwill appearances and charitable events in the next few weeks," I said. "I want you to think about limiting the balls-and-whiskey situations to private spaces. You can't take your picture with sick kids in the morning and then go buck wild at night. It's incongruent. People won't let you near the sick kids if your sac is all over social media." I gestured toward his lower body. His manspreading claimed two-thirds of the back seat. "Unless you'd rather we visit the testicular cancer floor."

He grabbed his crotch, shivered. "Why in the fuck would I want to do that?"

"Because the only reason you'd have your balls out in the middle of a bar—not a very good one, I might add—is to remind men to get them checked. Clearly, you're raising awareness about a disease that few discuss," I said. "With the exception of men growing beards in November."

He shifted, staring at me with a pensive expression creasing his forehead. "What are you talkin' about, lady? I don't grow a beard for ball cancer. I grow a beard for the World Series."

I bit my lip to hold back a laugh. "And here you are, raising awareness in April."

"I'm a hero. Obviously," he replied, still watching me with that confused look. "Who are you, lady? What's your story?"

I gave him a warm smile, dimples and all. "No story, McKendrick. I love the game. I love helping players position themselves for long-term success."

He chuckled. "That's a load of bull, honeycakes. That's something you read off a motivational poster or a fortune cookie. No one says shit like that and means it."

"I mean it," I replied, laughing. "I do love the game and I do love helping my players. Especially when they get into trouble."

"You might mean it but it's not your story," he said,

turning his attention to the window and the dark countryside beyond. "You married, lady? Kids?"

"No and no," I replied, wiggling my ringless fingers at him.

"You looking?" He gestured to his lap like he was a model on *The Price Is Right* and his dick was the showcase.

I worked hard at keeping my expression even. Experience had taught me that laughing at this moment was the *wrong* response. "I'm actually seeing someone." It was my standard response but it wasn't my usual stiff delivery. My voice softened, my head tilted to the side, my cheeks burned at the memory of Cal's tongue between my legs. I didn't expect any of it. I wasn't sure I liked it. "I'm seeing someone," I repeated.

McKendrick rolled his hand, wanting more. "You can't say that, honeycakes, and leave me hanging. I have the gym and my shenanigans. Nothin' else. No ball, no boys, no workouts with the team, nothing. I'm not even getting laid on the regular because someone won't let me socialize." He pinned me with a sour glare. "What's his name? What's he do? Where's it going?" He nudged me with his elbow. "Or is it a she?"

I gave McKendrick credit for asking if I was seeing a woman without a leer or suggestive tone. That was an accomplishment. "He. His name is Cal. He's a heart surgeon."

McKendrick drummed his fingers on his thigh. "And where is it going, lady? You serious? Will I get a plus-one to your wedding or will I have to plow all the bridesmaids to keep myself entertained?"

"I'm not inviting you or your scrotum to my wedding," I deadpanned. "I'm not getting married."

"That's a shame," he groused. "My Electric Slide is on fire." He rolled his neck from side to side, a loud crack accompanying each movement. "It's serious, huh? You're feelin' this guy?"

"I, uh, I don't—I don't know," I stammered. Fuck, why did I say that? Why did I say that? I made a point of keeping my personal life private. The last person on this planet who needed an update on the ongoing saga of Stella and Cal was Lucian McKendrick. Aside from the fact he was my client, he was gossipy as hell. "It's new. I'm not sure it's going to last."

Stellllllllla.

He regarded me for a moment before saying, "You wouldn't be thinking this hard if you didn't want the show to go on." He nodded, pleased with his assessment, and winked at me. "It's gonna last."

Because there were small miracles in this big world, the driver pulled to a stop at McKendrick's sprawling mansion. Another five minutes and I would've spilled the whole mess I'd made with Cal. Wanting him but not wanting him on my calendar because he'd never slide into that slot. Wanting him but not wanting the deep, all-encompassing relationship he offered. The one he craved. Wanting him and not being able to send him away, forcing him to do it instead.

That part was the worst of it. Cal's adoration was a drug to which I was already addicted. Even if I knew it was wrong, even if I knew I couldn't keep it, even if I knew it wouldn't last. And that was why I had to give him the scissors and force him to cut the cord.

"It looks like we're here," I sang. "My assistant will pick you up for your appearances tomorrow. Sleep tight."

The driver opened McKendrick's door and he stepped out. "It's gonna last," he called to me. "I'm gonna dust off my dance moves for you, lady."

IT WAS TOO late to change the sheets or start a load of laundry when I got home, and without that part of the back-from-business-travel protocol in place, I forgot to shower before flopping into bed. I scanned my calendar from under the covers, looking only for critical events and deadlines.

I noticed Harry's name later in the week. Deleted it. I promised myself I'd shoot him a text in the morning. I had a policy against texting after midnight. Even if I was texting to cancel on him, a one a.m. text screamed "thinking about you while in bed!" and I didn't want to go there. Instead, I set my phone in its charging cradle and burrowed under my blankets.

The next morning, it took me a solid minute to figure out where I was when I woke up. That sumbitch McKendrick. Fucking up all my systems.

I threw on a workout top and a pair of running tights that seemed mostly clean, didn't bother fixing the ponytail I'd slept in, and left the house without tying my shoelaces. I was groggy as hell and cursed myself for my strict adherence to routine. It was a good problem but it was still a problem. Once I got into a habit, breaking it was damn near impossible.

Thank god I'd never tried hard drugs.

As I maneuvered into a parking spot near the trailhead, I found myself staring at Cal's SUV. It was such a shock, I nearly backed into the car behind me. I'd spent the past few days convincing myself he wasn't coming. Of course he wasn't.

And yet here he was.

I stole a moment to fix my hair and run some tinted balm over my lips but that was the best I could do. "This is going to be great," I announced to my empty vehicle. "A nice morning. A good walk. Maybe a conversation with a man-brick. All good. It doesn't matter that I have nothing planned because I promised myself he wouldn't come here after that shit show in front of his apartment but it's going to be great. No worries."

Blowing out a breath, I forced myself out of the car and onto the trail. I found him just beyond the park gates, his hands clasped behind his back as he stared out at the pond. If I was in the business of staging advertising photo shoots, the picture in front of me would've sold a million pairs of track pants, running shoes, form-fitting shirts, anything. Anything, this portrait of quiet strength would've sold it.

As I neared, Cal glanced over his shoulder. A smile pulled at his lips and he turned, but he didn't approach me. No, that was on me. He'd done his part. He came and now it was up to me.

"Hi," I said, stepping closer to him.

"Hi," he answered.

I started to wave but that gesture morphed into me

opening my arms and wrapping them around Cal. Yep, I hugged him. I was hugging him. I was letting him hug me back.

That wasn't true. It wasn't a hug. It was an embrace like long-lost lovers and sex with your pants on. It was fingertips digging into skin, digging, *digging*. It was sucking in a lungful of manly pine trees and needing another hit. It was sighing at the feel of his hands on my waist, his chest under my cheek, his lips on my hair. It was the best thing I'd experienced in days and I could stay right here, just like this.

And that was why I broke out of his hold and rubbed my palms together. I was plenty warm but I needed something to do, somewhere to put all this energy. "It's good to see you," I said, hazarding a glance at him.

"I could say the same to you," Cal replied with a chuckle. "How was Los Angeles? Did everything go as planned? Did you slay?"

I thought about his question for a moment, the automatic slide back into comfortable territory. "Let's walk," I said, pointing down the trail. "I had an issue with a client last night and didn't get home until much later than intended so I really need to get moving if this day has any hope of staying on track."

Cal nodded, gesturing for me to lead the way. Once we got into a brisk pace, he asked, "An issue with McKendrick?"

I barked out a humorless laugh. "Seems like I didn't clean things up as well as I thought I did if you heard about his night on the town."

"I wouldn't jump to that conclusion," he said easily. "I haven't looked at the news today. It was a guess."

We continued along, silent for several minutes. When I couldn't take it anymore, I jabbed my finger into the hard stone of his bicep and blurted out, "You don't like ice cream."

Cal stopped but I didn't realize it until I glanced over and found him ten feet behind me. "Did you figure that out right now?" he asked. "Or did you know that night?"

I pivoted, traveled back to him. "I knew that night," I said. "When you suggested we share but didn't eat one bite."

"Maybe I was being generous," he argued, his eyes hard. "Letting you have both since you clearly enjoyed them."

"Maybe you were," I replied. "But I don't think that's the case. I think you let me believe you liked ice cream because I'd already announced it as one of my favorite food groups."

Cal dropped his hands on his hips and stared at the trail. After a moment, he said, "This isn't about ice cream."

I shook my head. "A little bit. But no. Not really."

"Could you help me out and tell me what it is about?" I didn't say anything. He tipped his chin up, toward the bend of the trail. "Come on. Keep walking."

I followed him and we fell into a companionable silence again. I would've been past the third or fourth song on my playlist if I was alone. Eventually, I said, "I like routines. There's not much predictability in my work so I need it in the rest of my life. I rely on my routines when everything else is chaos."

Cal squinted at me, fine pleats forming at the corners of his eyes. "You don't have to explain any of this to me, Stel," he said. "You walk at the same place, at the same time, in the same lime green sneaks every damn day."

"It's good self-care," I said, nodding toward the trail.

"Sure," he replied easily.

"I like routines," I repeated. "I also like having an active sex life. I don't need deep, complex reasons to justify either."

"No, you do not," Cal agreed.

"And if I do have reasons," I continued, "they don't have to define me. I am not my reasons."

"Agreed. On all counts."

"I can blame my work. I can blame my past relationships. I can blame my upbringing. But the truth of the matter is that I don't want to assign any blame. I don't have to. I'm allowed to enjoy sex. I don't have to be broken or fucked up."

"I get it," he said, and I believed him. Despite the fact I was tossing out random declarations that didn't neatly connect, he seemed to genuinely accept my comments. I needed that. "I can blame work. Past relationships too. And let's not even touch the upbringing. We'd need a marathon course to unpack that."

"But you're not," I said. It was more of a question.

He nodded. "No. I'm not." He gestured toward me. "As I believe you're aware, I can be painfully awkward."

"There's been a moment or two," I conceded with a smile. "I realized years ago that relationships aren't my thing. They don't work for me. They don't make me happy."

Cal hit me with a sidelong glance before asking, "What *does* work for you?"

This was easy. I had this one down to talking points. I'd smoothed it and evened it out over the years, eliminating terms like *fuck buddies* or *friends with benefits* because neither were appropriate. "There are a few men I see on a regular basis," I said. "It's casual and easy, and completely free from emotional attachments. No families, no friends involved, nothing too personal. There's some mutual fondness, sure, but no one is asking where it's going because it's not going anywhere." I glanced up at him, witnessing the exact moment when he turned to stone. If it was possible, even the morning sunlight shining down on him dimmed. "Everyone prefers it that way."

Silence settled around us for a few minutes. I expected the silence. I understood it. My statements offered no room for flexibility, no alternatives.

"You know your mind, I have no doubt of that," Cal said. I started to interrupt but he brought his hand between my shoulder blades, stopping me with a single touch. "But I doubt you're giving yourself a real chance, Stella, not to mention me. I doubt you're remembering that first morning when"—he paused, shaking his head by small degrees as he stared at the pond—"when everything happened. You felt it. I know you did."

I thought of fifteen different reasons why he was wrong. Rebuttals and arguments, anything to get him out of my softest, weakest spots. I thought of them all but I couldn't bring myself to deliver any of them. I didn't want the arguments. I didn't want to defend myself. I didn't want to say anything.

Then, I said everything.

"I was engaged once." Cal's gaze snapped toward me, stayed there. But I couldn't meet it. I couldn't let him see everything the way he always did. Instead, I stared ahead. "I lived at home through college. Paying for state school was a stretch for my parents. Campus housing was out of the question. So, I lived at home. Commuted to Bridgewater." I shrugged but my hands took on a life of their own, fluttering against my thighs as I spoke. "There was a boy from my neighborhood and—and we were together. Getting married seemed like the right thing to do. My younger sister was already engaged and I thought I was ready and I wanted it and it seemed like the right time but then—then I called it off."

Cal didn't say anything but he didn't stop staring at me either. Then he reached for my hand, folded it into his.

"I can't explain why but I did, breaking it off with him. I couldn't go through with it." He squeezed my hand like he was trying to transfer strength through his skin. "I'd worked hard at getting a good internship that summer but nothing panned out. At the last minute, a position opened up at a sports management firm in Seattle and I took it. I canceled my wedding and flew to Seattle and didn't come back for three months." With my free hand, I touched my forehead, traced a finger over my left eyebrow. "I didn't want to see the fallout so I left."

"You didn't do anything wrong, Stel."

I blew out a breath. "Maybe not," I said with a bitter laugh. "I couldn't hide in Seattle forever. I had to go back to school. I had to go home and I had to see him again. We talked and then—then we got back together. Got engaged all over again. It just happened. I knew it wasn't right for me but I let it happen. I knew I wasn't happy but I didn't know how to say that without making everyone else unhappy."

"This isn't going to end well," Cal said.

I shook my head. "He ended it that time. No explanation, no discussion. Nothing." I shrugged, forcing the weight of that relationship off my shoulders. "But he got married within a year. Ten months after demanding his ring back, if I remember correctly. He gave it to her. The woman he married. That was awful. Just fucking awful. I knew he wasn't the one for me but it still hurt to see it go down. It hurt worse to see it without a whisper of explanation." Another shrug. "Not that I'd really given him an explanation. I gave what I wanted and I got what I gave, you know?"

"I'm sorry," he said. "I...I'm sorry you had to experience that."

"Thank you," I replied. "I'm pretty sure I would've filed it away as a bad start to my twenties and moved on but then the pattern kept repeating. Not that I got engaged. Jesus, no. I've learned my lesson there. But I got back out there and dated someone else. We were clicking. It was good. Then it ended. Five months later, he was engaged. It happened one more time after that. Dating, clicking, everything. Then it was over. He was married within a year."

"So," he started, "you don't do this. I get it now."

"I don't do this. Yeah," I agreed, a hint of defensiveness in my tone. "Those relationships were disorganized train wrecks and I'm happy—no, fucking thrilled—I'm not married to any of those guys. But please don't look at me and think those times broke me. They didn't. They helped me figure a lot of shit out and now I get to have fun. I get to make myself happy. I don't have to worry about anyone else."

"And there's no future," Cal said.

"I'll figure out the future when I get there," I argued.

"Right now, I like my life. I like what I have going." I squeezed his fingers. "And I like you too."

But he didn't want the things I had to give. I knew he didn't. And I didn't want it with him. Cal was altogether too intense for a slot on my calendar. He demanded too much, played too hard, adored too deep. He wanted everything and he couldn't help himself.

Worse yet, I couldn't help myself around him.

"That's something to consider." His words were tight, as if I was asking him to choose which type of poison to ingest.

"Yeah," I agreed. "Think about it. You know where to find me."

He offered a noncommittal murmur but said nothing else as we rounded the last quarter of the trail. He didn't need to say anything. He hated this—as I knew he would—and I hated it for him. Cal wasn't like Stephen, Leif, or Harry. Even when he had me on the tailgate of his SUV, treating my scrapes and being bashful, I knew he didn't function that way. He vibed on a different level, my man-brick. He wasn't meant for anything but full-out, balls to the walls, unrelenting intensity when it came to work, women, even burgers. His whole damn life moved at that level. All or nothing at all.

And what a treat that full-out, balls to the walls, unrelenting adoration would be. But it wasn't meant for me. Not for now, not for keeps.

I knew it but that didn't stop it from stinging worse than some well-placed bites to the ass.

I pointed at the park gates as they came into sight and a

gangly creature hunched over an abandoned coffee cup. "Is that my raccoonasaurus?"

"No, Stella. That's a plain old raccoon. A little one too. No dinosaur lineage whatsoever," he said with a laugh. "It's not even the same animal from last week. That was a beaver. This is a raccoon. I'm sure of it."

"I swear to god, it was at least three feet tall and speaking in tongues. That thing wanted to enslave humans, starting with me."

Cal laughed. "You're fucking adorable." He shook his head, hitting me with a smile hot enough to thaw an ice sheet. "All right, Stella. That's our walk for today." He stepped back, pointed to the gates. "The beast has scurried off now that he's had his morning mocha."

"Thank god," I said, starting in that direction. "If that's the price, I'll pick one up on my way over tomorrow. I don't mind paying off the bouncer."

Cal stopped near my car, crossed his arms over his chest. *Oof.* Walking by his side protected me from the full frontal. I glanced across the street, down at my nails, up at the brightening sky. Anywhere but the gun show. Because I couldn't help myself. I really could not.

"What do you have going on today?" he asked. His question came out stiff, as if he didn't know how to talk to me anymore. "Do you get any downtime after working straight through the weekend?"

"Downtime, no," I said, laughing. "After the draft, there's a day or two where everyone breathes and the players are busy bathing in champagne and buying fancy cars. Unless they combine the champagne with the fancy cars, I'm usually off the hook. But after that, it's right back to the mayhem." I lifted my hands, let them fall. "What about you?"

"My schedule is light. That's always a cause for concern," he said, his knuckles running down the line of his jaw. "The shit always hits the fan when I have time on my hands."

"Because you invent your own trouble?"

He shook his head. "When it comes to hospital life, downtime attracts trouble. If it's quiet, wait a few minutes and all hell will break loose."

"Hmmm." The light hit his beard scruff and I was pretty sure my ovaries catcalled him. I rolled my eyes at myself but went straight back to admiring his scruff.

Stella don't Stella Stella Stella don't go there.

Cal shifted, unfolding his arms and setting his hands on his hips. "Any late meetings or calls tonight?"

I blinked away, mentally paging through my calendar. "Nothing after eight, assuming McKendrick's babysitters succeed in keeping him confined."

He stepped closer to me, moving into my space the same way he did before I left him on the sidewalk in front of his building. I could smell those manly pine trees. I could feel his skin, warm under my touch. I could almost taste his lips. God, I wanted to kiss him.

Don't do it don't do it don't do it Stella don't do it don't don't don't.

"Then I'll meet you for dinner at eight thirty," he announced.

No awkward. No shy. No bashful. Just my man-brick, disregarding the fuck out of my routines and systems and entire world order.

"Eight thirty," I repeated. "No ice cream."

Stellllllllla. What the fuck.

He pulled a smirk. "Just because I didn't eat the ice cream doesn't mean I didn't enjoy it."

Looking away for the sake of my ovaries, I patted his forearm. "That's not strange at all, Cal."

"I'll text you," he promised, backing away.

"Yeah," I murmured, pressing my fingertips to my lips. My head was spinning. What the fuck just happened here?

I watched him hop into his SUV and drive away. His taillights faded from view but I didn't move. Not for another minute or two. I replayed all the words I'd spoken, the truths I'd divulged. Some hadn't seen the light of day in years. A decade, maybe.

I couldn't remember the last time I'd talked about my broken engagements. I hated the disorganized, frenzied way I'd expressed myself. Talking was my job. I knew how to say things to get a desired effect but instead of doing that with Cal, I couldn't get a message across any more than I could handle myself around raccoons. Or beavers. I was full of contradictions.

Then my phone buzzed with a new text message. My first thought was Cal and his promise to message me. My second thought was Flinn and Tatum and McKendrick, and a fresh new disaster. "Heaven help me," I muttered, removing the device from my armband and swiping it to life.

Harry: Hey. Sorry we couldn't connect last week. On for this week?

"Um, no. No, thank you," I said to myself. I was typing faster than I could think. I didn't want to see him this week and I knew that before arriving at the trail this morning. But now I knew I needed a break from him.

Stella: Yeah, sorry about that.

Stella: So, I have a new client and my life is insane right now. I know I'm going to be tied up this week and next.

Harry: No worries. We'll reconnect in May.

Stella: You're too sweet, thank you.

Stella: I know I'm going to be high-touch with the client for a bit and I don't want to make plans but end up breaking them at the last minute. How about we hold off a little longer than that?

Harry: Yeah. Cool. Hit me up when you're free.

Stella: I hope it goes without saying but if anything changes for you and you want to go a different direction, just let me know.

Harry: Of course. Same goes.

Stella: Take care.

Harry: You too.

16

CAL

As easy as that, I managed a standing date with Stella every morning at the Jamaica Pond trail and another nearly every evening. We were going on two weeks of mornings and evenings, walks and after-work meals, and all I had to do was stop asking permission. Take what she wanted to give but wouldn't let herself have.

For as easy as it was to will this into reality, it was equally difficult.

On more than a few occasions, she was called away from our walks or dinners to handle issues with her clients. Lucian McKendrick and his inability to stay home weren't scoring any points in my book. Neither were her mysteries. She wasn't available on select evenings but never offered a hint of explanation. The notion of her seeing another man on those nights burned me from the inside out. I had no right to demand all her time, all her attention, but I damn well wanted it.

I wanted to touch her too. Touch her, laze in bed with her, waste hours on nothing more than dragging my fingers through her hair, winding those strands around my palm and then watching them unfurl on my pillows, my chest. I imagined her hair would slide and pool like silky ribbons. And that was just her hair. One fantasy about one part of her. Oh, I wanted all of it. All of her. I wanted to hold her and taste her and keep her.

But our interactions knew nothing of the heat we'd shared that first day. She opened her arms to me—seemingly in spite of herself—every time we met and parted, and that would suffice until she asked me for more.

The name of this game was outlast.

I'd waited a long time to approach Stella—such as it was. And I could wait a bit longer while I picked off the other men in her life. Whatever she had with them, it wasn't what we had. Not even close. I'd outlast McKendrick too. I was counting down the days until he was back on the mound and Stella claimed her promotion.

Then I'd claim Stella.

It was as easy—and really fucking difficult—as that.

I MET Stella at an underground restaurant a few blocks from her Copley Square office. It wasn't socially underground like some kind of off-book speakeasy only known to the cool kids. It was actually underground—in a basement. But probably a cool kid hangout nonetheless. She swore I'd love this spot and I stopped myself *this* short of telling her I loved her.

"Everything is so fresh," she gushed, spreading both hands over the assortment of salsas and guacamole. "And flavorful. You think you know what flavor is and then you eat here and realize you know nothing."

She reached for a chip and dug into the guac. She hummed, sighed, moaned. All that from some mashed avocado. I was torn between offering a stray but undeniably filthy comment inviting her to handle my avocados and clearing the table, taking her right here and giving her something worth moaning over.

Two strong options. Unfortunately, Stella beat me to it, saying, "Did you know the term avocado comes from the Aztec word for testicle?"

I took a long pull from my beer before replying, "Yep." Another sip. There wasn't enough beer in Boston to drown my arousal but I was going to give it a good shot. *Outlast.* "I do."

"*Ahuácatl,*" she said, her smile twisting around the word. "I can see the similarities but I don't think I could handle two at once." She held her open palm up, her fingers spread wide, wiggling as if she was struggling to cup some, ahem, avocados. "That's a whole lot of *produce*, you know?"

I choked on the beer, which was bad enough, but Stella shot out of her seat, rounded the table and stood at my side, patting my back like I was a three-year-old struggling over a bowl of sliced grapes.

"Arms up, open the airways," she said, still rubbing. "Isn't that what you told me last week? When that super sweet wine went down the wrong pipe?"

"You always forget you don't like Moscato," I said through a cough. I recovered after draining a glass of water but Stella didn't stop. And if she wasn't stopping, neither was I. I curled my arm around her waist, bringing her closer. She went stone still but—then she softened. Leaned into me. "Thank you."

She didn't respond for a moment. Then another. I was starting to think we were going to dine like this, with Stella standing at my side and my arm anchoring her there. I would've been content with that setup. But then she said, "I always think it's rosé I don't like."

"It's Moscato." I rested my temple against her belly. "Don't worry. I'll remind you next time."

"Thanks," she replied. "I take it testicles aren't your favorite dinner topic."

I laughed. "Warn me next time. Especially if you plan to use that hand gesture again."

"Got it." She moved her hand to my shoulder, patting once. Stella returned to her seat, her lips folded together and her gaze focused on the small dishes between us. "What's going on with you? How was your day?" she asked, hitting me with a dimple-popping smile.

I stared at her for a second, taking in her dark hair, dark eyes, dark olive skin. God, she was beautiful. Just fucking gorgeous. "It was all right," I said, captivated by the shape of her lips. It was like a bow, a heart, a fuckdoll fantasy right across the table. "I spent most of my time involved in a heart transplant case."

"But," Stella started, gesturing toward me with a chip, "isn't that good news? Someone got a new heart, right? Or did it not go well?"

"The outcome was positive," I replied with some reluctance.

"Then why aren't you pleased?" she asked.

She was still holding that chip. I curled my fingers

around her wrist, tugged her toward me as I leaned forward, and ate it out of her hand. Then I washed it down with the last of my beer. Not asking permission. "I don't like harvesting organs."

"Why not?" When my shoulders sagged with a deep sigh, she continued, "I'm truly curious but we don't have to discuss this if you don't want."

I ran the napkin over my lips, stifling another sigh. Today was a tough one. My patient needed a heart. Wouldn't have seen the end of the week without one. The donor was out of time too.

"I don't like harvesting organs. I prefer saving lives," I said. "Harvesting organs is the end of a life. Removing a heart, a set of lungs, putting them on ice—that's the end."

Stella nodded once. "You don't like it but you still do it."

"I do it for two reasons. One, I don't like transplanting organs after someone else retrieved them. The stakes are far too high for the work to be anything short of perfect. And two, that loss divides itself. At the end of the day, the donor is still gone. A family goes home short a loved one. Nothing will ever minimize that loss, but a life—usually more than one—is saved. That's why I do it."

She brought her drink to her lips. "I've never thought about it that way."

"Most don't," I replied. "It's not part of the average person's thought process. Not until they're faced with needing donor organs or consenting to give them." I shoved my hands through my hair. "Nothing is without consequences."

"Oh, trust me," she said, her voice heavy with meaning. "I know all about consequences."

I watched her for a minute, studying the way she tucked her hair behind her ears, reached for her water glass, straightened her silverware, checked her phone. All without making eye contact. Finally, I asked, "Do you punish yourself? For breaking your engagement?"

"I don't think so, no," Stella replied, all warmth absent from her tone. She speared me with a quick glance before focusing on the salsas. "Why do you ask? Are we donating his organs? I mean, I'm not his biggest fan but I don't want him dead."

"Right, right," I conceded. "It's just that, sometimes, you mention consequences or knowing better, and how you're well versed in both. Makes me wonder whether you're referring to your ex-fiancé or"—she turned her attention away from the bowls, hitting me with a cool stare—"or just being cryptic. Because that's fun too. There's a guy I work with—"

"The miserable one?"

"Yes, that one," I said, laughing. "Sebastian Stremmel. He's cryptic as hell. I actually believe he was meant to live in a different era. He's dark and tortured, like Dracula. Heathcliff on the moors. Poe and the damn raven. Sherlock Holmes and all his shenanigans. He belongs in a period of time where it's acceptable to turn your collar up and wander along the river at night."

"I feel like that could be any time period. We could do that right now and no one would find us suspect," Stella replied. "But I do know a few players like that. They aren't the media darlings who give good face on gameday but they show up, put in the time, make the plays."

"That's Stremmel for you," I conceded. "He would've dug

graves during the plague and then robbed them during the Enlightenment. I still think he's stuck in the wrong era."

"You also think I still punish myself for the mistakes of my childhood," she added, her words cloyingly sweet. "That's what I call it, by the way. Childhood. Or baby adulthood."

The server arrived then and we stopped talking to rearrange the table to accommodate the entrees we'd selected for sharing. When we were alone again and Stella was finished humming her excitement over every plate, I asked, "Do you? Do you feel like you deserve to be punished?"

She scooped an enchilada onto her plate. "Yeah, I deserved to be punished," she said, her gaze focused on her food. "Punished for letting myself accept proposals and agree to weddings—not just once but *twice*—all while knowing those were the wrong choices for me. Yeah, Cal, I blamed myself. But that was a long time ago and I don't do it anymore." She seesawed her fork between her fingers. "There was a time when I thought my penance was dating men only to see them leave me and meet their wives. But that confirmed for me that I didn't want to be in the dating-to-find-the-one game."

"For what it's worth, I agree with you," I said. "Dating is...it's fucking awful. I mean, *awful*. Fix-ups and apps and hell, all of it."

"And you've been in a war," she added. "You've been shot."

"That's what I'm saying. Dating is still worse than war and gunshot wounds. That's why I don't do it."

Stella tossed an unconvinced glance in my direction.

Her lips parted to say something but she thought better of it, shoving a forkful of rice in her mouth. Half of it didn't reach the destination and ended up raining down the front of her dress. She brushed it away with an eyeroll. Then, her hand shielding her mouth, she said, "Are you sure about that, Cal?"

I grinned, nodding. "I'm sure."

And I was sure. I wasn't dating to find the one. I'd already found her. She was sitting across the table from me, a clump of rice stuck to her sleeve.

"This is good," I remarked, tapping my knife against the plate of chile rellenos between us. "You were right. About the flavor."

"I know what's good and I know where to find it," she replied.

I murmured in agreement while she listed a handful of hot new eateries co-owned by athletes. It was part of an investment diversification strategy popularized by some wealth managers on the West Coast. Athletes with restaurants made for good press, she insisted. It was more interesting than serving as spokespeople for sports drinks or watches or laundry detergent.

But then the conversation wasn't about athletes and their income streams anymore.

Stella put her fork down, leveled me with a serious stare. "I meant what I said a few weeks ago. I'm not broken, not wounded. It's in the past. I had a bad experience when I was twenty. *Twenty*. I'm almost thirty-six. Soon enough, that bad experience will be more than a half a lifetime away." She shook her head. "It's not wrong for me to want things this way. Plenty of men do and for no other reason than enjoying their freedom. No one asks them if they're punishing themselves for anything."

"You're right about that," I said. "About the double standard."

She peered at me, her lips drawn tight in a line and her brows pinched. "Okay—"

"I shouldn't have brought it up again," I interrupted. "I don't mean to dredge up ancient history."

Stella reared back, holding up both hands while exaggerated shock played on her face. "Wait a second there. What—or who—are you calling ancient?"

"Stop it. You don't look a day over twenty-eight and you know it," I replied with a shake of my head.

With her fork in hand, she pointed at me, saying, "Good save." Then, "I want your ancient history."

"What?" I asked, glancing around as if I'd understand her meaning by glaring at other diners. I did not.

"You know everything about me."

Not hardly. I didn't know where she lived, I didn't know her ex-fiancé's name so that I could hate every guy with that name on principle, I didn't know what she looked like first thing in the morning, before the ponytail and leggings and lime green sneaks. I didn't know whether she watched reruns of 90s-era sitcoms before falling asleep, I didn't know whether she was a neat freak in the bathroom, and I didn't know what she wanted from this one, glorious life.

"I've shown you mine"—also untrue as there was plenty I had yet to see—"now I want you to show me yours." She motioned toward me with her fork, poking at the air as if that would spur me to speech. "You're a doctor. You're hot as fuck. Like, god*damn*." I almost fell off the chair at that.

"You're smart and successful, which hides the awkward real well. You're rumbly-grumbly but that only cranks up the fuck-hot factor as far as I see it. You're a catch, my friend. Why hasn't anyone caught you?"

I wasn't sure how I managed to stay seated while she spoke. I was either falling out of the chair and flopping on the floor like a fish on a line or tossing her over my shoulder and rushing toward the first enclosed space I could find. I'd make up for what I lacked in finesse with a fucking that robbed her of sight and speech for a time.

But then Stella continued, "Maybe someone did. She caught you but she didn't keep you. Or you didn't keep her." She gave me the sad-faced head tilt. "That's what happened. Isn't it?"

I stared at her for a beat or two then looked down at the dishes between us. I picked at a few, depositing a bit of this and some of that on my plate without much thought. All while I regretted the topic at hand, the one I forced.

"Ah ha," she whispered. "That is it."

"Basically," I replied, still dropping food on my plate. "I had a relationship while I was in Ranger school, down in Georgia. Ranger school ended. I deployed. She promised she'd wait for me but definitely didn't as evidenced by her moving up to North Carolina and marrying a Green Beret while I was overseas."

"I fucking hate her."

My head snapped up at Stella's sharp tone but it was her icy glare that hit me hardest. "You—what?"

"I fucking *hate* her," she repeated, a slight laugh edging into her words as she reached for her phone. "Give me her name. I hate her and I'm going to spend the rest of the night making snotty comments about her Instagram posts."

I couldn't fight the warm smile pulling at my lips. Stella —the woman who swore up and down she didn't do *this*, didn't like attachments, didn't want anything but drama-free fun—wanted to snark on my ex's Instagram.

"The name, Cal. I want it."

"It's in the past," I said lightly. If she heard me repeating her words back to her, she didn't acknowledge it. "Half a lifetime ago."

"Doesn't make me hate her any less," Stella replied.

"And now you know how I feel about that ex-fiancé of yours," I said.

She blinked at me. Her lips parted but no sound came out. I didn't think it was possible but in walking the length of this circle, I'd stunned her into silence.

"Like you said," I continued. "Not broken. Not wounded. Ancient history."

Stella stared at me for a long moment. "And you believe that?"

I nodded. "As much as you do."

17

STELLA

"I don't understand what you don't understand about this," Flinn snapped.

"And I don't understand why you can't answer a question without reminding everyone you're the smartest guy in the room," Tatum replied.

"It's not my fault people are idiots," he said.

"Now you're calling me an idiot? Really?" she whisper-shrieked.

"I'm not calling *you* an idiot," he replied. "I'm just saying this isn't complicated stuff and capable people should be able to understand it without hand-holding."

"So, you're saying I'm incapable," she said.

I rolled my eyes at my office door. It was closed but that didn't save me from today's rendition of Tatum and Flinn Hate Each Other. It was sibling-styled hate, the kind they turned on anyone who threatened their little cabal.

"I'll walk you through it if you want," he offered. "I don't mind."

"You don't mind wasting time on idiots? How good of you," she replied.

With that, I reached for my earbuds. There was enough noise in my head without those two. I'd spent the morning shepherding McKendrick through one goodwill photo op after another and my schedule was suffering from it. Remediating his image held the keys to my promotion but he was only one of many clients on my roster and the day still maxed out at twenty-four hours. Making it work was becoming more difficult.

Another area of difficulty: Cal Hartshorn.

It wasn't so much difficulty as *what the fuck should I do here*? Because I didn't know. For the first time in years, I didn't know what to do with a man. I looked forward to walking with him at sunrise. I thought about him during the day. I shared meals with him—damn, that boy could eat —on most evenings. And I dreamed about him at night. Those appearances were rather *spirited*. He was everywhere, occupying every corner of my life.

The toughest part was realizing I liked it. Realizing, accepting, believing. I liked Cal knocking me over and dragging me away from the safe predictability of my color-coded calendar. I liked him forcing his way into my life and telling me how it was going to be—while still giving me plenty of space to twist myself into overly complicated knots.

Over the ambient noise coming through my earbuds, I heard a thud on the other side of my door. Then a slam, another thud, and a bang. It wasn't loud enough to be an all-out brawl and I didn't have the time to investigate if I intended to leave here as scheduled. Cal and I planned to meet up for tapas—a recommendation from one of his colleagues—and I hated arriving late.

A minute passed without further commotion and I shifted my attention back to the interview copy sent over by a reporter. As I scanned my client's responses, I saw an incoming message flash on my phone's screen. The newest text was from Flinn, announcing his relocation to the other side of the floor for the remainder of the afternoon. Then I noticed another message, one I'd missed earlier in the day.

Harry: Hi there. Still alive?
Harry: Thought about you today and wanted to check in.

I GROANED loud enough for Tatum to inch the door open and poke her head in, asking, "Everything okay?"

"Peachy," I replied. "Please don't kill Flinn in today's cage match."

"He's an asshole," she argued.

"He's our asshole."

"That's...that's not a statement I'm comfortable supporting," she said.

"Nobody dies today." I shot her the sternest glare in my arsenal. "I need you to finish that slide deck. Now, close the door."

Stella: Hey! Sorry! I've been swamped and just saw this now.

Harry: It's all good.

Harry: I'm free next week if you want to connect.

I FROWNED AT HIS RESPONSE. First, because I'd told him May was going to be crazy busy—and it really was—and second because I wasn't interested. Not at all. I didn't want to see Harry. I was annoyed—irrationally so—that he was demanding my attention when I had no interest in dividing it. That part wasn't his fault but that didn't stop me from directing some blame his way.

Stella: Eek. I'm really busy this month. This isn't a good time for me.

Harry: Cool cool no worries. Another time.

Stella: Like I said, it's not a great time. I don't want you waiting for things to change with me.

Harry: I don't mind the wait.

Stella: That's kind of you. But I don't want you waiting.

Stella: If anything changes with me, I'll reach out to you. Otherwise, I think we should do our own things.

Harry: Are you ending this?

I SET MY PHONE DOWN, glanced up at the door. I could've used some commotion to distract me right now. Anything to get me out of answering Harry's question. It wasn't that I didn't know how I wanted to respond. I did. I did, and that response scared the shit out of me. Saying it out loud—or typing it in a text—made it real. It took it from hanging out with a dude who starred in my naughty dreams to acknowledging I had something substantial going on here. But then another message hit my inbox.

Cal: Still on for Toro at 8?
Stella: Works for me. You?
Cal: Yeah, I'm right on schedule today.
Stella: I'll meet you there.
Cal: What are you wearing? Just so I recognize you.
Stella: You know what I look like.
Cal: I do but I'll be able to spot you quicker if I know I'm looking for a blue dress or a yellow skirt or that goddamn green raincoat.
Stella: It's 72 degrees and sunny. No raincoat.
Cal: Thank god.
Stella: Don't be so quick to hate on the raincoat. I seem to recall a favorable turn of events where that raincoat was involved.
Cal: Yeah. For you.

MY CHEEKS BURNED red and I couldn't force the smile from my face.

Stella: Oh, please. You enjoyed yourself.
Cal: Truth.

I DIDN'T ALLOW myself a minute to think better of it before holding my phone up and snapping a selfie. I fiddled with the filters for a second—a girl's true best friend—then sent it off to Cal. There was nothing amazing about this shot. I looked fine and that was it. My hair was loose around my shoulders, a bit frizzy from the rising humidity. My black and white print dress seemed to blend into the darkness of my desk chair. The window behind me was the best part, showing off the sunny day and Boston's skyline.

Stella: Here you go. Now you'll be able to locate me without extraordinary measures.
Cal: Black and white today.
Stella: Correct.
Cal: I'm getting some green raincoat vibes there.
Stella: In what way?
Cal: In the wanting to get underneath it way.

I DIDN'T KNOW what to do with Cal but I didn't want to find out what I'd do without him.

CAL DIDN'T GET under my dress that night. He might've if I hadn't left dinner early to pluck McKendrick out of a karaoke bar near Northeastern University. Even if

McKendrick hadn't slipped out unnoticed and stirred up collegiate trouble last night, I wasn't sure I wanted to get physical with Cal again.

I mean, I *wanted* to. I really did.

But Cal wasn't like me. Hell, I wasn't like me these days. But I knew I couldn't have sex with him and continue with business as usual the next day. He wouldn't allow it. He'd want—he'd want everything. Right away. He'd want it to mean something and I didn't trust myself to not want the same thing.

That meant I dodged. Every time he looked at me like he wanted to eat me—and I knew how well he *ate*—I ducked the topic. If there was one thing I could manage with ease, it was spinning a conversation the way I wanted.

And that was how I found myself inviting him to a brand launch party.

"I like seeing your legs," he said, his gaze hidden behind dark sunglasses as we traveled the far side of the pond. "I liked those leggings but I like seeing your skin now that it's warm."

In a rare moment of out-loud insecurity, I replied, "My calves are thick."

To be clear, I had plenty of insecurities. A laundry list of them. But I didn't speak those insecurities. I didn't put that noise out in the world because it didn't need any validity. My mother—bless her heart—would've taken that comment about my calves and assured me I had a pretty face. That was the precise form of well-intentioned validity I didn't need. And I didn't need Cal shooing away my issues either. The opinions of others didn't factor into loving myself. I didn't allow it.

"Yeah, they are," Cal replied from a step behind. Where he was studying my calves. "They're great."

That was a surprise. "I mean, I can never find tall boots. Because of my calves." I had no idea why I was leaning in to this fight, especially when I worked hard at being kind to myself. "They're thick. And not cute."

Cal arched an eyebrow up as he appraised my legs again. "I don't know anything about boots but I'd happily die with your legs around my neck."

"Oh," I murmured, fussing with straightening the hem of my t-shirt. It was perfectly flat, not a wrinkle to be found. I kept smoothing. "Oh, okay then." I glanced over at him, careful to avoid staring at his arms for fear of liquefying here on the trail. Talk about thick. My god. And stealing glances at the tattoo hiding just under the cuff of his sleeve was my favorite trail game. I noticed something new every time I looked. "One of my clients is the new spokesmodel for an athletic wear brand. It's launching at the Newbury Street shop on Saturday. The media portion of the event starts around three and then there's a private party at six. D'you want to go?"

Cal stretched his arms over his head, making it impossible for me to hear his response over the choir of angels singing at the line of golden hair running down his abs.

"Stella?"

"Yeah what?" I replied, dragging my gaze up to his face. He laughed, running his hand down my ponytail. He twisted the strands around his fist, tugging just a tiny bit. "You're going to have a problem on your hands when you have to spoon me off the trail."

He shook his head with a laugh. "I don't know what that means."

"Nothing, nothing," I said, quick to shift gears. "You know, you don't have to do this. You prefer running."

"I prefer walking with you," he replied. "If I find myself in need of a run, there are plenty of stairs at the hospital."

"But you used to run," I argued. "This must be boring for you."

What I really wanted was a little more of his sugar. Another sweet word, another casual touch, another request for more than walks and meals and sex-with-your-pants-on hugs. I held him at a distance because I didn't know how to do anything else, but fuck, did I want him.

"I promise you, Stel, it's not boring." He glanced at me, his eyebrows lifting over the rim of his sunglasses. "Am I boring you?"

"What? No," I said, swatting him with the back of my hand.

"What did you do before?" he asked, pointing at the phone secured in my armband. "You listened to—what? Podcasts?"

I snorted out a laugh. "More like The Backstreet Boys." I reached for the phone, called up my music streaming app. "Here. That's what I listened to."

Cal took my phone, scrolled through the playlist. "Stella's Best Boy Band Jams, Summer 2012," he read. "This is—it's something. And slightly out of date."

"I stick to what I know and like," I replied.

"And that's the truth of it."

"It kept me moving," I said. "Until you came around."

"Yeah. Well. About that party. It sounds great," he said. "But the neurosurgeon I work with—"

"Nick," I supplied. "His wife is the climate scientist."

"Right, those two," he said. "They're hosting a dinner party on Saturday night. They're very chill people so it's not one of those dinner parties with place cards or anything like that."

A laugh burst out of me, louder and harder than I expected. "That's where you draw the line? Place cards?"

He waved me off but said, "You'd like Nick and Erin."

"I'm sure I would," I replied. "And now it sounds like we both have Saturday evening events. I wish there was a way to make it work." I pressed my hands to my face as I gasped. "Oh my god. I just assumed you were inviting me to your dinner party. Shit, that's embarrassing. I didn't mean—"

"Stop." Cal dropped his hand on my shoulder, squeezed. "I was inviting you."

I peeked up at him through my fingers. "Then this was even more embarrassing."

He gifted me one more shoulder squeeze before lifting his hand. "This is good," he mused. "I hover around this level of awkward whenever I'm with you. It's only fair you experience fourteen seconds of it."

"So pleased I could hand you this reprieve," I said, laughing. "If I could get out of this media event, I would. From everything you've told me, your friends sound awesome. Would I get to meet Stremmel? I really want to meet Stremmel. I want to put a face to the misery."

Cal gestured toward me, the back of his right hand grazing my left arm in the process. "Why not split the differ-ence? I'll meet you at your thing and we'll do that. Then we'll go to my thing. I've never once been on time to a party at Nick and Erin's house. Why start now?"

I bobbed my head in agreement. I didn't know what else to say. Cal was introducing me to his friends and colleagues—more than the quick hellos we'd shared on the sidewalk last month—and I couldn't pretend we were merely trail buddies or dinner companions or people who shared a fondness for ass biting. We were none of those things.

What we were...I wasn't ready to say that.

18

CAL

I COULDN'T STOP MYSELF FROM LOOKING AROUND THE ROOM, staring at the athletes and industry professionals as if I'd be able to identify who owned a no-attachments spot in Stella's life from sight alone. And if they didn't belong to her current cadre, had they in the past? Were they hoping to belong in the future?

Stella and I shared several evenings each week but not all. Work commitments claimed some evenings but I was left wondering about the others. I rarely saw Stella on Sunday. Did she spend that night with any of these men? Tuesdays were also tricky. Was she with someone then?

I shot another glance at the crowd, careful to assess everyone without making direct eye contact. But then I noticed a man approaching on my left. He was average height and on the slim side, the way young guys seemed to be these days. As if their goal weight was a size medium t-shirt and they enjoyed pairing skinny jeans with a jacket layered over a sweater over a shirt. In the springtime.

He ran a hand over the crown of his head, down to the

short ponytail that corralled his thick, dark hair. He walked straight toward me as an unpleasant idea hit—what if Stella had told the other men about me? And why wouldn't she? She'd told me about them, opaquely. It was only logical. I couldn't imagine why she wouldn't.

And what if he was one of them?

He stopped at my side, close enough to communicate his intention to strike up a conversation. Or a pissing contest. Hell, I'd win that. This kid looked scrappy but he was just that—a child. What he offered in stamina, I made up for in style.

"Hey," he said, holding out a hand. "Flinn Martin. Stella's media coordinator."

I took his hand, pumped it vigorously as I worked on holding back a relieved sigh. "Cal Hartshorn," I said, eventually releasing the man's hand. "I've heard a lot about you."

"Now that's scary," he said, staring at something over my shoulder. He beckoned in that direction and I shifted, following his gaze toward a strawberry blonde with two martini glasses in hand. "What is she doing? I told her I'd get my own damn drink."

He didn't wait for me to weigh in on the matter, instead bypassing me entirely and plucking a glass from her grip. They exchanged words—and eyerolls and head shakes— on their way back to me.

"Cal Hartshorn," Flinn started.

"You're the stalker," she continued.

Groaning, Flinn hung his head. "May I introduce Tatum Altschul."

I nodded, extending my hand as Tatum shifted the drink

to her other hand. "Nice to meet you both," I said. Even with the stalker barb, I was thrilled to assign this man to the staff column and eliminate him from the bedfellows column.

"What do you think of all this?" Tatum asked, tilting her glossy bob toward the models and athletes.

"It's really—"

"Don't answer that," Flinn interrupted. "No one cares. It's all the things and no one cares. We want to know how it's going with Stella."

I'd heard he was direct but this was heat-seeking. "Good. Great. Everything is"—I scanned the crowd again, my gaze cooling at the sight of her hand settling on a man's forearm —"really good."

Flinn followed my stare. He chuckled, saying, "Don't worry about Robertson. There's an extra bicep in his skull but no brain. Not an ounce. He needs a little handholding from time to time but that's it. That's where it ends. Bruh might even be a virgin."

"You would know," Tatum muttered.

He cleared his throat, spared her a sour glimpse. "Save it for later, Tate."

She hid her annoyed glare behind her drink. Then she asked, "What do you want to know? We're here, we're greased up on the good vodka, and we spend more time with Stella than anyone else. *Anyone* else."

This was a trap. It was an IED hidden in roadkill. Flinn and Tatum—through their special blend of hate-love— shared a knowing grin. Definitely a trap.

"That's a generous offer," I replied. "But I'm not lacking for information, thank you."

"Because of the stalking," Tatum offered. "I can see how that would be ripe for content."

I shook my head, smiling. "I come by it honestly."

Flinn caught me watching the crowd again, saying, "None of them. She doesn't bring anyone she's seeing to work events." He lifted his glass in salute. "Save for yourself."

Stella chose that moment to catch my eye from across the room. She spoke a few words to the group surrounding her before smiling, full dimples, and heading toward me.

And she was beautiful. Just too damn beautiful for words. Her coral-red dress fit like a sunburn and her hair spilled over her shoulders in long, loose waves. As if that wasn't enough, she looked bright and fresh—and happy.

Even better, she didn't bring men to work events. She'd said as much previously but hearing it confirmed by Flinn nailed the truth all the way to the front door.

"Hi," she mouthed as she approached, offering a quick wave. "Sorry I've been so busy. This wasn't an event we managed so—"

"So it was a hot mess shit show," Flinn interjected.

"With a side of train wreck," Tatum added.

"Not a problem." I brought my hand to the small of her back. "Not at all."

She smiled at Flinn and Tatum. "I see you've met my offensive line."

"We prefer special teams," Flinn said.

Stella gifted them with a sweet smile before shifting closer to me. "I have to say two things to one person, and then I can go," she said, glancing down at her phone. "Are we super late? Or just really late?"

I rubbed my hand up her spine, thought about skipping that dinner party altogether. I could stand here all night, touching my woman and grinning over the fact she didn't bring dudes to work events. Until now. "Doesn't matter," I replied. "Nick and Erin aren't waiting on us. We'll get there when we get there. Unless you'd rather skip it."

"Nope, not skipping it," she replied, shooting another glance at her phone. "Just give me five minutes to handle a few quick things."

I shifted my hand down as she spoke, over her waist to pat her backside. Squeeze. Pinch just enough to remind her she enjoyed it. Especially there. "Take your time."

She walked away but not without lobbing several heated stares over her shoulder as she went.

"Mmhmm," Tatum murmured, watching Stella. "Yeah. Okay, then."

I blinked at her, confused. "I'm sorry?"

Flinn shook a hand in my direction. "Don't mind her. She's just—"

"She's just admiring some very subtle and very effectively executed public affection," Tatum said, cutting him off.

I wasn't positive but it seemed like these two didn't know how to speak without interrupting each other.

He harrumphed out a sigh, turning his attention back to the crowd. "I'll call Stella's car service," he said, mostly to himself. "They'll pull up right outside and notify me when they're here. That saves you from getting stuck talking to people on the curb, and people on the curb always insist on dragging you along to the after party and then the after-after party, and you don't need that hassle in your life." He tapped his chest. "I do. I enjoy the hassle. When I'm not enjoying other hassles or generally beating my head into walls."

"Thanks, man," I said, offering my hand. That was my game plan: thank him for the assistance, ignore everything else.

"It's the least he can do," Tatum said, sparing Flinn an impatient glare as he pecked at his phone. "We want to see you around again. You're the *only* one we want to see."

"Thin ice, Tate. Thin fucking ice," Flinn said.

Then Stella was at my side, her arm sliding around my waist and her smile warming me through. "Ready?" she asked.

You have no idea, sweet thing.

STELLA WAS A WONDER.

I couldn't name the seven wonders of the world but I knew without a doubt she was one of them. How else could she hang with my people—Nick and Alex, and Stremmel and a handful of other random docs and residents—and make it look like she'd known them her whole life? How else could she charm a lopsided smile out of Stremmel, that stone-cold bastard?

She was a wonder and all I could do was hang back, watching her cast spells on my people. I nursed a beer while she peppered Stremmel with questions about his time in California. He gave as good as he got, hitting her with questions about—of all things—the Dallas Cowboys cheerleaders.

This was everything I wanted out of a Saturday night and I didn't have to weigh the possibilities of running into one of Stella's past or present hookups here. Motherfuck it, I didn't want to claim this emotion as my own but I hated —*hated*—the idea of her being with other men.

Not that I had clear evidence she was with them but she hadn't said anything to the contrary. If she'd stopped seeing them, wouldn't she tell me? Wouldn't she run up to me at the trail one morning and announce she'd stopped spending time with her regularly scheduled dudes which meant I didn't have to grind my molars to dust every time the thought of them crossed my mind anymore? Wouldn't she show up at my apartment, gesture up and down her luscious body and then tell me she wasn't for sharing?

I needed those news bulletins. I needed the green light.

And I needed Lucian McKendrick to keep his damn hands off her too. I knew he was a client and I knew there was nothing between them but hell, I couldn't deal with another photo of them together. The smart move would've been for me to stop seeking out the photos but now that I'd started, I couldn't stop visiting the sports news sites and blogs.

As I pondered this, Nick shuffled to my side, tapped his beer bottle against mine. "This is nice and cozy," he remarked. He tipped his chin toward the kitchen island where my future wife entertained my problem child and my excessively diligent resident with a true account of the locker room drama at last year's Super Bowl game. "She's great."

I shot him a sidelong glance. "Glad you think so," I replied. "I know you had your doubts."

An annoyed grimace pulled at his face as he shook his head. "Would you stop it? You have to admit this is a complicated case."

I waved him off. I didn't want any of Doctor Acevedo's logic tonight. Especially not when his scenario was an even more complex case. At least I lived in the same state, country, and continent as Stella. It'd taken him the better part of two years to claim the same.

"Where is your brother-in-law this evening?" I asked, referring to Alex's fiancé Riley. He and Nick's wife Erin were siblings. They came from a big family that threw fabulous parties. Any time the Walshes invited me, I went.

"Riley had a work issue," Nick replied. "Something flooded and something else shorted out and that's the extent of my intel on the matter. I'm told he'll be here eventually and I wouldn't put it past him to show up soaking wet. Or naked save for the drop cloth he found in his trunk and fashioned into a toga."

"Looking forward to that," I replied.

From across the room, I watched Stella peek at her phone and frown. She typed out a quick message before returning to her conversation with Stremmel and O'Rourke but I knew she was distracted. A minute later, another message came through. Then the screen lit with an incoming call. She rejected the call, shot a quick eyeroll at the device, and stepped away from the group.

Holding up her phone as she headed toward me, she said, "I have to take this." She glanced toward the sliding glass doors that led to the deck. And the rain beating against them. "Is there a laundry room or somewhere quiet I can duck into without bothering anyone?"

"Head upstairs," Nick offered, pointing in that direction. "There are several empty rooms available."

"He actually means empty," I added. "He's got a bedroom and his wife has an office, and aside from that, there's no furniture to be found."

Nick jerked a shoulder up as he glared at me. "So fuckin' what, Hartshorn? Since when are you the interior design police?"

"I'm not," I replied. "But you've lived in this house almost a year. Isn't there a point at which you decide to do something with your empty spaces?"

"No," Nick answered. "No, there's not but you can be sure I'll be coming to your house one of these days and making comments about your shit."

Stella folded her lips together as a laugh shook through her. "Upstairs it is," she said. "I'll only need a few minutes."

"Take your time," I called.

As if Stella's urgent call could set off a chain reaction of urgent issues, Nick and I reached for our phones. Alex joined us, asking, "What's going on? Why do we look worried?"

"No reason," I said. "Just checking on things."

The three of us scrolled through our messages in silence and then returned the devices to our pockets.

Nick said, "I like her. She's what you need."

"And what is that?" I asked, taking a sip of my beer.

He followed suit, bobbing his head as he drank and considered my question. Finally, he said, "Warm."

"As in alive and breathing?" I sputtered. "Or—"

"As in"—he circled his arms in front of him, miming some form of embrace or wheat harvest, I wasn't sure

—"*warm*. You know, pleasant. Generous. Outgoing. Kind. Capable. Good head on her shoulders." He made another grain-gathering motion. "*Warm*."

"You need a better vocabulary," I said, mostly to myself.

"You do," Alex agreed.

"You need to lock that lady down," he replied.

"You say that," I started, "but you don't seem to realize it's unusual to marry women the same day you meet them. You're also missing the fact many women aren't willing to go along with that kind of crazy."

"Truth," Alex said.

He barked out a laugh. "Some women invent that crazy all on their own. Now, those are the ones you need to lock down. Hold on tight and never let go because they're the best of them."

"My god," she muttered.

"I'll work on it," I grumbled. "Your feedback is always appreciated, Acevedo. Even if you're out of your damn mind." I pointed my bottle at the residents gathered near the pantry chalkboard, where they were busy drawing a set of kidneys and arguing over surgical methods. "Perhaps we should ask them to run an EEG on you this week. Maybe a psych consult. You need a good talk session."

He made a sound in his throat, something rude and contrary. "Oh, that would be fun."

"I don't agree with the substance of Acevedo's argument but I think you should consider the overall thesis. Think about it this way, Hartshorn. How did you introduce her tonight? Oh, right. 'This is Stella,'" she said, dropping her voice as she imitated me. "She's Stella. That's it. If I was

Stella, I'd be climbing out the guest room window right now and finding a better situation."

I stared at her, unblinking. "You don't believe she's actually doing that."

Alex made a face, something between *yeah, I totally believe it* and *who the fuck knows*? and said, "Probably not. I've been on some rough dates and never climbed out a window to escape. Not a second story window, that is."

"Alex," I snapped.

"Cal, chill out," she replied. "I'm sure everything is fine. You're great, she's great, everything is great. But maybe think about framing your relationship in less wishy-washy terms when introducing her to new people. That shit matters, dude."

Nick frowned, jerked both shoulders up. "She's been gone awhile. It's a short drop to the roof of the porch. I figure it's easy enough to make it down from there."

"For fuck's sake, Acevedo." I set my beer bottle on the countertop with as much care as I could muster, glaring at Alex. "And you."

"What did I do?" she asked.

"Nothing," Nick said. Another frown, another shoulder jerk. "You should probably go check on her."

They didn't have to tell me twice. I charged up the stairs two at a time and poked my head into every door I could find. More doors than anyone would ever need. Barren rooms by the dozen. Linen closets, laundry closets, closet closets. And then—finally—Stella standing in an empty bedroom, her phone pressed to her ear, her arm braced against the far window as she stared at the rain.

"Is there any way you can resolve this?" she asked, her

voice low. Impatient. "I'm looking for you to handle this situation without my intervention."

I stepped inside, shut the door behind me. She glanced over her shoulder, offering me a tight grin followed by an exaggerated eyeroll. My shoes were soundless against the floor but the old hardwood sent up a creak and grunt as I moved closer to her.

"This is one of those opportunities, Flinn," she continued, "where I'm expecting you to be a problem solver rather than a problem identifier. Before you rattle off a list of everything else you've solved for me, I'd like you to recognize that complete client management doesn't allow you to deal with only the tasks you favor."

I moved closer, settling right behind her and bringing my hands to her shoulders. She was tense, her muscles bunched and tight under my touch. I gathered her hair, shifted it to one side. Dropped a kiss on the newly exposed skin. Then I pressed my thumbs to the base of her neck, kneading as she held the phone away, sighed, whispered, "Oh my fucking god."

But that moment was short-lived. She stiffened as she returned the device to her ear. I leaned into her, dragged my lips from the crook of her neck up to her tender spot behind her ear. Goose bumps rippled down her arms, over her chest. From this vantage point, I saw her nipples harden against the bodice of her dress.

"If anything, me stepping in at this point will only publicly validate the idea you aren't capable of resolving minor crisis situations as they develop," she said, her breath hitching as she spoke. "That's not the path to you identifying yourself as a competent client manager."

Stella paused, listening to the rapid-fire argument coming at her, and I put real effort into loosening those muscles. She shot a glance at me over her shoulder, mouthed, "Thank you."

I responded with another open-mouth kiss and the barest hint of teeth scraping over her neck. That earned another glance, this one hot, wide-eyed. *Interested.* I was hard before she could blink.

"Listen to me, Flinn. I cannot continue giving you prime chances to lead if you are not willing to take them. I want you to make this better and I want you to do it without me hovering over you. If you need support, get Tatum involved. She's quiet but she makes things happen when they need to." She murmured as he spoke, shook her head. "Call me if the situation does not improve *and* you've exhausted the tactics I proposed."

Stella didn't wait for a response. She stabbed the red button on her screen, ending the call, and dropped her head back to my chest.

"That sounded fun," I remarked. "McKendrick?"

"Yeah. Flinn is dealing with it. Somewhat." She blew out a breath. "But my pal Lucian is back on his shit again."

I had to ask, "When is he not?"

"There are moments. Not many of them but they're essential to the preservation of my sanity nonetheless."

"He sees more of you than I do," I said, immediately hating the way those words sounded.

"That's not true," she said with a laugh. "There's plenty of me he hasn't seen."

A growl sounded in my throat. "I rather enjoy it that way."

"No argument from me," she said. "Whatever you're doing back there, keep doing it."

"Yeah?" I asked, ducking my head to taste her skin again. "This is good?"

"Amazing," she breathed, roping her arm around my waist.

Her backside connected with my crotch as she pulled me closer. There was no way she could ignore the erection lengthening under my trousers. "Is this hard enough?" I asked, my thumb digging into the knots along her shoulder blade. "Or can you take it harder, Stella?"

"I can take it," she said, a laugh ringing in her words. "Trust me, I can take it."

We stayed there, her ripe backside nestled right up against my cock as I smoothed out her kinks and dotted kisses over her skin. We didn't say anything and there was no need. We were alone, once again the only two people in the world. This was where we were at our best—when reality fell to the shadows and our only obligations were to each other.

She shifted her hand to catch hold of my belt, twining her fingers around the leather at my hip. Jerking me even closer. "I need something to do," she whispered.

"Right now?" I asked, my teeth grazing the back of her neck, just below her hairline. "Or in some larger context?"

"Right now," she replied. "I'm just standing here, doing nothing, while you're busy untangling my stress."

"No, sweet thing, you're rubbing your ass all over my cock. You're quite busy," I said.

"This is good?" she asked, feeding my words back to her.

"Amazing." I groaned into her neck as the roll and slide

of her hips increased, and I was nearly convinced that I needed to mark her. Bite, suck, anything. But then better options took over.

"I'm not sure how you knew I needed this but thank you," she said, her head lazing to one side. "Today has been a thousand times more stressful than I'd expected and you really know how to use those hands."

I kissed her again, right at the spot where her shoulder started and her neck ended. "Would you like me to do that? Use my hands?" I asked against her skin.

She nodded, dropped her mobile phone to the floor. It clattered against the hardwood, landing faceup. "Yes, please."

On a different night, things would've been different. I wouldn't have cornered her in an empty bedroom. I wouldn't have initiated this at Acevedo's house, where I had no guarantee of extended privacy. And I wouldn't have done this without a bed.

But I had tonight and Alex's words whipping the back of my mind and Stella in my arms. This was my night and I wasn't passing it up.

I ran my palm down her flank, over her hip, to her thigh. I gripped her dress, bunching it in my fist and yanking it to her waist. "Tell me again," I ordered.

She knew what I wanted. She didn't need any explanation.

"Yes, please," she repeated.

I growled in agreement as I pushed my hand under her panties. For a second, I thought about taking it slow, petting her, making her ache and want the way I did. But then I found her wet and swollen and I couldn't help but head straight for her clit. I'd succeeded in getting her there before and I meant to do it again. Fast and hard, and this time, we'd make it to the second act.

Two fingers circled her clit as I kissed her neck. "You need this," I whispered. "Don't you, sweet thing?"

"So much," she said through a groan. "It has been—oh, fuck, keep doing that."

I almost stopped if for no other reason other than determining how long it had been for her. Almost. I wanted to know who touched her like this, but more than that, I wanted to keep doing it. I wasn't going to deny her this pleasure because I needed some info. "It's not the same. Not the same as your toys, your fingers. It's not what you need."

Her head lolled against my shoulder as she said, "Not even close."

I pushed my foot against hers, widening her stance. "You need this." But I was a weak, weak man and she was so damn close to coming apart in my hands. I continued, "How long has it been, Stel? When was the last time someone made you feel good?"

"You know how long it's been." A quiet shriek burst from her throat and I felt a new rush of wet on my fingers. The sound of her arousal and my hand was obscene. If someone walked in here now, they'd know what we were doing even with my body sheltering hers.

"I don't, I don't," I repeated. Her body shuddered as I circled her clit, pushed my fingers inside her. She held back, doing everything in her power to resist. And I did everything in my power to send her flying over the edge. "How long? Tell me how bad you need this."

"The door," she cried, slapping her palms against my legs. "The door. Your apartment. The door."

"Because you belong to me," I said, dragging my teeth over her neck. I pressed, just enough for her to feel me there. And she broke like a wave hitting the shore. I kept up the pressure between her legs, stroking and circling as she trembled in my arms.

But that didn't last long. She swatted my hands away, stepped out of my hold, turned to face me. "Your turn," she announced. "It's your turn now. Okay?"

"Yes." I didn't have to think about it. "Yes, fuck, yes. Stella, get over here and get on your knees."

She reached for my belt and zipper, and before I could complain about her leaving my arms, she dropped to the floor with my cock in her mouth. I flailed a bit, nearly overtaken by the heat of her tongue and the rush of sensation. But then my hand connected with the wall and I steadied myself. As much as possible. Her hand slipped between my legs, sliding up my thigh and cupping my sac. My hips surged forward and a noise that was equal parts howl and holler rattled up from the pit of my stomach.

I wanted to hold back a bit. I wanted to enjoy this as long as possible. And I wanted to let her run the show. But I couldn't take more than three, maybe four minutes of her championship-caliber sucking and stroking before pure electricity fired through my blood. I was out of words, left with only desperate murmurs and choked pleas, and a steady stream of obscenity. Nothing meaningful, just a wild torrent of

fuuuck, fuuuuck, fuuuuuuck

your cunt

suckkkkkk
take my cock, take it
give me
want you
need
fuuuuuuck
need you
your cunt
need you, Stella. Need you.

Then I reached for her, tangling my hand in her hair and tugging. Pulling. "*Stella.*"

That was the best I could do but she didn't require further explanation. She bobbed her head, worked her tongue along the underside of my shaft, and took me to the back of her throat. Her forehead brushed against my belly and she gave my balls a little tug of encouragement.

Maybe it was a *whoa there* tug but we were past the point of analysis.

My body vibrated under her hold, every single cell of me turned up to full blast as her tongue moved over me. She kept one hand anchored on my thigh, her nails biting into my skin, and that twinge snapped my hips in uneven thrusts.

There was nothing nice about this moment. Nothing civilized, nothing loving. No tenderness or affection. Just flat out cocksucking, rough and ugly and not nice at all.

It was amazing.

My release arrived with a snarl, a noise that belonged in a jungle or forest. In a cave. I sounded raw, inhuman. With my hand on her neck, I traced small circles into her skin while I pumped into her, emptying myself into her mouth in long, hot spurts. I shook as my cock pulsed and twitched on her tongue, shuddered as my orgasm spilled over her lips.

I loosened enough buttons to tug my shirt over my head and then reached for the t-shirt underneath. I pulled it off, balled it up, wiped her face.

We stared at each other, Stella on her knees and me stroking my thumb over her suck-plumped lips. This was a moment. This was a time for confessions and promises and proclamations. This was when we stopped fucking around and got real with each other. No more playing games, no more wait-and-see. This was the moment and I wanted to say everything. Shake my truths out and see where they fell.

"Stella," I said, as determined as ever. I was taking her home tonight. Taking her to bed, keeping her there. Keeping her with me.

A shuddering breath blew past her lips as she blinked up at me. "I know, Cal, I—"

Brightness filled the room as her phone buzzed to life. A photo of Flinn appeared on the screen. We stared at the device as it skittered over the hardwood, the sound amplified by the uneven surface. Neither of us moved.

The vibrations ended but started back up a second later. From her knees, Stella said, "I have to take this. And... I have to go. He wouldn't be calling if things were fine."

I slapped my hand against the wall, dropped my head back against my shoulders. My dick was wet and my blood was thrumming and I hated Lucian McKendrick. I knew it was her job and I knew her promotion was on the line but fuck me, I hated him. I wanted to throw that phone out the window and then pick her up and take her home with me.

I blinked at the ceiling for a second while I dug deep to find the right words. *No, you don't* and *no, you aren't* weren't the correct sentiments but that didn't stop them from burning the tip of my tongue.

Finally, I reached for Stella, saying, "Up you go, sweet thing."

"I'm sorry about this," she whispered. "As soon as I get him back in the game, everything will change."

I shook out the balled-up t-shirt, folding the damp spots in on each other until it formed a smooth rectangle. "Don't apologize." I wrapped my arm around her waist, kicked her feet apart, ran the t-shirt over her slit. "But I'm not letting you leave here with a sopping wet cunt, Stel."

She rested her forehead on my shoulder as she released a breathy laugh. "Thank you." Her phone started vibrating again but I didn't stop. No, I wasn't rushing this job. "I think. I need to review the girl power bylaws on this one."

"Nope," I replied, my hand still working between her legs. At this rate, I'd have to scrub the scent of her off my skin. "The regs are clear. This belongs to me."

19

STELLA

N<small>OTHING GOOD HAPPENED AT</small> T<small>HE</small> L<small>IBERTY</small> H<small>OTEL</small>. N<small>OTHING</small> I'd ever witnessed.

The old jail-turned-hotel hot-spot seemed to shout "trouble be found here" and tonight was no exception.

As Flinn promised I would, I found McKendrick in Alibi, the trendy drunk tank-slash-watering hole, kicked back at the end of the bar. His body consumed as much real estate as possible. His arms were draped over stools on his left and right, his legs were spread wide enough to block anyone who tried to pass without his express desire. And three members of the hotel's security team loomed near him, physically separating him from the other patrons. And there were plenty of them, all edging against the human barricade to get a look at—and a photo of—Boston's reigning bad boy ballplayer.

At the other end of the bar sat Orrille Whitelock, a recently retired NFL wideout I'd repped through a PED scandal a few years back. He held a rocks glass in one hand, a bag of ice pressed to his eye in the other. The stools around him were missing. I was hoping they were removed to give him space and not as a result of damage. These guys could afford a few stools without issue but neither of them needed to add bar brawling to their résumés.

I nodded to him but that was all he was getting from me tonight. He wasn't paying me and I didn't clean up after athletes for the fun of it.

"Hey, lady," McKendrick called as I waded through the crowd.

"Here I am," I replied. Even at a distance I noticed his lip was split and swollen. "As requested."

He gestured to my dress with his beer bottle. "Did you get all fancy for me? You didn't have to do that."

"Sorry to get your hopes up but this is not for you." I glanced around, hoping to find an adult in the room. Head of security, management, anyone. The bartender tipped his chin up in greeting but offered nothing else. When I arrived at McKendrick's side, I said, "Pay your tab. White-lock's too. We're leaving."

He draped his arm around my shoulder. "I'd do that, honeycakes, if I had any cash." He aimed a surly glare across the bar. "But don't worry. Whitelock's picking up this round."

"The fuck I am," Whitelock called. "Not after you fuckin' decked me, dude."

"I'll add it to your bill." I yanked my corporate card from my wallet, pointing at both men as I slapped it down on the hardwood surface. When the bartender approached, I said, "These two gentlemen are finished for the evening." I glanced over at Whitelock. "Head on home now, Orrille."

He was a nice guy. Truly. He made tons of bad decisions but he was a nice guy.

"Maybe I wanna press charges," he yelled, loud enough for the whole damn bar to hear. "Maybe I'm not done with you, McKendrick."

"We're friends, Orrille. We don't need to call the cops." I leveled a pointed stare at McKendrick's split lip. "I don't think it makes sense to spend the night filing charges and giving statements when you could be"—I tipped my head toward the throng of women willing to kiss it better —"somewhere more pleasant. Don't you agree?"

Whitelock grumbled to himself and then slammed his glass on the bar. He craved attention just the way McKendrick craved it. Giving him that attention wasn't the solution. Not tonight. But that was the trouble with athletes who'd lived most of their lives as superstars—they didn't know how to exist without a constant feed of praise and adoration. They didn't care if that adoration came in the form of negative press or acquiring a bad reputation. When the drug of choice was fame, it didn't matter where the fix came from as long as they got it.

To be fair, I didn't know how I'd transition from playing in packed arenas before thousands of screaming fans and signing multi-million-dollar mattress spokesmodel deals to being a semi-regular person who used to be famous. I wasn't sure I could adapt to that rise and fall, the momentary luxury of people tending to my every need and maintaining my body like it was a machine, followed by nothing. Retirement wasn't nothing but it was a big drop off from the intensity of a decade in the NFL.

Part of me wondered whether McKendrick worked this

hard at screwing up because he wanted to get out of the game. If he wanted to play, he had another six or seven good years in him. But it seemed like he wanted the fall, wanted the sudden drop into semi-obscurity.

I signed the check and pocketed the receipt for my expense report before motioning to McKendrick to follow me out. He grumbled too and left Whitelock with an earful of foul parting shots, but he walked with me—and the security team—through the hotel's front lobby.

"There will be videos," I said as we waited for the car service to come around. "Videos of whatever led to Whitelock's shiner and your split lip, and the hearty goodbye you gave him just now."

He tugged a beanie from his back pocket and pulled it low, past his eyebrows. "And your fuckin' point, lady?"

"Oh, no point. Nothing to worry about here." I gestured toward the car as the driver pulled into the portico. "Though I will ask you to refrain from using the phrase cum-dumpster when we visit the elementary school in Chelsea later this week. Gotta know your audience, Lucian."

The security team moved forward to open the vehicle's doors and shuffle us inside but McKendrick wasn't having it. He pushed one of the men away, yelling, "You wanna swallow those teeth or what? Back the fuck up."

"Seriously," I hissed at him. "Just get in the car."

McKendrick held the door open, bowing dramatically. "After you."

I climbed in, scooting to the far side while he joined me. Once the door was shut, I said, "There will be a video of that too and the owners are going to love it."

He snickered as he sank into his seat, his legs open at an obtuse angle and his hands folded behind his head. "Did you leave your doctor-man to tell me that?"

I glanced out the window to get a sense of the traffic. Storrow Drive seemed clear but the Massachusetts Pike was always a gamble. "As a matter of fact, I did," I replied. "When my client gets into a fistfight at The Liberty and refuses to vacate the premises with anyone other than me, yeah, I leave the doctor-man." I turned back to him, shrugged. "You didn't give me much choice tonight."

"Nah," he drawled, long and loud. "That's made-up drama. Fake news."

My phone buzzed, drawing my attention down to a message from Flinn. No text, only social media screenshots. McKendrick and Whitelock drinking, arguing, throwing punches. McKendrick's bloody lip, Whitelock's black eye. McKendrick following me through the lobby, pushing the security guard, holding the car door open for me. In certain images, we appeared to be walking side-by-side, our shoulders nearly touching. It was a trick of the angle—but it still looked like we were together.

I prayed Cal didn't see any of these images.

I held up my phone, showing my client the photo of his fist connecting with Whitelock's face. "This is what not to do."

"But it's Saturday night," he wailed. "Gettin' in fights and bein' wild is my thing."

"Unless you want to be finished with the relief pitcher thing, those cannot be your things."

McKendrick huffed out a groan. "You should've stayed

with your man. I don't need you pickin' me up and tuckin' me in at night."

I laughed at that, a full-on laugh that shook my shoulders and brought a tear to my eye. It wasn't funny. It was fucking exasperating. I'd done everything in my power to avoid picking him up and tucking him in tonight. I'd wanted one night off from fixing and managing and juggling. I wanted one night where I could be the girl in the empty bedroom, the one who didn't get called away and didn't get lost in the definition of her relationships.

"I *am* hysterical," he said, his chin lifting with pride. "It's about time someone noticed."

He was a major pain in my ass and the only hysterical thing about this was the shortage of dick in my life right now but I wasn't telling him that. He needed the praise, even if it was hollow.

20

STELLA

I LOVED MY JOB. I MEAN, I *LOVED* MY JOB. I LOVED IT WHEN IT was stressful and annoying. I loved it after a messy night that turned into a morning of bad press. I loved it when I didn't think I loved it at all.

But goddamn, I hated being in the office on a Sunday. Working in professional sports meant the weekends weren't my own but I wasn't usually tucked behind my desk during the brunch rush.

"How should we deal with the noise about you and Lulu?" Flinn held up his tablet, tapped the screen showing McKendrick's arm around my shoulders. "We know it's bullshit but we also know the bloggers and gossip columnists have a mind of their own."

"And they've decided it's legit," Tatum added.

"Ignore," I replied with a quick shake of my head. "Can't whack all the moles."

"Hmm. That's folksier than your usual," Tatum replied. "And it's not going to put out any fires or decrease McKendrick's visibility right now. In case you haven't noticed, people are always interested in knowing who is hooking up."

Flinn snickered at that, shielded his face with the tablet.

"No more than refuting it," I argued. "Acknowledging a rumor means we care enough to comment and we'd only care if it was within a shade of the truth."

"And if we field inquiries about your relationship status?" Tatum asked.

"Ignore," I repeated. "Not a topic up for discussion. I'm not a public figure."

"Question for you, boss." Flinn pointed his pen at me while staring down at his tablet. "What's the deal with your quartet of men?"

I took a second to sit back in my chair, fold my hands in my lap. "I beg your pardon?"

He looked up, waved the pen in a small circle. "Your men. Stephen, Leif, Harry, and Cal. We've noticed you deleting individual appointments but you haven't deleted the recurring events."

Tatum bumped his forearm with her elbow, shaking her head. "Cal's not on there. By itself, that's an interesting point to consider."

He bumped her back. "I recognize this. Considered it too. Thank you." He turned his attention to me. "Would you like me to delete Harry? You haven't seen him since the last week of March."

"As I've mentioned before," I started, working my damnedest to keep my voice even, "you are not responsible for looking after my personal engagements. I'll change my calendar viewing permissions if that task is too complicated."

"But you need to drop them," Tatum whisper-yelled. "The calendar boys. You can't hang on to them if you're seeing Cal." She held up her hands when I sighed in response. "And before you tell me I'm not supposed to get involved in your personal life, I just want you to know we think Cal is really great and you should focus only on him."

"And we're already involved in your personal life," Flinn added. "Your mother sends us Christmas cards and I follow your sister's dogs on Instagram."

Tatum nodded in agreement. "Right. What Flinn said."

He glanced at her, his gaze chilly. "Oh, you're agreeing with me now? Funny how you see reason when it suits you."

I wagged my pen at them. "None of this conversation is Sunday morning critical," I said. "I don't want a lecture on my relationships and I don't want to referee the two of you."

Tatum folded her arms over her chest, elbowing Flinn in the process. "Sorry," she said, not sorry at all. "Didn't see you there. It's tough, you know, because you're not consistently in the same place."

Flinn cleared his throat, crossed his legs. His shoe tapped Tatum's calf. "My bad," he murmured. "I hope that didn't hurt. Would you even notice? I mean, how could you? You don't have normal, human feelings."

"Oh my god," I muttered to myself. "Here's the story, friends. I'm touching base with Travis Veda soon and you're hitting the phones to turn up the volume on McKendrick's apology tour. Get me every friendly, softball interviewer you can find. I don't care if it's a sports columnist from the Andover High School newspaper. As long as they can keep the conversation on the predefined topics, we'll grant the interview and do any promotional spots they want."

"Got it," Flinn replied.

"I'm not actually calling the Andover High School newspaper, right?" Tatum asked.

"You would ask that," Flinn said under his breath. "You never listen to clear, honest words when they're spoken directly to you. Doubt everything because it's easier than trusting someone. And why bother trusting anyone when you don't see a reason to rely on anyone but your own damn self?"

I pushed to my feet, sending my chair rolling back into a low bookshelf. "I do not have the brain space to care what's going on between you two. If you make me care, we will have a serious problem that will result in someone leaving this team. Solve it and move on. We have a handful of games left until McKendrick is back on the field and we don't have the time to dick around. Understood?"

"Yes," they replied.

Another elbowing and calf-tapping unfolded but they managed to keep quiet. About fucking time. "Thank you," I said.

"Fire me if you want but I'm going to say this." Tatum looked up, her bottom lip snared between her teeth.

Flinn sank back in his seat, his eyes closing on a groan. "Don't," he whispered. "Don't, Tate."

Tatum ignored his advice, continuing, "I know you don't want to hear this right now but you need to end it with your calendar boys." Her eyes crinkled as she grimaced, an expression I interpreted as *What don't you understand about this*? "You don't even see them that much. Why are they so hard to give up?"

I fetched my chair, tucked it under my desk, and stood behind it, my arms resting on the back. I thought about sidelining the conversation, but knowing Tatum and her quiet bulldog tenacity that would only tighten her hold on this bone.

"I haven't thought about it," I said, and that was the real, undiluted truth.

I hadn't thought about Stephen, Leif, or Harry much. Harry hadn't crossed my mind since the last time he texted me and—*oh shit*. I'd never responded to him. But no response still qualified as a response. Definitely. It was as good as ghosting.

"But you're deleting all of the appointments," Tatum argued. "I check your schedule on Sunday nights when I'm work-planning for the week and I've seen you canceling your standing Harry every time."

She was right about that. I deleted those appointments but they barely registered as proof of a thin but existent tie to those men. But...so what? Where was the problem here? I wasn't misleading anyone. No one was in the dark. Cal knew where I stood. If he wanted me standing somewhere else, he knew how to start a conversation.

"I promise I will put the appropriate time into reevaluating things once we've cleared the biggest hurdles with McKendrick." Another undiluted truth. My brain was at max capacity right now. I needed a few more weeks before I could engage in any soul-searching or priority shuffling.

Flinn cracked an eyelid. "Wouldn't you recommend dealing with an issue when it's first identified rather than putting a rug over it? Don't we know from years of experience"—he swiveled toward Tatum, gave her a one-eyed glare—"that pretending the issues don't exist is a terrible offense? It requires the defense to work overtime when the shit starts spinning, and someone always finds out that we've been sitting on the info all along."

Tatum met his glare and shot one back at him. "As much as I hate to admit when he's right," she said through gritted teeth, "you shouldn't wait."

"Wow," Flinn muttered under his breath. "So you can acknowledge when you're wrong."

"How am I wrong about anything?" she asked him. "I was the one who raised this topic when you were slouching into your chair and telling me to shut up."

He closed his eyes again, crossed his arms over his chest. "I never told you to shut up."

"Yeah, basically," she replied.

"Not really," he argued. "You should listen to the things I say to you, Tate. Maybe you'd realize they're not the bullshit you've cooked up in your head."

"Now you're saying I'm delusional?"

"Oh my fucking god, no," he cried. "Do you see this, Stella? This is what I'm talking about."

"I'm telling both of you to shut up." I pressed my thumb to my temple as I ran a finger over my eyelid. I hated being in the office on Sundays. "Thank you for the impassioned commentary. You need to learn how to work together again. If you can't, I'll send you to a Myers-Briggs retreat. The easier solution would be to reassign one of you but—as this weekend meeting should illustrate—I don't have time for a game of musical assistant chairs. Is that what you'd like? A day full of exciting reflection activities and teamwork exercises? Strategies for working with your personality type?"

Without consulting Tatum, Flinn said, "Neither of us want that."

"But neither of us want you driving your personal life off a cliff," Tatum added.

I glanced at my phone. I couldn't text Harry now. I couldn't. It had been weeks since he'd asked if I was ending it with him and responding now was the wrong tactic. As for Cal, I could deal with him tomorrow. On the trail.

"Again, thank you for the commentary. We need to get through this month and then we'll have some breathing room." Hopefully, in a much larger office. "I'm sure these issues will keep until then."

Flinn and Tatum shared an eyeroll that should've told me I was dead wrong.

21

STELLA

"QUESTION FOR YOU," I SAID, BRIGHT AND EARLY MONDAY morning. May mornings were the best. Sunny but still cool enough that I didn't feel gross as a result of simply walking outdoors.

"This weekend would be fine," Cal replied. "Assuming I can get my mother on a flight. I'm sure I can make that happen. She'll bring something old. She always has something ridiculously old hanging around."

I peered at him, confused. "For...what, exactly?"

He aimed a lopsided grin in my direction. "Once again, we are not talking about the same things," he replied, laughing. "What did you want to ask, Stel?"

"Are you okay with this?" I'd dedicated the better part of my Sunday to figuring out the right way to broach this topic with Cal. I wasn't sure this was the way but it was the best I could do. Since I had an evening event with McKendrick— one of several this week—Cal and I weren't meeting for dinner tonight. Not that hashing this out over food would've been easier, but wine helped many things and I sensed it would help this. "With us? With this—thing?"

I didn't want to say *arrangement* or *relationship* or *agreement* or anything similar because it wasn't like that and I didn't want those words in our world.

"Last weekend," I continued, "it seemed like you had some thoughts and I want to make sure I hear those thoughts. If you have them. And want to share."

I glanced over at Cal as I chewed my lower lip, not sure which kind of response I wanted from him. No, that wasn't true. I wanted something totally strange, completely unfamiliar. I wanted him to want me. To insist this thing wasn't all right, we weren't okay. None of this was good enough because it was a flimsy excuse for everything—and he wasn't settling for anything short of that.

And what a mess of contradictions I was. Just a big, damn mess.

"I enjoy spending time with you, Stella," he replied, his gaze fixed straight ahead. "That's my only thought."

No, it wasn't. It couldn't be. Unless Cal had fallen and bumped his possessive head, he wasn't content. He wanted to lock it down and wife me up. He didn't *enjoy* an empty-bedroom blowjob and then shake it off like it was nothing.

"Ice cream," I whispered. Then, more loudly, "Ice cream, Cal. Speak up or get stuck with another bowlful of black raspberry."

"But I like watching you suck on the spoon," he replied with a knowing smirk.

"I'll suck anything you want if you tell me the truth."

"Whoa." Cal reached over, pressed his palm to my belly, stopping me in my tracks. "Don't play like that, Stella."

"Don't tell me what I want to hear," I shot back.

The best part was that he *wasn't* telling me what I wanted to hear. Far from it. I didn't want to languish in another month of walking and talking and wanting each other like a sickness we couldn't cure. I wanted him to give all of him and demand all of me because he knew I couldn't. I couldn't jump off that cliff again, even when I believed I wouldn't hit the ground this time around. He could take me with him but I couldn't jump alone. I couldn't meet him on the other side; he had to come around and bring me there.

"I'm not doing that," he replied, dropping his hand from my belly. We started walking again. "I'm telling you what I think. I enjoy spending time with you. I'd enjoy more time but I know your schedule is demanding right now."

"Mmhmm." I bobbed my head. Pushing at a different seam, I said, "My assistants liked you."

"Did I pass their tests?" he asked.

Yes. Flying colors. They liked you so much they staged a small coup.

When I didn't respond, Cal tugged on the hem of my t-shirt. "What did they say?"

I removed his hand from my shirt, laced my fingers through his. "We didn't get a chance to discuss you in depth." That was true. We discussed everyone else on my calendar. "But you made quite the impression on them."

"Is that typical?" he asked. "Making an impression?"

I heard the question he wasn't asking. *How did I fare against the others?*

"Hard to say," I replied with a shrug. "I've never intro-duced anyone to them before."

"Not even..." His voice trailed off. He wasn't going to say it. He wasn't going to come out and acknowledge the existence of the other men in my life.

"Nope." I glanced up at him. "Not even."

Another truth. I didn't mix work and sex. I didn't hook up with men from the sports world and I didn't bring my calendar boys to professional events. Not even playoff games when tickets were worth my body weight in gold. I didn't blur those lines.

Not until now.

"Good," he replied, giving my hand a squeeze. "Good."

"Hey," I started, "it looks like the Bruins will go to the Stanley Cup this year. My firm usually gets a couple tickets. If they make it, will you go with me? I mean, I'm not sure if you like hockey or—"

Another squeeze cut off my words. "I'll be there, Stella."

I BLEW through emails and texts while the car service headed northwest, toward McKendrick's estate. I'd spent the past four hours of this Friday night at his elbow, clearing my throat when his language grew colorful or his commentary veered into inappropriate territories. The children's health and athletics foundation fundraiser at a craft brewery outside the city should've been an easy appearance but my client was in rare form.

I'd expected him to do the basics—meet and greet with big-dollar donors beforehand, red carpet and rope line, and then a bit of schmoozing and a quick exit. He came through on the meet and greet and the red carpet but seemed determined to shut the event down, lasting three hours longer than I'd anticipated. Everyone who wanted a wild Lucian McKendrick story got one plus another for the road.

The only upside was the complete lack of black eyes and busted lips.

"You're in a mood tonight," McKendrick remarked. He rested his arm on the window ledge, leaned his head against his hand. "That's a real mood you're rockin'."

"It might surprise you to hear this, Lucian, but I have moods just about every day," I replied. "If I'm lucky, several moods. It's one of my many gifts and talents."

"It's not a gift today, lady."

This, from the man who wasn't allowed within ten feet of a bottle of Hennessy.

I shifted, stared at him. "You're suggesting my temperament is an issue?"

"I don't know what the issue is," McKendrick said, drumming his fingers on his knee. "But you gotta fix that shit. That's what you do, lady. You fix what's broke and you do it with a fuckin' smile. You know why? Because when you smile, everyone else smiles too. Smile more, honeycakes. Does a body good."

I couldn't decide what to handle first—the uneven, unsettled state I'd found myself in this week or the fact McKendrick picked up on it. There was also the matter of my smiles and their impact on him. "Is that—are you complimenting me?"

"Oh my god," he groaned to the window. "Is it wrong for me to want something nice to look at?"

On principle alone, I worked a scowl the remainder of the ride to McKendrick's estate. And the ride back into the city too. I held on to that scowl and not simply because my client demanded a smile. I felt scowly. Uneven, unsettled, and scowly. As if I couldn't find a comfortable position no matter how many times I shifted.

This was unusual for me. I didn't get lost in my feelings too often. There were reasons for that. I had routines, I had structures, I had those ducks marching in line. No need for deep, contemplative moods when my life was ordered and my calendar color-coded. And this was why I'd kept it that way—I didn't want to devote a minute of my day to wondering how a guy felt about me and whether he was being completely truthful when I asked about our relationship.

All of this time and energy wasted on thinking about another person's thoughts, and for what? I asked Cal if he was all right with our—whatever this was. What else could I do? If he wasn't going to come out and demand something different, why should I spend my week struggling through the uncertainty of our connection?

I shouldn't. That was the bottom line. I shouldn't spend any time on this. I needed to go home, start a load of laundry and write a grocery list, and fall asleep with the sports highlights.

But that only worked when I dropped all the blame on Cal. He didn't insist I marry him and bear his children at any point this week so clearly this unsettled mood was his fault. Unless it was my fault and Cal was merely holding up the mirror, reflecting all my problem areas and weak spots back at me. And maybe it wasn't about problem areas or weak spots but climbing out from behind the fortress of my routines and structures, and letting go of the ducks. Of the fears.

That was the root of it: fear. For everything I said and all the times I insisted I wasn't rusty in my long-healed cracks, I was afraid. Of the unknown. Of being wanted more than I could live up to. Of being rejected. Of getting left behind all over again. Of allowing myself to care for a man only to end up hurt.

Tucking all this noise away and starting fresh tomorrow was the right approach. Instead of doing that, I leaned toward the driver. "Change of plans," I announced. "I'm not going back to the office. I'm heading to Beacon Hill. Here's the address."

22

CAL

Stella: I can't believe I'm typing this but...are you up?
Cal: Yeah
Cal: What do you need?
Stella: Maybe you could let me in?
Cal: Let you in...where?
Stella: I'm outside your building.
Cal: What?!?
Stella: Maybe let me in first and then we can discuss the hows and whys, okay?

I CHUCKED MY PHONE ON THE COFFEE TABLE AND DARTED toward the door, into the vestibule, out into the cool night air. Stella stood on the sidewalk, her hands shoved into her raincoat's pockets and her tote bag slung over her shoulder. "Hi," she called with a shrug. "Can I come in?"

Shuffling back to hold the door open for her, I said, "Yeah. Get your ass in here."

She gifted me with a sweet smile—all dimples—as she slipped past me and into my apartment. "Thanks," she said. "I wasn't sure you'd be awake."

I pushed the door shut and locked it but stayed rooted there, staring at the knob for a long moment. "It's not even midnight." Turning, I continued, "What's up, Stella?"

With her phone in hand, she hooked a thumb over her shoulder, her brows drawing down. "Should I go? I don't want to intrude."

I stepped toward her, wrapped my fingers around the belt cinched around her waist. That damn raincoat. I tugged her closer. An inch or two at first, then all the way to my chest. "What's got you on edge, sweet thing?"

She rolled her shoulders, tucked her phone in her pocket. Set her bag on the floor. "Nothing," she murmured, glancing down. Not meeting my gaze. "I just had a long night with McKendrick and that sumbitch is trying my patience like whoa and do you want me? Like, really, really want me?"

She tipped her chin up then, meeting my eyes. Worry creased her forehead, flattened her lips. No dimples for me now. "I didn't realize that was a question I'd left unresolved," I replied. "But yes. Fuck, yes. I've wanted you for—god, I don't even know how long."

"Would you put up a fight for me?" she asked, lifting her chin as she spoke.

I traced her belt around her waist, slipped my hand under the band at the small of her back. Frustration and arousal warred inside me. I wanted to shake her, to make her see the way I adored her. And I wanted to fuck her senseless. Perhaps the two were more similar than I thought. "If you don't know the answer to that, I'm doing something terribly wrong."

"Maybe I just want you to say it," she whispered.

I ran my hand along her waist, loosened the belt's knot. Then I went to work on the buttons, all seventy-four thousand of them. "Maybe you just want me to show you," I said, finally pushing the coat over her shoulders. It fell to the floor, leaving a rustling *whoosh* as it went. "Maybe you came here because you want me to pick you up, take you into the bedroom, show you what it looks like to belong to me."

"I belong to myself," she countered.

"No argument there," I said, blowing past frustration and heading toward exasperation. "But you didn't come here for that. That's not what you want right now." I ran my hands down her arms, settled on her hips. She shook her head once before flattening her hands on my chest. "Give me the words, Stella. Nothing is happening until I hear them."

She nodded, her head bobbing barely enough to notice. "I want that. I want"—she glanced up at me, her bottom lip snared between her teeth like an offering—"you to pick me up, take me to the bedroom."

Her eyes met mine when the word "bedroom" passed her lips, wide and dark and sparkling. That one word contained a million others. She knew it too. She knew this wasn't going to be a quick tumble in the sheets.

I brought my hands to her backside, squeezed. Squeezed a little harder. "Let me tell you what's going to happen next."

One corner of her mouth quirked up. "Please do."

I boosted her up, kept one hand on her ass, the other

between her shoulder blades. "You and me, Stella? We don't go easy. It's all or nothing, and it always has been." Her legs tangled around my waist and I did my level best to hold back a growl but failed. Miserably. "I'm taking you in there and I'm giving you everything I've got and it's you and me. You and me, sweet thing."

"You and me," she repeated with a nod.

My eyes widened as a wave of surprise hit me. I wasn't sure she'd give me this much. I wasn't sure she'd give me anything. But here she was, giving everything.

"Talk to me about pro—"

"Condoms," she interjected. "I seem to recall you telling me you had that under control."

"And I do," I agreed. "I definitely have it covered."

Her knees pressed into my flanks as she laughed. "Thank you," she said. "For covering it. I appreciate that."

"Your standards are too low if you're thanking me for using a condom," I said, pivoting toward the bedroom. She took this opportunity to yank my t-shirt over my head, fling it out of sight. Her nails raked over my shoulders, down my back. Goddamn if I didn't nearly roar. "I promise you'll appreciate far more than the rubber when I'm done with you."

My bedroom was seven steps from the sofa. I knew this because I'd called this apartment home for more than a handful of years and I'd shuffled to bed while seventy-five percent asleep after working multi-day shifts. I knew this but somehow the distance seemed to multiply when getting Stella on a soft surface was my only purpose in life. I couldn't be bothered to look up from the crook of her neck or separate my hands from her body to gauge my location in the apartment but that didn't stop me from grumbling over the distance.

After wandering for an eternity, I stopped beside the bed.

"I need to be on top," she whispered. "I can't—I can't get there unless I'm on top."

"If that's what you need, you'll have it." I ground her against me, raking her body over my aching length. It was like scratching a bug bite. Oh, it was relief but it was going to hurt something fierce if I kept at it. "I'm not going to tell you how your body works, Stel, but I'm still going to make it my mission to get you there on your back," I bit out, rocking her center where I needed it. "Against the wall. From behind." *Hurt so good.* "And if I don't succeed with any of those, I won't close my eyes until I get you there, sweet thing. I won't."

Stella grinned at me, her dimples lighting up like sweet little fireworks. "It's easier if you let me be on top. Less work. Faster too," she said.

"Why the hell would I want to speed things up?"

"You wouldn't," she replied. Her lips tipped up in a way that suggested she knew something I didn't. Or understood something I was missing. Wasn't that always the way with this woman? "But I want to make it good for everyone. That's all."

"If there's one thing I can promise you, it's that." I was breathless now. Aching, aching, aching. "Studying your body and understanding how to make it hum is not work, Stel. It's a privilege." Speaking directly to the tender skin at the base of her throat, I said, "I want to tear this dress off you. I want to fucking destroy it."

She shimmied out of my hold and knelt on the bed, reaching for my belt as she smiled up at me. "If you did that, I'd have nothing to wear home."

"There's always the raincoat," I replied as she unbuttoned my jeans. "One of these days, I want to strip that raincoat off you and find bare skin."

My jeans hit the floor. "Interesting," she mused, her gaze fixed on the bulge beneath my boxers. "The naked raincoat idea, not this." She nodded at my erection. "This is interesting but in totally different ways. Good ways. *Great* ways."

Her fingers traced the band of my boxers, and that devilish, dimpled smile playing on her lips had me rock-hard in a matter of seconds.

I nodded, reached for the zipper at the nape of her neck. "Since you don't want me ripping it, how do I get this off?" I asked, tugging at the sides of her dress.

Stella snorted out a laugh. "I was hoping you'd know how to get *this* off," she replied. "That's why I'm here, Cal."

I gathered the skirt up, easing it over her head as she held up her arms. Her breasts came into focus, full and heavy in a pale pink bra. Damn, I wanted to tear that too. Just shred the fuck out of that lace. I didn't have a clear reason for this surge of violence in me. It wasn't anger or hostility—I just wanted her naked. And naked such that she'd never be clothed again.

It was crazy. I knew that. But so was biting a starburst pattern into her ass.

"Do not doubt that I'll fuck that mouth," I said, carefully setting her dress aside.

"I'm glad we're on the same page about that," she said, a laugh winding through her words.

I reached out, curling my fingers around the middle of her bra. I could almost hear it ripping, feel it shredding in my hands. But I pulled the cups down instead, baring those beauties. I cupped her breasts, my thumbs circling her dark, dusky nipples. They were already hard but my treatment pulled them tighter.

I bent, my palm cupping her breast and my thumb circling her nipple, and I bit. Just a small bite, barely a nip. She smelled like warmth and sex and tasted just as good. Better.

"Cal," she whispered, her fingers twisting in my hair while I closed my teeth around the underside of her breast. "*Cal.*"

"Yes, Stella?" I dragged my lips up, gliding over that tight peak with the barest touch. I traced her there, exploring before my teeth scraped over a new section of her glorious skin. Even in the darkness, I saw the hot flush rising from her skin. It was going to throb and burn and sting, and she was going to explode when I pushed inside her.

"If it's not too much trouble, I'd like your cock in my hand for this," she said, her words pitching up as I bit her again, again, again.

"No trouble," I said, easing my boxers down. I'd have to kick them and my jeans off eventually but that could wait. I had my hands full—truly—with bountiful breasts. "What's mine is yours, sweet thing."

Her fingers wrapped around my length, moving up and down in a slow, feathery motion. Almost too light but much harder and I'd lose focus. Hell, if she got frisky, I'd lose the ability to stand. *If.* That was hilarious. If Stella was anything, she was frisky. And I loved it.

I loved her but that was not on tonight's menu.

"Good to know," she breathed, dragging a hand over my head and bringing my lips to hers for a fast, impatient kiss.

"I'm not done here," I promised against her jaw, her throat, her collarbone. I plumped her breast in my hand, finding the exact spot where I'd left off. "Not done."

"Neither am I," she replied, sliding that whisper of a caress over my cock.

I groaned into her skin at her touch, my teeth coming down harder than necessary. Everything was harder than strictly necessary. But I wasn't stopping. I was biting all the way around her nipple, covering her breast in swollen ridges and valleys and then—when there wasn't a millimeter of skin left for me to claim and she couldn't live another second without me inside her—then I'd stop.

The rich, delicious scent of Stella and the creamy texture of her skin lulled me into an unhurried pace where I tasted and teased her. I tried my damnedest to tune out the gentle stroke of her hand, relegate that pleasure to the back corner of my mind as if I was working on getting through a surgery before acknowledging my hunger. But I failed. Failed miserably. Every few minutes I'd rest my forehead on her chest, groan into the sweet valley between her breasts, and indulge in the early pangs of orgasm curling around the base of my spine. I'd murmur obscene notions of filling her belly button with my release, of making her hold still and keep it from spilling while I devoured her cunt, of flipping her over and letting my wet stick her to the sheets while I dug my fingers into her cheeks and fucked her ass.

But then I'd spy a new patch of skin in need of torment

and go back to work.

"Cal," she said, her fingers squeezing me at the root. My head dropped back to my shoulders. "Where are the condoms?"

I stared at her breast, turning my head to study every angle. Her skin was pink, swollen. Her nipple was nearly screaming for attention. The only thing I could think about was sucking on that tip when I slammed into her. Sucking it through the rise and fall of her release. Sucking it while she swore up and down she couldn't take any more but took it, hoarded it, begged for more.

But the condoms were in the bathroom and we were here, in the bedroom, and fetching them meant leaving this blessed spot where everything we did and everything we said was right. Maybe it was superstition or maybe it was all my experiences with having single perfect moments with Stella and then losing them to real life. I wasn't leaving her only to come back and discover her dressed and ordering a car service home.

I kicked off my jeans and boxers, yanked her panties down in the process. Then I patted my abs, and said, "Hop on. You're coming for a ride."

"Yes, thank you," Stella replied, lacing her arms around my neck. "I think we're on the same page now."

We were not on the same page, not ever. But that was another issue I wasn't remedying tonight.

I hooked my arms around her backside, forcing her bitten breast against my chest. The contact had her crying out, her nails scoring my shoulders, her legs locking around my waist. "You're trying to make me burst into flame again, aren't you?" she asked.

"It's one of many goals, yes," I replied, shifting toward the bathroom.

I knew it was only a handful of steps to the left but just like getting to the bedroom, it was longer and more complicated than expected. And the whole time I worked at delivering us there without incident, Stella was busy kissing my neck, murmuring "hurry" and "please" in my ear, rocking her heat against me.

This was the true payoff for my Special Forces training. This right here.

When we reached the bathroom, I edged her backside onto the countertop, balancing her there while I pressed myself between her legs for one glorious moment. "Just need to feel you," I said, the gravelly words bursting out with each buck of my hips. "Just for a second."

Stella's hands slipped under my arms, anchored over my shoulders. "I want more than a second from you, Cal," she breathed. "So much more than a second. Everything. I want—I want all of your everything."

And that was the end of my patience. My control. My goddamn mind. All of it—gone, over, done.

I moved fast, ducking down to snatch the box of condoms from under the sink, making a mental note to move them to a more appropriate spot because no one preferred sex in the bathroom. The cardboard was in shreds when I stood, long snakes of shiny packets in a pool at my feet. I held one up, dragged it down the breast I'd ignored. The edges rasped over her nipple as she shuddered and moaned and the scent of her arousal filled the air between us.

"Can you take care of this for me?" I asked, the sharp

corner of the packet pressed into her skin. "Can you do this, Stella? Or do you want me to handle it for you?" Her eyes flashed as I dropped that challenge on her. If anything, it was a challenge for me. I was the one who'd have to watch it happen. But I wanted to know what she was willing to give me tonight. How much control was she surrendering? Where were the limits? "Is that what you want? You want to spread those legs and let me take care of the rest? You want me to take care of you?"

"Yes," she whispered.

If I hadn't felt her breath on my skin, I wouldn't have believed she said it. I tapped the packet against her nipple once more, nodding. "Yes?"

"Yes," she replied, a bit louder this time. She looked up at me, met my gaze, opened her legs. "Yes."

Perhaps it was superstition. Perhaps I could've left her on my bed and retrieved the protection without incident but this was better. Her awkward position on the counter-top, the mirror over the sink reflecting the luscious line of her body back at me, the harsh overhead light. The way my cock pointed straight at her as if it knew its way home. This was better. The awkward and harsh and perfectly right was better.

I tore the condom open and suited up. Took myself in hand, teased her folds. A rush of arousal met me, slicking my cock, my hand. "Yes?" I repeated.

"Yes," she repeated. I dragged the head of my cock around her clit. Watched the exact moment when I got it right and her gaze turned cloudy. If I glanced up to study myself in the mirror, I'd find a smug grin staring back at me. "I want—*yes*."

I brought her knee to my waist, anchored it there. Pressed my hand to the small of her back to keep her steady. Bowed my head to her breast, the one I'd marked and claimed and now planned to conquer. Closed my lips around that bud, licking at first and then sucking. Sucking hard. Slammed into her in one rough, starved motion.

I stayed there a moment, my tongue tracing the round of her nipple and my hips flush against hers, and I remembered it. The feel of her, the overwhelming heat, the orgasm pulsing inside me, the tsunami swell of emotion. I steadied myself just enough to remember this moment because I knew I'd carry it with me all my days.

"Cal," Stella groaned, her nails making half-moons on my skin. "Oh my god, Cal."

I pulled back slowly, dragging my cock from her channel and releasing her nipple with a loud pop. As I moved, I looked down at her belly, at the thatch of dark curls on her mound, at the place where I lingered inside her, where her flesh stretched to accommodate me. I nearly came at the sight of us, thick, wet, throbbing.

But I returned to her nipple, sucking like I wanted to draw the very essence of her out through that tight bud. She whispered to me, a chorus of *ohhhh* and *yesssss* and *fuuuck* and *more* and *Cal, Cal, Cal*. And I thrust, hammering her hard enough to rattle the cabinets and knock my toothbrush to the floor. I wanted more, wanted deeper, wanted her body spasming out of control.

"You are so beautiful," I said, the words faltering as her inner muscles pulsed around me. My hips rolled against hers, fast and demanding. In the periphery, I heard water running, felt droplets on my hand. I didn't stop to connect those sensations to an origin. It could wait. Everything could wait. Everything else in the world could wait while I fucked my woman like I could make her mine if I hit deep enough. My teeth closed around her nipple, biting harder than before and—and then I felt it. The throb of her cunt, the rush of wet and warm. I didn't stop, didn't slow down as her body quaked.

That I'd lasted this long was heroic.

"Please," she whispered. "Please don't stop."

"That's amusing. As if I would." I looked up, ran my scruffy chin over her breast. The ripple and pulse of her inner muscles sent a shiver through my shoulders and a laugh tumbling from my lips. It wasn't funny—it was overwhelming. It was every sensation sparking to life, circuits overloading. "Fuck me, Stella, do that again. Do it again and I'll give you the world, the whole fucking world."

"Me? You do it—oh, fuck, yes—you do it again," she hissed.

I twisted my hand around the band of her bra, using the leverage to work her over my shaft. "This is what you want, isn't it?" I asked, the words ground out through my rigid jaw. "You want me using you, using this cunt any way I please. This is what you came for. Isn't it, sweet thing?"

"Yes, yes, yes," she chanted.

Her words were the red flag and I was the bull, and my release barreled through me with an angry snarl. I wanted to bury my face in her hair, her breasts—but I had to watch. I had to watch while I pumped myself into her, wishing for the first time in my life that we didn't have a thin layer protecting us from each other. Wishing I could mark her cunt the way I'd marked her breast.

A soft, sated grin swept over across her face, popping her dimples, parting her lips. "Yes, yes, *yes*."

I was spent. Words, thoughts, breath—all of it, gone. I stood there, Stella's legs around my waist and my palm wrapped around her bra, panting into the crook of her neck while my cock pulsed and twitched inside her. Stella said nothing, only smoothed her hand down my back and rubbed her lips over my jaw, my chest, my shoulder.

Goddamn. Just...goddamn.

"Are you all right?" I asked, my lips covering the birthmark under her ear.

"All right? Yeah, that's one way to put it," she laughed. "I knew you were going to murder my vagina."

"I still don't know what that means."

Stella huffed out a laugh, her breath warm on my skin. "It means I'm going to need you to carry me to bed because these legs are not so steady." She glanced between us. "And I'm looking forward to the creaming portion of these games."

"Honey, that happened a couple of minutes ago," I said. "You were busy scratching the shit out of my back and screaming at the ceiling."

"The other creaming," she drawled. "The one where you're gonna use that thick baby lotion on my boob—the one you ate as a midnight snack—and then I'll go full cowgirl on you."

"Is that what's happening?" I asked.

"I mean, I'm here for it," she said. "It would be great if my ass stayed dry for that go-round though. I've experienced far too many instances of ass wetness—and not the fun kind of ass wetness—since meeting you."

For fuck's sake. The water *was* running. I must've knocked the faucet at some point, turning it on and bathing her ass. I nudged it off, reached blindly for a towel to dry Stella's backside. "Sorry about that."

"I don't know how you can apologize at a time like this," she replied. "Would it be weird to high five? That would be weird. We shouldn't do it. But that's where I'm at—I want it up high and down low and I want to dump a cooler of Gatorade over your head."

I groped her bra to find the clasp, finally releasing it. Our bodies trapped the lace in place but I was more interested in softening my grip on her. Holding her instead of pounding her, caressing instead of biting. A bed and blankets rather than the bathroom countertop and accidental waterslide.

I held up my hand. She glanced at me, a sparkling smile pulling at her lips, and slapped her palm against mine. "I want to do this again," she said.

"Yeah, you do," I growled. "You're going full cowgirl next."

She ducked her head, laughing. "No, I mean," she started, her hands warm on my flanks, "I want more than tonight."

"It was never tonight," I replied, the words quick and rough. "You didn't come here for tonight."

She nodded once. "I know. I know." Another nod. "But this"—she wagged a finger at the bathroom—"definitely confirmed it."

It did. It definitely did.

23

STELLA

"All I'm saying is this doesn't require an expert," Flinn said, both hands held up in condescending surrender.

"But you're the one person who can do it," Tatum replied.

"I don't want anyone else fucking up my systems," he argued. "I don't want to hand over my documents and spreadsheets to some idiot without the common sense to preserve my formulas. I'd end up fixing it and spending twice as long as I would've if I'd done it myself." He wagged his hands, one last burst of surrender, before slapping them down on the arms of the chair. "But it doesn't require an expert."

"Not an expert but not an idiot," Tatum snarked. "Got it."

I blinked at them, not sure I knew what they were arguing about this time. Not sure I cared. More often than not, Tatum and Flinn debated everything down to the time of day and color of the sky. They were also the best support staff I could find and I'd looked. They got the job done, they did it well. Who was I to complain if they also sparred every free minute of the day?

"Stella, I'm eager to hear your thoughts on this," Flinn said. That was the corporate-speak version of "Mom! Tatum's being mean to me!"

"I don't have thoughts on the matter," I replied. "If you're electing to add work to your plate, that's your choice. As long as that choice doesn't interfere with our team and our priorities, I don't care."

I reached for my phone, turning my attention to the screen as Tatum launched another attack on...something about Flinn's time management that she considered relevant. Devoting this much of our morning huddle to winless, fruitless debate wasn't great time management either but we'd handled the essentials and I had a ton of new messages and alerts flashing at me.

McKendrick wanted scrambled egg whites and felt the best way to meet that need was a group text to—basically—everyone he knew. Awesome.

My boss Rebecca wanted a status report on two other clients but made the entire email about McKendrick and my promotion and how nothing was definite until my client was back on the field. Fabulous.

A sports news (but mostly gossip) blog wanted me to know they planned to run photos of me and McKendrick looking "cozy" at a number of public events last week. *Cool cool cool.*

It wasn't entirely unexpected after avoiding the world for a weekend. Save for handling a few calls and texts, I barely got out of bed. Not that Cal gave me many opportunities.

That man, he wasn't like the rest of them.

And I was gradually walking myself around to the realization that I liked it that way. Cal was a species all his own —genus *man-brick*—and while I'd known that from the very start, I embraced it now. I wanted him this way, rumbly-grumbly and demanding as fuck and obscene. My god, was he obscene. I knew some filthy guys but Cal was running some multi-dimensional dirty talk game.

But the biggest thing—bigger than everything else— was the complete lack of chaos. Right or wrong, I believed the world would turn upside down if I deviated from my carefully curated sex-only lifestyle. So far, the earth hadn't flipped on its axis and I wasn't driving any struggle buses.

I was sitting on a pillow again but that was a small price to pay for the best weekend I'd had in years.

It was also the first weekend I'd spent with one man in years. The first bed I'd shared for sleep *and* sex. The first time I wasn't thinking about getting dressed and going home the minute he pulled out. The first time I didn't rush to enforce the boundaries when he inquired about seeing me next.

Cal was all my firsts. All the ones that mattered.

"Did you want to weigh in on this, Stella?" Flinn asked.

I looked up. "No," I replied. I didn't know what they wanted but I did know they had to handle more issues on their own. "I'm sure you have it covered."

"Mostly, yes," Flinn drawled. "This situation really does require your stamp of approval though. We wouldn't want to rush to action."

"Please," I said with an expansive wave. "Rush. Act."

Tatum winged a folded paper at me. "We're talking about lunch."

I plucked the menu from my lap, glanced at the items. "I'm sure you know what I'd like. I trust your judgment, Tate."

"Mmhmm," she replied, a cheeky grin cutting across her face. "That's what you get for daydreaming."

"I was not daydreaming," I cried. I was working hard at the faux indignation. "Thoughtful work requires deep thinking."

"Real smooth, boss," Flinn quipped. "Like butter." He pointed at my chair and the decorative pillow under my ass. "Are you doing all right? Or are you *all right*?"

I had to fold my lips between my teeth to keep from laughing. "Not your concern," I said. "But yes, I'm just fine."

That was the truth. And no one was more surprised about it than me.

24

CAL

Every flu season, popular news outlets liked to cobble together lists on how to stay healthy. Most of them centered around drinking plenty of water, sleeping an adequate amount, eating fruits and vegetables, exercise, flu shots. The norm.

The earthy, crunchy ones touted garlic and elderberry and an assortment of essential oils.

But it was the racy outlets that recommended sex. They claimed a healthy sex life was like an infusion of vitamin C. An orgasm a day kept the viruses at bay.

As far as my professional opinion went, I landed somewhere in the middle. But I liked to believe the one about sex.

Unfortunately for me, sex wasn't enough to protect me from Stremmel and his fragile West Coast immune system. He was the fucking angel of death. He picked up every damn cold and flu and passed them to everyone in a fifty-mile radius. Even though I never got sick—I couldn't remember the last time I'd had more than a mild cold—I found myself knocked on my ass with a bitch of a late spring flu.

And here I thought the sex was going to save me.

I was half awake, half fever dreaming when I heard a knock at the door. I figured it was part of the dream and rolled over, pulling a pillow over my head to block out the afternoon sunlight. I was contagious and woozy, neither of which belonged in the operating room today. I'd skipped the trail this morning too. I hated doing it but the last thing I wanted was infecting Stella. Or worse, orchestrating another accident by virtue of sinus pressure fucking up my inner ear and equilibrium.

Five minutes later, I heard the door swing open and snick shut. I thought I heard it but it was possible the virus was fucking with my senses. Yeah. Probably that. No one was breaking into my apartment. And if they were, I didn't have the capacity to fight them off. I was too far removed from my Ranger days to manage anything like that.

Then I heard Stella's voice. She called, "It's just me and I'm putting a few things on the stove. You stay where you are, with your germs."

I was certain it was Stella. I'd heard that. Real, live Stella. Not a fever dream.

"Who let you in?" I asked. Because that was the only way to greet the woman in my life. Firing off rude questions about how she came to invade my home.

"Don't talk, you sound awful," she replied. "Riley let me in."

I didn't realize Riley had a key but puzzling through that required more energy than I had to spare. Instead, I went back to the fever dreams. I slept in fits of hot and cold, alternately whipping the blankets off me and then huddling under them. Weird scenes played in my head. Nothing I understood. A traffic jam of balloons on Commonwealth Avenue, dogs with bananas for tails, a dark-haired beauty wielding an enormous knife.

When I woke up, it was dark outside and I was drenched in sweat. My apartment smelled like spices. I couldn't name flavors from scent alone and I was too congested to discern much of anything, but my stomach offered a rumble of interest as I stepped into the shower.

I stayed in there for longer than I'd planned but the hot spray did wonders for me. I felt human again rather than a discombobulated cluster of limbs, organs, and virus. As I toweled off, I hoped Stella was still in the kitchen but I wouldn't blame her for getting the hell out of here.

Emerging from my bedroom in a fresh t-shirt and sweats, I found Stella stirring a large pot of wonderful. She pulled her earbuds loose as I approached and offered me a concerned smile. "How are you?"

I shrugged. "I've been better but I've also been worse." I pointed to her phone. "Are you on a call?"

"Just wrapped up a few minutes ago. I've been listening to the Red Sox game."

I gestured toward the flat screen television mounted on the wall. "Is that a nostalgia thing for you or did you not want to watch it?"

"I didn't want to wake you," she replied.

"Don't worry about me," I said, pulling together all my macho. There wasn't much of it right now. "I went through Special Forces training, Stel. The flu is a mild annoyance." I edged closer to get a look at the pot. "What is this goodness?"

"It's not soup," she said. It was delivered as both warning and apology. "In my family, we don't do soup when you're sick."

"I didn't ask for soup," I replied.

"It's typical, the soup," she continued. "Everyone thinks chicken soup is the best remedy. But that wasn't my upbringing."

I shook my head. "Can't be. Not when there's"—I took the spoon from her, stirred the contents—"this."

"Spicy peppers, roasted garlic, and red sauce. And some spicy sausage," she said. "My father's family on his mother's side is Sicilian and they're big believers in peppers and garlic. His father's side is from northern Italy but they also believe a big bowl of spicy peppers will cure anything that ails you. My grandmother on my mom's side, she tried to adapt this and give it a *pollo guisado* twist. That was one of her mother's recipes and she went to her grave angry that she'd never perfected it." Stella slipped a pair of mitts over her hands and opened the oven. "I baked some warm bread too. No messy story about grand-mothers and Sicilians or northern Italians, just some dough I picked up from the North End. It's good for sopping up the sauce."

If I didn't know I was in love before this point, I knew it now.

"You made this," I said, glancing around at the utensils and cutting boards on the counter, the dishes in the sink, the homemade bread coming out of my damn oven. "You did all this. You cooked for me."

Stella turned to set the bread on a rack. "Didn't think I had it in me, huh?"

I didn't see her expression as she spoke the words but I tasted the bitter bite in them. "No, I don't doubt you at all. You have everything inside you."

"Go sit down," she said, glancing at me as she shucked the mitts. "You're gray and clammy, and now is not the time to bathe me in compliments. I'll bring a bowl over—"

"And some bread, please," I said.

She pressed her hand to my chest, nudging me toward the sofa. "A little bit of everything," she said.

"Will you stay? We can watch the game," I said, giving zero fucks about how pathetic I sounded. "I'll sit on the other side of the room and breathe away from you."

"Go sit down," she repeated. "Listen to me, Cal. I'm not putting up with your rumbly-grumbly sweaty pine tree thing tonight and I'm pretty sure I can knock you over with a light push."

I coughed for a solid minute. Motherfucking Stremmel. He wasn't going to hear the end of this. "Your point?"

She blew out a breath, sending the loose hairs around her face flying. "I don't remember," she said, tossing up her hands. "But I did tell you to sit down."

"You also said something about sweating trees," I added. "Right? Did I imagine that?"

"It's an inside joke," she answered, turning back to the stove.

"And here I was, thinking I'd been inside you," I replied.

Stella dropped the spoon to the countertop as she backed away and bent at the waist, shaking with laughter. She wrapped her arm around her middle and wiped tears from her cheeks with her free hand. "I'll give you that one, Cal. I'll give it to you," she said. "But if you don't get your ass out of this kitchen in the next five seconds, I'm going to walk this pot of sausage and peppers upstairs to Stremmel. The bread too. Is that what you want?"

I took a big step back, effectively leaving the small kitchen. "No, ma'am," I replied. "I don't want you sharing any sausage with Stremmel."

"How do you do this?" she asked, her gaze trained on the sauce in front of her. "You're dying of the flu but also throwing out obscene comments like you're angling to take a bite out of my ass tonight."

"Not dying," I said through a cough. "Nah. I'm fine. Probably shouldn't eat your ass for a few days."

"Sit," she barked, holding back a laugh.

As I flopped down on the sofa, I heard her chuckle in the kitchen. It was a tiny, tiny moment. A single heartbeat. But it was the best thing I'd experienced in a long time. Me, sick and pathetic while the most beautiful, talented, generous woman in the world made spicy peppers and bread. The best.

It wasn't the domesticity of it. It wasn't about her cooking or caring for me.

It was the attachment. The one we shared.

Stella handed me a bowl. "Only because it's shaping up to be a good game and I'm starving," she said. "But if you get me sick, I'll send the raccoon after you."

"The caffeine junkie? Nah, he's my pal."

"I'm sure he is," she replied. "He's everyone's friend except mine."

"What about the beaver?"

She gave me a narrow-eyed glare while her lips twisted into a smile. "What about it?"

"Another friend of mine," I replied.

"Mmhmm." She nodded, laughing. "I bet."

She tucked herself into the opposite end of the sofa, her phone seated on the armrest and her bowl balanced on her lap. She didn't do any of the things I might've expected but that was how she operated. Never what I expected.

She stayed there long after we finished eating. She stayed, narrating the plays on the baseball game better than the commentators and cursing the players like they'd insulted her lineage. She stayed, handling the dishes during commercial breaks.

She didn't tidy the apartment or wrap a blanket around my shoulders when another chill hit me, but she stayed. I might've anticipated those moves from a different woman but not Stella. And I didn't miss them. I wanted her heckling the refs and dropping juicy insider details about the players, the managers, the team owners. I wanted her to stay.

But then I looked down at my empty bowl, the one without a drop of leftover sauce because I'd sponged it all up with that bread, and I realized this was the first and possibly last time she'd cook for me. Because I could lose her. All this time, all this waiting could end with her choosing someone else. Choosing no one. After all, she didn't belong to anyone.

I loved her and I could lose her.

25

STELLA

IT TOOK CAL A FULL WEEK TO SHAKE OFF THE FLU. THAT translated to more than a full week since getting naked with him. Not that I begrudged that time—no one wanted to visit Pound Town only to cough up a lung during the visit. But it served as a little timeout for us, an "are we good here?" pause.

And yeah, we were good. Mostly.

On the morning he'd promised to meet me at the trail and resume our regular walks, he slept right through his alarm. And my texts. Calls too. And a full minute of me banging on his door.

That man.

I'd never devoted this much time and energy to another human being since...ever. I'd never done this. I'd never cared this much. Not even when I was engaged—twice!—to be married.

I wasn't sure what I thought about all this yet. I wasn't sure how I felt about this newfound sensation of caring about another person to the point of my heart lodging in my throat and every terrible scenario possible flashing through my mind when he didn't answer that door right away.

And that was just a minute. A *minute*. Plus all the minutes on the frantic drive to his apartment from the pond. Plus the minutes of waiting for him at the pond. Plus the weight of caring for a person as much as I cared for myself.

I didn't know what I thought about that and I wasn't quite ready to sit down and sort it out. But he was on the mend now and busy gushing about a new surgeon at his hospital. A lady surgeon. A lady surgeon who taught him some snazzy new tricks today.

"She's really talented," Cal continued, awe tinting his words. "I'm amazed how her little pointers make such a big impact on minimizing scarring in major procedures."

"Great, great," I said, forcing a smile. What was wrong with me? Honestly. He was allowed to work with women. It wasn't sexual for him. Much like understanding my reaction to him sleeping through his alarm, I didn't want to unpack this one. I just didn't want to know what I'd find.

"I'm having Shap lead a skills lab session for my residents. They need as much of her teaching as they can get. Hell, I need it."

This was what I'd avoided all these years of scheduling men and snipping attachments before they took root. Misplaced, illogical jealousy. A sense of competition with a woman who probably wasn't trying to seduce Cal by doing a really good job at a surgery thing.

Stelllllllllla. Seriously. Get a fucking grip on reality and chill the fuck out.

"You'd like her," he said, plucking a lone piece of sashimi off my plate. "She doesn't put up with any shit."

"As she shouldn't," I said. Then, with a hearty laugh, "It comes with age, you know. Most of us don't know any better when we're younger or we're not in a position to do anything but shovel someone else's shit. But the older I get, the more willing I am to walk away from shit-shoveling situations. I didn't know how when I was younger. Didn't know that I could." I reached for my drink, held it up but didn't bring it to my lips. "I bet your surgeon friend knows what I'm talking about. I bet she's put up with so much shit she goes a little crazy if anyone tries sending it her way. I bet she's only allowed to take no shit because she's good at her work."

"She is good at her work," Cal conceded, shooting a glance at his beer bottle.

Probably easier to look there than my crazy eyes but goddamn it, I hated hearing about women who were strong and tough, the ones who didn't fuck around. Women didn't need anyone rubber-stamping their strength, and we didn't need anyone calling it out as rare or unique.

"And you admire her work," I said. "You want your students to learn from her."

"I do. I want them to think about the cuts they make and the ways in which they close them up, and I want them to be as patient-centric as possible in that thought process," he replied, hitting me with a quick smile before rummaging for more food. I couldn't decide if this was another incident of Cal eating everything in sight because he was roughly the size of a black bear or him avoiding me.

Then I realized it didn't matter. I cared about this man

263

and he cared about me. I could tell him difficult things without hiding behind good girl manners. I didn't have to be a smiling face that said the right things, kept the uncomfortable topics to myself. A man who cared about me didn't need—or want—that kind of people-pleasing, peace-keeping behavior. A man who cared about me wanted my raw opinions and my ugly spots and my needy, wobbly moments. He didn't want me filtered.

"Then you have to use your position as the dude on the magazine cover to make sure your residents see her as an effective surgeon and not a bitchy surgeon," I said. "And it's the *dude* on the magazine cover who can do that. Make it about her abilities and knowledge, Cal. Don't make it about her not putting up with any shit. And when you hear them referring to her as the bitchy surgeon—because they will—tell them how much they're missing out on by relegating her to that corner. That their inability to cope with a woman who doesn't wrap her requests in honey means they're focusing on the wrong things and they're passing up an opportunity to learn."

He stared at me a moment, his expression even. Then, he said, "I can do that." He popped a piece of California roll in his mouth, nodded. "I still think you'd like Shap. You could probably trade stories about people underestimating you."

I hadn't planned on testing him like that. If anything, I was more concerned with corralling my ridiculous, outrageous, need-to-get-my-head-checked jealousy. But it was a test—and he passed.

"We all start off taking some shit," I said, softening my tone as much as possible, "and then doing better. Learning the lesson. Now that I'm older, I can definitely say I've learned the lesson."

"The only one getting older here is me," he said. "You could pass as twenty-something, Stel. I'm shocked you don't get carded. I'm just waiting for the day someone asks if I'm your—I don't know—uncle. Or something."

I took a sip of water. Set the glass down. Went for it again. My god, Cal as my uncle. I needed to wash that thought away fast. "Honey, you're not that much older than me and you look"—I gestured toward him, circling my hand at his upper body—"you're fine as fuck."

He ducked his head as his cheeks heated. Ears too. God, I loved it when he blushed all the way to his ears. Like an elf, if elves were huge and obscene. And dressed in a suit made for remotely detonating ovaries. No tie, shirt open at the collar. Fine as fuck.

"Good to know," he said.

For absolutely no good reason, I announced, "My birthday is coming up."

Cal glanced up at me, his eyes round and curious. "When?"

I sucked in a breath as if I was preparing for a plunge into cold water. Maybe I was. My birthday never included the men in my life, not since my fiancé. There'd been no reason to include them. We didn't have the kind of relationship that extended to birthdays, holidays, or anniversaries.

"May twenty-fifth," I replied.

He blinked at me, a slow smile pulling at his lips. "That's—that's this weekend."

"It sure is."

He stared at me as if I wasn't connecting the dots. "What

do you usually do to celebrate?" he asked. "What does Stella's Natal Celebration involve?"

"Well, we don't call it Stella's Natal Celebration to start," I said, laughing. "I don't do much. I'm not over-the-top about birthdays."

"Neither am I," he replied. "Are you all right with nearing the top? Approaching but not going over?"

I barked out a laugh, pressed my hand to my chest. "I guess that would be fine," I said. "My family always has a birthday dinner at my parents' house. It's been that way since we were kids. We'd get to choose the menu and no one could object to our choices because it was the one day we could have whatever we wanted. My older sister Sophia always wanted something ridiculous. Fancy and ridiculous. She's always been obsessed with the finer things. One year, she requested beef Wellington. I think she was eleven, maybe twelve. She'd read about it in a book and insisted my mother make that for her."

"How'd that go over?" Cal asked, laughing.

I shook my head. "My mother had to ask everyone in the neighborhood if they had a recipe because it wasn't part of her usual Sicilian-northern Italian-Dominican fare. It was fine. It was fine and we ate it but I hated Sophia's birthday dinners." I lifted my drink, drained it. "Serina, my younger sister, always wanted cheeseburgers and tomato soup from a can and Funfetti cupcakes. To this day, she'd choose grilled cheese over anything else."

Cal smiled at me a moment, his gaze warm and his eyes shining. "Well?" he asked eventually. "What's your birthday meal?"

I returned his smile with a shrug. "Nothing crazy," I

replied. "You should come. Come to my birthday dinner at my parents' house."

"I'd love to," he said. "Count me in."

Really, Stella. Really. Way to take it all the way there and back again.

CAL WAS on call tonight and—predictably—had to return to the hospital not long after finishing dinner. But it was good. I needed to call my mother. She'd kill me if I brought a guest to dinner without adequate warning and five days barely qualified as adequate in her book.

"Hi, Mom," I sang when she answered. "Is it okay if I bring someone to dinner this weekend? For my birthday?"

"What do you mean, is it okay?" she asked. If her tone could be trusted, she was totally fucking mortified that I'd asked. She'd also be totally fucking mortified if I hadn't. There was no winning this one. "Are you fuckin' kidding me? Yes, you're welcome to bring someone. Is it Flinn? That boy needs a family unit, Stella. I've told you before. He needs a damn family. Or Tatum? She's a sweetheart. She's always welcome. You don't have to ask. You know that."

"Not Tatum. Not Flinn," I said. "Someone new. His name is Cal. He's a doctor. Surgeon, actually."

There was a long pause. Long enough for my mother to walk out of the house, down the street, and into oncoming traffic. Not that she'd do that but what the hell *was* she doing?

Then, "George? George! Goddammit *George*!"

In the distance, I heard my father saying, "Just kill it with a broom, Christina. I'll be there in a minute."

"Not a spider, George," she yelled. "Stella's bringing a boy to dinner."

It didn't matter that Cal was very much a man. Holy fucking fuck, he was all *man*. But in my parents' book, any guy I brought home was a boy.

"What? What about Stella? Where is she? She's bringing what? She's here?"

"She's not here," my mother shouted.

I held the phone away from my ear. The driver shot a curious glance at me over his shoulder. "Sorry," I whispered.

"On the phone, George. She's on the *phone*," my mother yelled.

Chances were good my mother was standing in the middle of the kitchen. That was her spot. At any point in the day, my mother could be found standing there, trying to remember why she went into the kitchen. Chances were also good my father was in the basement. That was his spot. He kept an old television down there—the kind with rabbit ears —and every copy of *Sports Illustrated* published since 1975. He also had a punching bag he never touched and a recliner that would one day digest him into the dark abyss of that chair.

"What does she need?" he yelled back.

The problem with their kitchen/basement spots was the acoustics. He couldn't hear a damn thing down there and she believed he wasn't trying hard enough.

"She's bringing a boy to dinner," my mother called.

"A what?"

"Dammit, George. She's bringing a boy home."

"What's wrong with her? Where is she?" he asked.

"She's on the *phone*," Mom repeated.

I heard another extension pick up, probably the old wall-mounted phone near the washer and dryer in the basement. It was a terrible place to take calls because the washer rattled relentlessly and the dryer—which was always fluffing something—smothered the area in white noise. "What's happening?" he asked.

"I'm—" I started.

"Stella's bringing a boy home for her birthday dinner," she cut in. "Can you believe this? I looked outside just now and I don't see any pigs in the sky so I don't know what's going on."

"You better not be pulling one over on us, Stella," he warned. "This sort of thing isn't a joke."

I laughed, not certain I understood the unrestrained shock from my parents. "I'm not joking," I replied. "I called to make sure it was all right to bring him and—"

"Oh, would you stop it with that?" Mom snapped. "We'll need the folding table unless we seat Toby with the kids in the kitchen."

"Good place for him," Dad muttered, referring to Serina's husband. Nice guy, Mets fan. Couldn't get past that one.

"And we need to get some good wine. Not the shitty kind you usually buy," Mom continued. "What kind of wine does he like, Stella? Red or white?"

"Men drink red wine," Dad argued.

"Enough of that," Mom chided him. "I'm asking Stella."

"Red wine is great," I replied. "Or beer. Honestly, you

don't need to worry about Cal. He'll be fine with whatever you have."

"I'll get red wine," Dad said. "Beer too."

"You don't need to do anything different," I cautioned. "Really. He'll be fine."

"Stella, please," Dad replied, his tone heavy.

"You need to cut the goddamn grass," my mother announced. I assumed that was directed at Dad. I didn't cut grass. The small patch of lawn at my house was handled by a professional and I preferred it that way. "We should get those flower boxes filled too."

"Really, guys. It's not necessary. Cal's not going to base the dowry on the flower boxes. It will be the size of the meatballs."

"Oh, okay. I'll have to make them bigger," Mom replied.

No one had ever been this serious about meatball size.

"Oh my god," I whispered. "That was a joke. I'm going to be thirty-six and dowries don't exist in today's society and the flower boxes do not matter at all. Sure, get the good wine because Sophia won't complain about it all night and yeah, make those meatballs as big as a planet because that sounds awesome but please don't do anything different on account of Cal coming to dinner."

There was a pause filled only by the distant sound of the eighties music my mother played in the kitchen. Then, "Stella Marie, we are not putting up with your comedy routine," she snapped. "Now, your father and I need to discuss the fuckin' front yard. We'll talk to you later. Love you. Goodnight."

And with that, my parents hung up on me. But I'd bet anything they were still talking on the phone, a dial tone vibrating between them as they spoke from inside the same house. Because I was a glutton for punishment and still confused about my parents' reaction to my guest, I opened a group text with my sisters.

There was no sense in calling them. Not unless I wanted to listen to dogs barking, children crying, and significant others yelling in the background.

No, I was maxed out on all counts.

Stella: Hey. I'm bringing a guy to dinner next weekend.
Sophia: Flinn is not a guy. He's the little boy who works for you.
Serina: What she said.
Stella: Not Flinn...why does everyone assume it's Flinn?
Serina: Because he's the only man who's been in your life for more than a hot second.
Sophia: Only one we've met since (ahem) you know who.

WE DIDN'T SPEAK my ex-fiancé's name. I wasn't sure when that tradition started but I liked it. I kept it going.

Stella: Right well it's not Flinn. His name is Cal.
Serina: Age/location/profession
Stella: Early 40s, Beacon Hill near Charles Street, cardio-thoracic surgeon.
Serina: Winner, winner...
Sophia: How long?

Serina: She's not asking about penis length. You can give me that info in a separate text.
Sophia: Why do straight women mythologize the penis? It's the ugliest, most bizarre, unreliable organ.
Stella: This one's reliable. It's really reliable. It's pictured in the dictionary next to the definition of reliable.

SERINA REPLIED with a string of heart eyes, praise hands, and drooling faces. Thank god for emojis.

Sophia: I'm just going to say this. My strap-on doesn't get performance anxiety.
Serina: Oh my god stop talking about your damn strap-on.
Stella: Back to the topic at hand. It's been a couple of months.

THAT WASN'T the most accurate accounting of our relationship but my sisters were tough nuts to crack. I didn't want them looking at my relationship with Cal as something new and insignificant. To them—happily married women going on years of wedded bliss—two months was nothing. And I couldn't bear it if they brushed off Cal as nothing.

Cal wasn't nothing. He was my—

Holy shit, Stellllllllla.

This was a really big deal. Cal was coming home with me. Meeting my parents, my sisters, my nieces and nephews—both human and canine. On my fucking birthday.

Stella Stella Stella, what have you done?

Serina: And you're bringing him home? Do Mom and Dad know?

Stella: Yeah. I just got off the phone with them.

Sophia: Wait wait wait.

Sophia: You told Mom and Dad you were bringing a male home and you didn't conference us in?

Serina: I really wanted to hear the screaming.

Sophia: Is Mom rewallpapering the bathroom? She's been complaining about that bathroom for a time.

Serina: No, she's down at the church. Praying to Saint Marguerite d'Youville, the patron saint of marriage.

Stella: I'm not getting married.

Sophia: HA. Hahahahahaha.

Serina: You know what? This is like the hometown date episode of The Bachelorette!

Sophia: Do you think he's going to ask for Dad's blessing?

Serina: omg that would be adorable. A little man chat down in the basement where Dad asks him about his intentions. Love this so hard.

Stella: Seriously. I am not getting married.

Serina: Of course you're not, Stellaluna. You're just bringing a guy home for the first time. Happens every day!

THIS MAN. He had all my firsts.

26

CAL

THE KNOCK AT THE DOOR SOUNDED AS I SHRUGGED INTO MY suit coat. I stole another glance in the mirror before making my way through the apartment to open the door for Stella, cursing myself for not giving her a key.

I'd remedy that soon enough. She could have a key to my apartment while I went on not knowing where she lived. I was nothing if not consistently ahead of the game.

I swung the door open, saying, "I'm getting you a key so you can let yourself in. But not today. That's a poor excuse for a birthday gift—and happy birthday, sweet thing."

She stepped through the doorway, her shiny yellow shoes whispering against the hardwood floor. She looked damn cute. She wore a short black dress, the kind made from t-shirt fabric that skimmed her curves and made her tits look like they needed to be devoured. A little jean jacket too, the cuffs folded up to her forearms. Just too fucking cute.

The kind of cute I could only acknowledge by burying

my head between her legs and admiring her dress from underneath.

"Look at you, making me open my own doors. And they say chivalry is dead," she replied with a lopsided smile. But then her eyes widened, her lips parted. A sound rattled in her throat. She lifted her fingers to her lips, held them there. "Oh, shit. Look at you."

Most days, I interpreted that reaction as positive. Stella was a big fan of suits and that was why I wore them as often as possible. But this didn't seem altogether positive.

I glanced down, expecting to discover a blob of toothpaste on my lapel or a rip in my trousers. I found neither. "What's wrong?"

She stared at me, her fingertips pressing her lips hard enough to turn them white. "You're wearing a suit."

"Yes," I replied, gesturing toward myself.

"You can't wear a suit." She shook her head. "You—you can't."

Before I could respond, Stella was off, marching into my bedroom and digging through my closet. I followed, watching while she held up shirts and mumbled to herself. Since this suit wasn't happening, I slipped the coat off and set it on the bed.

"My parents only get dressed up for church," she said from inside the closet. "Funerals, weddings, baptisms. They're more casual for Sunday morning mass."

"Okay," I said, nodding. "You're saying I'm overdressed."

Stella barked out a humorless laugh. "I'm saying my father has one suit. He bought it fifteen years ago when Serina got married. He wears it to funerals, weddings, and baptisms. Combined, he's probably worn it fewer than ten times in those fifteen years. He's definitely not wearing it tonight." Another wry laugh. "He's probably wearing dungarees. That's what he calls them. Dungarees. Every pair he owns is older than I am and as we know, I'm thirty-six. But he wears dungarees when he's at home."

"Sure." I kicked off my shoes, reached for my belt. "That works for me."

Stella emerged from the closet, two hangers clutched in each hand. Her gaze dropped to where I worked my belt loose, unbuttoned my trousers. And then—*fuck me*—she dragged her tongue over her upper lip. Slow, like she was sucking a flavor off her skin.

"Stella," I warned. "You have to—we can't—not right—stop it with the tongue."

She tossed the clothing to my bed and moved toward me. "Stop what?" she asked, sliding my belt free. It hit the floor with a muffled clang, right before my trousers. She smoothed her hand down, over my lengthening cock. "What did I do, Cal?"

"*Stella*." She glanced up at me, all dimples. I could drink whiskey out of those dimples. I could jerk off into those dimples. *Fuuuck*. "I'm not going to shake your father's hand with the scent of you still staining my skin."

"Then don't use your hand." Her fingers curled around me, light at first and then tighter. "I'd rather have"—tighter —"this."

"We'll be late," I argued. What the hell was wrong with me? There was no earthly reason to argue with this woman. I wanted whatever she wanted and that was the truth of it. But I also wanted to do this right. Show up on-fucking-time. Meet her parents, wear the suit, charm the sisters.

Demolish her history and every memory of men before. "We'll be late to your birthday party, sweet thing."

"It's *my* party," she replied, her lips turning up in a pout. I felt that pout on the head of my cock. "I'm allowed to be late."

"Are you allowed to show up with cum on your tongue? Because that's what's going to happen."

"Like I said," she replied. "My party."

She hooked her thumbs under my boxers but I caught her wrists. "No," I said, my hands shaking as I squeezed her. "No."

Another pout. I gathered up all the strength I had, all the stern. And still, it wasn't enough.

I dragged my hand up to her elbow, whirled her around. "Get over here," I snapped, tucking her ass against my boxer-covered cock. I banded my arm around her waist while my free hand yanked her skirt up, covered her mound, teased her through her panties. "You want this?" She nodded. "Words, Stella. Give me words and I give you what you want."

She pressed her lips to my arm. I felt her breath straight through the fabric of my shirt, felt it all over. "Yes, please."

I shoved my hand under her panties, between her folds, ground the heel of my palm against her clit. She cried out against my arm. "Is this what you want, sweet thing? You want to rub that thick ass on my cock while I teach this clit how to come for me?"

"Yeah. This works," she replied with a giggle. "If you don't mind, I'd like it a little harder."

I pinched her. I pinched her clit and I almost blasted

into my boxers from the sounds she made alone. "How's that for harder?"

A frustrated groan tore from her lips. "Will you let me suck your cock when I'm done?"

I pushed two fingers inside her, teased the spot that made her cross-eyed, pulled out. Added another. "If you can talk, I'm doing something wrong."

"May I remind you it is my birthday?" she panted. "You should let me suck your cock."

"Goddamn it, Stel," I said, my lips on her neck. "If you don't get there right now, I swear to you, I'll leave you like this."

"You won't," she said through a moan. "You—oh, *fuck.*"

A warm wave of arousal coated my fingers, my palm, as she shook in my arms. A low cry rumbled through her as she broke apart but I didn't stop stroking her. Not when her inner thighs quivered and cunt clamped down around me. Not when her clit pulsed against my palm and she screamed into my arm. Not when her head lolled to the side and she sighed with more bliss than I'd ever heard.

But then, "On the bed. I'm not in the mood to kneel on the floor."

I almost objected. Almost reminded her we had to go and even though I was late to every dinner party and event to which I was invited, I wasn't going to be late to meet her parents. I almost made that case. *Almost.* "I'm not in the mood to come in your mouth unless you're sitting on my face while I do."

She glanced up at me, her eyes bright. "I can work with that."

27

STELLA

"Okay, birthday girl," Cal said. He rested his hand on my thigh—upper, definitely upper—as I drove past the Public Garden. "What am I getting myself into here? Prep me for the medieval torture."

Oof. My family. My birthday dinner. I was *this* close to calling it off and staying home and being naked with Cal. Because holy shit, I was still boneless from the past half hour. I couldn't believe we'd managed to leave each other alone long enough to get dressed and get out of the apartment.

And just like he'd promised, I could still taste him on my tongue.

I started to respond but pressed my free hand to my lips, stifling a laugh. "Have you ever seen Virgin-Mary-in-the-bathtub statues?"

He swiveled toward me. "Have I—what?"

"Yeah, you know, a Virgin Mary statue where she's enshrined in an upright bathtub. It's a thing around here. For believers, that is. And my mother, she's a believer. It's kind of funny how it came to be, actually. Around here, many of the folks who keep a shrine are of Irish, Portuguese, or Italian descent. My grandmother was Dominican but she grew up in an Italian neighborhood. Over the years, she and her family adopted a lot of Italian traditions and customs. She married an Italian guy and passed this crockpot of culture onto my mother who also married an Italian guy. And that's how a miniature Madonna came to live in our front yard."

"Right. Virgin Mary in the bathtub. Got it," Cal said.

"My mother is highly religious but not in the ways you might expect. She works at the local Catholic church— she's the coordinator there. She schedules masses, marriages, baptisms, last rites. She keeps the priests' sched- ules and manages the whole joint. She runs a tight ship and she loves her work and that parish. But Cal, she swears like a gangster. She pretends it's a one-off thing but it is not."

He nodded but he didn't understand. How could he? This wasn't altogether reasonable.

"It's not just the swearing. That's just the most obvious part. If you asked after her politics, it would sound like she was speaking to you from the far side of progressive island. But don't try to reconcile any of it. Somehow, she's able to keep a strict interpretation of a centuries-old text that was potlucked together after the fact while also loving and supporting my gay sister, marching with her pink hat, demanding better from those who try to rob women of bodily autonomy. I don't know how she threads that needle and I don't think I could do it myself but she does and I love her for it. I love that she can have these ideals, ones that run in direct contradiction at times, and do it without breaking a sweat. I admire it."

"I know physicians like that," he said. "It's hard to believe in anything other than science after all the years spent in med school, internship, residency. It's tough to hold on to faith." He shrugged, his gaze still on the road ahead. "Or so I've heard. But many do. Many believe even when the science gets in the way of those beliefs."

After a pause, I said, "I believe in football."

"You should believe in better helmets and hit restrictions," he replied, squeezing my thigh. That thumb of his, it was edging into the hot zone. "You're not going to have much football if your players keep hammering their heads."

"Don't mention that to my father," I said. "He thinks CTE is a conspiracy perpetrated by overprotective mothers. The South Americans too. He thinks they're trying to replace American football with fútbol and he's not having it."

Cal barked out a laugh. "Really?"

"Not all the things we believe make sense," I said with a shrug. "And on the topic of my dad—have you ever spent more than five dollars on cheese?"

"Per pound or total?"

"Doesn't matter," I replied. "Either or."

"Then...yes."

I glanced in my mirrors as I merged onto the highway, shook my head. "Don't mention that to my father," I said. "If he sees me with a Starbucks cup—or anything other than black, hot Dunkin'—he says I'm being careless with my money."

"You do well," Cal said, the statement delivered with a

hint of a question. "As a publicist, you do well. You don't worry over the price of matcha, right?"

"I do well," I agreed. "But my parents, they've always struggled to make ends meet with a house full of girls. Like I said, Mom's a church coordinator. Dad's a high school football coach. They work hard. They don't understand why I'd spend more than five dollars on cheese even if I can afford it because they'd save that money to fix the roof or replace the boiler or finally go on the cruise they've been talking about for ten years."

"I get that," he replied. "My mom's a physician but rural medicine is a rough situation. She's one of only a few doctors in the entire county. Most people don't realize that access to health care is extremely limited in rural and remote areas. There are no urgent care clinics, no emergency rooms, no medical parks crammed with doctors' offices and labs. It's not an exaggeration. Some areas of the country are hundreds of miles away from a critical care center and that is just too far for most emergencies."

"Wow. I had no idea."

"Her world consists of house calls and setting up shop in shuttered clinics a few days each week. She plays the role of general practitioner, obstetrician, pediatrician, emergency specialist, mental health counselor, hospice coordinator, and everything in between."

"Why does your mom do it? Why not move to a region with more lucrative opportunities?"

He shook his head with a grumble. "Because she knows no one will fill the void. She doesn't want to leave women with high-risk pregnancies and kids with diabetes and seniors with chronic heart failure." Another grumble. "And my dad, well, he's another story. He works with wood. Mostly tinkering but sometimes he sells a piece or two. My sister—"

I held up my hand, interrupting him. "Ada. She lives in Portland. Right?"

"Right," he replied. "She set him up to attend some farmers' markets and art fairs in the area. She talks about an Etsy shop but my dad doesn't believe in the internet. It's his South American chronic concussion conspiracy." Another grumble. "He has PTSD. He hasn't worked steadily —hasn't done anything steadily—since returning home from the first Gulf War. Whether he's following through on counseling and meds is a different story but I get it. I get that things are tough. My parents don't own a television. Or a microwave."

"You could send them a microwave," I said. "Or a television. Or both."

"And you can ship your parents off on that cruise or pick up some good cheese."

"I do buy the good cheese," I replied, laughing. "But I tear off the sticker, hide the receipt, and lie about the price. I tell them I found a new market near my house and everything is really cheap. My mother is devoted to her local grocery store and wouldn't consider leaving it so they never question me and my affordable cheeses."

"And I lie and tell my mother pharmaceutical reps drop off all the samples and supplies and new equipment I send her each month."

"Lies," I said, laughing. "Sometimes they're a good thing."

"The intentions are good," he said. "I imagine they wouldn't be thrilled if they knew the truth."

"Do you think they do?" I asked. "Perhaps they realize what we're doing and go along with it because they're proud and we're generous, and calling these lies on the carpet injures everyone in the process?"

"Maybe," he said. "It wouldn't kill me to tell my mother I want to restock her supplies. She won't take a microwave. Honestly, she wouldn't use one and my dad hates anything that beeps. But she'd accept a portable sonogram if it showed up on her doorstep."

"But it's the lie that allows her to keep her pride, Cal," I argued. "She doesn't want you to think she's struggling. No one likes to admit that. When my parents drove down to Florida to visit my uncle last year, my sisters and I hired a handyman to fix up a few things around their house. We said it was their Christmas gift. They appreciated it but they also hated it. They didn't want us replacing their kitchen sink. It didn't feel right to them and it doesn't matter if it's tied up in some weird layer of parent-child financial politics. People don't like feeling small."

He squeezed my leg. Lower this time, as if he knew we were nearing my parents' home and couldn't finger me in their neighborhood. "I don't disagree with you, Stella."

"Don't mention anything about cheese or concussions to my dad. If he asks, change the subject. Talk about the Patriots' depth chart. He has strong opinions on the matter."

"Should I expect that? A conversation about cheese?"

I shook my head slowly. "It could happen. Stranger things have."

It was his turn to hesitate. "Okay. Mary in the bathtub and the price of cheese. What else do I need to know?"

"Those are the biggies," I replied. "I mean, my older sister Sophia and her wife Kailey are hardcore into the dogs-as-children thing. My younger sister Serina has been known to throw hands over that but otherwise, no worries. Just don't weigh in on the dog-children topic if you want to get out unscathed."

"Right. The Madonna. Cheese. Dog-children. Got it." He nodded. "What's the long-story-short on your sisters?"

"Sophia is"—I blew out the exaggerated sigh that accompanied my older sister—"an executive life coach which basically means she helps CEOs and other high-ranking folks sort out their shit."

Cal glanced at me, his brows quirking up. "How does one get into that line of work?"

"Well, you start as a professional organizer," I said. "You go to people's houses and deal with their clutter. Then you move on from the clutter in their closets to the clutter in their heads."

"Fascinating," he murmured.

"Truly," I replied with a laugh. "She's been married about five years now. Her wife is a pastry chef and they have two dog-babies. Yorkies named Nemo and Dory. She has a low-key drinking problem in the sense lots of professional women have 'Isn't it cute that I'm drunk all the time?' drinking problems. She's functional, she never drinks before five o'clock on weeknights, and she never, ever gets incoherent or blackout drunk but she definitely needs that cocktail every night. She'll cut the bitch who gets between her and the Grey Goose. Serina and I keep going back and forth on what to do about it. We haven't solved that one yet."

I turned down the street leading to my parents' house, fighting back a quick swell of nerves.

Stella Stella Stella Stella. It's fiiiiiiiine.

"Serina runs a mom life blog. According to her, it started out as a fun thing she did to display photos of her kids. But I know she went to work on building it out and monetizing it. And she's succeeded. I don't know what she earns but I know it's decent. I think it covered their fully loaded, bells-and-whistles trip to Disney last year and it's paid for some really high-end photo equipment. To be honest, I think she started the blog as a way to cope with postpartum anxiety. She doesn't talk about it. She works hard at keeping a happy face regardless of how she's feeling, and I know she's on medication so that helps. Her husband Toby is great. He installs windows and roots for the Mets—"

"What?" Cal cried. "You allow that? You hated me because you thought I had Clemson laces."

"I did not hate you based on the Clemson laces. I just didn't have an interest in talking to you." I laughed. "Believe it or not, my father is the biggest Boston fan in my family."

"Wow," he replied. "Toby must have some balls of steel."

"I can't speak from personal experience but I'm told his balls meet expectations," I said. "They've been married forever. Serina's the youngest but does everything first. Married at nineteen. Pregnant at twenty." I shook my head, laughing. "They have three kids. Georgia, Preston, and Blaine." My parents' house came into view. "Don't worry. You'll do fine."

"Oh yeah?" he asked. "You don't sound too sure. You sound like you're feeding yourself some lies right now. How many have survived the Allesandro family inquisition without falling into the aforementioned death traps?"

I came to a stop in front of my childhood home and gulped down a surge of bile at that question. I had to press my fist to my lips to assure myself it wouldn't come back up. "You're the only one, Cal."

28

CAL

THIS WAS A BIG FUCKING DEAL. I'D KNOWN THAT GOING IN BUT to hear Stella say I was the only one to make her family's acquaintance? *Fuuuuuck.*

Obviously, they'd met the guy from before. The fiancé turned ex-fiancé turned fiancé turned dickhead. They knew him but, as Stella liked to put it, that was half a lifetime ago.

Fuuuuuck. That was all I could think as we climbed the front steps of her parents' home.

"If you want to score some points," she said under her breath, "mention the flower boxes."

I followed her gaze to the planters overflowing with early summer blooms on either side of Mother Mary in her bathtub shrine. "Noted," I murmured, bringing my hand to her lower back.

The door opened before we reached it and a wave of noise billowed out from the house. Dogs barked, children yelled, and Stella's family crowded the entryway. They all talked at once, shouting over each other and leaning forward to make their point heard and tossing impatient glares at each other.

Stella leaned into me as we stepped inside. "This is normal," she said. "Just go with it."

"I'm good," I replied, turning my head to speak directly into her ear. Her family was still fussing around us—dogs, children, adults—all wishing her a happy birthday and asking after the traffic because there had to be traffic for us to be late. "Are you all right?"

"After two orgasms, I better be," she said. "Don't blush unless you want them to know what we're talking about."

"It's a physiological reaction," I said. "You can't turn those things off."

Stella hit me with a grin before saying, "Hi, everyone! Yes, there was traffic. I didn't expect it on a Saturday evening and it slowed us down getting out of the city."

"They're always working on something," her father muttered. "Or they shut down three lanes to change a light bulb. Insanity."

"Always," she agreed. "And thank you for the birthday wishes. Like I've said, I'm not getting older, I'm just getting more fabulous."

"But you'll always be older than me," a woman—probably the younger sister Serina—said.

"Thanks," Stella drawled. "So good of you to mention that." She gestured toward me. "And this is Cal." She scooped up a small girl, no older than four or five, and set her on her hip. "Cal, this is Georgia. She's my favorite niece."

"Only niece," a little boy bellowed.

"That's Preston," Stella said with a nod toward the boy. I

waved. That seemed like a safe response. "And his older brother Blaine is over there, looking bored because he's eleven and we're *really* lame." She sent up a smiling eyeroll. "These are my sisters, Sophia and Serina. Serina is the youngest and she won't let you forget it."

I reached out to shake their hands. "It's great to meet you," I said. "I've heard the best things about you both."

"None of it is true," a man shouted from the back of the house. He headed toward us holding a small plate. His Mets t-shirt was hard to miss. "Hey, man," he called, a meatball halfway to his mouth. "I'm Toby."

I waved—he was too busy with the meatball to shake hands—while Serina said, "He's starved for dude friends so you'll have to forgive him if he gets a little clingy."

Sophia stepped forward, wagged a finger at Toby. He ignored her, taking Georgia from Stella's arms when she tried to wiggle free. "Kailey has served as a fine dude friend."

Glancing around the group, Stella asked, "Where is Kailey?"

"She's catering a big wedding tonight," Sophia replied. "If she can swing it, she'll be here later."

Stella pointed at the older man and woman who seemed to vibrate with excitement. "Cal, these are my parents, George and Christina. Mom, Dad. This is Cal."

George stuck out his hand but pulled me into a hug-backslapping-handshake combo. "Good to meet you, Cal," he said. "Thank you for sharing Stella with us on her birthday."

As she'd promised, her father was wearing jeans that had survived decades. He paired them with a t-shirt heralding a Patriots Super Bowl win from a handful of years ago and a Red Sox World Series hat.

"Thank you for having me," I replied. "Your flower boxes are remarkable."

That earned me another slap on the back and thirty more seconds of handshaking.

"Cal," Stella's mother repeated. "Is that your Christian name or is it short for something?"

"Mom," Stella warned. "No one calls it that anymore. Not unless they work in a Catholic church."

"I'm only wondering because Cal seems like a nickname and I want to make sure I type the right thing into the fuckin' Facebook and the goddamn Google when—"

"Oh my god," Stella said, her fingers flying to her temples. Serina made noise about swearing in front of the kids but Christina only waved her off. "Mom, okay. First of all, don't say that. Don't do it either. Just have a normal conversation with us. Second, I, uh"—she glanced at me, her eyes wide as wine bottles.

I reached out, pressing my palm to the spot between her shoulder blades where her muscles were tight and bunched. "It's Pascal," I said.

Stella swiveled her head toward me. "How did I not know that?"

I dug my knuckle into her lower trapezious. "You never got around to taking a picture of my driver's license, I guess."

"This moment is," Sophia started, her arms spread wide, "simply delightful."

Christina reached for us, grabbing me and Stella by the hand and leading us toward the dining room. "Time for supper," she said. "We'll talk at the table." As she delivered us to our assigned seats around the oval table, she shouted to the rest of the family. "Come on, everyone. You too, Blaine. You can make that sour face at the table. Toby, you make a plate for the baby. Sophia, don't think I can't see you pouring another drink. Put the vodka bottle down. Switch to water for a bit. We don't need you face-planting in your spaghetti and meatballs."

I shot Stella an arched eyebrow. "Balls?" I mouthed. "That's your birthday dinner?"

"All about those balls, 'bout those balls," she mouthed back. "No sausage."

I dropped my forehead to her shoulder as silent laughs shook my entire body. "Don't worry, Stel. I'll give you plenty of it later."

"I should hope so," she said, feigning some indignation. "But I really do love balls."

And I love you.

I almost said it. Almost ripped that truth from my mind and thrust it into existence. But a pair of dogs chose that moment to attack the hem of my jeans and Georgia shrieked about requiring a different bowl and Sophia slammed a cabinet shut and I wasn't certain she'd believe me. If I knew Stella, I knew she'd look at this everyday chaos and laugh away my words.

Hell, if she said those words to me right now, I'd laugh too. I'd hear "I love you...for coming here. I love you for putting up with this crazy. I love you for letting me make songs about balls—and sausage. I love you for walking past that Mary on the Half Shell without batting an eye."

But wasn't that it? Wasn't that the heart of it?

So, I did. I said it. I lifted my head from her shoulder, stared into those dark chocolate eyes, and whispered, "I love you."

Her cheeks tightened, her dimples popped. And she laughed, just as I'd suspected. Hoped, even. "Good," she replied. "Hold on to that sentiment. You're going to need it."

She didn't speak them back to me and I hadn't expected that. But it wasn't bittersweet. No, that response was perfect. It was everything I needed from her.

"What can I getya to drink?" George called to us.

"Red wine," Stella whispered. "Red wine and no one gets hurt."

29

STELLA

"WHAT ARE YOU THINKING ABOUT?" CAL ASKED, RUMBLY-grumbly as ever.

I glanced over at him as we drove back to the city. He had his arm on the lip of the passenger window, his head leaning on his palm. A smile played on his lips and his eyes sparkled with heat and I felt things. Big things. Really big things. Storage locker the size of Vermont things.

He'd told me he loved me. That didn't escape my notice. And he said it in that rumbly-grumbly way of his, a little bashful, a lot sweet. I just couldn't help myself with him.

But I said, "Nothing much. I have a busy week coming up. I'm due in New York for a few meetings on Tuesday and Wednesday." I looked at him again. I wasn't sure what I hoped to see there but he went on smiling and sparkling and making me feel things. "If everything goes as planned, McKendrick should be pitching next weekend."

"That will be a relief," Cal said. "For both of us."

I nodded. "Yeah." But then, thinking better of it, I asked, "What do you mean?"

He held up a hand, let it fall to his lap. "I mean, he's sucked up a ton of your time. You're always getting calls and texts. Running off to rescue him from himself. Chaperoning his ass all over town." He lifted his hand again. "I want him in the game just as much as you do. That's all."

I stared at the road ahead for a moment, lost in my feelings. There were so damn many of them. None I'd asked for, none I'd invited. But they were here now, crawling over me and gobbling up the air between us. If I had my way, I'd live a happy life without any of this hassle. And I wouldn't devote a single second to wondering whether Cal was wrong about this. Whether he was wrong about me. Whether I was the last stop on his way to finding the woman he was supposed to love. Whether I was the one before The One.

I'd be fine without all of this. Totally fine.

I avoided these feelings and attachments because I didn't want to be left behind anymore. But more than that, I didn't want to have this only to lose it. And that was the problem on my hands now. I had Cal and his bites and his grumbles and his quiet declarations at all the wrong times. I couldn't do without those things now. I had them and I wanted to keep them, claim them as mine—only mine.

Stellllllllla. Easy there.

I had to hold on real tight, blink back the fear of being passed over, and trust I'd make it through. I would. I'd make it through.

Eventually, I said, "You knocked it out of the park tonight."

"I had a good coach," he replied. "You sent me in warmed up and ready to hit."

I shrugged off his praise because Cal would've nailed it regardless of whether I schooled him on matters of the Madonna of the Bath and dog-children and pricey cheese. My family loved him because I loved him.

I wanted to panic at that. Pull over on the highway, jump out of the car, and shake the love bugs off. I wanted my life back, my happily calendared existence where I didn't have to think or care or do anything but smile my way through. But yet, I didn't. I didn't want that at all.

"The game did go into extra innings," I said, stepping all the way into this metaphor. "I figured the little rookies would've hit the benches sooner."

"The infusion of triple chocolate cake kept them in the game," he said. That cake wasn't on my birthday menu—I favored Dominican cake—but when my mother had the chance to coax a fudgy smile out of Blaine, she went for it. She also liked sending her grandchildren home buzzed on sugar and chocolate because Serina barely allowed either. "It kept me going after your father opened that fourth bottle of wine."

I laughed at that. "My parents were freaking out over the wine. They hung up on me the other night so they could argue about it."

"It is your birthday," he said mildly. "They're allowed to freak out over spoiling you."

That earned him another laugh. "It wasn't me they were worried about. It was you," I replied. "That's why the flower boxes were overflowing and the bathroom ceiling was freshly painted and my parents basically flailed over you for three hours."

"It's still about you, Stel," he replied. "They want you happy."

"Is that what I am? Happy?"

He paused, tilted his head to stare at me from a different direction. "I hope so," he replied.

I stared at the highway ahead. Delivering Cal to his Beacon Hill apartment meant meandering through Chinatown or taking the Tunnel to Storrow Drive. But the exit leading to Brookline's Buttonwood Village neighborhood was up ahead, beckoning us home.

My tiny Cape Cod style house was my sanctuary. A little spot I'd made my own over the years, fixing it up as much as I could, hiring out for renovations when I had the money. It was mine and never anyone else's. No calendar boys. I preferred it that way. I liked that separation of church and state.

I frowned at the exit one more time.

And then I took it.

As we traveled down the ramp, Cal asked, "Detour?"

"Sort of," I said.

We drove the rest of the way in silence, me with my gaze fixed on the road and Cal shooting curious glances at me. I didn't meet any of those glances. I couldn't. I couldn't see the fascination and adoration and love in his eyes without losing my will to do this. To bring him home and give him the last hidden pieces of me. Not yet.

When I pulled into the driveway, I wanted that panic back. I wanted to grab onto it and remind myself of all the reasons I'd reached this point. I wasn't broken. I was not. But I was afraid of breaking. I was afraid Cal would love me and leave me, and I didn't think I could bear that.

But I couldn't reach that panic. I couldn't get it back.

"Do you want to go in?" I asked, finally shifting toward him.

Cal studied the darkened house. "Maybe," he replied. "It depends on whether this is the super-secret lair of Stella Allesandro or you'd like to commit some birthday breaking and entering."

I dropped my head back against the seat as I laughed. "Is that how you celebrate your birthday, Cal? Breaking and entering?"

He unbuckled his seat belt, shook his head. "Yeah. That's how former Army Rangers do it."

"That's funny," I replied. "I thought that little performance in your bedroom was how Army Rangers did it."

"Yes on both counts." He reached over, cupped my cheek. I leaned into his touch. "Take me inside, Stella."

"Are you speaking about this"—I gestured down the length of my body—"or that?"—a nod toward the house.

"Yes on both counts," he repeated.

I melted into his easy touch, sighing in relief when he leaned forward and brushed his lips over mine. It was a gentle kiss, patient and unhurried as if he knew we had all the time in the world.

But...did we? Did we have time? Or was this bound to end like everything else always ended for me? My head was fogged in, thick with questions and doubts and hopes.

Cal released my seat belt and whispered, "Stay there. I'm coming to get you." As if I could've moved after that. He climbed out, rounded the car, his fingers gliding over the hood as he walked. He opened my door, took my hand as I gained my feet, and held out his palm. "Keys, Stella."

I handed them over as he swatted my backside. This was the kind of chivalry I wanted: open my door, smack my ass. "It's the one with the red nail polish. The side door," I said, nodding to the narrow set of stairs and small porch. "I only use the front door on Halloween."

"You must get a lot of kids in this neighborhood," he said, swinging his gaze up and down the quiet street. "This is nice. I can see why you'd keep it to yourself."

We walked up the driveway, our fingers laced together. He unlocked the door, held it open for me. A single light shone over the sink, the one I switched on every time I left home. I frowned at it for a moment, struggling to remember the last time I cleaned the bathrooms and changed the sheets. But Cal closed the door behind him and turned the lock, and none of that mattered. We stared at each other, smiling as if we were alone for the very first time.

Cal placed my keys on their hook. He took my bag from my shoulder, set it down. Then he brought his palms to my hips, pulled me close, pressed a kiss to my forehead. I looked up at him in the low light, nodded. "Come with me," I whispered. "I want to show you something."

I led him through the house, upstairs to the bedroom that had never before welcomed a man. I closed the door behind me, leaned back against the hard plane of wood. He turned in a slow circle, taking in the all-white space. White walls, white blankets, white pillows, white furniture.

"If you'd asked me," Cal started, "I never would've chosen this for you. But now that I'm here, I get it." He turned toward me. "I get it."

I kicked off my ballet flats. "What do you get?"

He tipped his head to the wall where four square canvases hung, each with a single curved line of black giving rise to the shape of a woman's body against the flood of white. "You," he replied simply. "I get you." He gestured to the bottom right canvas, the one hinting at the dent of a waist, the cleft of a backside. "I get the calm of this space. The absence of noise."

I shrugged out of my jean jacket, tossed it at the bench at the foot of the bed. I wasn't sure whether it landed. I was too busy staring at Cal, here, in my calm. I reached for that panic. Tried to get my hands around it one more time. But it wasn't there.

"I get your quirks," he continued, nodding at the abalone shell mermaid lamp on my bedside table, the one sporting a solid D-cup. "I get your mind, your heart."

I pushed away from the door, toward Cal. I went to him hands first, grabbing at his shirt and pulling him against me. "How?" I asked. "How do you do that? How do you know?"

I walked him back until his legs hit the bed. He sat, drew me between his legs, shifted his hands to my waist. Squeezed me there, like he wanted my skin to remember his fingertips. "I've always known. Even when it didn't make sense."

"That's crazy." I tangled my fingers in his hair while his hands shifted to my back, my thighs. "It's crazy, Cal."

"And yet here we are," he said with a lopsided grin.

"Here we are." My hands skated over his shoulders, down his arms and then up again. I brought my fingers to the buttons at the base of his throat, glanced up to meet his gaze. "Yes?"

He nodded. "Yes, Stella."

I freed each button while he studied me. His breath came in short, quick bursts against my cheek and that was enough to keep me from going in search of that panic again. At the end of the placket, I pushed the shirt over his shoulders before reaching for his belt. "Yes?"

Another nod, another, "Yes, Stella."

He leaned back, his hands anchored on the bed behind him as I worked his jeans open. His gaze never left me as I peeled his clothes from him. When his boxers hit the floor, I reached for the hem of my dress but he grabbed my wrist, stopping me.

"My turn, sweet thing," he said. The dress was up, over my head, gone in the blink of an eye. My bra and panties followed, separating from my skin without ceremony.

I smoothed my hand up his flank, over his chest and shoulder, pausing at the Army Ranger tattoo on his bicep. With my free hand, I reached between us, closed my fingers around his length. "Yes?" I asked, stroking him just enough to send his eyes rolling back.

"Yes, Stella. *Yes*," Cal answered.

He sucked in a breath as my lips ghosted over his neck, jaw, shoulders. I kissed every inch of skin I could reach and then went back for more, for every bit of him I could keep for myself. *Mine*. I squirreled away each rumble and grumble that slipped past his lips, all his sighs and hums and growls.

I edged onto the bed, planting my knees on either side of him. He nudged at my opening and I groaned at the feel of him, hot and hard and *mine*. But then, "I don't have any, um, I don't keep any because I don't, I mean, I never, not here—"

"In my wallet," he gritted out.

I blew out a frustrated breath and leaned into Cal, our foreheads pressed together. "Okay," I murmured, nodding. "I'll do that, you get comfortable."

"The only thing I need for comfort is your cunt so hurry up."

Oh, my rumbly-grumbly man-brick.

I hopped off his lap and went in search of his jeans. They were on the other side of the room because I couldn't simply strip his clothes off and leave them nearby, I had to fling them away like an insult. I dropped to the floor, patting the fabric for his wallet and then holding it in both hands when I found it.

"I meant what I said, Stella," Cal called. I spared him a glance and found him kicked back on the middle of my bed, voluminous pillows at his back and blankets like an avalanche around him. The rigid line of his jaw refuted his casual pose. The hand curled around his cock too. "Hurry up."

Flipping his wallet open, I smiled at the driver's license announcing his full name but went straight for the condom tucked in with the cash. I made a quick dash for the bed, straddling his legs as I opened the packet. I tipped my chin down, toward his shaft. "Yes?"

He gave me a slow nod as he shifted his hands to my hips. "Yes," he said. The way he gazed up at me, it was the most magnificent heat I'd ever known. Like he could warm me through with nothing more than a stare.

And hell, I wanted to do that for him. I wanted to fill him with all the things he needed.

His hips bucked when I reached for him, rolled the condom down his length. Once it was in place, I shifted, dragging my breasts over his chest, up to his mouth as I crawled to him. He sucked my nipple into his mouth as I guided him into me. He rested his hand on the small of my back, holding me in place and then pulling me down as he surged into me.

I looked down, watching as his body met mine. I'd never felt as powerful and beautiful and desired as I did when he was inside me, his grumbles and growls mixing with my sighs and whispers until we were one sound, one body. I closed my eyes, focused on the rasp of his teeth on my nipple and the fullness of his cock and the need in my blood and the love in my heart. And I stopped thinking. Stopped looking for my panic, my escape hatch. Stopped bracing myself against the inevitability of heartbreak. Stopped holding back, keeping safe.

I pushed up to straddle his hips, my hands flat on his chest and his cock fully seated inside me and his gaze burning me, branding me. My body moved on its own, knowing what we needed without direction or thought.

Cal's eyes drifted shut and then opened again, searing right through me as he thrust up, stole my breath, stole everything I had to give.

"I think," I said, my words panting out in jagged sylla-bles and tears filling my eyes, "I think I love you."

A snarl sounded in his throat. He reached up, thumbed away my tears, saying, "I think you do too."

30

CAL

Stella rolled off me with a high-pitched "Whoa" as she hit the mattress.

"Yeah," I agreed, reaching for her. "Whoa."

My hand connected with her belly, the underside of her breast. I wanted to look at her, see the damage we'd done to each other. But that required turning my head and I'd spent the last of my strength on blasting into the condom like I was trying to incinerate the thing.

I'd thought about it, more than once. Thought about what Stella would feel like with nothing between us. What she'd look like with me spilling out of her. And I thought about it now as I eased the rubber down my shaft and deposited it in a wad of tissues.

There was no explaining my desire to bite her, to watch my seed splash on her skin. Never had these urges presented themselves before this woman. When I really thought about it, nothing before Stella was worth remembering. It'd been satisfying, a bit basic. I'd never felt starved for a woman, never wanted to possess a woman in every way possible, never felt unleashed by her nod, her "yes."

But even at forty-two, there was a first time for everything. There had to be, because I'd never wanted to rip off a condom and pound into a woman while she told me she loved me before tonight.

I'd heard the words before but they sounded different this time around. Felt different too, as if there was a space deep inside me meant to hold them, keep them. A space I'd never accessed before.

Stella curled into my side, nestling her head on my chest. Her cheek was still damp. They seemed like good tears, happy tears, great sex tears. "Are you all right, sweet thing?" I ran my knuckles down her face. "What's happening here?"

"I don't know," she whispered. "I might be dying. Maybe it's a heart attack. I don't know."

I reached across my body, pressed my hand between her breasts, just over the organ hidden behind layers of tissue and bone. It pounded fast, steady. "You're fine," I said. "Just well-fucked."

"That's all," she answered. "Like I'm not still seeing stars and remembering what my face feels like."

I glanced down at her with a grin. "Like I said, you're fine. You're just perfect."

"I want to tell you something but it might change your opinion of me," she said. "I need you to prepare for that."

"Unlikely." I brushed her hair over her shoulder, trailed my fingertips down her spine. Nothing could change my opinion of her. "Out with it, sweet thing."

"Okay, okay," she said. "Even though we just had a ton of

spaghetti and meatballs the size of Georgia's head and an entire chocolate cake, I could really go for some pizza right now."

As if on command, her stomach sent up a loud gurgle.

"You're probably thinking to yourself, 'Wow. This girl is a bottomless pit,'" she continued. "And that is true but you have to agree this"—she gestured to the sheets ripped clear off the corners of the mattress and the pillows piled on the floor—"was a little athletic. Like a marathon. I basically burned off all that pasta."

"And now you're ready for pizza," I said.

"That's right."

I kissed the top of her head, breathed in the scent of her. This moment right here—us naked and spent, the bed in shambles, the bond between us unbreakable—was only the beginning. There were years and years of this ahead of us.

"You stay here," I said, shifting her head onto the one pillow we hadn't lost in the struggle. I caged her in, my hands on her wrists and my knees tight on her hips. "I'll find my phone and order some pizza. Unless you threw my pants out the window."

"I might've," she said, laughing. "Things got a little rowdy."

I dropped a kiss on her lips. Went back for another. I couldn't imagine how it was possible but I felt my cock stiffening on her thigh. *Fuck me.* I was mad for this woman. Just fucking gone for her. "I like you rowdy."

She glanced down the length of my body, stared at my cock long enough for it to throb for her, and then smiled, hitting me with the full force of her dimples. As if she required that last inch of my surrender. "I wasn't the only rowdy one."

I tipped my head to the side, offered a small shrug of agreement. "You didn't seem to mind."

She shook her head, pursed her lips together. Peered at me as if she was trying to see me with new eyes. "What do you want, Cal? What do you really, really want?"

I dropped my head between her breasts, scraped my teeth over her skin. "You're all I want, Stella."

"Yeah, you've mentioned something like that before," she said. "You're going to let me up and I'm going to the bathroom. When I get back, we can keep being rowdy and honest and real."

I murmured my agreement, not ready to part ways with her breasts. "I'll order that pizza."

"Let me find my phone," she said, wiggling away from me. I dropped onto the mattress, buried my face in her pillow. "Use my food delivery app. It's easier since my address is plugged in." She took my hand, placed the device in my palm. "Here you go. Make good choices."

"Is this a test?" I asked, shifting away from the pillows. "If I order the wrong thing, will you send me packing?"

She bobbed her head from side to side as she considered this. "I can think of some truly heinous pizza toppings but I know you. I know what you like." She pointed to me. "And you know what I like."

I watched while she pulled on a short, dark green robe with little white pompoms along the edge. The fabric skimmed over her body like an oil slick. "I do," I replied, still captivated by the wide flare of her hips, the luscious curve of her breasts. I wanted to wrap that thin belt around my fist while I fucked her from behind.

Fuck me.

But the truth was, I'd feel this way about every piece of clothing in Stella's closet. I'd see ratty old sweatpants and want to rub her clit through them. I'd see a dress and want to yank it up, sit her on my cock. I'd bite her nipples through thick winter sweaters and slide my fingers up the leg of summer shorts.

"Order wisely." She slipped out of the room, her silky robe fluttering as she went. I stared after her for a moment, too love drunk and cock hungry to do anything else.

And then her phone vibrated in my hands.

It was habit that drove me to look down, read the messages flashing across her screen.

Harry: Hey. Wanted to say hi. I miss your face.
Harry: I want to see you this week. Monday night. Just come by my place when you're off work and we'll hang out.

HABIT DROVE me to read those messages but a gut-punched blend of curiosity and horror drove me to go looking for others from Harry. Who I fucking hated. Who the fuck was named Harry anymore? Awful fucking name.

There was only one previous message, dated a couple of weeks ago.

Harry: Are you ending this?

THERE WAS no response from Stella. No response.

I stared at the timestamp, the date. I'd spent more than a month's worth of mornings walking with her at Jamaica Pond when that message had arrived. I'd shared at least twenty evenings with her. I'd tasted her cunt and bitten her ass and asked her to marry me and she hadn't responded.

I dropped the phone as if it'd stung me.

Suddenly, the rucked-up sheets and scattered pillows that represented every one of my dreams and desires now chafed my skin. I darted off the bed, snatched my clothes from the floor. My shirt was inside-out but I didn't care. My only concern was getting the hell out of here.

I couldn't stay. I couldn't look at Stella after tonight—after everything—without demanding an explanation. But I knew what was coming to me. I'd accepted the terms. I'd known her conditions. And I'd stayed in spite of them. I'd believed I could outlast those men and I thought I had.

But it wasn't the men I was working to outlast. It was Stella.

I shoved my hands into my pockets, hoping to find my phone. The one with a stunning shortage of women asking me to "hang out" with them. When I located it, I went straight for the car service app and thanked all the deities for GPS because I didn't know which fucking town I was in right now. And why would I know where Stella lived? Why the fuck would I know the name of the street she lived on or the number of guys who begged her to hang out in any given week?

I ordered the first driver I could find and went in search of my shoes. If I didn't find them in the next nine seconds, I was leaving without them. Fuck shoes. Who needed them? Shoes, women who told you they love you, orgasms that made you believe in heaven. None of it was necessary. Fuck it all.

Then Stella stepped inside the bedroom, her skin rosy and her hair gathered on the top of her head. She looked like a fucking angel and I hated Harry even more. In that moment, I hated Stella too. Hated her for being honest with me from the start, for letting me fall for her, for standing by while I built this fantasy world where all I had to do was love her harder, love her better than those guys. And I hated her for loving me in return because why bother if she wouldn't end it with Harry? Why say it if she couldn't be bothered to tell Harry it was over? Why allow me to belong to her if it wasn't meant for more than a minute?

Her smile faltered as she took in my jeans, my inside-out shirt. "What's wrong?" she asked. "Did you get paged?"

Yes. That was the answer. Far better than *You're still seeing other guys and I told you I love you and you said it back and now I have to kill a douchebag named Harry.*

"Yeah. I'm leaving," I replied, the words exactly as sharp as they needed to be. "I have to go."

"Okay," she said, pulling her robe tight. "Do you want me to drive you or—"

"No," I snapped, still looking for my damn shoes. Even with my gaze glued to the floor, I saw her recoil at my words. "No, Stella. I'm going and you're staying right there."

She banded an arm over her waist, gathered the lapels of her robe in her other hand and held it to her breastbone. "Oh. Oh, okay." She nodded as if she understood—she didn't—and lifted a pillow, revealing my shoes. "Here you go."

I didn't look at her. Couldn't. Couldn't melt for those dimples again. Couldn't see forever in her eyes and then walk away. Couldn't risk accepting the pittance she offered me because I would. I'd take this fractional part of her life and pretend I was okay with it. I'd do that until the day I lost my shit and actually killed Harry. And that day would be tomorrow.

"Thanks," I barked.

It sounded like a slap and the way she stumbled back told me it landed that way too. Good. I wanted her to hurt.

"Do you want to come back? When you're done?" she asked. "I don't care if it's late. I'll give you a key and you can—"

"No," I replied. "No, I'm not coming back here."

"All right," she said slowly. "What about tomorrow? Do you want to get brunch or go for—"

"No," I repeated. "Not tomorrow. Definitely not tomorrow."

"Definitely not tomorrow," she repeated. "Okay. What about Monday? Will I see you Monday at the pond? Will you be there like usual?"

I jerked a shoulder up while I tied my shoes. "It depends on how the weekend goes, Stella. I can't predict what will happen with my patients and they come first. You can't expect anything more from me."

Out of the corner of my eye, I saw her bobbing her head

as she processed my words. Through the dull ache of this moment, I knew I was being harsh. Excessively so. But I was too fucked up to protect her feelings. If anything, I wanted to wound her. I wanted to hit her with all the harshness I had in me, just rip her the fuck open. I wanted her to know what it was like to be kept in the dark. To be left scrounging for scraps.

"Cal, I don't know what's happening," she whispered. "What did I do?"

I spied my wallet on the floor, plucked it up before glancing at her. I shouldn't have. Fuck, no. Should've ditched the shoes and the wallet and skipped that last look because it broke me. My chest was heavy and my head pounded and I couldn't manage a deep breath and it fucking broke me.

But I looked again, stared at her this time. I memorized her big, dark eyes and the tears shining back at me. Her pinched brow, her bottom lip snared between her teeth. Her glossy hair sliding loose from her bun, one tendril after another. Her arm folded over her waist, the other across her chest as if protecting her vital organs.

Stella broke me and I'd asked for it.

I cut a wide swath around her, calling over my shoulder, "You can let Harry know you're free this week."

31

CAL

"Hey."

I opened my eyes and found Stremmel staring down at me, his arms folded over his chest.

"What are you doing here? Tonight's game seven of the Stanley Cup Finals. Doesn't your girlfriend get free tickets to those things? Shouldn't you be with her?"

"Not my girlfriend," I answered, shutting my eyes again.

I'd managed to steer clear of this conversation in the handful of days since running out of Stella's house like my hair was on fire. It meant dawdling in post-op and spending an excessive amount of time drilling my residents during rounds and inviting myself into a few cath lab cases to avoid lunch with my friends but I didn't count that as a loss. No, the real loss would've come in the form of Nick and Alex blinking at me with a mixture of pity and *we told you so*. Them reminding me I'd spent eight months imagining her, and in the two months I had her, never relinquished my Stella-in-the-sky ideals. Never believed her when she told me where she stood and what she wanted.

"I don't care if she's Joan of fuckin' Arc, if she can get you into that game, you're morally obligated to go," he cried. "Can she get tickets for me? If she did, I'd be her personal pony and let her ride me down to the Garden tonight."

You and Harry.

I wanted to slap myself. I hated the noise in my head right now. Resenting her for doing exactly what she told me she did wasn't helping anyone. But I was finished hating her. If I ever did. Probably not. I missed her and I ached for her, and I wanted things to be different. I wanted to be enough for her. I wanted to change her too, but only this one small issue.

It was small but it was major.

"That paints a picture," I grumbled.

"Hartshorn," he snapped. "Seriously. What the fuck is going on with you? What are you doing on the floor?"

I pressed the heels of my palms to my eyes with a groan. God, I was tired. Even with claiming an extra hour of sleep because there was no fucking way I could go back to the pond, I was exhausted and sore. I'd never known the pain of heartbreak, never considered it manifested itself as true physical distress. And this was one heart I couldn't fix.

"I'm on the floor because I dropped my pager and I didn't feel like getting up after I put it back together."

He circled his hand at me, wanting me to elaborate. "Why are you here?"

I shrugged. "I'm here because I was paged."

Stremmel rolled his eyes at the ceiling. "This exchange is not amusing," he said. "You're not on call. Who paged you? Better question, why are they paging you when you're not on call *and* you should be at game seven? Have we no values around here?"

I considered him for a moment. "You're a hockey fan, Stremmel? Wouldn't have guessed that."

Another eyeroll. I could almost hear it, like winding an old-fashioned clock. "I'm a fan of championship games," he said. "That shit is far more interesting than slogging it out through the regular season. I know that knocks me down a few pegs as far as true fans go but I won't apologize."

"Wouldn't ask it," I replied.

"Who paged you?" he asked. "I want to know who doesn't respect protocol. I want to yell at someone."

I waved him off. "It's not that," I said. "My resident paged me instead of the on-call attending because he knew the on-call wasn't going to handle the issue the way I wanted. My resident did everything right."

"Which one?" he asked, glancing down at his phone. "O'Rourke? Or Popov?"

"O'Rourke. How'd you guess?"

"Your favorites are easy to spot. For a guy with your background, you're not so good with the poker face." Stremmel motioned toward my clothes. "Whatever it was, it couldn't have been that important if you haven't changed. And I'm still annoyed you're here over a page that didn't require scrubbing."

"You keep on being annoyed," I replied. "It works for you."

He peered at me, his head tipped to the side. "I think you're looking for an excuse to hang out here."

"You know all about that. Don't you, Stremmel?" I asked, pushing to my feet. I stood for a second then dropped onto a bench. "You think I don't notice you coming in on your days off?"

"None of those days featured the final game of a playoff series." He glanced at his watch then back at me. "God-damn. I was supposed to leave three hours ago. Are you finished here or what?"

"Yeah," I replied. "I'm not scrubbing tonight."

He held up his hands. "Since you're obviously not going to the game, you can buy me a beer."

"I'm not the best company tonight."

Stremmel pressed his palm to his chest. "I've never in my life been good company. Hasn't stopped you from dragging me to holiday parties and happy hours and everything in between."

"That's what I do, Stremmel," I snapped. "I drag people along and make them do things even when they tell me they don't want to and it's not their way and it's never something they'll want. I figure they'll start to like it."

He snapped his fingers, motioned for me to stand up. I didn't. "You can buy me a beer but I have conditions," he said. "I don't want to talk about anything. At all. Ever. We're just having beer. We're not discussing your problems or my problems. No teachable moments, no life coaching, no management conversations about five-year plans or growth potential. Just beer."

Stremmel turned toward his locker as he changed out of his scrubs. I glanced down at my phone, hoping to see a text from Stella because I'd hoped for that since the minute I left her house. I wanted her to send me long messages about misunderstandings and it not being the way it looked and correcting my assumptions. I wanted her to tell me I was wrong and I wanted her to be right about that.

"I mean it," he continued. "No mentoring, Hartshorn."

"I take it you've noticed my efforts," I said.

"They're hard to miss, dude," he replied. "You're pretty overt about your intentions. If you're trying to do something, it's difficult to tune that shit out."

"Thank you for humoring me," I said. "I'm realizing I'm not as successful at bending people to my will as I thought."

He turned, his shirt bunched under his chin as he buckled his belt. "You're decent about it," he said. "I've met some real assholes but you're decent." He smoothed his shirt down, shoved his phone and pager in his pockets. "You're not about preaching at people or wrist slapping. You're not a douche. And it's not all about the ego with you either. You're not a leapfrogger, you don't use people. You're just a decent dude who puts in the work without expecting much in return."

I pointed toward the door. "So, that's what you're doing with this feedback. Awesome."

Stremmel shook his head, muttering to himself, "I'm not in LA anymore."

"I guess it's a market. I don't know. They sell ravioli," I continued, "but they have a counter in the back. You have to buy some pasta first and put a good tip in the jar, and then ask for a seat. All cash. I don't think it's completely legal but they'll hand you a jelly jar of wine to go with the raviolis. Heavy pour and they keep it full. Things aren't so bad with a jelly jar of wine and some noodles."

"That sounds like going to confession."

"Not far off," I replied.

"You want to get ravioli and wine," he said, as if it was the strangest thing he'd ever heard. "You and me in a back room in the North End, drinking some under-the-table wine. During the National Hockey League's championship game. That's what you want to do."

"Well, I don't have tickets to the game and I don't want to watch the game because with my luck, I'll probably see a shot of Stella in a private box with a douchey guy named Harry all up on her and then I'll throw a massive clot and die of an aneurysm. So, yeah. I want to eat some fucking ravioli and drink a gallon of fucking wine, and I won't want to talk about a fucking thing."

Stremmel crossed his arms over his chest as he stared at the ceiling, nodding to himself. Eventually, he said, "This Harry guy. You need me to get some sodium thiopental and some potassium chloride? Make it look like an accident? Army Ranger style?"

My shoulders fell as I blew out a sigh. "While I appreciate your willingness to be an accomplice, I'd rather not kill the guy." I brought my hand to the back of my neck, rubbed the ceaseless tension there. "I don't even want to see him. Or any of the others."

He stared at me for a moment, his eyes narrowed and his brows knit. Then he said, "Is it good wine? I can't drink shitty wine. Gives me migraines."

I bobbed my head. "I've only been there once but it was decent. Better than decent, actually."

"All right," he conceded. "I guess we're getting wine and ravioli because I don't want to have your aneurysm on my watch."

We made our way to the North End, walking in companionable silence while the city around us held a collective breath through the final game of the hockey championship. We circled the block twice before finding the tiny shop with *Fresh Ravioli* painted on the window. After arguing about our order for longer than was logical, we found ourselves seated at a low bar with old wicker chairs.

Stremmel held up his makeshift wineglass. "We have nothing to toast. We won't be doing that," he announced. "If you need to talk about something, you can tell me about battlefield surgeries."

I split a ravioli open. It felt good to stab something. "No," I said simply. "I don't want to talk about the war right now."

"That's disappointing," he said around a mouthful of pasta and cheese.

"You know what's really disappointing? Falling in love with a woman only to find out she doesn't believe she's meant for relationships or monogamy or marriage. How is that even fucking possible? Yeah, sure, everyone's had a few bad ones. That doesn't mean you can't pick yourself up and move on. Doesn't mean you can't have a good one. But to avoid them altogether? Foreclose the possibility because your ex got married ten minutes after ending it with you? No. No, I don't buy it. I can't."

"I am literally the last person you should be asking for relationship advice, man." Stremmel glanced around the shop. "Let's grab the ravioli lady or someone off the street to talk to you because they'll be more qualified for this conversation than I am."

"Yeah? Who fucked you over?"

He glanced away, bringing his attention to the wine, the food, the odd surroundings. He was silent for a long beat, and then, "No one. No one fucked me over. I did it all by myself." He pointed to the front of the shop. "But I'm serious about pulling someone off the street because the only advice I can give you is on the topic of treating crush injuries."

"I don't need advice," I said.

"Neither do I but you keep giving it," he replied with a laugh.

"Then we won't talk," I said.

"Perfect," Stremmel said.

IT WAS LATE when I got back to my apartment. After midnight but before dawn. I had no sense as to which was nearer. I didn't return home with much sense at all. To make matters worse, the wine was playing tricks on my mind. It had to be the wine. Why else would I spend ten minutes standing in the middle of my kitchen, reaching for a woman who was only there in my mind? But I was convinced she was there. I believed it. I could see her at the stove and smell the spices and hear her talking. I wanted more than anything for it to be real rather than a memory.

That desire sent me to the bedroom. I wanted to find her there, to feel her under me. I flopped facedown onto the bed, desperate to find the scent of her lingering in the sheets and pillows. I found none. But I should've expected that. I should've known she'd leave and take everything with her. I should've known I wasn't playing for keeps.

Dragged down by that bitter realization, I surrendered to sleep with my shoes still on and the bed linens rucked up around me. It was just like being in Stella's bed. But a thousand times worse.

32

CAL

I STORMED OUT OF THE OPERATING ROOM, RIPPING MY surgical gown off as I pushed through the double doors. The surgery was successful, my resident performed competently, the patient was likely to recover without incident. Regardless, I was holding on to this foul mood. I was doing my damnedest to keep it localized rather than dumping it on the people around me. But this door, this gown—they were free game.

Stremmel fell in step with me. "I know I'm the last person to suggest this," he said, shoving his hands in the pockets of his white coat. "But you might want to fix your face. People are worried."

"About what?" I snapped, forcing another pair of doors open.

"Nothing much," he replied. "Nearly ripping doors off their hinges is fine. Everything is fine."

"I don't care about the door. I've been in surgery for nine hours and I need something to eat," I said. Even through the fog of this mood, those words sounded needlessly sharp. "Fuck it. I'm going across the street. To the park."

I'd managed a full week without discussing my crash and burn with anyone, save for Stremmel. Not that he allowed me to say much. I'd also avoided the pond. I'd driven near there three mornings ago but quickly turned around and headed for the gym. I hated the gym.

Stremmel made a sound of disapproval as he stepped in front of the next set of doors. "I can't recommend that," he said. "Emmerling and Acevedo are talking weddings and honeymoons. Just speaking for myself here but I can't stomach that shit."

"Oh, hell," I grumbled. With Stremmel blocking the door, I was forced to pace. "I'm not hungry anymore."

"Unlikely story," Stremmel replied. "I'm blowing off the happily coupled table. I found a place around the corner with decent pizza by the slice."

"Would we be friends or whatever this is"—I gestured toward him—"if we didn't get food together?"

He jerked a shoulder up. "Is that a problem? I can't see how it is. It's not like I can eat three meals a day in the cafeteria while also putting up with your moods."

I swung a glance toward him, tapped my chest. "*My* moods?"

"It's just a slice of pizza, Hartshorn. One I'm expecting you to buy," he continued. "It's not like we're taking yoga classes together. Does it matter that we only hang out when there's food involved? No. Would I hang out with you if you weren't picking up the tab? Also no." He snapped his fingers. "If you don't mind, I spent the morning putting a pair of fools back together after they fell off a bridge trying to take a selfie. I need some carbs and caffeine to make me happy."

I stopped wearing the linoleum thin, tossed a frown in his direction. "The carbs and caffeine are going to make you happy? That's the magical combination?"

He rolled his eyes. "As happy as I get, Hartshorn." He beckoned toward me with both hands. "I'll go without you if you don't get your shit together right now."

"Are you inviting me to join you?"

He dropped his head back against the door, shrugging. "Only if you promise to keep your problems to yourself."

"I can do that."

Stremmel kicked the doors open and gestured for me to follow him. "Starting now," he warned, "you can be miserable but don't involve me in your misery."

We walked in silence, down the stairs, out of the building. The sun was high in the sky and the air was warm and scented with summer. Objectively, it was a nice day. But I couldn't appreciate any of it. Just like the song said, there was no sunshine when she was gone.

Halfway through devouring his slice, Stremmel announced, "I like this crust."

I stared at the pizza but couldn't recall tasting it. "Yeah," I agreed. "It's all right."

"Not like California pizza," he continued. "But I dig it."

I looked up at him, my brow pinched tight. "I hope you didn't strain yourself admitting there's one thing you like about this town."

Stremmel considered his pizza with a quiet chuckle. "I might deserve that."

"How do you do it?" I asked. "How are you miserable every damn day?"

He didn't answer right away, instead finishing his slice, thoroughly wiping his hands, and draining a can of soda. "Are you asking for pro tips? Lessons?" He looked me up and down. "Doesn't look like you need my help."

"It's not advice I want," I replied. "I want to know how you live this way. My head is a fucking minefield and I can feel my arteries hardening from bitterness alone. I hate everything. I scowled at a dog this morning and I don't even know why. How do you handle this—this condition? I've been at it for a little more than eight days and I'll do anything to make it go away."

"If you find the remedy, let me know," he said. "I've been at it for a little more than thirty-eight years."

33

STELLA

Four things happened after Cal walked out of my house.

I broke my long-standing routine of walking at the pond every morning and acquainted myself with the gym on the ground floor of my office building.

McKendrick's suspension ended. He followed up his first appearance on the mound by conducting locker room interviews in a towel with one foot propped on a stool while the family jewels peeked out at reporters.

I earned my promotion, though to hear Rebecca tell it, she gifted it to me out of the goodness of her cold, dark heart. The little office party she threw for me was also a gift, one I wasn't allowed to forget. I sobbed over my cake and champagne after everyone left.

And I ended my relationships with Stephen, Leif, and Harry. Of all these things, that was the easiest. So easy I couldn't believe I'd waited this long to do it. But that was my problem, wasn't it? I stuck with things even when I knew they weren't working. I held on long after it stopped serving me.

I accomplished all that and endured multiple phone calls from my sisters and parents. They were too hopped up on their newfound obsession with Cal to keep their gushing contained to texts. Everyone wanted to know where was it going and would I bring him around for another family dinner and wasn't he wonderful?

Yeah. He was.

Serina insisted Cal was ready to wife me up. I laughed at that, both the phrase and the constant reminder I wasn't The One. Not for Cal, not for anyone.

Sophia said I deserved a man like Cal after all of my "bad luck." That I'd put my vision for a healthy relationship out into the universe and the universe sent back Cal. I laughed at that too because it was hilarious in a cruel, painful way. I'd never asked for Cal and I'd kept that fact in the foreground of my mind right up until the night he walked away.

Mom begged for Cal's mother's phone number. That yielded another hearty laugh. She wanted to befriend my future mother-in-law and who could blame her?

My father was the worst of them because he simply said he was happy for me. I didn't laugh. I cried. Ugly, snotty sobs punctuated by shuddering breaths and sniffles and hiccups. Dad thought they were happy tears and I didn't have the heart to tell him otherwise.

But really, I didn't have the heart to say it out loud. Didn't want to tell them I'd lost another good guy, and not just a good guy but the best guy. The very best of them. The one who accepted me as I came, who waited for me, who wanted me all the way.

Cal was the best of them.

———

DESPITE GETTING McKendrick back in the game, I wasn't rid of him. Not yet.

His contract with me ran through the end of the calendar year which was good for the purposes of continuity but terrible for my patience. It was hard to keep a smile on my face when I woke up to nineteen text messages from him, all relating to the whereabouts of his scrambled eggs.

It was even harder to keep that smile while he refused to prepare for his first major on-air interview since returning to the mound. We were in Bristol, Connecticut for a taping of SportsCenter and my client was too busy doing pushups to review talking points.

"We have half an hour before you're in makeup," I said, rolling my eyes as he launched into jumping jacks. "You're going to sweat through that shirt—"

"Then find me a new one," he replied.

Ignoring him, I continued, "and you need to clean up your response about learning from your mistakes."

"No mistakes, no remorse," he panted out with each jumping jack. "If they got a problem with that, fuck 'em."

I reached for my water bottle with a sigh. "While I happen to believe fuck 'em is a great philosophy, I can't let you lead with that on ESPN."

He stopped, reached for the floor, and pushed into a

handstand as he said, "You're salty as fuck today." From his upside-down perch, he shot a glance at me. "What's wrong with you, honeycakes?"

"Just off the top of my head, you're doing handstands while I'm trying to run through interview responses," I said. "There's also the issue of you texting me your breakfast order as if your trainer isn't sending meals to your house every morning."

"Nah, that's not it," he drawled, kicking out of that position and into another round of pushups. "Are you havin' troubles with your man?"

Like I needed the reminder.

I wanted to put my head down and cry, right here in the green room. Instead, I said, "McKendrick, seriously. We don't have a lot of time and you need to nail this."

"Either you tell me about your man problems," he threatened, "or I drop my pants and go balls out on ESPN. You can tell them it's for my nut cancer advocacy."

I pressed my fingertips to my temples with a sigh. "Why did I ever give you that idea?"

"Come on, lady. This place is boring and I need something to entertain me. Tell me about this man." McKendrick stood, whipped his shirt off. "Is he jealous of me? Doesn't like me sliding into your messages every day and hangin' with you at big parties?" He watched as he flexed his bicep, grinning at the bulge. "I'd be jealous of me."

"Naturally," I replied. "But no, it's not about you. Not really."

His smile widened. "A little bit?"

"No," I said, but then, "I mean, you didn't help."

McKendrick patted his bare abs. "I'm hard to resist."

I spared him an impatient glare. "I'm resisting just fine," I said. "But I think we can agree you're a little extra, Lucian."

He ran his palm over his belly. "I'm a jackass. I like jack-assing. That's what my ma calls it, jackassing." He shoved his hand under his belt. I looked away. "Sometimes I do some stupid shit and sometimes I jackass all over the place but I didn't mean to mess up your thing, honeycakes."

Oh, this was it. This was the moment when it all went to shit. When I cried in front of a client and let it all out in the ESPN green room. And it was Lucian McKendrick's fault.

"You didn't, McKendrick." I gulped down a rush of tears. "I'm the problem. It's me."

He zigzagged a finger at me. "Not from where I'm standing it's not."

I gained my feet, turning away from him. I went in search of tissues and when I found them, I made it my busi-ness to fold one into a perfect, crisp square. "It's sweet of you to say that but trust me, I'm the issue here. I'm the one who fucked it up. I always do."

"What's this shit?" he asked, right over my shoulder. "You're the fixer. You don't fuck nothing up."

I tossed the tissue square to the side, went for another. "Well, I fucked this up. And I shouldn't be surprised. Not really. I'm always the one they leave."

"You can't drop this shit and expect me to roll with it," he said. "Not without some explaining."

I balled the tissue in my fist as I whirled on him. "You want an explanation? Okay, cool. Cool. You're on camera within the hour but let's spend our time talking about me and how I don't do relationships but I went for it this time. I thought it would be different even though I was scared. I didn't want to get close to another guy only for him to walk away and meet the woman he's going to marry. But I did it and I fucked it up and now it's over."

An unpleasant noise rasped in his throat, something like phlegm and annoyance. "That's some *Cosmopolitan* shit. 'I didn't want to get hurt so I didn't put myself out there.' Like, 'I didn't believe in love until love believed in me.'" He pulled a scowl, shook his head. "I thought you were better than that."

"Not good enough to get out of my own way," I replied. "Sorry to disappoint you."

"But you're the fixer, lady. People fuck things up and you fix them. They fuck up again and you fix it better. Then you fix it harder so they can't step in the same shit a third time. You've gotta be able to fix your own things," he said, exasperated.

"It's not that simple—"

"Oh, it's fuckin' simple," he roared. "You just stop jack-assing, lady."

A watery laugh burst from my lips. "I did that already," I said. "I took the jackassery out back and buried it."

His eyebrow arched up. He stared me down like I was a rookie clutching the bat with sweaty palms. "And now you're gonna fix it with your man."

I rolled the balled-up tissue between my palms. "I don't think I can. I hurt him."

He gestured to himself with a showman's smile. "I've hurt tons of people, honeycakes. I've pissed on them too. But then I go on TV and flash my puppy dog eyes and promise to be a good boy. There's always a way to make it better."

I stared at the floor for a long beat. Too long for McKendrick's liking.

"Listen, lady. You're gonna stop with this advice column shit. Put *The Secret* down. When you get back to Boston, you're gonna fix it with your man."

"I appreciate the sentiment," I said, glancing up at him. "But it's not as though I can apologize and poof, everything is better. There's more—"

"Bullshit," he interrupted. "I'm living proof that people are willing to forgive just about anything. Before you tell me that you did something unforgiveable, please think about all the times I've done unforgiveable things and all the times I've been forgiven."

"Because you bring home wins," I argued, still worrying the tissue. "League wins. World Series wins. You are the guy who shuts it down and that's why they forgive you."

He nabbed the tissue from my hands. "How are we any different, lady?" When I didn't respond, he continued, "We're not different."

"It's been almost two weeks," I protested. "I haven't even reached out to him because—because what do I say at this point? Like, 'Oh, hey. Remember when I was awful and then did nothing to resolve the situation for half a damn month? Well, my schedule opened up and I'd like to resolve it now.'"

"Do you overthink everything or do you limit it to the dudes in your life?" he asked. "The romantic dudes, not the athletic dudes."

I gathered myself together enough to look affronted. "I'm not overthinking."

He snorted out a laugh. "This is the definition of overthinking. So what if a guy got married after ending things with you? That's fuckin' life, lady. Players get traded. Things change. You move the hell on."

"It happened more than once," I said, my voice as feeble as the argument felt.

"I watch a lot of game tape. My games, everyone else's games. But I don't keep playing that shit. I don't go back to my rookie year, pick my worst night of the season, and revisit every bad pitch. I don't spook myself out of bringing the firepower today because of shit from yesterday."

"I understand what you're trying to do and I appreciate having a conversation with you that doesn't involve bar fights, testicles, or scrambled eggs," I said, "but the situations aren't perfect comparisons."

McKendrick shook his head, chuckled. "This man of yours, he'll forgive you. Apologize, promise to do better, give him some good loving. I bet he's dying to see you."

I looked up at him. He had too much energy for one human, an unnatural fascination with putting his berries on display, and couldn't stop creating drama for himself. He was also the voice of reason.

"It's the bottom of the ninth. All tied up. Time to rally." He tossed my tissue ball into the wastebasket on the other side of the room. "Okay?"

I forced a smile, nodded. "Okay."

IT WAS HOT TODAY. Sunny, no clouds. It felt like summer. Lemonade and flipflops and fireworks an hour after sunset. I loved those things. I looked forward to them all winter long. But now that they were here, I couldn't summon any enthusiasm. I didn't want to watch fireworks alone. Didn't want to show off a new pedicure without Cal to compliment my toes. I didn't want to do anything.

But I had to—I had to fix this.

The middle of my team's late afternoon huddle wasn't the right time to formulate that solution but Tatum and Flinn had everything under control without the benefit of my full attention.

Or so I thought.

Flinn tapped Tatum on the arm and announced, "We're together."

I sat back in my desk chair, crossed my arms over my chest, and narrowed my eyes at them. "I'm sorry. What? What did you say?"

They exchanged a quick glance, some mouthed words. Tatum leveled a sharp glare at Flinn as she shook her head. He shifted in his seat, crossed his legs.

I didn't have the patience for this, whatever it was. I'd barely slept after returning home from the ESPN studios last night and I had other priorities to tend today. I went to the pond this morning with the hope of seeing Cal but he wasn't there. I'd dragged myself around that trail while listening to all the sad songs by The Backstreet Boys and then forced myself to walk another loop. It served the dual purposes of compensating for the rough night and allowing me to stick around in case Cal was avoiding our usual time.

It hadn't occurred to me he'd avoid our usual place.

After an exceedingly awkward pause, Flinn repeated, "We're together."

I swiveled my chair to the side and stared out at the city.

"Meaning what?" I asked, not looking back at them. "Don't leave this up to inference, Flinn. Specifics, please."

"Specifically, we are dating," Tatum said. "We've been—uh—hanging out, I guess, for a little while now and we"—I saw her motion toward Flinn—"decided to make it official."

I brought my hands to my face, pressed my fingertips to my eyelids. The rational portion of my mind knew their relationship had nothing to do with me. It didn't matter whether these two could make it work when I couldn't. Why would I bother comparing? But the other portion of my mind, the one that wanted to cry all the tears and eat brownie batter while watching *The Notebook,* wasn't on the same page. That part of me was ready to tell them they weren't allowed to make it official.

I continued gazing at the skyline because I didn't trust the rational side in this fight.

"We've also decided I should be the one to leave," Flinn said. "If someone has to leave the team because of this, it should be me."

Brownie batter. That was the only solution. "How magnanimous of you," I mused.

"What Flinn is trying to say without any coherence or connection to the talking points we planned last night," Tatum started, "is we understand if you don't want us working together while dating."

"'While dating,'" Flinn parroted back to her. "'While dating.' You say that like I didn't tell you I wanted to do this, wanted to work at it." A frustrated snarl sounded in his throat. "How am I supposed to believe you're committed to this thing when you won't even make a clear, definitive statement now?"

"I'm sorry if I'm coming across as not fully committing," she replied evenly. "But it's hard for me to accept that you want all the things you tell me you want. I've heard about the men and women in your life for years. I've heard all the stories about how quickly you hopped from one person to another. How no one seemed to matter to you. No one lasted." She sighed. "I don't want to sit here and tell Stella we're together, we're doing this, only for it to fall apart in a few weeks."

"You matter to me," he said softly.

"And you matter to me," she replied.

"You will always matter to me," he continued. "But I'm not the only one holding this together. If it falls apart, it's because one of us dropped our side. I'm promising you I won't do that."

"I won't drop my side," she said.

"I need you to believe I'm here to stay," he said. "I need you to show me that, Tate."

I saw it. I knew what I had to do.

After a weighty pause, Tatum said, "Stella, this thing with me and Flinn is serious. We know it's probably awkward or unprofessional for us to work on the same accounts. If that's your perspective on the matter, Flinn is prepared to leave. Or I can go. We'll do whatever you want."

I pushed out of my chair, grabbing my things from my desk. "I have to go," I announced, shoving my phone and notebook into my bag. "I need to leave. I have things to do and places to go, and I'm turning my phone off for the rest of the day. I'll see you tomorrow."

"Both of us?" Flinn asked as I rounded my desk.

"Yeah," I replied from the doorway. "But I'm serious about turning my phone off."

"Okay," Tatum said. "So, we're not fired?"

"Just don't have sex in the office," I called over my shoulder.

34

CAL

I LEANED AGAINST MY LOCKER, STARED DOWN AT MY PHONE. Nothing to see there but I went on staring. I knew I couldn't will a message from Stella into existence but that didn't stop me from trying.

Out of the corner of my eye, I saw Stremmel move through the room toward his locker. He kicked his shoes off, one thudding on the floor after another. "Hey," he called. "How'd that dissected aorta go?"

"Not great." I dropped my head back, stared up at the ceiling. "What about that stabbing? Did you pull that one out of the fire?"

"Just barely," he replied.

I shoved my phone in my pocket. "Better than not."

The door swung open and Acevedo stepped through, his surgical gown billowing around him. "Come on, losers," he yelled, slapping his hand against the doorframe. "We're going running."

"I don't run," Stremmel groused. "Not intentionally."

"It's a good thing I'm not giving you a choice," Acevedo

replied. "Let's go. Up. Both of you. I can't take all this pissing and moaning."

"The beatings will continue until morale improves?" Stremmel asked.

Acevedo waved him off. "Sweat is the solution to many things."

I pulled my phone out again, glared at it when I found no new messages. Nothing in the past minute. "Sweating isn't saving the day."

"This? From you?" Acevedo cried. "If there's anything you believe in, it's a good, long run. What happened to you, Hartshorn?"

"Lost myself looking after an asset," I said, mostly to myself. Then, louder, "Yeah. All right. Let's hit the pavement."

Acevedo brought his hands together in a loud clap, saying, "Yes. That's what I'm talking about." He pointed his clasped hands at me. "I'm giving you ten minutes to suit up and meet me across the street. We'll start at the park and follow the Charles into Cambridge and back around again. Ten miles. Twelve if we push it."

"That sounds like a death march," Stremmel grumbled. "No offense but I'm going to accidentally forget to meet you there."

"God help me, Stremmel, you're running," Acevedo replied. "You need to burn off some of your bitter."

Stremmel banged his locker shut and turned a well-practiced glare toward the neurosurgeon. "I've tried that. Burning, drowning, strangling. Every way you can kill a witch, I've tried it."

I headed toward the door, beckoning for Stremmel to

join me. "It's no use," I said. "We're doing this. If we're lucky, we'll be too tired to be miserable later."

He followed but asked Acevedo, "Where is your wife? You wouldn't be doling out corporal punishment if that spitfire was at home."

"And how long is she gone?" I asked.

"New York," he replied. "Lucky for you two, she gets home tomorrow afternoon."

Stremmel nudged me with his elbow. "These mother-fucking married people," he grumbled.

I tried to protest. To offer another explanation for Acevedo and his exuberant concern for dragging us out of our foul moods. But I didn't have it in me this time. I wasn't sure I had much of anything left in me.

I WASN'T certain but it seemed like Acevedo ran us all the way to the state border and back.

This was a perfect night for it, light until nearly eight o'clock, clear skies, warm but not humid. And everyone was out. If Stella and I hadn't fallen apart—or whatever happened—we would've been relishing in summer's arrival and following the path along the river with everyone else tonight. We would've walked and talked, and she would've bought an ice cream cone or two and I would've watched her eat them.

But Stella wasn't here and Acevedo taunted us better than a drill sergeant. After two months with little more than brisk walking as training, every mile felt like five. And Acevedo was right about the sweat doing us good. Or doing me good. Stremmel muttered something about moving back to Los Angeles if anyone conscripted him into another half marathon.

As I shuffled toward my apartment, my shirt soaked through and my muscles numb, I cursed Acevedo for plotting a course that forced me to think about Stella. But then another thought niggled loose. What if it wasn't Acevedo's fault? What if everything in this damn world reminded me of Stella? Even the street outside my apartment was built on interactions with her. I didn't want to move but I couldn't manage sucker punches like this one on a regular basis.

And dammit, it smelled like her. Not her hair or her skin but things I'd come to associate with her. Spice and garlic and herbs. It wasn't the typical cauldron of city scents. No, it was like an apparition, one rising from my building and leading me into temptation.

That was, if composing and deleting texts while watching the baseball game on mute to save me from imagining the way Stella would call the plays constituted temptation. It probably qualified as self-destruction or at least a healthy dose of mental torture.

Stremmel led the way into our building and said nothing more than a chant of "Fuck" as he climbed the stairs to his third-floor apartment. I waved to him as I unlocked my door, tried to ignore the rich, heavy aroma around me. It was my imagination, I was positive. Scent imprinted itself on memory and I'd never forget the night Stella came to me when I was sick, all fierce and defiant about chicken soup.

I laughed at that as I opened the door. Stella wasn't

chicken soup. She wasn't the standard option. She was surprising and a bit strange. Unexpected in every way. She was complicated too. Her history was loaded with disappointments and she distanced herself with sweetness and smiles, using that warmth as a shield to keep everyone at an arm's length.

And she was here, in my apartment.

I leaned against the doorway into the kitchen, a little dizzy, a little dazed, my muscles pushed past the point of fatigue and still aching in the places where I broke for her. I wanted to stand here, wanted to stare as she chopped vegetables and force my brain to confirm this as reality. But my body wasn't sure about staying upright. I had to brace my hands on either side of the door to keep from sliding to the floor.

After seven or eight hours of me gazing at her, unblinking, she peeked over at me. Offered a small smile, no dimples. "Hi."

"Hi," I replied.

"Riley let me in. I hope that's all right," she continued. "I'm making some sauce."

I didn't respond. I didn't know what to say or how to say it because I knew I'd launch into a big, awkward speech that would invariably include another proposal of marriage and a dozen other things best kept to myself.

"Okay," she said, mostly to herself. "Food is—I don't know how to put this—food is about people. You know? It's not basic nutrition. It's tradition and family and giving something to the people you care about."

She was so beautiful it hurt. More than everything else already hurt. This was another ache, on top of all the others. She wore a dark purple dress and those pretty yellow shoes, and she had her hair tied in a ponytail. Nothing about her appearance was remarkable. She wasn't trying to win me over with an epic display of tits and ass, or piled on layers of seductive makeup.

She looked like she just came from a long day at work and she was perfect. Her eyes appeared tired and her shoulders were tense and I loved her. I loved her and she came for me and that was all I needed to know.

"Maybe that's not your experience," she continued. "But it's mine. For me, food *is* family. It's spicy peppers and sausage when you're sick and Funfetti cupcakes on Serina's birthday and it's lasagna when I've fucked up so bad the only answer is cheese and extra sauce on the side. It's intertwined in a way I'll never be able to unravel. I tried unraveling it last night. I was in a car for three hours and spent most of that time—"

"Why were you in a car for three hours last night?" I asked.

She swung her gaze toward me, her fingers still curled around the handle of a knife. It was clear she hadn't planned for an interruption at this point in her speech. "I was in Connecticut. At ESPN."

I shrugged. Nodded. Motioned for her to continue. When she didn't, I said, "I want to hear the rest of this. You can tell me about ESPN later."

"Later?" she echoed.

Ah. Now I got it. Since I couldn't manage more than a flat stare and had myself braced in the most aggressive position possible with my arms straight out and hands holding up the walls, she thought I wasn't happy to see her. "Yeah. Later."

After a blink, she turned back to her vegetables picking up where she'd left off. "On the drive back here, I tried to figure out how I care for people. What is it I do to express that?"

It was a rhetorical question, one she wasn't interested in me answering. But I could spend all night ticking off the ways she did it.

"And it occurred to me that I communicate for a living," she said with a rueful laugh. "I'm all about the right words in the right way at the right time. But here I am, wondering how to show someone I care about him. That I care about him—about you—more than anyone else." She set the knife down, shifted to face me. "I've never had the right words for you. Never in the right ways. Definitely not at the right times." She rolled her gaze to the side, twisted her fingers together. "I'm trying to get better at the words but until then, I'm here. I'm cooking. For you."

She motioned toward the pots on the stove. I hadn't noticed them until now. Honestly, she could've torn down the walls and put my furniture in storage and I wouldn't have noticed because the only thing I could see was Stella. Nothing else existed for me.

"But I don't do this too often. I don't cook for anyone but myself, not much," she continued. "Food is family to me. It's special and personal and—and I've never done this. Not for anyone else." She lifted her fingertips to her forehead for a moment. "I have my sisters and my parents. Maybe Flinn and Tatum. It depends on the day with them. But no one else. There is no one else, Cal. It's only you."

A rough breath whooshed past my lips but I offered no additional response. I needed to replay her words, listen to them back one more time before I believed them.

Stella glanced back to the stovetop, speaking as she stirred. "I didn't have the right words for you. I'd felt it all along. God, that first morning on the trail. At the coffee shop. I'd felt everything but I didn't want to let myself feel it. No matter how many times I swore I wasn't broken, I was still afraid. Afraid of being forgotten again. And I didn't know how to be scared and vulnerable out loud. Not when I'd worked my ass off to bury it along with the rest of my baby adulthood. I didn't have any of the words, Cal, and I'm not sure I have them now. Instead of trying to make sense of it all, I'm cooking for you. I only cook for my family and you're going to be my family." She looked up, met my gaze. "If you still want that. If you'll belong to me."

Those statements, they knocked me back a step. I pushed away from the door and walked a slow circuit around my apartment. I needed a minute to gather her words, swallow them down. When I returned to the kitchen, I said, "Isn't there a game tonight?" I shot a pointed glance at the television and Stella's phone on the counter-top. "Why aren't you watching?"

"The balls can wait," she replied. "They won't always be able to wait but they're waiting now. I have a lasagna to prepare and some more words to struggle through, and those are my priorities at the moment." She looked away from the stove, studying the floor for a beat. "If you're okay with that."

"With the lasagna?" I asked. "Or you struggling through words?"

She lifted her shoulders. "How about both?"

I bobbed my head, felt a smile tugging at my lips for the first time in forever. "Do I get the crispy corner piece?" I asked.

"Honey, you get all the corners," she replied.

"I don't want it that way, Stel." I advanced toward her, my hand outstretched. "If I can't share them with you, I don't want them. I don't want anything if I can't have it with you."

A strangled laugh-sob stuck in her throat as she closed the distance between us. "Okay," she whispered, knuckling away a few tears. "We'll share."

I wanted to sweep her into my arms and press her up against a wall and get my hand under that dress. Just to feel her. All I needed was thirty seconds and I'd be there, my skin against hers and the world sliding back to rights. But then I remembered my sweat-soaked t-shirt...and everything else sweat-soaked. "Not to end this before it starts, but I need to shower. I ran several hundred miles and I'm gross. Nothing about my appearance is acceptable."

She stepped back, looked me up and down, and belted out a laugh. "Oh my god, yes. You are completely filthy, Cal." She frowned at the mud caked to my shoes and splattered over my legs. "Where have you been?"

"Vermont, maybe," I replied with a shrug. "Acevedo likes inventing his own trails."

"Go. Wash." She pointed toward the bathroom. "The sauce needs a little more time."

I reached for her hand, closed it in both of mine. "I'm sorry."

Her eyelids drooped, her shoulders rising and falling as

she exhaled. "You don't need to say that. You did nothing wrong and I—"

"We made plenty of mistakes. Both of us." I stroked my thumb over her knuckles, offered a small smile. "We'll talk about it when I'm not covered in trail funk, okay?"

Stella nodded, repeating, "Go. Wash." And then, "I'll be here when you're finished. I'm not going anywhere."

I knew hearts didn't swell, not outside cardiomegaly. I knew hearts only seemed to lodge in one's throat and only while experiencing severe palpitations. I knew the organ's every corner and flutter. And I knew love didn't live in the heart, didn't start there and didn't grow there.

But I knew Stella owned mine.

I WAS under the shower's hot spray no more than two minutes before Stella threw back the curtain and joined me. She said nothing, asked nothing, only stepped inside and wrapped her soft around my hard.

She rested her head between my shoulder blades, clasped her arms over my torso. I layered my hands over hers. We stayed there, twined together as the water pounded down on us and the steam rose.

Eventually, she said, "I want us to be the people who collided at the pond. I want us to be open and honest and not afraid of a single thing. Except demented raccoons."

"It was a beaver."

She groaned her disagreement into my skin. Then, "I want us to be the people we were that morning. When we shared that scone and almost agreed to forever because—because it felt right."

I turned, took her into my arms, tucked her head under my chin. "I am sorry and you do deserve an apology." When she started to object, I cupped her chin and pressed my thumb to her lips. "The way I left, it wasn't right."

"I would've done the same thing," she mumbled against my thumb.

"You told me how it was," I continued, using that thumb to trace her plump lips. "I knew and I didn't have the stones to tell you I didn't like it."

"And I didn't have the big girl panties to end it with them," she added. "I need you to believe me when I say you're the only one, Cal. Even before that day with the crazy raccoon—"

"Beaver," I said under my breath. "It was a beaver, Stel."

"—I hadn't seen any of them for weeks. You were the only one then and you're the only one now." She glanced up at me, her cheeks wet. "My phone is unlocked and you can read anything you want at any time and it wasn't a beaver—"

I kissed her. I dragged my hands across her shoulders, down the line of her spine, over her ass cheeks. Squeezed them both. I ran my knuckles between her legs but only for a quick moment. She responded with a gasp, a thin, breathy sound that went straight to my cock. I didn't think I had an ounce of energy left after the overexertion of this evening but somehow my body was ready to demolish this woman.

My woman.

"You're mine," I whispered against her lips. "You belong to me, Stella."

She pushed up on her toes, caught my lower lip between her teeth. Nipped, hummed, turned my cock to stone. "You belong to me."

I reached for her breasts, covered her nipples with my thumbs. "We're not doing this here," I announced. "The water will run cold and your skin will shrivel before I'm done with you tonight. And don't think I'm stopping with one night. You still need to marry me." I bent down, closed my teeth around the underside of her breast and then delivered the same treatment to the other side. "Yes?"

Stella stared at me, her lips parted. "Yes," she answered. "And *yes*."

EPILOGUE

STELLA

I SAID *YES* BUT WE WAITED A YEAR TO SAY *I DO*.

There was a hot second when eloping sounded awesome but then we realized we didn't want to rush this part. We had the rest of our lives to be married.

But there was one thing we rushed. One precious, little thing we were keeping to ourselves until after returning from the honeymoon.

And that was why Cal was slumped back in the passenger seat while I drove us home after my thirty-seventh birthday dinner. Since we wanted to keep my pregnancy quiet until after the wedding next month, Cal covered for me by drinking my wine. And his.

He was just smooth enough to pull that ruse off and get totally hammered in the process.

He tipped his chin up, a sloppy smile warming his face. "How are you doing, sweet thing?"

"I'm good," I replied, a laugh thick in my words. "I'm really good."

"Feeling all right?" he asked.

"I am," I said. "I'm tired but I'm all right. It was a good day."

I'd worried about making it through the meal without setting off suspicions. Since peeing on the stick last month, my appetite had vanished. All I wanted was toasted cinnamon raisin bagels or corn flakes with almond milk. Nothing else interested me. But I'd tolerated Mom's cooking well enough. She sent us home with leftovers to last the week and a Dominican cake with pineapple filling she'd whipped up just for me.

That smile of his, it was sloppy as ever. "You're fucking beautiful."

"I appreciate you saying so. Especially since I've been a bit gray and wobbly and—"

"And fucking beautiful," he said, catching a lock of my hair between two fingers. "I'm not putting up with any of this gray and wobbly bullshit, Stel. You've never been more amazing than you are right now."

I loved him. Like, crazy, wild, boundless love. There was no structure to it, no routine. And the heat of his adoration, it was everything. It was a light that never went out. I didn't know I could love someone else this way. Didn't know I could open myself to the kind of vulnerability that came with giving and receiving love.

But Cal made it easy. He made it worth the risk and all the uncertainty.

And he guzzled wine to keep my parents from noticing I wasn't drinking on my birthday.

"Honey, you're drunk." I laughed as I turned into our neighborhood. I was still learning the shortcuts and back ways to our new house in Cambridge. For the first time in my life, I lived north of the city. For a south-of-Boston girl, this was a big change. It was practically a different state up here.

We lived a few blocks from Nick and Erin Acevedo now. We'd debated the merits of my little Cape house in Buttonwood Village over his postage stamp apartment in the city but the choice made itself when we decided we wanted to try for a baby right away. As cute as my house was, it was cute and *small*. And my husband-to-be is a man-brick.

"I know I'm drunk. I drank"—he held up all his fingers and mumbled out a few numbers as he stared at them—"all the wine."

"Thank you for doing that, Cal." I pulled into the driveway and turned off the car. "But you didn't have to drink so fast. That's why my dad kept refilling our glasses."

"He's so happy when I drink the wine he buys," he argued. "I figured it would be a good distraction if you lost your appetite again."

My parents were still obsessed with Cal. I wasn't sure but I think they still mowed the lawn and filled the window boxes before we visited. And my dad seemed to think this wedding hinged on plying my future husband with "the good wine."

But I waved him off. "Like I said on the way over, we're getting married in a month and I'm allowed to watch what I eat. Can't risk the wedding dress not fitting. If anyone really pushed on the topic, I was ready with some spin."

He held out his hand for the keys as he gifted me with a warm, lazy grin. "I cannot wait to fuck my wife."

I dropped them in his hand, ran my fingertips over the inside of his wrist. "What about your fiancée?" The only answer he offered was a growl. "Your rumbles and grumbles are not words."

He jingled the keys in his palm and reached for the door handle. "Stay there. I'm coming to get you."

He rounded the front end of the car, his steps uneven. He really did drink all the wine for me. He helped me out of the car, grabbed my ass in the process, and then steered me toward the door. It took him a few tries to get the key in the lock but then he whisked me inside. He had me against the door before I could switch on the lights.

"I love you," he whispered, his lips on the corner of my mouth. "I fucking love you."

"And I love you," I replied, lacing my arms around his neck. "Fucking love you."

This was *it*. The scary, strange, amazing thing we'd found on that trail more than a year ago. I hadn't wanted it and I hadn't believed it was for me, but now I knew better because a better man taught me.

"I want to fuck you," he announced, his scruff doing the best things to my neck, "but I will need a nap before I can do anything but lean on you."

"Then we'll nap," I replied. "We have all the time in the world."

THANK YOU FOR READING! *I hope you loved Cal and Stella's journey.*

Join my newsletter for new release alerts, exclusive extended epilogues and bonus scenes, and more.

If newsletters aren't your thing, <u>follow me on BookBub</u> for preorder and new release alerts.

Visit my private reader group, Kate Canterbary's Tales, for exclusive giveaways, sneak previews of upcoming releases, and book talk.

Aʀᴇ ʏᴏᴜ ʀᴇᴀᴅʏ ғᴏʀ ᴍᴏʀᴇ? *Keep reading!*

Iғ ʏᴏᴜ'ʀᴇ *ready for more of Doctor Alex Emmerling and Riley Walsh, Preservation, is also available!*

Two lonely hearts.

Just once, Alex Emmerling would like to be someone's first choice.

She's strong-willed and spunky, but she's left picking up the pieces from her ex's lies and manipulations, and daydreaming about taking a scalpel to his scrotum.

Flying under the radar is what Riley Walsh does best.

He's laid-back and loyal, but he wants the most off-limits woman in his world, and nothing will ever make that a reality.

An arrangement of mutual benefit.

Two months, four dates.

Five, if things go well.

Five at the most.

But possibly six.

Definitely no more than six dates.

Only the appearance of a romantic relationship is required, and they expect nothing more from their time together. There will be none of those benefits involved.

One wild weekend.

After waking up in bed together—very naked and even more hungover—the terms and conditions of their arrangement no longer apply. Now they're faced with something riskier than exposing their fake relationship: letting go of the past and zipping up the future.

Some things have to fall apart before they can be put back together.

Preservation is available now. Turn the page for an excerpt!

Nick and Erin's story, ***The Spire, is now available!***

Rebel, runner, recluse, rich girl.

Nine years ago, Erin Walsh ran away from everything.

Home.

Family.

Secrets.

Tragedy.

Herself.

The only permanence in her life is catastrophe.

She travels from country to country, chasing disaster, teasing fire, playing with poison. She guards against real connections, and shuns the only family she has left.

She holds everyone--even her siblings--at a mile-long distance. It's the only way to protect herself.

But she can't protect herself from Nick Acevedo.

He's the ice to her fire, and he's willing to sacrifice everything to bring her home.

The Spire is available now. Turn the page for an excerpt!

ALSO BY KATE CANTERBARY

The Walsh Series

Underneath It All – Matt and Lauren
The Space Between – Patrick and Andy
Necessary Restorations – Sam and Tiel
The Cornerstone – Shannon and Will
Restored — Sam and Tiel
The Spire — Erin and Nick
Preservation — Riley and Alexandra
Thresholds — The Walsh Family

Walsh Series Spinoff Standalone Novels

Coastal Elite — Jordan and April
Before Girl — Cal and Stella
Missing In Action — Wes and Tom
The Magnolia Chronicles
Boss in the Bedsheets — Ash and Zelda

Talbott's Cove

Fresh Catch — Owen and Cole
Hard Pressed — Jackson and Annette
Far Cry — Brooke and JJ
Rough Sketch — Gus and Neera

Get exclusive sneak previews of upcoming releases through Kate's newsletter and private reader group, The Canterbary Tales, on Facebook.

AN EXCERPT FROM PRESERVATION

ALEXANDRA

He pointed at the plate between us. "These are my favorite pretzel bites in the city. Try some."

I shot him a sharp look. "Are you just trying to get me in a good mood?" I asked. "I *did* eat lunch today."

"Oh yeah?" he asked, dipping two pretzels in the accompanying sauce. "What did you have? Based on you yelling at me about noticing your shoes, I'd say it was an iced venti skinny latte."

"Almonds," I replied. And an iced venti skinny latte but I wasn't copping to that just yet.

Riley tried to fight a laugh, failed. "Almonds?" he repeated.

"Chocolate-covered almonds, yes." I folded my arms across my chest. "It was an appropriate amount of calories, fat, protein, and carbs."

He shook his head and ate another pretzel. "I don't want to live in a world where a few almonds—chocolate or otherwise—are lunch." He pointed to the plate and pushed his beer toward me. "Eat. Drink. Please."

I glared at the pilsner and pretzels. I hated being told what to do. Just fucking hated it. But then my stomach growled—goddamn digestive muscles—and Riley shot me a pointed glance.

"People think that a rumbling stomach is the sign of hunger," I said, reaching for his glass. I drained the beer and then selected a pretzel for dipping. "It is not. The muscles of the stomach and small intestines are always contracting, and those contractions make more noise when the organs are empty."

Riley gazed at me, his expression flat. It gave me a moment to study him while choosing another pretzel. He was wearing jeans, a tailored shirt with the cuffs rolled up to his elbows, and a pinstriped vest, and his hair was a wreck. It looked like he'd been tugging the dark strands in every conceivable direction. His eyes were rimmed with a bit of red and his lids heavy, as if he'd been rubbing them or hadn't gotten much sleep. Perhaps both. There was a small notebook beside his phone, and a mechanical pencil tucked into the spiral binding.

And he was still more attractive than I knew how to handle. Even tired and irritable, and ordering me to eat his pretzels and drink his beer, he was hot as fuck. I bit into another pretzel and offered him a small smile.

"Would you say the chip on your shoulder is massive or epic?" he asked. There was no hint of amusement in his tone, and he was staring at me with more ice than I'd believed he could muster. It didn't feel like we were sniping at each other anymore. "It might be semantics to you but I'm trying to get a feel for what I'm dealing with here."

But then one of his big hands found my leg under the

table. He squeezed and rubbed his thumb along the hollow of my knee, and I started to believe I'd been all wrong about this man. There was the player and there was the overgrown kid, but there was so much more than that.

Preservation is available now.

AN EXCERPT FROM THE SPIRE

NICK

"Call me Ishmael," she said, following my gaze to *Moby-Dick* scrawled across her chest. She was the kind of girl who wore a t-shirt well, and she didn't seem to mind me noticing. "Funny story, *Moby-Dick*. It's all about chasing down the thing that haunts you, but in that chase, losing everything else."

"Yeah, now that you mention it, I do see the humor," I said, failing to rip my eyes from her shirt. Yes, all right, it wasn't the *shirt* that had my attention. It was the woman wearing the shirt, and everything I could infer from the way she wore it. "Death at sea has always been hilarious."

"Well, no," she said, shaking a hand at me. "It's revered as this tale of good versus evil, man versus nature, blah, blah, blah. But it's really just a swan song for the good old days of Nantucket whaling. A sermon to the sea, and all of its machinations. Most people blame the rise of petroleum, the depleted stock of whales, and the seizure of northern ships by the Confederate Navy during the Civil War for the decline of the American whaling industry, specifically the decline here on the Cape, but it was actually the development of more efficient Norwegian ships. Instead of catching up to the Norwegians and furthering the decline of the entire species, American interests turned to railroads, mining, conquering the west."

I blinked at Erin while she studied the dark road before us. "Do you do that often?" I asked, scratching my chin. "Make odd observations about one thing and then drop a maritime history lesson like you had that information on the tip of your tongue?"

She shrugged. "Sometimes."

"Right, yeah. It was kind of amazing," I said, "and a little intimidating."

"I told you," she said. "I don't do small talk." Erin looked away, out her window, but then cut an up-and-down glance back at me. It was quick, but the smile that followed was more than enough to telegraph her interest. Okay. So it wasn't just me. "Take Route 6."

We rode along the far eastern arm of Cape Cod in amicable silence, and found a harborside tavern that screamed local-but-not-tourist. Not that I cared, but Erin knew what she wanted. As far as I was concerned, we could sit on a curb all night, so long as she kept talking and let me bury my face in her hair to find that scent again.

Once seated at the bar, I stole every opportunity to gaze at her. She didn't put much on display, but that didn't matter. When the Lord gave to Erin, he gave with two hands. She was small. Narrow, even. But that t-shirt showed off the curve of her waist in a manner that made my fingers itch. And her tits were a crime. They were that soup ladle shape that was too rare to be real, but there wasn't an ounce of artifice on this woman.

What you see is what you get.

Except it wasn't, not by a mile. I leaned back in my seat and draped my arm over the edge of hers. My fingers were drawn to her shoulder. No, that was bullshit. Complete bullshit. I was drawn to all of her, and touching her shoulder was an entry-level way of saying *I dig you, darlin'.*

She glanced at my fingers and then back to me, her eyebrow arching. I didn't respond to her unspoken question, instead staring at her pink lips. She'd be sweet there. Sweet but tart, too.

"What are you running away from tonight, lovely?"

She shook her head. "Nothing new," she said.

Her fingers tangled in the thin chains circling her neck, and she toyed with the small stone that sat in her jugular notch. "What is that?" I asked, pointing to the gem. "Onyx?"

"Carbonado. Black diamond. It's the toughest natural diamond form in existence. I found this one in Brazil."

"I've never heard of those," I said, my gaze drawn to her neck. I wanted to taste her there. I wanted her in nothing but that necklace. I wanted to wrap my fingers around that necklace and feel her pulse thrumming against my skin while I moved in her.

Oh, *shit*. Shit, shit, shit. I could *not* think about her naked. Not here. Not yet. And it wasn't about the touch-and-go nature of public erections. No, it was that I wanted to do this *right*.

"It's not quite clear how they came to exist," she continued, her voice taking on new authority. Her words were clear and efficient, and even her gestures rang with professional fascination that bordered on obsession. "They possess no mantle minerals, and that's fucking weird, but what's more strange is the lack of high-pressure minerals, like hexagonal carbon polymorph."

"No hexagonal carbon polymorph?" I asked. I had no idea what we were talking about. I mean, sure, I knew my share of chemistry, but this was beyond my share. "That's crazy."

"I know, right?" she said. "Fun fact—their isotopic values are low, which isn't how diamonds are supposed to behave. Some researchers have suggested that radiation was involved in their formation, given the presence of lumines-cence halos, but that calls into question a spontaneous fission of uranium and thorium."

"Right," I murmured, nodding in thanks as the bartender placed two beer bottles in front of us. "The lumi-nescence halos. Of course."

She held up her index finger, pressing pause on the black diamond mystery while she sipped her beer. "Oh, sorry," she said, tapping her bottle to mine. "Here's to... surviving this weekend."

Here's to evading your big brothers. What they don't know won't hurt them. Right?

"To surviving the weekend," I said. I took a sip, but then returned the bottle to the bar top. Reaching over, I pulled her chair closer to mine. Fuck cool and friendly.

"Right, right," she said. She was looking down, inspecting the way I had us pressed together, and then back up at me. "What's this about?"

"You." I pressed my thumb right there, to the tender hollow where the stone sat. It was just a moment, a fleeting touch. A second longer and my hand would've moved up her neck and into her hair, and then we'd never hear the end of this wonky explanation because my mouth would be fused to hers. "You were telling me about this," I said, my eyes locked on her lips.

"Yeah..."

She eyed me for a wary beat, then pushed her glasses up her nose and leaned into me. *Leaned the fuck into me.* Her shoulder was on my chest and her head was tucked under my chin, and this, *this* was what I needed after the week from hell.

Patting my knee twice as if I was a well-behaved golden retriever, Erin blew out a soft breath. She relaxed in pieces, her shoulders sagging first, and it moved down her body. Back, hips, legs. I imagined her toes uncurling inside her boots. From this angle, I could see her lashes brushing against her cheeks, and I didn't even think about it when I pressed my lips to her temple. It was natural, for both of us. This was what she needed, too.

"So, carbonado," she said, patting my knee again. God, she was fucking cute. "The theory that keeps me up at night is this one—that it was formed deep inside an early genera-tion giant star, one that exploded forever ago into a super-nova. Which makes this"—she tapped the stone—"an artifact of forever ago. Of a time before words and thoughts and anything at all."

"That's...incredible," I whispered into her hair. Her voice did things to me. Really good things. And the nerdy science talk? Oh, shut the fuck up. I was done when I saw her, and I was well done now.

Her tongue darted out and ran along her top lip as her

shoulder jerked. "Whenever the world is too much for me, I remember that this rock might have been thrown out of interstellar space when time began. Before the world was anything, this ball of carbon was flung into earth's atmosphere in one of the cosmos's greatest tantrums. I've had a lot of bad days, but never one as bad as this rock."

She really did know things I couldn't begin to comprehend. I hadn't expected it to involve black diamonds or supernovas but the means didn't matter. It was the method that had me entranced. And I wanted—no, *needed*—to know her.

"Is the world too much today?" I asked.

A quick nod. "A little bit, yeah."

She offered nothing more, and that was okay. The world was kicking my ass right now, too.

I tapped the tiny stone winking at me from her nose. "And what's this?"

"Diamond," she said. "The kimberlite variety. Nothing interstellar here."

"Boring," I murmured, and that earned me a hearty laugh. "Hawaii. Italy. Grad school. Volcanoes. Tell me everything. When do you finish?"

In other words, when can I keep you forever?

The Spire is available now.

ABOUT KATE

USA Today Bestseller Kate Canterbary writes smart, steamy contemporary romances loaded with heat, heart, and happy ever afters. Kate lives on the New England coast with her husband and daughter.

You can find Kate at www.katecanterbary.com

ACKNOWLEDGMENTS

To the readers who first met Cal Hartshorn in early 2016, when the man-brick was little more than a hunky, hulking character who distracted me from a great number of things —thank you for waiting. Thank you for waiting while I found him and Stella again. Thank you for bearing with me while other characters jumped in and claimed my attention. Thank you for knowing they'd be worth the wait. Thank you.

To the people who allow me to swirl around in my doubt and always have the right words (and sometimes, the right kick in the ass), thank you.

To my husband, who sent me off to write at Panera on a Saturday night and asked "are you still working on that?" far too many times, it's done. You're welcome.